Dear Reader,

What happens when you take one sexy diner waitress, put her directly in the path of a hot Marine on leave, create a phosphorus-burning chemistry and then tell them they can't have sex? Well, read on....

In *Distinguished Service,* active duty Marine Mace Harrison is back in Colorado Springs for two purposes: to be awarded the Navy Star for courageous deeds he views as only doing his job, and to feel out old friend Darius Folsom's new security firm Lazarus, where he hopes to work in six months when he retires his uniform. What he doesn't bank on is meeting irresistible beauty Geneva Davis. They click on every level from the moment they meet. Problem is, Geneva is in no condition to get involved with anyone, and he is in no position to take on anyone in that condition. So they strike a bargain: pretend to date for the duration of his leave to clear out unwanted emotional clutter from their lives. A platonic arrangement that finds them exactly where they shouldn't be—setting fire to the bedroom sheets...

We hope you enjoy Mace and Geneva's blazing-hot, emotional journey toward sexily-ever-after. Curious about upcoming Tori titles? Visit www.facebook.com/toricarrington.

Here's wishing you love, romance and *hot* reading.

Lori Schlachter Karayianni

and Tony Karayianni

aka Tori Carrington

Tori Carrington

DISTINGUISHED SERVICE

&

EVERY MOVE YOU MAKE

HARLEQUIN®
entertain, enrich, inspire™

ISBN-13: 978-0-373-79722-6

DISTINGUISHED SERVICE

Copyright © 2012 by Harlequin Books S.A.

The publisher acknowledges the copyright holders of the individual works as follows:

DISTINGUISHED SERVICE
Copyright © 2012 by Lori and Tony Karayianni

EVERY MOVE YOU MAKE
Copyright © 2002 by Lori and Tony Karayianni

Recycling programs for this product may not exist in your area.

CONTENTS

ABOUT THE AUTHOR

RT Book Reviews Career Achievement Award-winning, bestselling duo Lori and Tony Karayianni are the power behind the pen name Tori Carrington. Their more than fifty novels include numerous Harlequin Blaze miniseries, as well as the ongoing Sofie Metropolis, P.I. comedic mystery series with another publisher. Visit www.toricarrington.net and www.sofiemetro.com for more information on the couple and their titles.

Books by Tori Carrington

DISTINGUISHED SERVICE

This book is dedicated to dear friends
Cris Gaytan Beck and Deb Leahy Dunphy,
whom I think of fondly every time I see my right foot:
You both are tattooed on my heart.

LAZARUS SECURITY WAS EXACTLY the type of well-oiled engine he could see himself willing to get his hands dirty with.

Mace Harrison squinted into the watery early November sunlight where he stood near the back of the training center strategically located behind the building. Everything at the company was top of the line, including personnel. Situated on several acres just outside Colorado Springs, Lazarus was an extraordinary operation that in a short time was already gaining notable momentum within the private security industry.

It was one of the reasons why he was there.

The other was Lazarus partner Darius Folsom.

He nodded at his old friend now.

How far did they go back? Fifteen years, at least. To the first time Mace's parents had shipped him and his older brother Marcus off to live with his paternal grandfather for the summer? Their military family had moved to yet another house in yet another city and he'd been young enough to need supervision, and old enough to cause trouble because he'd hated moving. And then there was his need to escape the shadow his brother cast that threatened to suffocate him. Dari and his family had lived around the block from his grandfather and he and Mace had become fast friends.

They'd enlisted in the Marines at around the same time—by that point Mace choosing to live at his grandfather's house, which offered him greater independence—but they hadn't been stationed together until the past year.

Darius Folsom had recently completed his second tour, but Mace still had a six-month stretch ahead of him. He was back home for a brief week break, investigating job opportunities, Lazarus at the top of the list.

Of course, it was also possible he'd take on that counterterrorism desk job he'd been offered in Washington, D.C.

And he was purposely ignoring the fact that he was also there to accept an award he didn't deserve and didn't want.

The Navy Cross...

A small bit of metal that might as well be the size of a Humvee as far as he was concerned.

Of course, some brave men and women went their entire lives without receiving such an honor.

He supposed he should feel guilty for not wanting it. But considering everything...well, many had made the ultimate sacrifice and received nothing more than a military burial.

How would his brother feel about the medal? He imagined Marcus would give him one of his trademark smirks and slap him hard on the back. "Still running after me, little bro? Think you'll catch up? You might want to pick up the pace."

Of course, Mace could only guess at what he'd say. Because Marcus wasn't there. Not anymore.

But Mace still felt shadow hands choking him from behind, a sensation that was even stronger when he was within a hundred miles of his parents.

A time like now.

"So what do you think?" Dari said hesitantly, after having given him the nickel tour of Lazarus Security, apparently having noticed the darkening of his expression.

"Impressive," Mace said, shaking off his thoughts although he knew better than to try to rid himself of the shadow; that would be there forever. "Very impressive."

Darius's grin was his response.

"Good job, old pal." Mace squeezed his shoulder. "This is really something. You can tell you've put a lot of work into it."

"Thanks."

It still amazed him that Dari drew such words close to heart. Oh, not from anyone. The big, tough Marine wasn't easily flattered. But when it came to his friends… Amazing. "Don't let the success go to your head," he teased now.

Dari laughed. "Don't worry. This is a joint endeavor and I had very little to do with the start-up. I was too busy overseas getting my ass shot and saved by someone we both know."

Mace grimaced as he glanced at his friend's leg. "You'd have made it out on your own."

"Maybe. Maybe not."

What went unsaid was that several of their team hadn't made it out.

And it was that incident that not only still gave Mace— and very likely Dari—nightmares, it was what had ultimately earned him that damn medal he'd be accepting at some sort of bigwig event that Saturday.

He wondered if it wasn't too late to hop onto the first transport out. He'd take full-on assault from enemy forces over what he was facing in days.

"That's how you earned it," Dari said.

"I was just doing my job."

"No, Mace, you always do more than your job."

"You'd have done the same."

"Would I have? I'd like to think I would. But I don't know. While I would have ultimately done what was needed, I would have likely hesitated that split second to assess the situation before diving in. You…" Dari fell silent, undoubtedly reflecting on that late afternoon in the mountains of Waziristan when they'd been lied to by villagers and surrounded by enemy forces the instant they were outside town. "You charged straight in, to hell with the consequences."

"Some would say that's stupid."

Dari squinted at him. "If you had hesitated, a leg wound would have been the least of my worries. And you'd have returned home to attend a very different event."

Mace didn't even want to consider that possibility. Not then, not now.

"What's done is done," he said. "I'd prefer it if everyone looked forward rather than back."

Dari half-smiled. "Yeah." He nodded. "Yeah."

Mace shifted his weight from one foot to the other, wishing the subject done.

"Come on," Dari said, seeming to pick up on his mindset. "Let's go into town and grab some grub. I've got a favor to ask. Oh, and I hope you don't mind, I told Megan we'd meet up with her at The Barracks afterward for a drink."

Mace nearly sighed audibly in relief. "Fine with me." He'd known Dari's wife since she was little more than the reason his friend bought acne cream when the occasional zit popped up on his face. He'd only been in town for a few days and he'd enjoy the chance to catch up with her, find out what both of them had been up to outside their working at Lazarus together.

"She'll be alone, right?" he asked, a thought occurring to him.

"What?"

Damn.

His friend had never been any good at lying. "Hell, Dari, I'm not in town for that long. I'd like to spend some time with my friends before heading back."

"Surely there's a little room for some friendly company."

"No. There isn't."

"Aw. She's a real sweetheart. I promise you'll like her."

That was the problem, he thought.

He didn't want to like anyone. Not right now. Not without knowing where he was going to land in six months, if, in fact, he landed at all.

Not after what had happened the last time he'd tried to make a long-distance relationship work.

"Sorry," Dari said. "I know you asked me not to do it. And I really haven't. It's Megan's idea. I know how you feel about people knowing your business, so while I made your feelings on the matter known to Meg, I didn't tell her why you felt that way. Without that…"

Without that, she couldn't understand why he was adamant about not dating while on this leave.

"You'll understand if I pass on that drink then," he said.

Dari looked disappointed, but finally he nodded.

They walked back to the main structure, passing armed recruits making their way out to the state-of-the-art shooting range along the way. He shared his friend's disappointment. He truly would have enjoyed having a beer with him and Megan tonight. But to be placed next to a woman hoping to be swept off her feet, one who looked at him with big doe eyes, who promised forever and then moved on to someone else while he was overseas…

No.

And that meant a long night stretched out in front of him with nothing to do but stare at his motel room walls.

He could go over to see his grandfather again, but he'd gotten into hot water with the nursing home attendants for having stayed past regular visiting hours once already. He didn't want to risk having his visitation privileges revoked.

His grandfather…

Mace grinned even as he shook his head. The old man had one foot in the grave and still somehow managed to chase around anything female like a spry twenty-year-old.

Well, okay, maybe a spry twenty-year-old with a walker.

He remembered their last conversation. "Give me something, kid," Dwayne Harrison had requested that morning. "Good-looking stud like you? Them skirts gotta be falling all over you. Surely you could send some sweet stuff my way."

Mace had merely smiled.

Oh, he planned to date again. Hopefully soon. Once he was able to get rid of the bad taste Janine had left in his mouth.

Of course, he could always go over and visit his parents. They'd settled back in his father's hometown five years or so ago when his dad finally retired.

Still, somehow, he didn't look at their house as home.

And the shadow hands tightened at the thought.

Dari cleared his throat. "I don't think I've had a chance to say it yet, but…well, I was sorry to hear about Janine. You deserve better than what she did to you."

Mace turned his head so quickly to stare at Dari, his neck cracked. It wasn't like his friend to mention something so personal in such a casual setting. At least, not without downing a few beers first.

"What?" Dari asked.

Of course, his friend couldn't know that Mace had no sooner switched his cell phone on after his flight than he'd received a voice mail from the woman in question. He'd stopped dead in the middle of the airport terminal, staring at the notification. He hadn't heard from her in nearly eight months. What could she possibly want now?

He'd found out soon enough. Her words still reverberated through his mind.

"Welcome home, Mace. I know I'm probably the last person you expected to hear from, but… Well, I just wanted to say I'm sorry…again. And to tell you I'd love to see you while you're in town. Call me…please."

Curiously, hearing her voice hadn't moved him in the least. But her apology and her request to see him again had elicited a very specific response: Hell no.

He opened the door and stepped aside so his friend could precede him inside. "Something tells me you're getting a bit soft around the middle."

Dari rubbed a rock-hard six-pack.

"Not that middle."

They chuckled and walked back to Dari's office in the front of the building.

While Mace could make light of his relationship woes when the situation called for it, there was nothing but heaviness in his heart at the memory of Janine's betrayal.

"So, Rocky's Diner after I close up shop here."

He nodded. "Rocky's Diner. Meet you there in an hour."

They shook hands and gave each other a bro hug. Then Mace headed out to the parking lot where his rental car waited, trying not to think about Janine…or the phone call he'd gotten from her that morning.

He failed.

GENEVA DAVIS TOOK three meat loaves out of the industrial oven, swiping the back of one of the oven mitts across her brow after placing the last on the stainless-steel counter. Two of the kitchen staff had called in sick this afternoon, leaving her and one of the other waitresses to pick up the slack at Rocky's Diner. Monday's Meat Loaf Mania was one of their busiest nights when all staff was present. Handling it with two people short was going to make the evening hell on earth.

Trudy Grant, the mercurial owner who was a combination of Betty White witty cuteness and Bea Arthur brashness, hung up the phone on the wall near the door. "Cindy just called in." She shook her head. "This damn flu is going to put me out of business."

Make that three people short.

Of course, Trudy's proclamation was an exaggeration; something or other was going to put her out of business at least three times a day. Still, somehow she'd managed to keep the diner's heart beating for the past twenty years when she'd bought the previous owner out.

Tiffany, the other waitress, breezed by with warm pies to stock the counter displays in the other room. "Cindy ain't sick. Cindy has a blind date tonight."

Geneva shared a smile with Mel, the main cook, but didn't say anything as she slid off the mitts and gave the large pot of homemade mashed potatoes a stir. As expected, Trudy went off like a bomb, filling the kitchen with inventive curse words. Everyone moved around her, giving her the wide berth she required. They all knew the steam would dissipate and Trudy would be operating on full throttle again soon without risk of being scalded.

Geneva moved around Mel, where he tossed burgers, to turn off the alarm for the French fries. She took the basket out of the oil and hung it on the rungs above to drain.

"Oh, and Gen?" Tiffany poked her head back inside the kitchen. "Your Baby Daddy Dustin just took up residence in his usual place at the counter,"

Geneva stood perfectly still for a moment, staring unseeingly at the golden potatoes, battling back a sudden surge of nausea.

"You okay?"

She glanced at where Mel had leaned in to quietly ask the question.

"Yeah. Fine." She smiled. "Thanks."

She removed her hand from where it lay against her stomach, a spot she often found it resting lately, and then tipped the fries out onto two plates and salted them.

Lately, it was getting harder and harder to face Dustin. She didn't know how to explain in a way that would register with him that just because she was pregnant, it didn't mean they were a couple. And that she didn't expect anything more from him but to be a good dad. But he seemed determined to make something out of nothing. And his unwanted attention was eroding what had once been a great friendship.

A friendship that had accidentally become more for five whole minutes a little over two months ago.

It wasn't that the sex had been bad…

Okay, maybe it had been.

But that wasn't the reason she didn't want to be anything more than a joint parent with him. They were friends—period.

And the one-nighter had happened on the day she'd buried her mother in the ground and her sadness in a bottle of tequila.

"I remember my wife couldn't even keep crackers down during her first try," Mel said, putting two cheeseburgers onto buns and then handing the plates to her.

"Thankfully I haven't been sick once." She smiled as she dressed both burgers and then balanced all four plates on her arms. "I only feel like I'm going to be."

All…the…time.

Trudy gathered her wits. "With my luck, your first time will be all over one of the tables. A full one."

"Knock wood," Geneva said, edging through the swinging doors to deliver the burgers to Table 6, passing Tiffany as she went.

"Trade you Table 7 for 3," the too-pretty nineteen-year-old said.

That meant there was someone male and attractive at Table 7, one grouped in her regular station. She didn't even glance that way. Instead she took in Table 3. A crowd of rowdy teenagers.

"Pass."

"I'll share the tip with you. Fifty-fifty."

Geneva kept walking.

"And you can keep the other tip."

She let her silence speak for her.

She genuinely didn't have it in her to deal with the other table just then. Not after pulling a double shift and working all last night to get in a rush job to design a last-minute sales flyer for Johnny's Jalopies car dealership.

She said hello to Dustin as she passed without stopping to hear what he might have to say, then waited with a smile for the couple at Table 6 to move their joined hands before placing the burgers and fries down in front of them.

"Anything else I can get you for now?" she asked.

"Ketchup," the girl asked.

"On the table."

"Oh. Thanks."

"Are the pies fresh?"

"Always. Today there's blueberry, apple and, of course, Trudy's chocolate marshmallow."

"I'll take a piece of the blueberry," the girl said.

"And I'll have Trudy's," the guy added.

"Very good. You want them now or after you've finished?"

"Now."

"After."

"I can do both," Geneva said.

She got the coffeepot, which unfortunately happened to be near where Dustin sat, and the blueberry pie. After delivering the pie, she moved on to Table 7, filling the two cups that had been turned up to indicate coffee would be appreciated.

"Welcome…gentlemen."

Wow.

Okay, so she didn't normally agree with Tiffany's taste in men, which seemed to run from blond kids with mohawks to tattooed motorcyclists. But this time, the fickle teen was spot on.

She recognized Darius Folsom. He came in to the diner often enough and was a great guy along with a great-looking one.

But his tablemate was new.

And he was hotter than a July Colorado Springs day.

She silently cleared her throat. Not that she was interested. After all, she was an expectant mother. But she did still have a pulse.

And, apparently, a sex drive. Something she hadn't anticipated, given her condition. Which probably explained her unusual, spellbound response.

Just looking at this guy made her think of sweaty sighs and hungry kisses.

"Hi, Geneva," Dari said with a smile. "It's crazy in here tonight."

She made an effort to ignore her curiously overwhelming chemical reaction to his friend. "It always is. What can I get for you today?"

"Meat loaf, of course."

She looked at his guest…and nearly lost her breath.

God, did eyes come any browner?

And the way he was looking at her…

"Well, if he's game, so am I. Meat loaf."

She smiled, probably bigger than the situation called for.

"Meat loaf it is, then. Are you sticking with the coffee? Or would you like to add something else?"

"Milk," Dari said. "A nice, big cold glass."

"Make that two."

"You got it."

She turned from the table feeling something other than nausea stir her stomach. It was a welcome change. Not overly so—while she wasn't and had never really been involved with Dustin, she wasn't shopping either—but nice nonetheless. It had been a long time while since she'd felt anything other than expecting.

"I hate you," Tiffany said as they passed again.

"I love you," she said back and then disappeared into the kitchen.

She leaned briefly against the wall inside, savoring the very female feelings while she could. She knew better than anyone that she'd soon have to nip them in the bud.

"You all right?" Mel asked after seeing her face. "You look a little flushed."

"What? Oh, yes. I'm fine. It's just hot in here."

How long had it been since she'd experienced that unmistakable spark of attraction? Long enough for her to have forgotten what it felt like. Even though she knew exactly how long: since before her mother fell ill a year and a half ago.

She briefly closed her eyes, willing the sudden cold away.

How alive it made her feel, that spark of shared attraction. Hot summer sunshine seemed to course through her veins even though it was a chilly and rainy November day. And twenty pounds at least had been lifted from her feet.

"It's not like you to waste time daydreaming," Trudy said as she passed with a mop.

Geneva blinked.

No, it wasn't like her.

And like that, the moment to nip the sexy sensations had arrived. Time to return to the real world where sexy strangers didn't exist.

Damn.

2

"I KNOW YOU SAID you don't plan to be in town long, but about that favor I wanted to ask…" Dari said.

Mace found himself following the pretty waitress with his eyes. She was all curly light brown hair, tanned skin and long legs, even in the unattractive white orthopedic shoes she wore.

He bet her thighs were toned and strong and could grip his hips like nobody's business.

And that mouth…

"Hmm?"

He looked to find Dari grinning at him.

"Thought you weren't interested in dating," his friend said, indicating the waitress.

"I'm not." He sipped his coffee, which was surprisingly good for diner fare. "I might, however, be interested in getting laid."

Dari howled with laughter. "I stand corrected."

"You're sitting, but I get your point." He put his cup down. His words were meant as a joke, but just barely. The waitress did stir something in him he hadn't felt in a while. And while it was physical, there was more to it. There was a genuine quality to her smile, a kindness. "Are you really asking for a favor already? I've been in town, what?" He looked at his watch. "Five minutes?"

"I meant to ask you the first minute."

Dari's expression, more than his words, got Mace's attention. It wasn't like his friend to exaggerate. Whatever he was going to ask was important.

In his career in the military, Mace had come to understand how important it was to immediately recognize who he could count on…and, more importantly, who he couldn't.

Going back to their teenage years, he'd always been able to depend on Dari.

He grimaced, wishing his friendship skills extended to relationships. Maybe he would have had better luck.

His hand instantly went to his cell phone where another voice mail waited from Janine. He didn't expect it to be much different from the first one.

"Shoot," he encouraged now.

"Okay. I've given you a brief rundown on how quickly Lazarus has grown in such a short time. And with that, comes growing pains. Most notably, we're attracting some high-profile contracts I'm sometimes afraid we're not prepared for yet. This one falls solidly into that category." He paused. "There's an ex-general, now a political radio pundit, coming into town the day after tomorrow for a three-day stay, including two public rallies. We've been hired to handle security for the public end of his schedule—transportation, et cetera—in cooperation with his personnel and local law enforcement. While I'm sure we can handle it, well, it would be stupid not to utilize our assets. And I see you as a definite asset in this case, what with your background and your connections."

He nodded. "Go on."

"Well, in a nutshell, I was wondering if you would consider sitting in as co-lead on this one?"

Mace sat back, carefully considering what Dari was saying...and not saying. His friend went on to share some additional details, such as the name of the dignitary. He was familiar with the guy. Hell, nearly everyone in the western hemisphere was familiar with him, if only because of his skill at gaining attention, usually by exhibiting offensive behavior.

"Okay, I get the military connections and the growing pains. But this job sounds pretty run-of-the-mill, tooling around with a political celebrity. What is it you're not telling me?" Mace asked.

"There have been threats."

"Threats."

"Yes. Specific to his visit here."

For the past few years, Mace's military career focus had been counter-terrorism, so this was right up his alley. But...

"And...?" he led.

Dari chuckled and pointed a finger at him. "Never could get anything by you. Truth is, these threats are serious enough to concern his security personnel and serious enough to concern me." He checked the cell phone he had on the table next to his wrist. "And...well, if I'm hoping that by pulling you in on this job, it'll convince you to sign on with us when your tour's over in six months... that's between me and the wall."

Mace considered him.

Dari grinned. "Did I mention that it won't hurt business to have a Navy Cross recipient on board with us? No? Well, then there's that."

He grimaced at the reminder.

"By the way, Megan and I are looking forward to attending the ceremony Saturday."

"You're going?"

"Of course, I'm going. My ass is part of the reason you're getting the sucker. What makes you think I wouldn't be there?"

He took a deep breath.

"I plan to sit up front and center."

"Refill, gentlemen?" a knockout blonde smiled at him suggestively as she held up a coffeepot.

Mace found himself looking for the pretty brunette even as he and Dari held up their cups. The waitress topped them off then hovered for a moment before finally moving away.

"You didn't even look at her," Dari said.

"Sure I did. She's too young and too…"

"Eager?"

"That, too."

They shared a laugh.

"Okay," he said.

"Okay what?"

"Okay, I'll do it. Where do you want me when?" He laughed and looked around the diner again.

There she was.

He found himself relaxing in to the booth as the waitress who'd garnered his attention came through the kitchen door looking even more attractive.

She brought their meals quickly despite the busyness of the place. They ate while Dari outlined the specifics of the assignment.

This beat the hell out of staring at the cracks in his motel room ceiling, feeling guilty about not spending more time at his parents' any day.

And it made him forget about those shadow hands pressing against his neck for a much-needed while.

Mace's gaze followed their waitress where she bussed the table next to theirs, even as another couple moved to occupy it. She was calmly efficient and attentive, smiling warmly despite the obvious crowdedness of the diner as she took their drink orders.

He couldn't help noticing that there was a guy about his age seated at the counter who kept trying to get her attention for more than a second at a time…and that she did everything politely possible to avoid giving it to him.

She briefly glanced in his direction and their gazes met, inspiring something a little more than respect in his response to her.

He smiled and she returned it before she moved on to another table then went back into the kitchen.

Oh, he'd bet she was the type who'd be up for anything, any time. A challenge, a new experience, a new restaurant, it wouldn't matter; she'd be in…and make it doubly worth it just by being there.

"Okay, I'd better get moving," Dari said, edging from the booth. "Megan's already at The Barracks." He stood, pocketing his cell phone. "Thanks for agreeing to come in on this job for me, Mace. You have no idea how much of a relief it will be having you aboard."

"You haven't seen what I charge for babysitting a political big mouth yet."

"Whatever it is, I'm sure you'll be more than worth it." He peeled off a couple bills to pay for his half of the meal. "Sure you won't change your mind and join us for a drink?"

"I'd rather step directly into enemy fire."

"I believe you would." They shook hands and agreed to meet at Lazarus the following morning, then Dari left.

Mace sipped on his coffee and watched his friend through the front window of the diner, even as more customers approached.

He glanced around. The place was more than busy, it bordered on chaotic. At different times, he was aware of a woman swearing in the kitchen, a couple of tables complaining about the lateness of their meals and from what he could tell, there wasn't a busboy to be found.

His cell phone vibrated in his pocket. He fished it out to find Janine's name highlighted again. He sat and watched the screen blink until her call finally rolled over to voice mail.

Why was she being so persistent?

He couldn't even begin to guess. So he didn't try.

He slid the cell back into his pocket without checking the message.

"Dessert?" the pretty waitress asked.

He looked up at her. Despite everything, she managed to treat him as if he was her only customer, where the other waitress practically shooed people from the tables the instant they took their last bite.

"Trudy's chocolate marshmallow pie is the house specialty."

He took her in, noticing how the world seemed to rush around her in a blur while she stood perfectly still.

Of course, that could be just him.

The vintage jukebox in the corner. Definitely the jukebox. He'd play a song—an old one—pull her into his arms…lean her against the machine and work his hand up her skirt to find out just how sweet those thighs and what lay between them were…watch her smile melt into a sexy sigh.

"Maybe later," he said.

He didn't detect any flicker of disappointment that he wasn't leaving to free up the table for another diner.

"And only if you promise to have a piece with me. It'll be my price for having leant a hand..."

THREE HOURS LATER, Geneva was even more impressed with Mace Harrison than when he had first slid from the booth, introduced himself, then asked for an apron and bussing tub.

What guy did that?

None that she knew of.

And certainly not a complete stranger. She'd verified he was new in town since none of the staff nor Trudy could remember seeing him in there before, much less knew him.

And certainly not a completely hot stranger who made her feel like a wanted woman instead of the host of other titles to which she'd grown accustomed lately.

Refusing his generous offer hadn't even entered her mind. Truth was, they were busier than she could ever remember being and Trudy's usually easily dismissed sounds of dismay had begun turning into very real ones.

Mace had been as good as gold, a natural as Mel had noted, his sheer size and impressive presence not interfering with his assisting without being asked, and doing at least two of the jobs for which they were short staffed, lightening the load for the rest of them.

Was he military? She guessed yes. And that normally would have counted as a strike against him in her personal notebook, considering her experience with members of the armed forces.

But what had happened tonight was anything but normal.

And what was happening to her fell solidly into the same category.

Finally, one by one, satisfied customers began to ease to a workable trickle, and then the staff began to leave, including Trudy herself, who begged off with a migraine. Thankfully, Dustin had given up trying to corner her an hour ago and left, as well. Only Mel remained. But seeing as closing time was in ten minutes, he had only one order to finish up and she knew he'd be leaving, too, as he always did to get home quickly to his wife and family.

Now, as Mace stood spraying dishes to go into the washer, she couldn't help staring at his hands. He'd rolled up the sleeves of his crisp white shirt while the full-body white apron covered the front from his chest down to his knees. If his feet hurt in his dress shoes, she couldn't tell, even though he'd been on his feet all night.

Her own dogs were barking loudly and she wore the equivalent of gym shoes.

Geneva absently wrapped up the little that remained of the meat loaf and mashed potatoes, not realizing she was still staring at Mace until he asked, "Did I spill something?"

She met his gaze, reading the telltale grin there, then smiled herself. "Sorry. It's been a long day."

Tiffany had left in a huff about the same time Dustin had, apparently disappointed that her obvious flirting wasn't gaining her any more attention from the unhired help than Mel got.

Actually, Geneva was pretty sure she'd gotten less.

Interesting. Not many men were capable of refusing the pretty blonde's charms at normal speed, much less when she amped them up. And she'd definitely set her sights on Mace.

A few minutes later, Mel removed his apron and grabbed his jacket. "Well, it's that time again, kids."

Geneva held up the paper bag she'd readied for him and he took it, giving her a loud kiss on the cheek.

"Thanks, doll. See you on the morrow."

"Tell Alice hi."

"Will do. 'Night."

"'Night."

And just like that it was only her and Mace.

Well, and three people at two tables in the other room.

He finished up the dishes while she closed the last of the garbage bags then washed her hands.

"How about that pie?" he asked.

"How about it? Take a seat at the counter. I'll join you in a minute."

"Deal."

She watched as he did as suggested, trying hard not to stare at his tight rear end and failing.

All right, she could be forgiven this once, right? For being selfish? For being needy?

For being a woman?

She went about wrapping up and putting away a few other items. It had been a long day. Still, strangely she didn't feel tired.

She peeked around the window that opened up into the dining area, catching Mace's gaze.

"Be right there," she said.

"Take your time."

She ducked back away and caught her breath.

Okay, she could do this. All she had to do was serve him pie and coffee and tell him she was pregnant. That was sure to douse whatever spark had ignited between them but quick.

Only she was hoping it wouldn't...

3

MACE CLEANED UP after the last of the customers, then fed change into the vintage jukebox that had remained pretty much silent all night, selecting a few '50s classics before sitting back down at the counter. He glanced at his watch. Twenty minutes had passed since Geneva had said she'd be right there. He'd noticed an employees' locker room off the kitchen and guessed she'd taken advantage of it. He realized he was still wearing the borrowed apron and took it off, laying it on the stool next to him.

The past few hours had passed in a welcome flurry of activity. The best decision he'd made was to trade his night of motel sitting for lending a hand at the busy diner. He'd never done very well left with too much time on his hands. And even he could jog only so long before his muscles protested.

Bussing tables and doing dishes and occasionally filling coffee cups had given him something productive to do. And feeling like a part of a team hadn't hurt.

If Geneva's gratefully surprised and sinfully sexy smile every now and again had anything to do with his sense of satisfaction, he wasn't copping to it.

"Sorry," she said, finally coming out of the kitchen. "I just wanted to finish a few things up."

He blinked. She still wore the same gray uniform and ruffled white apron, but she looked...different somehow. Refreshed. And hotter than hell.

She put down something in a bag and then moved to the pie case while he rounded the other side of the counter.

"Coffee?" he asked, holding up a pot.

"I'd love a cup of decaf."

"One decaf coming up."

He poured two cups and placed them on the counter while she took not one, but four different pie plates out of the display case. Each held at least two pieces. She reached into the fridge and pulled out a can of whipped cream, placing it next to them.

He sat down and she took the stool beside him.

He was abnormally taken with the can of whipped cream; the thought of licking a line of it off her skin from collarbone to toes, stopping for longer stays along the way that seemed particularly tempting.

He wondered what she'd say if he suggested it...

"I figured since you wouldn't let Trudy pay you, you're entitled to as much pie as you want." She handed him a fork.

"Part of the deal was that you join me."

She held up her own fork.

He chuckled, watching as she dug into what he guessed was the chocolate marshmallow one. Damn, but she had a sexy mouth. What made it even sexier still was that she didn't appear the least bit aware of the effect she was having on him.

"So, tell me," she said around a bite, "are you from around these parts, soldier?"

He chose the blueberry. "In a manner of speaking, yes."

"Dubious answer to a yes or no question."

To his surprise, he found himself explaining his being a military brat and staying with his grandfather as a teen. Even more surprising was the casual way in which he did so. He wasn't usually given to sharing information with anyone. But she made it easy, her face open, her interest unselfish.

There was something strangely…intimate about sitting, just the two of them, in an empty retro diner, '50s music playing on a jukebox, the street beyond the front windows quiet and dark.

Even as they talked, he watched her eat, something he found strangely erotic. He couldn't remember enjoying watching a woman eat. Then again, he could barely recall a woman eating in his presence, unless she was a colleague or a friend.

But watching Geneva savor the blueberry pie didn't qualify as either.

"Which branch?" she asked after he'd fallen silent for a moment, reflecting on what he'd said; reflecting on her.

"What?"

"Which branch did you choose?"

"Marines."

"Same as your father?"

He paused. "No."

Curious, he'd forgotten having chosen a different path than his parent.

Funny how things worked out.

"I can relate." She got up. "I could go for a glass of milk. How about you?"

Surprisingly, the idea appealed to him. "Sure."

She poured them two large glasses then sat down again.

"I take it that means you're from around here in a manner of speaking, as well?" he asked.

She nodded, then licked a milk mustache from her upper lip. Mace felt his pants tighten at the innocent move.

"I followed…someone here five years ago. I've been looking for a way out ever since."

"He still around?"

She smiled. "Who said it was a guy?"

"I did."

Her smile widened. "No, he was history two months in."

For reasons he couldn't be sure of, he was glad that not only was the guy part of her past, but she didn't seem to have a problem with leaving him there. "Where are you from originally?"

"Ohio. Toledo. Whipped cream?"

She shook the can and then held it above the pies.

Mace felt the urge to reposition the tip above her lips so he might kiss it from them.

"Sure," he said instead.

"Tell me when…"

She began spraying…

And spraying…

Covering what remained in all of the pie pans.

"When?" she asked.

"Huh?"

She stopped spraying and laughed. The sound was deep and husky…and made him want to kiss her all the more.

"I was waiting for you tell me when."

He chuckled and switched his attention to the cherry pie, taking an extra-big bite to assuage the growing desire to run his fingers up her knee, which was left nicely bare by her skirt.

"So tell me about the other guy," he said.

She held a hand under her cream-dripping fork as she moved it toward his mouth. "What guy?"

He began to refuse the bite of chocolate marshmallow

pie, or rather her offering of it, then did the opposite by opening his mouth instead.

"The one at the counter panting after you all night," he said with his mouth half full.

"Dustin? Dustin doesn't pant. He moons." The smile eased from her face and she suddenly avoided his gaze.

Then she appeared to make her mind up about something and her expression opened up again.

She brushed her hands together then went to the register, taking out a handful of change. The jukebox had gone silent while they talked.

"Any requests?"

"B-17."

She laughed.

He liked that she got the reference.

"Who sang that song?" she asked. "No, wait…don't tell me. I'll get it."

"I'd tell you if I knew. Female, I know that."

"Olivia Newton-John."

"Yeah…yeah. I think you're right."

She made her selections then came to sit down again. "I know I'm right. B-17 is the song."

They shared a laugh as she picked up her fork again.

God, but he couldn't remember a time he'd enjoyed an evening more. Her easygoing demeanor, sexy smile and revitalizing openness made Geneva great company.

And, he hoped, great in bed.

"So, does it always get that insane in this place?" he asked.

"You'd be surprised by how popular Meat loaf Mondays are." She smiled and licked her fork. "It's usually pretty busy all the time, but right now the flu is knocking down a few more staff than usual." She sipped her milk, reminding him of a kitten lapping cream. "Well, that and blind dates."

"Excuse me?"

"One of the missing waitresses had a blind date, I guess. At least that's the rumor." She toyed with a bit of crust. "I hope it's not true or Trudy might fire her."

"Can she afford to?"

"Afford to or not, she will. Trudy's funny that way. You could break every glass in the place, but if you're honest and here on time, she'll keep you on."

"I'm thinking honesty is important in a business of this nature."

"Yeah." The song changed from an upbeat to a slow tune on the jukebox. "So how long are you in town?"

"A week."

The reminder of why he was back here was enough to loosen the fit of his pants a bit, but not much.

"You staying with family?"

He shook his head. "Nah. Bunking at the motel on University. You?"

"I live here."

He chuckled. "Right. Sorry."

"My mom and I did live together for a while, though…"

Something in her voice captured his attention.

She cleared her throat. "She passed a little over two months ago."

"I'm sorry to hear it." Damn. Talk about a pants-loosening change in conversation.

"Thanks. She was sick for a long time. Lymphoma. She was diagnosed shortly after she moved here."

He didn't know what to say, so he said nothing.

They ate in silence for a while.

Then she leaned back and groaned. "God, I can't believe I ate so much of this. I feel like I'm going to burst."

Mace looked at where they'd nearly polished off all four

pies. "I can't believe it, either. Although I think I have a ways to go before I reach bursting stage."

She smiled. "I may have room for a bite or two more."

Geneva Davis was unlike any woman he'd met in a good long while. By now, most of the women he usually dated would have checked their lipstick at least twice and made one run to the ladies' room to check on the rest of their appearance.

Of course, he allowed that this wasn't much like a date, either.

Still…

"Are you career?" she asked.

"Military? Nah. Six months to go."

He found it interesting he'd answered in the negative. When had he made the decision not to sign up for another tour?

Just then, he realized. No matter what happened at Lazarus this week, he knew he didn't want to exchange active duty for a desk job in Washington.

"Thank you," he said.

"For what?"

"For asking me that. I didn't know what my answer would be until you did."

"You were considering staying longer?"

"I was."

"But not anymore."

He took in her pretty face. "Not anymore."

His cell phone vibrated at the same time hers rang.

They laughed. Mace took his out of his pocket even as she consulted hers.

Janine.

Damn.

He refused the late-hour call and put the cell back into his pocket, watching as she pretty much did the same thing.

Then she began toying with the crust again.

"Someone you don't want to hear from?" he asked.

She nodded. "You?"

"Yeah."

Then, surprisingly, he found himself telling her all about Janine and what had gone down eight months earlier.

He couldn't be sure how long he'd talked, or exactly how much he'd revealed, but she'd patiently listened, nodding when the situation called for it, making encouraging sounds when he needed them.

"So...just to be sure I'm following you," she said once he finally stopped talking and teetered on the verge of regret for having said too much. "She not only left you for someone else because you were gone too long... She was messing around with him while you were still a couple, even introducing him as a friend to you during your last leave and including him in things you did together.... And now that you're back, she wants to see you again?"

He grimaced. "That would be the long and the short of it, yes."

"How do you feel about that?"

He raised his brows and leaned back. "I don't know."

And he didn't. Not really.

He did know he didn't want to get involved with her again.

She fell silent.

"And your phone call?" he asked.

She blinked up at him. "Huh?"

He repeated the question.

"Oh. Dustin."

"Ah. The panter."

"The mooner." She rested her chin in her hand, her elbow propped against the counter. "Or, as the rest of the diner staff like to call him, my baby daddy."

She tilted her head slightly to look at him as if waiting for his response.

"Oh. You have a child together."

"No. Not yet."

He squinted at her. "Now I'm not sure I'm following you."

She looked away as if weighing whether or not to continue, then met his gaze fully, her chin coming up a tad higher than before. "I'm pregnant...and he's the father...."

4

THERE. SHE'D said it.

Geneva paid an inordinate amount of attention to the crust she was pushing in and out of the whipped cream that remained in the chocolate marshmallow pie pan. By rights, she should have said something much sooner. The minute they'd sat down at the counter. Maybe even found a way to casually mention it early on. Something along the lines of, "Gee, I can't remember my feet ever hurting this badly when I wasn't pregnant," or "Boy, if I wasn't pregnant, I'd take you back to my place and do all the naughty things I see playing out behind your sexy eyes."

She couldn't be sure why she'd been hesitant to say anything.

Yes, she could; she knew exactly why she hadn't shared the news: because for that short time, she'd enjoyed being just her. Just a single woman enjoying flirting with a hot, single man.

"You're…pregnant?"

The two words broke through her reverie. She tried to decide whether the emotion behind them was more of shock or regret, but all she seemed capable of concentrating on was now that the proverbial cat was out of the bag,

there was no getting it back in. You couldn't exactly retract
something like that. Pretend you were joking.

And why would she? For a frivolous, albeit surely hot
night between the sheets with a handsome stranger?

Wasn't that how she'd ended up as a single, expectant
mother in the first place?

She grimaced and found herself eating the crust, even
though she hadn't intended to.

Comparing what had happened between her and Dustin
two months ago and…well, tonight, was like saying the
satin of a wedding dress and the satin that lined a coffin
were the same.

She drank the rest of her milk to help wash the crumbs
down.

"Yes," she said simply.

Mace sat back as if stepping out of the path of a speeding truck. Not that she could blame him. Essentially, that's
what she was, wasn't she?

Not that she viewed her baby in that light. While unexpected, she'd instantly grown attached to the idea of
having a child growing within her. Her son or daughter.
And meeting him or her topped the list of things she most
looked forward to.

When it came to the opposite sex seeing her as dating
material, however…well, she could understand how that
would come as a major deterrent.

Was there such a thing as a pregnant-woman fetish?

She nearly laughed at the ridiculous thought.

What man in his right mind would want to make love
to a woman already pregnant with another man's child.

"So, you two were…are a couple?"

She blinked to look at him. "Dustin and I? No. We've
always been just friends."

He nodded slowly but she could tell he was not only not

following her, he was so far behind he couldn't make her out in the distance.

She propped her chin in her hand and tried to explain. Not that the confusing story was all that clear to her.

Taking care of her mother while her illness had slowly ultimately robbed her of the tiniest breath had hollowed Geneva out until sometimes it seemed only her beating, hurting heart remained. Her friends and everyone at the diner had been a tremendous source of support, but only she knew how deep her pain went. How watching her mom die by millimeters had profoundly impacted her.

Yes, she could have put her mom in a hospice. But she'd wanted to spend every moment with her that she could. And the only way she could work out how to do that was by having Hospice come to them at her apartment.

Then, suddenly, her mother was gone.

It still seemed…strange, somehow. The shock she'd felt at not having her mother there anymore. She'd been moving toward that end agonizing moment by agonizing moment, yet the moment she was finally released, Geneva hadn't wanted to let her go.

And Dustin had been there to hold on to instead.

"We met when I first started taking graphic design years ago at University of Colorado, Colorado Springs," she offered. "We'd always been friends and had never even considered dating," she said quietly. "And I know he doesn't want anything more now. Not really. He's projecting what he thinks traditionally should happen on to our untraditional circumstances. Trying to do what's right."

She looked to find Mace still nodding…and still somewhat behind her.

Finally, he smiled awkwardly and shook his head. "I'm sorry. My response probably falls just shy of rude…or is maybe full-out rude. It's just that I'm having a hard time wrapping my head around the fact that you're pregnant."

She smiled. "Stick around. It won't be hard in a month or so when I start showing."

She caught herself. Of course, he wouldn't be around in a month or so. He'd be off somewhere on his final six-month deployment. And even if he wasn't, there was no chance he'd stick around anyway.

She squinted at him. Was there?

Behind him, the jukebox clicked on B-17.

They both laughed.

"Okay," he said. "Time for me to stop acting like an idiot and accept the fact that I misread the signs."

"Signs?"

His gaze moved over her face and she felt herself blush. "Yes. The regular girl-guy stuff."

She smiled. "You didn't misread anything. I'm pregnant, not dead, Mace."

He wore that "speeding truck coming toward him" look again.

She reached over and touched his arm. "Sorry. You're obviously having a hard time with this. So why don't we just keep this simple." She held out her hand. "Hi, I'm Geneva Davis and I'm pregnant. Would you like to be friends?"

He stared at her hand, then her face, then her hand again. He slowly took it. "I'd love to be friends, Geneva Davis."

FRIENDS...

A good ten hours had passed since his late-night conversation with Geneva in the deserted diner, the jukebox playing in the background, whipped cream, pie plates and glasses of milk littering the counter in front of them, and all he could think of was, despite everything she told him, he wanted to be much more than friends.

"Sir?"

Mace looked at Jonathon Reece, one of Lazarus's personnel.

"Darius would like to speak with you." He held out a cell.

He took the phone. "Thanks."

He stepped away from the table in the downtown Denver hotel conference room. He'd been in there for an hour going over the sketchy schedule of the visiting dignitary with Lazarus reps and sheriff's deputies, waiting for Darius to arrive.

"Hey," he said into the phone.

"Hey, yourself. Look, I got called in on an urgent matter back at the office. Would you mind taking the lead?"

Mace glanced at the ten Lazarus reps, nine men and one woman, who were looking expectantly at him.

"I'm afraid it looks like it would be for the duration. I've got a kidnapping/ransom case out of L.A. that just came in…." Darius continued.

Mace grimaced. Not because he wasn't up for the job. But because he would only have today to build up a rapport with the personnel he would be overseeing.

He took in Reece standing military tall a short ways away.

"I'd rather not. Isn't there someone else you trust? How about Reece?"

"He's good, but I need someone with more experience. And I'm not talking security. One of Norman's reps will be there in an hour. He'll give you a full rundown of what we're looking at threat-wise. And the sheriff's office already has several routes mapped out."

"I've seen them."

"Good." Dari said something to someone on his end of the line. "I really wouldn't ask this of you unless it was absolutely necessary, Mace. I'd owe you big-time."

"Last check, your debt is already considerable."

Dari chuckled. "Got me there. Tell you what, I'll name my firstborn after you…"

Mace held the phone to his ear even after he'd signed off, the mention of children bringing Geneva back to mind.

Why, oh why, did she have to be pregnant?

He handed Reece his cell, took out his own and told the crew to take fifteen.

He'd gotten her number last night, but honestly hadn't intended to use it.

Why then was he running his thumb over the cell pad, the mere thought of hearing her voice making his pulse run faster?

The room emptied out and he sat on the edge of the conference table. He pressed the button to illuminate the cell screen only to find another voice-mail message from Janine.

He sighed and rubbed his face. At his motel, he'd finally retrieved her messages. Five all told. The first two had been quietly nice. The next two longer narratives—the last one, she'd simply said she really needed to talk to him.

He didn't like the sound of that. And, yes, he admitted, a part of him was afraid of how he'd react when he finally saw her, even though he knew, with everything he was, that he wanted nothing to do with her.

"Frank and I broke up… Well, I broke up with him… Almost immediately after you left for your last tour… Look, Mace, I know I have no right to ask you this, but it's important I talk to you… In person… Apologize…"

But it wasn't that message so much as the next one that proved the cause for concern:

"I've missed you…" A small, nervous laugh. "You know how hard that is for me to say, don't you? Me? Who's never wrong about anything." A pause then, "But I was wrong about this. Wrong about you. I should never have done what I had. You didn't deserve it. We didn't deserve it. I really need to see you. Please…"

It had been damn near impossible to get to sleep after that one. He hadn't heard a word from her in months. Then the minute he gets back into town, he's bombarded with calls.

He honestly didn't know what to do.

He caught himself running his thumb over the cell pad again, Geneva's name and number highlighted in his address book.

He smiled.

Yes, he did. He knew exactly what to do…

5

"BE MY GIRLFRIEND for a week…"

Geneva couldn't believe her ears. She was washing up her few dishes, trying to ignore how it would usually be double, but not now that her mother was gone.

She dropped a glass and it broke in two at the sink bottom. She hadn't realized she cut herself until she saw a perfect dot of blood on the tip of her left ring finger. She braced her cell phone against her shoulder, then ran the small wound under cold running water, wrapping a paper towel around her finger.

"Hello? Geneva? Are you still there?"

"Who is this?" she asked.

Silence.

She laughed. "Sorry. I know it's Mace."

She knew it was Mace because his name came up. She'd entered him into her address book the instant he'd given her his number before leaving the diner the night before.

Only she hadn't expected to hear from him.

Ever.

"So…" she said. "I'm still here." She turned and leaned her hips against the counter. "I'm sorry. I'm thinking it might have been better to begin that sentence with something like 'Are you sitting down?"

Mace chuckled. "Are you?"

"No."

"Then maybe you should."

"Maybe I should." She didn't budge from the counter, although she did look at the small table and two chairs set against the wall she hadn't used in over two months. "I'm sorry? Could you repeat what you just said?"

"I asked if you might consider being my girlfriend for a week."

His request made no more sense now than it had the first time he made it.

"Wait, I think I'm missing an important word there," he added.

"And that would be?"

"Pretend."

She squinted hard. "I'd like to say that helps, but… well, it doesn't."

He laughed again. "I'm working so I can't go into detail right now, but let me just say this. You want…what's his name? Dustin? To stop pursuing you. And I want my ex to stop her useless efforts. So, if we date, or pretend to, it should go a long ways toward helping us to that end."

"Ah," she said.

Okay. Now his meaning was beginning to sink in.

"What time do you get off tonight?" he asked.

"Seven."

"Okay. I'll pick you up at 7:15 at the diner for our first date."

"Okay. Sure. Date?"

"Pretend date. I'll take you somewhere I'm sure to run into Janine. And, I'm guessing, Dustin will be at the diner when I pick you up?"

"Probably." Most likely.

"Well, then…a win-win all the way around."

She heard voices on his side of the phone.

"Look, I've got to run. I hate to rush you, but, well… what do you say?"

She found herself incapable of saying anything.

The idea of spending time with Mace? For any reason? Phenomenal.

"By the way," he said, "if this is to work, we can't say anything to anybody about it. The fake part, that is."

"Of course." Funny he should say that. She'd been con- sidering asking for a little time so she could call Trudy and ask her advice. But he was right. If this was to work, they couldn't tell anybody. If Trudy knew, well, then so would Mel, then Tiffany…and within five minutes the news would reach Dustin's ears.

"So, is that a yes?" Mace asked.

She found herself smiling, imagining the possibilities. "Yes. I guess it is."

She swore she could hear him smiling. And her body reacted the same way it would have if he'd been standing in front of her—with a rush of heat.

"Good," he said. "See you tonight then."

He ended the call, leaving Geneva to remain standing at the counter, smiling stupidly at the opposite wall with- out complete comprehension of where she was or what she was doing.

"Oh, stop it," she told herself. "It's just a game." She pushed from the counter to get a bandage from the bath- room. "He needs to scare off his ex and I…"

Her hand went to her still-flat belly.

And she needed to convince Dustin that while he was welcome in her life as a friend and as the father of her child, the door was firmly shut when it came to anything else.

She passed her home office, which was essentially what would have been the dining room, got what she needed from the bathroom, then heard her active computer chime, indicating she had email.

She fastened the bandage to her cut and clicked to access the message. It was from Johnny's Jalopies. She'd sent them the copy they'd requested last night.

"Love it! But…" she read.

More changes.

She sighed and sat down in her swivel chair. Whoever invented the word "but" should be taken out back and shot. Multiple times. With a large-gauge shotgun.

She read over her client's suggestions—the fifth round—and wondered how an auto repair shop owner had gotten so picky. It was a Black Friday sales flyer, not a family crest.

Family…

She caught herself rubbing her belly again and smiled. If she needed a reminder of why tonight would only be for show, she had only to remember her condition. Of course, Mace wouldn't be interested in dating her otherwise. Why would he?

So she'd go out with him and help scare off her ex. Do what he wanted. Enjoy his company. Have fun. And he'd do what she needed. Which was…

She caught sight of the Harvest Dance flyer she'd helped design pinned to her corkboard then took it down. The event was this Sunday night. Perfect. She and Mace, dancing, obviously a couple, should be enough to persuade Dustin she wasn't interested.

She called the number listed on the flyer, arranged to pick up two tickets, then began writing Mace a text with the info.

She hesitated pressing Send, rereading the message five times.

Should she be friendlier? Perhaps act like a girlfriend? Maybe even ask him before arranging for the tickets.

She gave an eye roll and pressed Send.

Then she sat back, ordering herself not to check for a response every two minutes.

She tilted the cell phone so she could see the display then laughed at herself even as she got down to the business of responding to Johnny, trying to ignore the zing of electricity that seemed to course through her body...

DAMN, HE WAS LATE.

Mace checked his watch for the third time in as many minutes as he got out of the rental car he'd parked outside the diner. The meetings in Denver with the sheriff's deputies and General Norman's men had taken much longer than he'd anticipated. Simply, this assignment wasn't going to be quite the run-of-the-mill one he'd first thought.

Norman was receiving death threats, very plausible ones, in connection to his Denver visit.

It seemed the controversial radio show host, who was rumored to be considering a run for political office, was not only popular with his supporters, but with his haters, as well.

And more than a few wanted to see him dead.

His visit to the Mile High City was for four days and his schedule was jam-packed.

"What's being done to find the suspect?" he'd asked three hours into the meetings.

Everyone had stared at him as if he'd grown an eyeball in the middle of his forehead.

He held his hands, palms up, on the reams of documents in front of him. "It's just common sense to me. I mean, we're spending all this time arranging to protect Robin from an unknown threat when, maybe, we should be getting to know the threat better." "Robin" was Norman's agreed-upon security name, as in bird dropping in for a brief visit before heading south again.

That's when the meeting took a turn that had ended up extending it. And he'd still had the forty-minute commute back to Colorado Springs and a stop at his motel for a shower and change of clothes.

He glanced as his watch as he opened the diner door for exiting customers. It was just before eight. Geneva was going to be pissed. If she was even still there…

He stopped inside the door.

She was.

She sat at the end of the counter looking better than any one woman had the right to.

Certainly any one pregnant woman.

He swallowed hard. She wore what to anyone else might look like a simple fall flowered dress. But to him, it might as well have been a fire-engine-red teddy and garters. She sat on the stool with her long legs crossed and was half turned away from him, talking to the diner owner, her dark hair a sexy cloud around her face.

He felt the urge to loosen his tie, only he wasn't wearing one.

Then she saw him.

Oh, boy.

Maybe this hadn't been the brightest idea he'd ever had. Damn if he didn't feel like walking up and kissing her breathless.

She didn't get up. She merely swiveled her stool until she was facing him more fully. He noticed the V of the neck of her dress that revealed soft, tanned skin and full breasts.

He realized he hadn't moved since entering and forced himself to walk toward her.

"Hi," he said, holding out the simple red rose he held. "Sorry I'm late."

Her smile seemed to take up the whole of her face. "Forgiven."

He barely registered that the room had gone quiet. Everyone was watching them, a few customers at tables but mostly staff gathered around the counter…and Dustin, who sat closer to her now, but had likely occupied the same end stool he had the night before.

"Hi," he said, extending his hand to the guy. "I'm Mace."

The other man hesitated, then accepted his shake. "Dustin."

"Dustin? Nice to meet you. Geneva's told me a lot about you. Congratulations on the baby."

He appeared surprised, then wary. "Thanks."

For a moment, Mace felt sorry for the poor guy. He couldn't say he blamed him for wanting more. But it was Geneva's call and he had no cause to question the line she'd drawn.

"Ready?" he asked her.

"Ready."

She got up and he helped her with the light, fall raincoat she took off a neighboring stool. He caught a whiff of her perfume—the scent of something fresh and sexy—and was helpless to stop himself from humming as his fingers brushed her hair back over the collar.

"You smell good," he said.

"Better than meat loaf?"

"Better than meat loaf."

Her smile widened. "You smell pretty good yourself."

He was aware of the jukebox playing and wondered if

she'd made the selection. No, he didn't wonder. He knew she had. Because the song playing was B-17.

He offered his arm and she took it.

"Good night, everyone," he said as he opened the door for her.

"Have fun" was one of the many returns.

Fun. Yes.

Somehow Mace didn't think the word came near covering it.

6

GENEVA COULDN'T REMEMBER a time when she'd felt so... tongue-tied. She didn't have a clue what to say as Mace drove her to their destination. And where were they going again?

She found herself burying her nose in the bloom of the rose he'd given her, breathing deeply then smiling. There had been a minute or two when she'd been afraid he was going to be a no-show. And she hadn't quite known how to feel about that. Had it been a real date, she would have been upset. But because it was a pretend one...?

Then he'd stood looking at her in that way from the door. And all thought of real or pretend had faded away like the morning fog, leaving her happy he'd come.

Thankfully, the ride wasn't long. He pulled into the parking lot of a place called The Barracks, which appeared to be a pub she'd passed often but had never been to.

"Thank you," she said as he switched off the car.

He looked at her. "You're welcome. I think. What are you thanking me for?"

She held up the rose. "For this. For saying what you did to Dustin. For suggesting we go out."

His gaze caught and held hers for long moments, making it all too easy to forget this wasn't real at all.

"I'm thinking I'm the one who's going to come out ahead in our little arrangement. Stay where you are. I'll open the door for you."

He got out before she could ponder his words. Then he got her door, allowing her to climb out. Then he closed it behind her and offered her his arm again.

She took it and shivered.

"Are you warm enough?"

"Enough. Yes."

Truth was, her shiver had nothing to do with the chilly evening.

"I was hoping we'd have a little time before Janine arrived," he said as they walked inside the pub. "But I'm afraid my lateness isn't going to allow for it. I'm thinking she might already be inside."

"Have you told her anything?" she asked as he helped her with her coat.

"No."

"Mace!"

A man called out to him from a nearby table packed with other guys. Geneva stood smiling politely as he greeted each of them. It was easy to see they were long-time friends he hadn't seen in a while. That he took time to introduce them to her touched her in a way she was unprepared to acknowledge.

"Sorry about that," he said after he'd spoken to them for a few minutes, promising that they'd get together for a beer before he left town again.

"It's okay."

He led her to a free table and pulled out a chair for her. She sat down and thanked him.

"Have you eaten yet?" he asked.

"No. But that's okay. I had a big lunch."

Truth was, the heavy smell of all things fried was doing interesting and not welcoming things to her stomach.

"You sure?"

She nodded.

A waitress appeared. He placed an order for a beer and asked what she wanted.

"Tomato juice with Bloody Mary mix on the side, hold the vodka."

She looked to find Mace smiling at her.

"What?"

He shook his head. "Nothing."

She shifted in her chair, trying but failing to look casual. In all honesty, she felt anything but in Mace's presence.

"I have to admit, I feel a little sorry for the guy," he said.

"Who? Dustin?"

He nodded. "Yeah. I mean, I can't blame him for wanting more."

She felt herself blush. Which was stupid. "He just thinks he wants more. He feels he has to man up or some sort of thing."

He held her gaze for a long moment then shook his head. "No, Geneva. It's not something he thinks he wants. It's something he wants…"

She fussed with her skirt and recrossed her legs, readying an objection, but somehow couldn't find the words.

Then she caught sight of a knockout blonde at the end of the bar. The woman seemed intently focused on their table.

"Um, what does Janine look like?" she asked.

"Why?"

"Because I think she's already here."

His grimace spoke volumes. "I was afraid of that."

Geneva looked at him. "She's beautiful."

"Yeah. I guess she is. I just wish it went beyond skin deep."

"How long did you guys date?"

"A year."

"Well…it must have gone deeper than what you're saying to have lasted that long."

"Nah. I just hoped it did."

The blonde got up. "Don't look now, but she's heading in our direction," Geneva added.

She watched as he stiffened.

"Mace?"

He looked up and smiled. Only it wasn't the type of smile she'd seen him wear before. "Janine. Hi."

He got up and gave her a brief hug then turned. "I'd like you to meet Geneva. Geneva, this is Janine."

"Hi," Geneva said. "Nice to meet you, finally."

One of the blonde's perfectly penciled brows arched at the last word. Geneva couldn't help noticing the way Mace's smile broadened.

"Nice to meet…you, too. Geneva, wasn't it?"

"Yes."

"I'd like to say Mace mentioned you…"

"Well, we haven't exactly talked," he said.

"No. But I was hoping to talk to you tonight," Janine said pointedly. "Alone."

"Sorry," he said. "But if you'd like to join Geneva and I…?"

Geneva's stomach tightened at the thought of sharing their table with the pretty blonde, despite Mace's obvious coolness toward her.

"No, no. Go on ahead. I'll catch up with you another time."

"Okay."

"Have a nice night," she said.

"Thank you. I'm sure we will," Geneva said. "We always do."

Mace waited until Janine walked away then sat back down, his shoulders still stiff, his face tight.

"What's she doing?" he asked.

Geneva looked casually over his shoulder. "She appears to be…yes, she's leaving."

Finally, he seemed to relax. "Good."

She couldn't help relaxing a bit herself.

"Sorry to tell you this, but that's not the last you're going to hear from her, I'm afraid."

He reached across and covered her hands with his. "Why do you think I asked for a week of your time?"

His grin was all too warm…and far too sexy.

"Five minutes," he said.

"I'm not following you."

"Oh yes, you will. In five minutes. Through that door. I'm going to take you somewhere to get something proper to eat."

"Really, that's not necessary."

"It's completely necessary. No arguing."

Their drinks arrived, but neither of them touched them. She watched as Mace peeled off a few bills, placed them under his beer bottle, then got up to help her back on with her coat.

She was glad it was just going to be the two of them again. And their…friendship.

LATER THAT NIGHT, Geneva opened the door to her apartment. She didn't think twice about leaving it open for him to follow her inside. This wasn't a date and they'd spent the past two hours laughing and talking at a nice Italian restaurant up the street from The Barracks. She'd had minestrone soup and garlic breadsticks—something she'd never dare order on a real date—and accepted a couple of bites of his seafood linguine.

"Coffee?" she asked, shrugging out of her coat and stepping out of her shoes, leaving both by the door.

"I'd love some. Nice place."

"Thanks."

Her mom would have loved Mace, she couldn't help thinking. Besides the fact that he was hotter than any guy she'd ever dated, he was kind and smart and knew how to make a woman feel like a lady.

She put the coffee on, then got cookies out of the cupboard.

"Thank you."

Mace's quiet words caught her off guard.

At the restaurant, both of them had laughed over how successful their first night out as a "couple" had gone, joking about where they could take it from there. He'd agreed to attend the dance, so long as she went to some event or other with him on Saturday afternoon.

"You're welcome. Thank you back."

"You're welcome. But that's not what I meant."

She took mugs out of the cupboard. "Oh?"

"I really enjoy spending time with you."

She couldn't help a goofy grin. "Ditto."

She busied herself getting out the cream and sugar and arranging them on a tray with the cookies.

"Why don't you find something on the stereo while I get this ready?"

"What? Sure."

The moment he left the room, she exhaled, unaware she'd been holding her breath. The way he sometimes looked at her... She gave a tiny shiver. It was all too easy to think this—what was happening—had little to do with a fake relationship and everything to do with a real one.

She heard the soft strains of Harry Chapin and caught her breath. Moments later, she placed the tray on the coffee table in the living room.

"Is this okay?" he asked, turning from the stereo.

"Yes. More than okay. One of my favorites. One of Mom's, too."

"Are you sure? If it makes you uncomfortable…"

She shook her head. "No, it's perfect."

A week ago she might have burst into tears at the selection. Even now, her eyes moistened. But the rough edges of her grief were slowly beginning to soften and she was beginning to be able to appreciate things connected to her mother.

He joined her on the sofa and accepted his coffee cup.

"So, tell me…" she said carefully after handing him a cup. "Why do I get the feeling you're not over Janine?"

7

THE WAY MACE SAW IT, she could have dumped the contents of his coffee cup down the front of his slacks and she couldn't have surprised him more.

"I'm sorry. What?"

She sat back on the flowery sofa that boasted a ton of pillows and tucked her legs under her, looking sexier now than she had earlier. Which, considering what she'd just said, was a bit of a feat.

She picked up her coffee cup and shrugged lightly, although he got the impression there was nothing light about the question she'd just thrown at him.

"I don't know. The way I see it, if you're not truly interested in someone, then you feel indifferent toward them. And I think indifference is the furthest thing you feel when it comes to Janine."

Mace rested his forearms on his knees, cupping his coffee in his hands, carefully considering her words.

"Does that make sense?" she asked.

"To a certain extent, yes." But that wasn't all of it. "I suppose what you're saying is true in some ways. But not in the way you mean."

"Then in what way?"

He looked at her, hating the idea that she believed he still might be harboring emotions for his ex. "What remains in my feelings for Janine is hurt. And maybe confusion." He shook his head. "No, definitely confusion. A lot of it..."

He sat back as well so he partially faced her.

The apartment was feminine, but not overpoweringly so. While the sofa they sat on boasted a chintzy flowery upholstery, the rest of the furniture was almost mission style, and there wasn't another flower in the place. He'd noticed the dining room didn't boast the traditional table, but was rather an office...and a working one at that. He recalled her telling him she was also a graphics designer and that she had nearly built her client list up to the point where she could permanently quit working Rocky's. But she said she liked the routine, and could see herself still working part-time for some while yet, if just to make sure she got out of her apartment regularly.

Besides, she'd told him, some of her best ideas came while she was watching a customer's face as he or she tried to decide between the open-faced roast beef sandwich or the closed.

Of course, he could have done without that particular comparison; it made him think of edging something else open...

"It's complicated," he said, continuing his thread of thought. "I mean, I loved her. God knows I loved her. I would never think of doing to her what she did to me. It just wasn't a consideration. My parents...well, they've been married for over thirty years and to my knowledge, neither of them have ever looked at anyone else, much less been unfaithful."

Geneva nodded. "I understand. When you love somebody, well..."

She left her sentence unfinished.

So, he tried to put a period on both. "What I'm trying to say, I guess, is that yes, in some ways, you're right. I'm not over it. But the emphasis is on the 'it.' Not Janine herself, but what happened between us at the end of our relationship." He sipped his coffee. "I thought I was over it, had moved on. Until…"

"Until she called."

He held her gaze. "Yeah. Until she called."

"So I'm guessing you just tucked those feelings away into a neat little box—or tried to, anyway—and now, well, now the lid's off and they're tumbling back out at you again."

"More like a lasso around my ankles."

Her expression was so soft, so understanding, he felt something shift inside him merely looking at her.

"I wish it wasn't that way. I mean, who in their right mind would want to feel this way? But…"

"But it is what it is."

"Yeah. In a nutshell."

He watched the way she smoothed her hand over her tucked legs, back and forth, forth and back.

"Have you ever been in love?" he found himself asking.

Her hand stopped midcalf. "Pardon me?"

He smiled, knowing by her reaction that she'd heard him.

She looked down into the contents of her cup. He wanted to tell her she wasn't going to find the answers there. Then again, who was he to say? Maybe that's where they'd be. And he might be better served looking into his own cup before asking stupid questions like the one he just did.

"Yeah," she said. "Or at least I thought so at the time. The guy I followed here…"

The chirp of his cell phone didn't so much as cut her

off—he guessed she hadn't intended to go any further—as it did give him the reprieve he was looking for.

"I'm sorry," he said.

He took the phone out: Jonathon Reece.

"I have to take this."

"Go ahead. No need to apologize."

He got up. "Harrison," he said simply.

Upon leaving the Denver hotel earlier, he'd appointed Jon as contact. So he wasn't surprised now to hear that tomorrow morning's pre-event route run-through had been moved up a half hour by Norman's people.

"See you fifteen minutes before then."

"I'll be there. Oh, and look for the changes you suggested in your email box by day's end."

"Thanks."

He disconnected and turned to find Geneva staring off at something he couldn't see. A result of his question? Her earlier comment? Or something else entirely?

He couldn't be sure.

What he was sure of was he wanted to know more about went on in her mind.

"Sorry about that," he apologized again.

"That's all right. Everything okay?"

"Yeah." He sat back down next to her. "A friend of mine—Darius? I think you know him from the diner—asked me to take over a security detail for a visiting personality in Denver while I'm here."

"Anyone exciting?"

He told her.

She made a face. "I was hoping for Taylor Swift."

He chuckled and picked up his coffee cup only to find it empty. When had that happened? He glanced at his watch to find the hour later than he thought.

"Wow."

"I know. I was just thinking the same thing."

"I never really understood the whole 'time flies' thing, but…well, I guess it's true." He put his cup back down. "Well, except for the past half hour or so. That part of the night I could have done without."

She laughed softly. "Oh, I don't know. It's something you need to think about maybe. I mean, if you are still holding even an ounce of love for Janine…well, you owe it to both of you to find out."

"And do what?"

She shrugged slowly. "That's for you two to decide." She rubbed her belly, which was flat and unfairly showed no signs of the baby growing within her. "Then again, we all make mistakes. Maybe yours is fixable."

He squinted at her, wondering if she was trying to fix him and Janine back up.

But that didn't make any sense. Why would she try to do that?

Either it was the most unselfish thing a woman had ever done…or the dumbest.

He decided the first one was the case because if anything was clear, it was that Geneva was no dummy.

"So, you're saying I should give her another shot, then?" he asked quietly.

She dropped her gaze and something flittered across her beautiful face.

That's what he was looking for. Disappointment.

She didn't want him to reconcile with Janine at all. Rather, she was trying to make sure it was not something he wanted.

And he knew beyond a shadow of a doubt that he didn't.

As for what either of them did with that information from there…

He firmly tugged his thoughts away from that particular trail.

"I should be going," he said, getting to his feet. "Dawn comes early and I've got to be awake to greet it."

"Me, too."

She walked with him toward the door. He turned to face her.

Without her shoes, the top of her head came to his nose. Perfect.

"So," he asked. "What's the next step in the dating game, other than that dance you told me about?"

"I don't know," she said. "Maybe you can stop by the diner tomorrow night, say around dinnertime, if you wanted to?"

"It would have to be late. I probably won't be getting back from Denver until after seven or so."

"Okay. I'll hold some pie for you."

"Deal."

He knew he should be reaching for that door handle, letting himself out, but, dammit, he was having a hard time convincing his feet to move.

"Thank you again," he said. "You know, for tonight."

"You're welcome again. And thank you."

They both laughed at the sweet ridiculousness of their exchange.

He took a deep breath. "Okay, I guess this is the part where I leave."

"Yes, I guess it is."

His gaze fastened on her face. "Can I kiss you good-night?"

She was clearly amused by his question. "Is that something friends do?"

"It's definitely something friends do. You know, on the cheek."

"Okay."

He took her hands in his, the subtle scent of her perfume surrounding him as he leaned in. But somewhere between his genuine intentions and the actual act, right when he might have brushed his lips against her cheek, he rerouted and hit her full-on on the mouth instead...

8

Wow...

Geneva didn't quite know how to respond.

She'd be lying if she said she hadn't imagined this, what it might be like to experience Mace's kiss. She'd dreamed about it last night. Thought about it all day. Then each time, she'd told herself to stop because there was no chance it was going to happen.

Yet here he was...kissing her.

She stared straight into his open eyes as his lips pressed against hers. The meeting was soft...sweet...unexpected. Then something within her sighed and her eyelids drifted closed, allowing her to fully appreciate the sensations tingling outward from where they touched, however briefly.

He slowly pulled back and she nearly whimpered, only to feel him press against her again.

Geneva couldn't be sure how it happened... One moment they were saying good-night and he was joking about a friendly kiss on the cheek, the next their kiss pole vaulted into wickedly hot territory, with no mats around to cushion the fall.

Oh, wow. Just...wow.

He released his hold on her hands and she felt his fingertips on either side of her jaw. She skimmed her hands up the thickness of his forearms, heat unfolding deep in her belly like a long-forgotten love note. His tongue dipped out and she welcomed its wetness in her mouth, inviting him as far as he wanted even as she hesitantly explored his openness.

Had she ever been kissed like this? She felt breathless and so vividly alive she could barely stand it.

Then he touched her breast.

She was pretty sure the gasp she heard was her own. But she wasn't entirely clear. Somewhere over the past few minutes, she'd stopped being herself. Stopped being aware of anything but the thick pulsing of blood through her veins, the wetness between her thighs, the need for more—much more—building in her belly.

Yes…

Mace cupped her breast through the fabric of her bra and dress, seeking for and finding her stiff nipple. She bit her bottom lip briefly and continued kissing him. She was so very sensitive, so very aware of every nuance, every touch, in ways she hadn't been before.

He reached for the buttons that ran down the front of her dress and she shivered as his fingertips met with her bare skin. He found her breast again, tunneling underneath until her bra cup gave and her confined flesh popped free.

His barely audible groan fed the flames flicking over her, but paled by comparison when he ran his tongue over her nipple.

Geneva moved her hands to his shoulders for support, just in case her knees decided to give out under his slow, concentrated attention. His lips tugged at her, his tongue teased, his mouth tasted. By the time he moved back up to her mouth, leaving her fully damp and shivering, she was pretty sure she couldn't remember what her birthday was, never mind her name.

Then she felt the backs of his fingers against her stomach…

She sucked in air. She honestly didn't know if she could stand it anymore without…without…

His fingers touched the damp curls between her thighs through her panties.

She nearly passed out from sheer pleasure…

MACE COULD SMELL Geneva's scent, thick and musky, as fully as her perfume. And it was driving him beyond crazy with need.

No, he hadn't planned to kiss her.

No, he hadn't anticipated his hand moving to her breasts.

No, the thought of touching her womanhood hadn't been part of tonight's schedule.

But he'd be damned if he could stop himself.

Especially since she seemed to want to be touched as much as he wanted to touch her.

His fingers found the crotch of her panties and he groaned. She was soaked.

If he needed any more impetus to continue, that was it.

But as he worked his index finger inside the elastic to run the length of her, he knew a moment of pause.

He forced himself to drag his mouth from hers and pull his hand away. She made a small sound that nearly sent him straight back in.

Instead, he drew away to stare into her heavy-lidded eyes. "Is this…okay?"

"Okay? Yes. Oh, yes…"

He waited for her to register what he was asking.

"Oh." Her cheeks flushed even deeper as comprehension dawned. "Um, yes. I'm a fully functioning female for at least the next six months."

He couldn't help his grin. "Good."

He leaned back in and reclaimed her mouth.

God, she tasted, felt, smelled so good…

Of course, what he was avoiding was asking himself a very important question: whether or not he should be doing this.

He groaned inwardly, not wanting to stop. It had been a good long while since he'd wanted someone so intensely.

The touch of her hand against the front of his slacks chased the air from his lungs. He held it there, waiting, wondering. Her fingers lightly traced the outline of his erection and it was all he could do to keep his hips from bucking forward, seeking more.

He restlessly turned her, pressing her back against the door and reaching back between her thighs, his need surging to urgent within a blink. Geneva's return affections intensified his building need as she tucked her fingers into the waist of his slacks.

So hot, so wet…

Mace dipped his index finger inside her dripping channel, stroking back and forth before coming to rest at the delicious bit of flesh at the apex. He gave a gentle squeeze… and she made a sound deep in her throat and shuddered in a way that made him think she'd come.

Sweet heaven, he wasn't going to be able to stop himself.

He fingered her opening, then slid his index finger into her. Her tight muscles immediately contracted and she moaned, making his erection even harder.

If he had any doubt of her having achieved orgasm, he didn't now. He caressed and stroked her until her shudders began to subside and she melted against him, her beautiful face flushed, her lips trembling, her eyes huge pools of sated bliss.

He couldn't remember a time when a woman had been so easy to please. He didn't know if it was him...or her... or perhaps even them together, but whatever the reason, he decided he liked it.

Perhaps a little too much.

He slowly removed his hand from between her legs and kissed her deeply, leisurely tangling his tongue with hers, finding even that simple action almost painfully erotic.

His cell phone chimed once.

Geneva smiled at him. He smiled back.

"I have to get that," he whispered, kissing her again.

She nodded. "Okay."

He slowly removed his weight from her, making sure she could stand on her own before reaching into his pocket for his phone.

The text was from Reece: he had emailed him the promised travel routes for tomorrow.

"Important?"

He ran his hand over his face, the fog of desire slowly dissipating and reality returning. But not so much that he didn't register the scent of her on his fingers...or stop to appreciate it.

"Yeah," he said.

He searched her face, looking for what, he couldn't be sure. Something? Anything? Everything?

"I've got to go," he said quietly.

A brief flash of regret crossed her features then she smiled again. "Okay."

He lifted his hand and brushed her curls back from her face. She was still flushed, her lips plump and well-kissed, her eyes sleepy and sexy. "See you tomorrow?"

She nodded.

"Good."

She stepped away from the door and opened it for him, appearing to lean against it for support.

Damn, but she was beautiful. He'd give anything not to have to leave her.

"Good night," he said.

"Good night."

He forced himself to move through the open doorway, then down the hall, and the stairs, every step seeming to take superhuman strength to make until he reached the parking lot and his rental car. Before getting in, he glanced up to find her watching from her living room window. He raised a hand to wave. She waved back.

Then he climbed in and drove away, trying not to think about her going into her bedroom, stripping down and climbing into bed…alone.

Oh, boy. If this was what friendship was doing to him, he'd hate to think what would happen if they dated.

Then again, what passed between them felt absolutely nothing like friendship.

Oh, boy.

He lifted his fingers to his nose and breathed deeply.

Oh, boy, indeed.

He smiled and switched on the radio…

9

GENEVA LAY ON HER SIDE in bed, pressing her hot cheek against her pillowcase, cooling her skin as well as hiding her dorky grin. Which made her feel even sillier still since there was no one around to see it.

She sighed and rolled onto her back, her entire body seeming to vibrate.

Oh, how good it had felt to be kissed, touched, to the point where she no longer recognized herself. She liked, no loved, who she'd turned into. And she wanted to get to know her better.

Wanted to get to know Mace better. A lot better.

Of course, that was an improbability. But just having those few minutes with him earlier…

The power of her sigh seemed to bow the windows outward.

She found herself absently touching her belly in much the same way she had been in recent weeks, yet differently. There was life in her and life all around her. Rainbows bursting with color and light even in the dark of night. Bright passion reminding her she had needs beyond her usual day-to-day grind.

"Friends. We're just friends."

She grasped the extra pillow on her queen-size bed and hugged it close, breathing in deeply, imagining she could still smell his cologne, still smell him.

She rolled on to her side again and stared at the clock. It was after midnight. She needed to be up early to work the breakfast shift. Then she needed to finish the Johnson account, follow up on two important quotes and work on a new logo for Ames Green Technology.

Why did she have the feeling she wasn't going to be able to sleep?

And why didn't she care?

She moved the pillow to rest between her thighs.

Wow.

She restlessly licked her lips and then replaced the pillows with her hands.

Oh, yes. That was much more like it…

She imagined it was Mace's hand there still, stroking her, probing her, bringing her pleasure.

Her cell phone chimed once and her hands froze. Who would be texting her so late?

She rolled over to retrieve her cell from the nightstand.

Mace.

She held the bit of plastic and electronic wizardry against her chest and smiled that dorky smile again before even reading it.

"Really enjoyed tonight. Sweet dreams…"

She read and reread his words, taking notice of the ellipsis at the end, as if leading into something else.

"Stop it," she ordered herself.

She accessed the text again and responded.

"'Night night. Sleep tight."

She hesitated, then pressed Send.

She lay for long moments just holding the phone against

her chest, then forced herself to put it back on the night-stand.

This could be dangerous, a little voice whispered.

But it would be oh, so worth it…

MACE CHECKED HIS WATCH: one hour until transport.

The route from Norman's hotel to the hall where he was scheduled to address a political rally was exactly 1.354 miles, and he was walking it one last time before being picked up and driven to the hotel.

Having spent a great deal of time in Colorado Springs, he'd always viewed Denver as the city's older, bolder sister. Buildings were bigger, streets were wider and the citizens more nervy.

Having spent the majority of his career specializing in counter-terrorism, he knew a view from the street would help him note aspects he wouldn't otherwise see; side entryways into commercial courtyards, parking garages that couldn't be blocked, public buildings and private residences he couldn't hope to cover. He'd walked it the day before; he was walking it again.

He'd gone over the intelligence the Lazarus team had gathered on possible suspects behind the threats made on General Stan "The Man" Norman's life. The detail—including sheriff's deputies and Norman's private security—all had photos of the nine most likely, with special emphasis on the fact the threat could originate with more than one of them…or none.

The day was clear and seasonal for November, with temps around fifty degrees. Mace's plain black suit, white shirt and nondescript tie were enough to identify him to fellow team members, but weren't obvious enough that he stood out in the crowd. Of course, if someone looked close enough, his reflective sunglasses and earpiece could give him away.

He listened as final pre-event checks were made on those premises deemed the most vulnerable and okays issued, even as he noted additional weaknesses in the route and considered options to protect them.

He was seriously considering rerouting the rally drive, even though Norman himself had made it very clear this was the one he wanted to take, since there were at least two "support" gatherings along the way scheduled to watch his car go by. While Mace had never overseen nor participated in a similar occasion, he'd educated himself over the past two days enough to where he felt semi-comfortable.

And he didn't care for the changing variables.

In addition to the support gatherings, he was assured there would also be anti-Norman assemblies, as well.

Midmorning pedestrians walked the streets alongside him, commuters drove on the streets, bike riders zoomed by and delivery trucks came and went. Nothing looked out of the ordinary and he had every reason to expect everything to go smoothly.

Still, he couldn't help feeling he was missing something.

He acknowledged the sensation could stem from caution honed over his years in the service, time he'd spent stationed where anyone and everyone was a possible suspect, including women and children, in innocuous locations that appeared peaceful but could turn into hell within a blink.

Combine all that with natural instincts that had rarely steered him wrong and he wouldn't be comfortable until this assignment was over.

He reached into his pocket for his cell phone. He didn't realize what he was looking for until he didn't see it: namely, any calls or texts from Geneva.

Merely thinking her name made him hot for her all over again.

He slid the cell back into his pocket and ordered himself to get back on point.

The memory of her mouth, her soft cries, were enough to keep him up longer than he'd have liked.

If only Reece had texted him a little later, he would have taken her back to her bedroom and found out just how far her responsiveness went.

"Sir, check complete." Jonathon Reece's voice came through his earpiece.

He moved to press the button to allow him to respond when a man wearing a gray hoodie walked from one of those courtyards that caused such concern and cut in front of him, catching his shoulder.

Mace stopped, watching as the man unapologetically continued walking across the street with barely a look at traffic.

Awareness ran through Mace as he tried to match the man to any of the nine guys they'd identified as threats and came away with a negative.

Which meant little. Yet it could mean everything.

"Sir?" Jon's voice sounded again.

Mace pressed the button that was part of the earpiece. "Very good, Reece. Have everyone walk it again, this time from the opposite direction."

Silence. Then, "Roger that."

He released the button. He knew Reece disagreed with his orders. But he would do as requested, no questions asked.

The hooded man disappeared from view into another courtyard across the way.

Mace remained watching after him, then crossed the street to follow…

"So…"

Geneva wiped down the counter after the lunch crowd had mostly dissipated and the instant she reached the end where Trudy was taking her usual, post rush coffee, her friend and employer decided some conversation was in order.

"So, what?" she asked.

Trudy stared at her over her reading glasses where she read the daily paper, words unneeded.

The diner had mostly emptied out aside from a couple of lingering regulars and the help, including her and Trudy, the day cook and a part-time busboy who even now cleared the last of the tables and was preparing to mop before the dinner shift took over.

"Sit," Trudy ordered more than requested.

"I just wanted to finish—"

"Now."

Geneva poured herself a cup of decaf and sat.

In the time she'd worked there, Trudy had proven to be just as much of a second mother as she was an employer to Geneva. She had her own family, but everyone who worked the diner was an extended family of sorts…unconditional until someone violated the terms.

Like Cindy, whom Trudy had fired the next time the blind-date opting brunette had showed up for her next shift and had forgotten to feign the illness from which she'd claimed to be suffering that had kept her from work. Unfortunately, that left them short another pair of hands every day until Trudy found a suitable replacement. Something experience told Geneva could be weeks.

"So, does he know?" Trudy asked.

Geneva pretended that adding sugar and creamer to her cup required her undivided attention. "Who?"

Another over-the-glasses look.

"About the baby? Yes. Yes, he does know."

Trudy made a quiet sound. "And do you think he might stick around for a while?"

Geneva nearly choked on her coffee.

Trudy sighed. "That's what I thought."

Geneva felt inexplicably irritated. "I know you're concerned about me, Trudy. Really…I do. But this…Mace…" Merely saying his name made the butterflies that had taken up residence in her stomach flutter faster. "He makes me feel good. The way he looks at me…makes me feel not like a waitress, or a friend, or an expectant mother, but like a…well, woman…I like it. What's wrong with enjoying it while I can?"

"The problem is your hormones are running in circles…and it's important you not forget you are an expectant mother."

"Trust me, that's not something I can exactly forget."

"Oh? Because the way I see it, you're trying pretty hard."

Talk about pins and balloons.

Of course, what Geneva was leaving out of the equation was that despite last night's unexpected turn of events, she and Mace weren't truly dating, they were only pretending to date.

Not that she'd tell Trudy that. Aside from agreeing with Mace that they couldn't tell anyone in order for this to fly, she knew the instant she breathed word one to the talkative diner owner, everyone would know. Then what value would their agreement have?

She shivered for reasons having nothing to do with the temperature.

"Uh-huh," Trudy said, rustling her paper.

Geneva took a sip of her coffee. "We're dating. Nothing more, nothing less."

"Pregnant women don't date."

"Why not? Last time I checked, we're still human."

"No, you're not. You're hormonal."

"I'll give you the hormonal part. At any rate, what does it matter? In a week he'll be gone and everything will return to normal."

"Depends on how you define normal."

How did she define normal? What happened last night? The mere thought…

She couldn't help smiling.

Which earned her another Trudy frown.

She pushed her cup to the other side of the counter where she could collect it when she walked around.

"Are we done?" she asked.

"I am," Trudy said. "I think I've made my point."

With a fine-honed carving knife, Geneva wanted to add, "And I hope I've made mine."

She rounded the counter, dumped the contents of her cup into the sink and put it in the bussing bin. She caught Trudy watching her and could have sworn she was hiding a grin behind the paper she pretended to read.

Geneva shook her head and grinned back, then hurried off into the kitchen.

10

M ACE RODE in the trailing car in the passenger's seat, keeping an eye out and listening to route reports as Norman's limo drove under the speed limit ahead of them. That sense of wariness remained with him, even though everything was going like clockwork.

So far...

Ahead of the limo, Jonathon Reece rode in the lead sedan, and in the limo itself were two more security personnel, in addition to Norman's personal assistant and event organizer, who had met him at the hotel.

He resisted rubbing the back of his neck to smooth the prickling there.

General Stan "The Man" Norman had been presentable enough, direct and to the point, an extension of what had likely made him a successful general. More importantly now, he was content to let them decide what he needed to do...beyond his predetermined routes.

Mace didn't get it. While rumors surrounded the one-time general, now political talk show radio host's future political plans, he couldn't understand why the guy garnered so much attention.

"Have you listened to his show?" Dominic Falcone asked Mace from the driver's seat.

"No."

"If you had, then you'd know why. They don't come any more confrontational than the general. Name one group he hasn't manage to offend and I'll point how he managed to do it."

"Sticks and stones…"

"Yeah, well, we all know what words are capable of."

Indeed, they all did, as history and armed conflict bore out.

In Norman's case, it seemed many people were interested in stoning him simply for the words he chose.

Earlier that day, the man responsible for putting Mace in this position had called to consult with him. He'd reminded Darius of his mounting debt and assured him he had everything well under control. They'd talked a bit about the kidnapping case that had taken his friend away, and then Dari had asked about the girl he'd been spotted with at The Barracks.

If he didn't know better, he'd think that had been the true reason behind Dari's unnecessary call.

"Geneva?" His friend had sounded incredulous when he'd told him. "You do know…"

"Yes, I do."

Dari's silence had been louder than a car bomb. "Hey, far be it for me to suggest you don't know what you're doing, but, well, do you know what you're doing?"

"I'm enjoying her company."

Enjoying her company. Those words seemed to fall far short of the mark. Whatever he was doing, Geneva and her soft lips were there, along the fringes of his thoughts.

He'd texted her a short time ago to tell her he'd see her at the diner later.

She'd texted back with a smiley face and told him to be careful.

He'd nearly texted back saying he was always careful. But then he decided not to. Mainly because he wondered if careful entered anywhere into their situation.

Oh, he knew they were only pretending to date. That when she'd revealed her circumstances, a real relationship was out of the question.

But what had happened last night? There had been nothing fake about his actions...or her reaction.

He'd liked it.

More than liked it, he...

He set his teeth together.

He needed to keep his head in the game.

He and Dari had talked a little while longer, then his friend had signed off with a quiet, "If you need anything, call."

Mace suspected that Dari had been talking about more than his assignment.

They were nearing the point where he'd run into the hooded man on the street earlier. He went on alert, actively scanning the areas he'd seen the guy. Unfortunately, he'd lost him in the crowd. That meant one of two things: he lived in the area or he was the one they needed to watch out for.

"Damn."

"What is it?" Falcone asked.

He indicated the corner of the next block where a group of people with signs were gathered.

"Looks to be protesters," Falcone noted.

That's exactly what they were. Even at a distance, he could read the signs that ranged from, "Go Home and Be a Man, Norman!" to "Think Outside My Box!"

He'd allowed for the possibility of protestors. He just

didn't like that they were gathered so close to where he'd run into the suspicious character earlier.

"I'm getting out," he said.

"What?"

"Slow down."

He issued the command for the lead car to do the same, which would alert the limo driver to follow suit, allowing him to walk alongside the cars until he felt it was safe to move forward.

He climbed out, unfastened the protective strap of his shoulder holster and stepped up next to the limo, careful of traffic coming in the opposite direction.

He heard a woman's scream from his left, then a shot rang out.

Damn!

He watched as a bullet hit the limo's shockproof passenger's window and ricocheted off.

"Move, move, move!" he ordered through his earpiece.

The lead car took off and the limo followed, as did Falcone, protocol dictating the target be protected first, leaving him behind.

He ran in the direction the gunshot had been fired from...

GENEVA LOOKED at the wall clock that hung above the jukebox for the fifth time in as many minutes. Seven o'clock had come and gone, and other than the brief text that morning she'd received from Mace saying he'd see her later, she hadn't heard from him.

"What's the matter? He stand you up?"

The words came from Tiffany, who appeared a little too smug for her liking, and were loud enough for everyone—including Mel in the back—to hear.

She caught Trudy's gaze through the window from

where she worked in the kitchen and tried not to make a face.

She wasn't so much afraid of being stood up as she was worried about Mace's safety.

Word of the attempt on General Norman's life was all everyone was talking about. It dominated the news that played on the television in the upper corner of the diner that was usually set to a national news channel and muted so you had to read the scroll but it had been changed to a local station to keep up on developing reports on the event.

The goings-on had brought out more people than usual for a Wednesday night. Reactions ranged from "They shouldn't have missed," to "There are a lot of crazies out there."

All Geneva could think about was Mace's safety.

In the middle of refilling the coffee cups on Table 3, her cell phone vibrated in her pocket. She nearly spilled the hot liquid as she hurried to get it out.

"Sorry," she said, hurrying away.

Mace!

"Hey," he said simply when she answered.

"Hey, yourself. You okay?"

"Okay?"

"Yeah. What happened today is all over the news."

"Don't worry, I'm fine," he said, but she wasn't convinced. "Sorry, I'm late."

A thrill ran up her arms at the thought he was still coming. "It's okay. The diner's packed."

But she had reserved a booth in the corner after the last occupants had vacated it at six-thirty.

"Will you be long?" she asked.

"I'm here."

His words sounded both in her phone…and her free ear. She turned to see him behind her.

She was sure people around her thought her insane as she ran toward him and hugged him hard…

MACE HAD SEEN such welcomes over the years. At airports, on bases. He'd watched wives and girlfriends embrace their loved ones like they might never let them go.

But he had never been on the receiving end of one.

He couldn't help chuckling, breathing in the sweet scent of Geneva's hair. "If that's your reaction to my being late, I'll have to arrange to do it more often."

She drew back and smiled up at him. "I'd advise against it. Trust me."

Was it possible he missed her? Yes, it was. He'd missed her smile, her wit, her presence. It should have struck him as odd, but somehow it didn't.

"Sorry I'm late. Something came up at work."

She squinted. "I already figured that out." She indicated the television. He looked to see the scene from today being played out via someone's cell phone camera.

He frowned, watching the cars race off even as he ran after the gunman. But just as had happened earlier, he hadn't found him. Or her, as the case may be.

But he'd bet a year's salary the hooded man from earlier in the day was the one behind the shooting.

"Are you okay?" Geneva asked.

"What? Yeah. Yeah, I'm fine." At least he was now. Earlier, he'd been so worked up, he'd barely been able to speak without shouting. He couldn't help thinking they should have been able to prevent the incident.

He should have been able to prevent it.

"Come on. Let's sit down," Geneva said.

She led him to a corner booth and righted the coffee cup waiting there, filling it from the pot she'd put down before hugging him.

He watched the easy, fluid way she moved. Took in the concerned expression on her beautiful face. The way her hair curled around her head. The bow of her lips as she bit on the bottom one, caught herself, and then stopped.

"Hungry for anything in particular?" she asked.

You, he wanted to say.

He hadn't said it, but given the way her eyes darkened as she looked at him, he thought he might have.

"Surprise me," he said instead.

She twisted those lips he seemed inordinately fascinated with. "Anything you're allergic to? Dislike?"

"Nope."

"Okay. But no complaints allowed if I bring you something you don't like."

He thought she could bring him liver and he'd not only eat it, but enjoy it.

And he hated liver.

"Will you be joining me?"

She looked around, then back at him. "I'm already supposed to be off, but the place is packed…"

"That's okay. I understand."

"But I haven't eaten yet, so, yes, I will join you. At least for a meal."

"Good."

He sat back, watching as she filled a couple of coffee cups and delivered a check on her way toward the kitchen. She had the type of legs he'd love to run his hands over… but it was the memory of the tight wetness that lay between them that made him instantly hard.

He was glad he'd come to the diner. He'd seriously considered canceling, staying back at the motel to go over tomorrow's schedule, continue consulting with the team to find the man responsible…and devise ways to make sure the guy wouldn't get another chance to squeeze off a round.

As it was, he'd merely planned to drop by, do his part as Geneva's fake "boyfriend," then leave.

Now he hoped she'd let him come home with her.

Someone sat down in the booth opposite him. He blinked to find it was Geneva's friend, Dustin.

Damn.

11

"I CAN'T APOLOGIZE ENOUGH," Geneva said for the third time as Mace followed her out to her car an hour later.

The diner had pretty much emptied out in the interim, with the buzz of the day finally dying down like a caffeine high. One of the customers had recognized him as the one in the footage and quietly approached him, but he'd deflected the inquiry.

It had been Dustin he'd been more focused on.

"She's going to marry me," the other man had said.

Mace had stared at him as if Dustin had just told him he had a vest of plastic explosives strapped to his chest under his plaid shirt.

As far as guys went, Dustin didn't look too bad. A little soft around the middle, maybe. The type that would run from a fight instead of face it.

Well, except in this case, apparently. It appeared the guy had decided to stand up for Geneva.

"I'm sorry?" he'd said in response to his statement.

"You do know she's pregnant with my child."

Mace had nodded, experiencing a pang he couldn't quite identify but didn't like. "I do. I also know the circumstances surrounding the situation. And that she has no intention of marrying you."

The guy had looked so genuinely heartbroken, Mace had felt instantly bad.

"Look, no hard feelings, but she doesn't feel that way about you. And from what I understand, you don't feel that way about her, either. You two were friends, right?"

"Right."

"And that one night was an accident."

He didn't respond.

"I appreciate and respect that you want to do the right thing, Dustin. And I'm sure Geneva does, too. But I'd recommend you try to get the friendship back before you destroy even that. For the sake of the baby, at least."

Geneva had come up then, looking a little upset and worried that Dustin was sitting at his table. Then she asked what he was doing there.

Mace had raised his brow at the other man as if to provide a punctuation point. Then he extended his arm.

"Good seeing you again, Dustin," he'd said.

Dustin's jaw tightened, but he shook his hand and got up. But rather than taking his regular seat at the counter, he'd left.

"No need for apologies," he said to Geneva. "That's what all this was about, wasn't it? Getting a specific reaction?"

"What did he say?"

"Probably what you're thinking."

The night was chilly and he didn't think the light sweater she wore was protection enough, so after she unlocked the car, he opened the door for her.

"The chicken fried steak was great," he said. And it had been. Doubly so when he saw she'd had the same thing.

"Was."

He squinted at her. "Sorry?"

"You said that's what this was about. You know, Dustin's reaction." She hesitated getting inside the car. "Past tense."

He smiled. "Tell me why I'm not surprised you're one of those type of girls?"

"What type?"

"The type that easily reads people."

"So you're saying…"

He grinned at her. "That it's too cold to be standing out here. Get in the car, Geneva."

She made a face.

He chuckled and opened the door wider.

She climbed in and started the engine, but kept one foot outside so he couldn't close her inside. He couldn't help looking at the way her skirt hiked up, revealing a nicely shaped knee.

"Are you going back to your motel?" she asked.

He grinned. "I was thinking about it."

"Want some company?"

He didn't know quite how to respond.

If you had asked him what might come out of her delectable mouth next, her question wouldn't even have rated a spot on the list. In fact, he'd pretty much accepted he'd be spending the night alone.

She cleared her throat. "I have something I'd like to talk to you about."

"Okay."

"If you'd rather not…"

"No, no. Please, do come over."

She looked suddenly shy, sexily so. "I have to swing by my place, shower some of these food smells off me and change first."

"And I'll have to clean up the room."

She laughed. "See you in an hour?"

"An hour."

"Okay."

"All right."

She finally pulled her leg back inside and he closed the door for her then knocked on the window.

"Room 3," he said.

She looked so damn hot when she smiled he nearly kissed her. "See you there…"

He stepped aside as she put the car in Reverse and backed up before shifting into Drive and leaving the lot.

She wanted to talk to him about something.

He wondered what.

While they ate, he'd easily relayed what had happened that day in a way that didn't make him grind his teeth. Talking to her was so effortless. He couldn't imagine what she wanted to say. In private.

He blinked. Well, he'd find out soon enough, wouldn't he?

He walked over to where he'd parked a couple spaces up. He found himself hoping it was something that would find her lying in his bed.

He cursed under his breath.

First he needed to clear off the bed.

OKAY, MAYBE she was being too forward.

Geneva hesitated outside Room 3, her hand raised to knock. She curled and opened her fingers then dropped her hand back to her side, her courage abandoning her.

What was she thinking? Oh yeah, about last night…

She swallowed hard. Last night had been phenomenal. But had it been little more than aberration? A spur-of-the-moment thing not meant to be repeated?

Halfway through her shower, the anticipatory high she'd been running on had begun to dissipate, knocked back by

Trudy's words earlier, then Dustin's descent on Mace's table.

Was it possible Mace wanted to do more than fake their dating?

She closed her eyes and took a deep breath, releasing it slowly.

Oh, criminy, ask him already...

She lifted her hand and forced herself to knock.

The door opened so quickly, she nearly fell inside.

"Whoa," Mace said, steadying her.

She laughed. "That was fast."

"Yeah. I thought I heard something."

"My breathing?"

"That must be it."

She was running late, taking more than the hour she'd promised. Sixty minutes had been more than enough time to get ready and drive over. But then she'd started to wonder if she was doing the right thing.

Taking in the welcoming expression on Mace's handsome face, she felt instantly better.

"Come in," he said.

She did.

"I tried cleaning up, but..."

The place was pin neat. She'd bet he earned extra points in the service for his efforts.

"Okay, so it's clean."

And so was he, if his damp hair and fresh soap smell was any indication. Which explained why he'd changed. He wore a soft pair of jeans and a honey-brown T-shirt.

She walked in and he closed the door after her. The radio played on low—a local country station—but otherwise it was quiet.

She turned to say something to him at the same time he

stepped forward to say something to her and she bumped right into him.

But rather than apologize, Geneva did something she'd hoped they'd get around to, but certainly hadn't planned on doing now.

She kissed him.

And he kissed her back.

Wow!

If she thought last night had been something, well, now she was sure her skin was going to burn from the instant heat generated by the mere touch of his mouth against hers.

She made small hungry sounds she'd never in her life imagined she'd ever make, running her hands restlessly up his back then down over his hind end, then up again, tunneling under his T-shirt and the hotness beneath.

She'd changed into something as casual as what he was wearing. They plucked and tugged and pulled and kissed until they were half undressed and then fell onto the nearby king-size bed.

Geneva wrapped her legs around his hips, one of her jeans legs still half on, her T-shirt half off, one bra cup pushed up. He shook his leg to free himself from his own jeans, one hand cupping her exposed breast, the other reaching between her thighs.

Yes, yes, yes…

Had she said the words? She couldn't be sure. She was unaware of anything other than the thick pulsing of blood through her body and her white-hot need for the man even now sheathing himself with a condom.

She worked her hand between them, gently grasping his rock-hard erection and positioning it against her waiting flesh.

Her breath caught and held and she arched her back,

swimming in sensations that flowed over and through her like vivid colors.

Then he entered her...

She moaned so loud, the sound almost roused her from her dizzying state.

Almost.

He felt so good. So very good...

He withdrew, then slid in again, this time to the hilt.

Her back came off the mattress.

Had she ever wanted anything so much?

A hunger that surpassed anything she'd ever experienced rushed through her. She grasped his hips and tilted her own, taking him deeper still.

He thrust once, twice...

Then uttered a curse and went rigid.

12

"I'VE GOT TO...STOP for a minute..." Mace whispered into her ear. "Sorry..."

Geneva swallowed so hard she heard it. "It's okay."

She made a small sound as he rolled off her to lay flat on the mattress next to her.

She didn't know what she should do, so she did nothing.

She lay staring at the ceiling, wondering if what had just happened...well, had.

Had he really come that quickly?

Of course, last night she had nearly achieved orgasm by his merely blowing on her.

Well, a bit more than that, but still.

She fought to catch her breath and wondered if she should put her clothes back on, or take them the rest of the way off. She settled for a compromise as Mace pulled the covers over them both: she took off the jeans but left her bra and T-shirt on.

"Wow," he said so softly she nearly didn't hear him. "That's a first."

She laughed. She couldn't help herself.

At least he wasn't trying to pass off that he had intended to do that or that it hadn't actually happened.

They lay for long, quiet minutes. Geneva attempted to rein in her runaway emotions, but was having a hard time. She'd been a teenager when she'd last been left hanging this way.

Mace slid an arm around her shoulders and pulled her to him. She gladly went, laying her cheek against the warm granite of his chest.

"Just give me a minute."

"It's all right," she said.

And, she discovered, it was.

While she'd have preferred more, she really was okay with leaving things where they were. After all, there was always tomorrow.

At least she hoped there was.

Now that her breathing was returning to semi-normal, and her temperature cooling a bit, she found it was delicious just to lay this close to him.

He smelled so good.

"So," he said quietly, even as his hand smoothed up and down her back from her bare bottom to her neck. "What was it you wanted to talk to me about?"

She dragged her nose against his collarbone. "Huh?"

"Earlier, outside the diner—"

She struggled to clear the cobwebs crowding her brain. "Oh! Yes. Sorry."

She collected her thoughts and slowly rubbed her leg against his. But then he surprised her by touching her knee and then smoothing his hand to the back, pulling her leg over his and placing her sex in direct contact with his thigh…a thigh he maneuvered so it pressed against her.

She lost her breath briefly then bore down against his hard muscles.

"This," she rasped.

He moved his thigh. "This?"

"Uh-huh…" She bit on her bottom lip. "After last night, I was going to suggest that maybe we could add sex to our arrangement…"

He moved his leg back and forth against her clit.

"Sex?" he whispered.

"Mmm, yes." She arched into him, amazed by how wet he made her by doing something so simple. "We don't have to alter the agreement. We can still act like a dating couple. But we'll just be friends…"

"Friends who have sex?"

"Mmm-hmm…"

His hand took the place of his leg. She gasped at his touch as he ran his fingertip along her hungry opening then moved on, teasing her.

She reached to see if he might be ready to go again. He'd removed the condom and she happily saw he was mostly erect again.

And she was all too willing to get him the rest of the way there.

She wrapped her fingers around him and squeezed gently, then stroked him as confidently as he touched her.

Oh, yes…

She wanted to taste him so badly her mouth watered. His weight felt so good against her palm. She slid down the sheets until her mouth was at his waist level then slid her lips down over the tip of his erection, licking as she went. He tasted of desire. She took more of him in and his hips bucked involuntarily.

"Sweet hell," he muttered under his breath, tangling his hands in her hair.

Geneva licked him, stroked him until his breathing quickened and he appeared on the verge of coming again.

She hoped he would. She wanted to taste him fully…

Instead, he grasped her shoulders and pulled her up

until she was kissing him. She all too readily straddled him even as she focused on the talents of his tongue in her mouth, moving her wetness along the length of his erection then back again, holding off when he tried to enter. Finally, he'd had enough. He quickly donned a condom, then grasped her hips and thrust hungrily upward.

She gasped, her mouth opening against his, incapable of movement, incapable of words, incapable of doing anything but riding the delicious tsunami of sensation that rushed over her, through her, in her.

Yes…

Mace pressed his hand against her shoulder, gently moving her until she sat upright.

She rocked her hips, then again, leaning her right hand back against his thigh. He touched her breasts, lightly pinching her nipples, adding to the hot chaos swirling within.

She felt like she could do this forever, wanted to do it forever, feel his thick hardness filling her to capacity, ride him until they were both raw…

She wasn't sure how long she'd stayed like that, merely moving on top of him, but when she heard him groan and he grasped her hips, she braced herself…and welcomed him thrusting wildly up into her.

Oh, yes!

"Mmm…"

A while later Mace lay with Geneva curved against his side, enjoying the quiet, contented sounds she made.

"So," he whispered against her hair. "Is that an adequate answer to your question?"

Her giggle made him smile. "Mmm-hmm…"

Adequate didn't come near describing how he felt about the past hour. After a perfectly horrific start, he'd regained his momentum—with some hot help from Geneva—and the two of them had set the sheets on fire.

Her responsiveness? Mind-blowing.

Actually, he was coming to see everything about her was mind-blowing. For all intents and purposes, she was the perfect woman. Kind, sexy as hell, levelheaded, funny, wild in bed, smart, sexy as hell... Wait, he'd already said that.

Yes, well, it bore repeating.

How in the hell he ever thought he'd be able to keep his hands off her was a mystery.

Then he remembered...

He couldn't help gazing down at where she curved against him. More specifically, at her belly.

Flat and toned, it was impossible to believe a baby was growing within her. But there was.

He waited for some sort of feeling other than post-coital bliss to hit him...

Nothing. At least nothing associated with the guilt he expected.

He honestly couldn't say that outside his admiration for her for going ahead on her own, with no expectations, no grudges or regrets, that he felt anything but a growing physical need and fondness for her.

Which brought him to his next need for her appearance.

"I want you to meet my parents."

Her soft sounds stopped. So, it appeared, had her breathing.

Hell, at his poor choice in words, he found himself holding his breath.

"Wait...that didn't come out right," he said. "What I meant is that I'm having lunch with my parents tomorrow and I'd like you to come with me."

"Play the role of girlfriend? For your parents?"

She'd moved slightly away and propped her head up in her hand, her elbow planted on the bed. He missed her warmth and closeness instantly.

"Yeah," he said simply. "Oh, and you'll be meeting my grandfather, too."

She squinted at him. "Are you sure you want me to lie to them?" She shifted, appearing uncomfortable. "I mean, it's one thing to do this with friends, but…"

"Quite another with family?"

She had a point.

When he'd first considered asking her to go with him, he thought it was the perfect way to get his mother to stop hounding him about grandchildren. But now…

And, of course, there was always the situation surrounding his brother…

"I want you to come," he said. "We don't have to lie. We can just tell them the truth—that we're friends." He wished she'd bring her heat back. "They don't interact with any common acquaintances, so there's no risk of the truth getting back to anybody."

"The truth…"

He grinned. "We'd, of course, leave out the sex part."

"Of course."

He moved his fingers over her propped-up arm and encouraged her to come closer.

He sighed in gratitude when she did.

They lay like that in companionable silence for a while, her rubbing her leg against his, his hand caressing her bare back.

"I have to warn you, they'll probably talk about my brother the entire time," he said quietly. "And my grandfather will probably flirt outrageously with you." He chuckled. "No, no probably about it—he will."

"I didn't know you had a brother."

Mace winced, but didn't say anything immediately.

He was curious why he'd offered up the comment so easily. He hadn't mentioned Marcus until well into his relationship with Janine. And even then, she had found out via his parents…which is probably why he'd thrown up the warning now.

"I don't," he said quietly. "At least not anymore."

She tilted her head to look up at him, but didn't say anything.

"Actually, that sounds cold. And my feelings for my brother are anything but." He took a deep breath. "I don't know. It's complicated…"

"How did he die?" she asked quietly.

"9/11. He was one of the firefighters who'd gone into the Twin Towers…and never made it back out."

He could feel her shocked stare in the darkness.

"It's all right. You don't have to say anything. Everything's been said already." Over and over and over again…

He grimaced and ran his hand over his face.

How had his love for his older brother gone from something he cherished to a burden to be hauled around, forever a weight on his shoulders?

He realized it was somewhere around the time his parents had stopped living and had gone into a sort of prolonged mourning trance it took him a month to recover from whenever he visited.

He hadn't been aware he'd spoken the words aloud until Geneva said, "It must be very difficult for you."

He extracted his arm from around her and pushed to a sitting position on the side of the bed. "Yeah."

He didn't know why he'd said the things he did to her, shared emotions he'd never told anyone.

She gently touched his back.

"I'm going to go grab a shower. I have a long day ahead of me tomorrow."

He heard her gather the blankets around her. "Okay."

He switched on the bedside light, got up, grabbed his jeans and headed for the bathroom, not so much needing a shower as he did a moment to himself.

Marcus...

He turned in the doorway, taking in the somber expression on her beautiful face.

"I'd love to come with you," she said quietly. "You know, for lunch tomorrow."

He said nothing.

"If the offer still stands?"

"Thanks."

She smiled at him. "Sure."

"Don't go anywhere until I get out?" he said.

She nodded.

He quietly closed the door then silently banged his fist against the cheap wood.

What had he been thinking?

Obviously, he hadn't been.

He switched on the shower, hoping the hot water and few minutes to himself would give him back the balance he needed.

Yet, somehow he knew it wouldn't.

13

GENEVA SAT AT HER DESK the following morning, trying to finish up some work before Mace was scheduled to pick her up for lunch. But she wasn't having much luck.

Last night, well, last night was a mix of both the fantastic and the confusing. She and Mace…

Her mind broke off, veering from her attempt to control it, as it had so often since getting up that morning following minimal snatches of true sleep.

She released a bone-deep sigh, remembering the way Mace had kissed her, touched her, filled her, bringing her to climax again and then again. He'd moved her more than merely physically, touched something vast inside her that had everything and nothing to do with sensual pleasure. She'd felt somehow joined with him on every plane. Looked into his eyes while he was inside her and saw him, herself and everything in between, as if nothing separated them.

Then he'd shut her out as solidly as he'd closed the bathroom door.

She caught herself absently scratching her arm through her sweater and stopped.

The swing was extreme enough to leave her breathless.

She knew his emotional withdrawal was related to his brother. What had he said his name was? Marcus. Yes, that was it.

But after sharing so much with her, why had he moved away, more than just physically?

As he'd requested, she'd stayed in the room until he emerged from his shower. She'd dressed and semi-made the bed and was sitting in one of the two chairs near the window. But he'd looked the same when he came out as he had when he went in, puzzling her all the more.

She knew whatever he was going through had nothing to do with her. But she couldn't help thinking his distancing himself wasn't a good sign.

Baggage. Everyone carried around their fair share. She looked down at where she rubbed her belly. Would Mace open up and share his with her? Or would he move on, his psychological suitcase still securely locked?

Of course, she was assuming that they'd remain in contact when he returned to duty next week…

She squinted at the computer screen, finding the prospect of saying goodbye to him permanently somehow inconceivable.

Her cell phone rang. She fumbled to pick it up, almost desperately thankful for the distraction, reading the display screen. Not Mace.

She took a deep breath and accepted the call from her client. No doubt he wanted more changes.

Ah, well. At least it was the distraction from her thoughts she needed, if not wanted; perhaps it would spur her into action work-wise until Mace got there. Then she'd know more how to proceed with what was becoming an increasingly complicated situation.

Was it simply a speed bump? Or had the countdown to goodbye already begun?

She told herself it didn't matter, one way or the other.

But she hoped with everything that was in her it was the former and not the latter...

THE MORNING HAD GROANED by without a break, but the instant Mace saw Geneva coming out of her apartment building to meet him instead of waiting for him to come up, it was as if the rain parted, allowing for a sweet ray of sunshine to shine through.

He got out of the car to open the passenger's door for her.

"You look great," he said, appreciating her dress and heels, while trying not to stare at her sexy legs.

"Thanks."

She climbed inside and he closed the door after her.

In the little downtime he'd had since last night, he'd been dreading this lunch with his parents, as well as dreading what he might see in Geneva's eyes when he saw her.

Until now...

While he wasn't exactly looking forward to seeing his parents, the open and warm expression on Geneva's beautiful face served as an eraser to the morning's stresses. And his own worries.

After getting little sleep, due in part to the incredible woman seated in his rental car, he'd met up with Jonathon Reece at Lazarus to review footage of yesterday's events, trying to identify the gunman and apprehend him before Norman's next rally, which was later this afternoon. Neither the general's team, nor the Denver police department, had any clue who it might have been. Not even a bullet casing had been retrieved, indicating the gunman had either plucked it up after firing, or perhaps even shot through something in order to catch it, such as a Ziploc bag. And that meant they weren't dealing with a random nutcase as they had suspected, but a possible pro. Eyewitnesses hadn't been able to give any more description than he'd already discerned from his chance run-in with the suspect. The guy was a Caucasian male somewhere in his late twenties, early thirties, wearing a gray hoodie with the hood up and fastened tightly. They couldn't even say what color his hair had been, much less his eyes…and neither could he.

He climbed into the car.

"Are you sure you're up for this?" he asked Geneva.

She blinked at him. "I'm sorry?"

He smiled. "This lunch. It's not too late to back out."

She laughed. "Sounds like you're the one more likely to back out."

"That's because I know what awaits."

"It can't be that bad?"

"That's because you don't know what you're walking into."

She smiled back. "Well, then, it might be a good idea to put it behind us as quickly as possible."

He shifted the car into gear. "A good idea, indeed."

The restaurant where he'd arranged to meet was some five minutes away, making it an easy drive for him, yet far enough away from his parents' place that they couldn't press him into going home with them for an extended visit. The last time he'd gone, he'd barely been able to breathe. If it were possible, they'd turned the house into an even bigger shrine to Marcus's memory than it had been before, including photos he hadn't ever seen.

Within moments, he'd pulled into the restaurant parking lot. He wasn't surprised to see his parents' sedan already parked near the front in a handicapped spot since they'd picked up his grandfather en route.

His grandfather…

Now him, he was looking forward to seeing.

He didn't realize he'd turned off the car and was just sitting until Geneva lightly touched his arm.

"Ready?" he asked, taking the key out of the ignition.

"Yes."

And before he knew it, he was being led to his parents' table near the front of the restaurant where they'd undoubtedly watched him pull up. He introduced Geneva to them.

Sharon and Mike Harrison were a kind couple. Friendly to everyone with whom they crossed paths. And they openly welcomed Geneva now, as he expected they would. If they were surprised he'd brought someone along, they hid it well. But he noticed his mother, especially, smiled a little more widely.

But it was his grandfather who smiled the widest.

"Well, hello," he said in a way that would have been almost salacious had he been a younger man.

He watched Geneva for her response; her own eyes danced with the same playful light as his grandfather's. Which is what he'd hoped. Given her position as a waitress, he guessed she encountered more than her fair share of open attention. He was glad she wasn't insulted by his grandfather's.

Dwayne Harrison got up with a little difficulty, leaving his cane untouched as he pulled out the chair next to him with gallant flourish. "Please, if you could be kind enough to grace an old man with your pleasant company."

Geneva accepted while Mace returned his parents' curious glances with a smile.

"I didn't realize you would be bringing someone with you today," his mother said.

"Sorry, I invited Geneva late last night and didn't have a chance to tell you before now." The free seat put him between Geneva and his father.

He didn't miss his mother's expectant expression, indicating she was waiting for more.

He didn't deliver it.

His grandfather was busy charming Geneva who, indeed, appeared charmed.

"So, have you been dating long?" his mother asked.

Geneva nearly choked on her water. She quickly picked up a napkin and dabbed at her chin, giving him an amused glance under the thick fringe of her lashes even as his father suggested maybe the question was too forward.

"We're not," Mace said in answer to her question.

"I'm sorry?" Sharon said.

"Dating. We're not," Geneva provided. "We're just friends."

"Just friends…"

"Good," his grandfather spoke up. "That means the field's wide open for me. A man my age needs all the help he can get."

The men and Geneva laughed while his mother appeared appalled.

Menus were brought and orders placed, Mace silently counting the seconds when the meal would be over with and he could get out of there, even as he admired Geneva and the easy way she handled his grandfather and his parents. Things were going so well, in fact, he found himself relaxing, enjoying the company rather than suffering through it.

Sharon Harrison was still an attractive woman. A golf lover, she'd kept in great shape and could easily pass for a decade younger.

His father, on the other hand, looked his age. Dedicated career military, he'd seen his share of violent conflicts, both on the front line and commanding them.

Geneva easily conversed with his parents as if she'd known them for years instead of minutes.

His mother sighed deeply. "I wish you could have met our Marcus. You two would have gotten on famously."

And just like that the light mood fell through the floor...

14

GENEVA SLID A GAZE in Mace's direction at the mention of his brother. His body language couldn't have been any clearer: the smile vanished from his handsome face, his jaw clenched and his shoulders squared. And had he really just looked at his watch? Yes, he had.

The table fell silent at the mention of Marcus. But whether it was in deference or warning, she couldn't be sure.

"I'm sure I would have liked him, too," Geneva said quietly.

Sharon Harrison seemed to take that as some sort of cue and continued on Marcus, who instantly became not so much a memory but a palpable presence.

Even Mace's grandfather had gone quiet, pretending an interest in his soup.

Within a blink, everything had gone from light and happy to somber and heavy.

While Geneva genuinely wanted to know more about Mace's brother and his family, she had the feeling that the cloud descending on them all wouldn't help her in that endeavor.

"I thought you all should know… I'm pregnant."

The table fell silent.

Geneva supposed she should be appalled at her own forwardness. She usually wasn't the type to draw attention to herself. But the growing toxicity of the current environment was making her uncomfortable. More importantly, it was making Mace unhappy. And she'd do anything to prevent that. Even make a spectacle of herself.

Luckily, her words had the intended impact by distracting her tablemates from their dark thoughts.

Sharon coughed, apparently having trouble swallowing, while next to her, Mace's grandfather gave her a nudge even as he fixed a grin on Mace. "Harrison guns still firing straight, eh?"

Thankfully Mace laughed. Not the kind of polite, accommodating laugh but a full-out chuckle. "Wish I could take the credit, Gramps, but truth is Geneva and I met only a few days ago."

"The baby's not yours?" Sharon asked.

"The baby's not mine."

For reasons she wasn't entirely sure about, Sharon asked Mace to trade seats with her. A waitress appeared to help rearrange their plate settings.

"I hope you don't mind," the older woman said with a warm smile. "I've spent so much time around guys, well, it's just nice to enjoy female company. So tell me all about the baby…"

Geneva couldn't remember the last time she'd experienced such complete acceptance and excitement directed at her. Oh, Trudy and the girls were happy for her, but guardedly, realistically so.

On the plus side, Marcus's name disappeared from the conversation. On the minus, Mace's dad and grandfather seemed puzzled.

But it was Mace's reaction that mattered. Just as quickly

as he'd tensed up, he'd relaxed again. And when she looked to find him smiling at her, she swore she could feel it like a physical sweep of his hand against her bare back.

She wasn't sure what, exactly, she'd done...but she hoped that she did it again soon. Preferably the next time they were alone together...

"THAT WAS INCREDIBLE," Mace said quietly.

Geneva released her seatbelt after the nearly two-hour lunch with his family, trying not to feel too smug. She knew she'd saved the meal by offering herself and her pregnancy up as a willing distraction.

They'd ridden to her place in silence, but now Mace reached for her hand and held it fast in his.

Her heart hiccupped and she returned his grasp, reveling in the warm feel of his skin against hers.

"Thank you," he said.

"For what?" she asked as innocently as possible. "The way I see it, I should be thanking you."

"For what?"

"For a terrific meal. For a good time. For sharing your family with me."

He looked away and grimaced.

She got the distinct impression his reaction was a pre-programmed one. Because from where she sat, the only grimace material had been that brief period before she'd announced her pregnancy.

"Your family is wonderful, Mace," she said.

He looked at her, seeming to search her face for an answer she wasn't sure she had, but openly allowed him to search anyway. "I'd forgotten that," he said. "Thank you for the reminder."

"No problem."

They sat in silence for a few moments.

It was the middle of the day and they still held hands but there didn't seem to be a rush to leave.

But she knew he would be leaving. He needed to get back to work protecting that political bigwig.

But she'd be damned if she was going to remind him of that and miss out on sharing this closeness.

"I don't know how late I'll be tonight," he said.

She nodded.

"I'd ask you to wait up..."

She smiled at him. "If you did, I would."

He smiled back. "I'm thinking we could both do with a bit of sleep."

She looked down and nodded, trying to hide her disappointment.

He squeezed her hand and she squeezed back.

She didn't know how much time they had left together, but she wanted to enjoy every moment. Still, he was right: they did need some solid rest.

"Call you tomorrow?"

She nodded again. "Sure."

He leaned over to kiss her.

She was sure he'd meant to give her a brief goodbye peck, but the instant his lips met with hers, they lingered.

Geneva breathed deeply, taking in the sweet scent of him. How she was coming to look forward to his kiss, his smell, his touch.

He leaned back and she sighed.

"Let me walk you up."

She began to object but he'd already opened his door and was getting out.

She waited for him to open her door, feeling ridiculously touched that he liked to do these little things for her.

Before she knew it, they were standing outside her apartment door.

"Thank you again, Geneva." His eyes were earnest. "I can't tell you how long it's been since I've enjoyed my parents' company. Today, well, today isn't something I'm soon to forget."

"Good," she said.

She reached out and touched the side of his handsome face, smiling deep into his eyes. Then she leaned in to kiss him softly, communicating more than gratitude or sexual need or even friendship.

Long minutes later, he made a low sound in his throat and pulled away.

"If I don't go now, I'm afraid I won't."

"And your point is?"

He chuckled as he quickly kissed her one last time and slowly took his arms from around her. "Talk to you tomorrow?"

She nodded. "Talk to you tomorrow."

She watched him go, stopping every few steps to look back at her before continuing again. She didn't go inside until she heard the downstairs outer door close behind him. Then she closed her own and leaned against it, staring at nothing and everything. She told herself she should be concerned about her wistful state. But her heart was hearing none of it…

15

TOMORROW AFTERNOON'S RALLY was going to be far more dangerous.

Mace didn't like it. He didn't like it one bit. If his radar had been tweaked while walking the route on the first go-round, this time alarm bells were going off.

He told Darius about his concerns over the phone. His friend was still in Oregon working the kidnapping case.

"He refuses to cancel," Dari said finally.

"Well, then, we're just going to have to do the best we can to protect him. So long as you've outlined the risks and made your recommendations, that's the only course of action to take."

"We could pull out."

Silence.

Mace knew it was a radical solution that wasn't really a solution at all.

"Then we wouldn't get paid."

"I feel that strongly about this."

"I know you do."

He paced the length of the conference room then back again, the men around him giving him a wide berth.

Forget that the perpetrator from yesterday's rally had

yet to be caught; there were warning signs that tomorrow's event would leave Norman even more vulnerable.

First off, the venue was larger, harder to protect, not to mention the turnout was predicted to be quadruple, possibly more given the publicity received.

Second, well, the gunman had gotten a taste of fame himself. Who was to say he wouldn't make the next attempt bigger? Bolder?

A normal man might be scared off.

But they were dealing with someone who was far from normal here. Someone driven, someone insane enough to make the first attempt might be doubly motivated to make a second.

He took a deep breath and stopped pacing.

"Okay. I just needed to say the words," he said to Dari.

"Yeah, I know. And they would have been the same words I'd say if our roles were reversed."

"Yeah."

He doubted that, but he was grateful to his friend for saying it.

A few moments later they disconnected and Mace turned to face the guys. They had their work cut out for them.

But he had every confidence they could do it.

"Okay, let's get down to it…"

GENEVA'S CELL PHONE CHIMED. She rolled over in bed and squinted at the clock: it was just after five-thirty. Who would be texting her that early? Probably Trudy. She likely needed her to fill in again at the diner this morning.

She groaned and reached for her cell phone. She'd worked the dinner shift last night and with a football game running into overtime, they were kept busy until well into the night. She didn't get home until after eleven and while she'd made really good tips, she felt like she'd gotten maybe two hours of solid sleep.

She accessed the text and experienced an instant infusion of adrenaline.

It was Mace.

"I've got an hour to spare. Do you want coffee?"

Geneva tossed off the blankets even as she began texting back. "Where are you?"

"Outside your place."

She hurried to the window, instantly catching sight of him where he leaned against her car holding up two cups of extra-large coffee in white foam cups.

"I'll buzz you in."

She looked down at her faded flannels, grabbed jeans and a sweater, then hurried to press the buzzer to let him into the building. Then she opened the apartment door even as she dashed for the bathroom. She'd gotten on her jeans and was putting on her sweater when she heard, "Hello?"

She cracked the door. "Make yourself at home. I just need five."

She closed the door again then ran the water, washing up and upgrading herself to mildly presentable. Once finished, she stood staring at her reflection. What was she doing?

She found herself smiling. She didn't care. Right then, the only thing that mattered was that she had fifty-five minutes left to spend with Mace.

She emerged from the bathroom to find him standing in front of the living room window staring outside, sipping coffee. He looked so damned good in dark slacks and a crisp white shirt, his dark hair combed and neat. She, on the other hand, felt like a field mouse who'd just emerged from a dusty hole.

He sensed her presence and turned to face her, that grin of his lighting his face. "Hi."

"Hi yourself." She cleared her throat.

He put his coffee down and stepped closer, folding her into his arms. "I hope you don't mind my stopping by so early unannounced."

"No, no." She found she had a hard time breathing with him so close. "Not at all."

He smiled down at her then leaned in for a kiss. "Good, because I have another request to make."

Sleep still clung to the fringes of Geneva's consciousness, emphasizing her wholehearted response to his kiss. "Oh?" she somehow managed to say, even as her thighs vibrated as if he were licking them instead of her lips.

"I want to spend every moment possible of the next hour inside of you…"

MACE WASN'T SURE what had made him say the words. One minute he'd been on his way back to Denver following a long night and an even longer day ahead of him. The next he was pulling Geneva close and her sleep-enhanced scent made his need level surge.

She blinked liquid hazel eyes up to stare at him and he chuckled softly, trailing his fingertips over her jawline before leaning in to kiss her even more deeply.

She felt so good. Better than anyone had a right to. Holding her in his arms made him feel all-powerful yet grounded, hot as hell yet cool as could be.

And it made him want her with an intensity he was loathe to ignore.

He drew back and looked at her, waiting for her response.

He heard her swallow thickly. "I'm sorry. Was I supposed to say something?" she whispered.

He groaned and led her to her bedroom, drawing her close the instant they were inside. He kissed her then pulled off her sweater as she undid the first few buttons on his shirt and tugged it the rest of the way off. Within moments, they were stripped and breathless.

She turned, rubbing her bare bottom against him, then reached an arm back and positioned her head so she could kiss him over her shoulder.

Dear God, but she was sexier than any woman he'd ever known.

He curved his hands around and cupped her breasts.

She caught them in her hands. "Gently," she whispered.

He lightened his touch, kissing her more tenderly. Her quickening of breath told him she approved.

He snaked his right hand down lower, over her abdomen, lower still…until his fingers rested against the springy hair between her thighs.

Geneva made a small sound in the back of her throat then caught his hand. But rather than move it away as he was afraid she might, she budged it the rest of the way down until his fingers pressed against her dampness. Then she grasped his wrist as if to steady herself as he stroked her.

So hot, so wet…

He moved his fingertips back and forth and forth and back, lightly pinching her clit. At her gasp, he slid his middle finger between her silken folds, moving deep within her.

She went limp in his arms. He gently moved her toward the bed. She reached out until her left hand rested against the mattress, bending slightly, even as she continued kissing him over her shoulder. He increased the frequency of his thrusts, taking pleasure in the way she bore down against him. He lowered his other hand and stroked her outside even as he did inside.

"I…want…to…feel…you…" she rasped.

"You will, baby, you will." He thrust deeper. "Come for me now…"

She moaned, her hips rocking against him.

Geneva's mouth opened against his in a gasp. He breathed it in and kissed her deeply, feeling her slick muscles contract around his fingers. He continued stroking and caressing her, drawing out her crisis, supporting her weight as she surrendered to the sensations rolling through her.

"Please…" she whispered, kissing him languidly.

He didn't need any more encouragement. His penis was so erect it was nearly painful. Watching, bringing her to climax, had turned him on more than sex.

He sheathed himself then pressed against her soaked flesh. She kissed him, replacing his hand with hers, then took him in.

He nearly groaned aloud at the feel of her surrounding him, tight, still shivering. She reached her other hand out until she leaned completely against the bed. The sexy sight of her back, her hips, her rounded bottom made his erection pulse harder. He smoothed his hands down her spine then grasped her hips, holding her still as he surged into her. Her low moan echoed what he was feeling as he thrust again, then again.

"Yes, oh, yes…"

Each stroke brought him closer to her…closer to orgasm…closer to a euphoria that left him wondering with awe at its complexity and simplicity.

He slowed, afraid of coming too fast. Geneva bore back against him, shifting her hips hungrily. He reached around, finding her damp curls, and rubbed her lazily. She caught his wrist. Not to pull him away, it seemed, but to hold him there as her body stilled, her back arched.

Mace groaned and surged into her again, reaching for an unnamable something he needed more than he'd ever needed anything.

Then, suddenly, it was upon him…

His entire body stiffened, his blood roaring past his ears, through his body, making him feel totally, gloriously alive.

Geneva moaned.

Somehow, he found the will to thrust into her again, and again, harder, tilting his hips to change the angle of his stroke.

She went still and her breathing seemed to stop.

Mace grasped her hips tightly, moving in, pulling out…

Reaching out his hand and taking her with him as he toppled over the edge into sheer bliss…

16

GENEVA LAY BONELESS in bed, her hand resting against Mace's thigh next to her. They'd both ended up there, and somehow she'd managed to cover them both, but beyond that, she could do little more than marvel at the music pulsing through her body and focus on trying to breathe again.

She sighed and curved against Mace, who seemed to be wearing the same expression she probably did as he stared wide-eyed at the ceiling.

"You okay?" she whispered, kissing his shoulder.

"Hmm? Oh. Yeah." He grinned down at her then kissed the top of her head, rubbing his hand against her tangled hair. "I'm… I don't know how I feel…"

She sighed again and closed her eyes. "Yeah. Me, too."

They both chuckled then fell silent again.

She couldn't be sure if the spontaneous element of their lovemaking was behind her elevated reaction, but whatever it was, she wanted to do it again.

And again and again and again…

She guessed Mace would be in complete agreement.

"You need to be in Denver again?"

He nodded, his hand running lazy circles along her back. "Yeah."

"Oh, okay. By the way, I thought you should know, your mother called me last night…"

MACE WENT TOTALLY and utterly still in abject terror.

"What?"

He was incapable of any other verbal response. Only that one word.

Geneva gave a quiet laugh. "No worries. She just wanted to tell me how much she enjoyed meeting me."

Had his mom ever called Janine? He couldn't recall. In fact, in that one moment, he couldn't recall much of anything. His mind was frozen on the image of his mother calling Geneva…and Geneva picking up.

"I haven't even heard from my mother," he said.

Geneva shifted slightly. "Maybe because she thinks she's bothering you whenever she calls."

He tucked his chin against his chest so he could look down at her. "Is that what she said?"

"In so many words…yes. She did."

That was odd. He'd never considered that his mother might feel awkward about calling him.

"What else did she say?"

Geneva snuggled a little closer to him, putting her wet sex in direct contact with his thigh. He grew instantly hard.

What had they been talking about?

Oh, yeah. His mother.

"That's between me and your mother," she said in answer to his question.

He grimaced. "I can only imagine."

She shifted again, this time to prop herself up on one elbow so she could look at him. "Can you?"

"Mmm." The way she kept moving her sex against him was driving him to distraction.

"I'm not entirely sure you can."

"One word: Marcus."

She seemed to consider him for a long moment. "Not in the sense you're thinking."

He blinked.

"Let's just say I think there's a whole lot going unsaid between you two."

"Oh, I think everything's been said. And then some."

"Do you? Well, then I'm not sure which of you is more stubborn."

He raised his brows. "And you're an expert on my mother and me because…?"

She visibly winced then smiled. "I don't consider myself an expert on anything," she said quietly. "But I am a good listener."

"Most people hear what they want to."

Mace didn't particularly care for the words coming out of his mouth, but Geneva had touched on a sore spot… and refused to stop.

"Even if that's the case, I didn't have to listen to hear what she had to say."

Poke…poke…

"The day Marcus died…"

There it was.

"Your parents feel like they lost two sons, not one."

Mace experienced a sensation similar to a boulder being dropped onto his chest.

"I can see you're surprised."

"I'm also horny."

She nudged him with her closed fist against his chest. "That goes without saying."

He glanced at the clock then rolled her over so she was under him, her thighs spread wide. "I've got twenty minutes. Do you really want to spend them talking?"

He watched her gaze roll over his features then back up

to his eyes. She smiled and slid her feet around his calves and arched her back. "Oh, I think I've said all I need to. For now…"

Good.

He kissed her deeply even as he reached for another condom. This time when he made her come, he wanted it to be so hard she couldn't utter a word until sometime tomorrow…

GENEVA LAY BACK against the sheets, listening as her apartment door closed behind Mace. Every inch of her felt so vibrant, alive. She pressed her face into her pillow and breathed deeply, taking in his scent even as she ran her hands over her still-vibrating body.

What he did to her…

Her breasts trembled, her belly quaked and her thighs were saturated with the proof of her need for him.

Oh, how she would love for his semen to be there…

She shivered at the thought even as she lazily touched herself.

He'd loved her so thoroughly, you would think she'd be satisfied. Instead, she wanted more. Oh, so much more.

She couldn't remember ever feeling this…sexual before. Uninhibited. Needy.

She stroked her swollen flesh then inserted her fingertip inside, moaning as she recalled how he'd touched her just a short time ago.

Mmm…

Her cell phone rang.

She slowly reached for it.

It was Mace.

"What are you doing?" he asked.

She smiled. "Touching myself."

"Grr… That's my job."

"Yes, well, since you're not here to do it..."

There was silence for a few minutes while she continued stroking herself. Then he said, "I miss you already."

Geneva clutched the phone against her shoulder and closed her eyes before responding. "Miss you more."

She put the cell phone back on the night table then rolled over, bunching the sheets between her thighs and stretching languidly.

More...

She definitely wanted much, much more...

Was Mace ready, willing and able to give it to her?

She didn't know.

What was clear was how incredible things could be if he was.

Her cell phone chimed.

She saw a text message.

I Love You.

She blinked at the words. Then read them again.

Was it possible?

She was about to write back when another chimed in.

Sleep well. Talk to you later.

She responded with a smile then held the phone close to her again.

When she awakened a couple of hours later, she was still holding it there...

17

"ARE WE READY?"

Funny, was it really only yesterday he'd asked Geneva the same question prior to going to lunch with his parents?

Was it really that morning he'd said those other words he'd never uttered in his life?

I love you...

Not only had he said them, he'd typed them. They were in black and white, unmistakable, permanently evidenced.

Was it possible he'd never said them before? Not even to Janine? Not even to his parents? His grandfather? His brother?

Yet he'd texted them to Geneva.

And he'd meant them.

He scrubbed the back of his neck, trying to ease the tension there.

Love. He felt it. For his family. His friends. And he had felt it for Janine.

And now for Geneva.

But it wasn't something he'd thought about a great deal. It was an obvious statement that required action, not words, similar to his military lifestyle.

Then why had he been moved to say them this morning?

And were the words welcome?

He scrubbed his neck harder, fighting to review his checklist. Post-coital misstep. Yeah, that's what he could put it down to. The sex had been so incredible, he'd still been half out of his mind. Capable of saying anything.

Still, that didn't quite cut it. What was happening between them was different from the challenges he faced at work, even though they were no less intense. There were road signs posted all over the place. Unfortunately, he was spending so much time enjoying the ride, he wasn't really registering the signs until after he had passed them. And there were no U-turns to be had.

And if he could? He didn't know.

Reece came up. "Ready, willing and able, sir."

"Ready, willing and able."

And they were. At least as much as they could be.

When all was said and done, all they could do was their best.

"Good," he said. "Oh, and Reece? I want you to take the lead today."

The other man hesitated. "Sir?"

He grinned. "She's all yours."

"Are you leaving the premises?"

"No. But while I'll be listening in, I won't be in contact."

At least not unless there was an emergency.

He planned to move at will, no worries about calling shots and overseeing details: all those had been taken care of and Reece was more than capable of overseeing them.

He needed to be on the ground.

Alone.

"Very well, sir," Reece said.

"Good. There's an hour before departure. Do what you need to do to prepare your men."

Reece did as he was asked and Mace took the opportunity to slip from the room.

He ran into one of Norman's men outside the door. The guy had been looking for him.

He shook his head. "Sorry. The man to talk to is Reece."

He vaguely heard an objection but gave it little attention as he continued walking down the hall.

A TAKE ON the street hustler's shell game. Find the car, any car; which one held General Norman?

Except in this case the question wasn't which one, but rather did any of the five hold the man?

That was the tact Mace decided to take en route to today's lunchtime rally, scheduled to make the noon news coverage, not just locally, but nationally. He was coming to understand this was the way most of these rallies were done. Maximum exposure was the name of the game.

But with maximum exposure came maximum risk.

As he listened to the team communicate via his earpiece, he mentally reviewed the plans. The cars were due to pull out in five minutes. But that wasn't all that was on his mind; he'd been working hard to try to uncover the identity of the gunman from the last outing. While his sources had spat up a couple dozen likely suspects matching his physical description and MO, Mace had the feeling they were dealing with someone off the grid. For the guy to have felt comfortable enough to move so freely, he had to be relatively sure he wouldn't be easy to find.

Either that or he was psychopathic and was unconsciously looking to get caught.

It was a toss-up which was more dangerous…

He accessed his cell phone, checking for texts. He knew who he was hoping to hear from, but the queue was empty other than brief channel communications from Reece.

He rubbed his thumb pad over the keys then put the phone back into his pocket.

"We're rolling…"

Reece's announcement sent him into motion.

He'd changed from his security detail clothing into jeans, a green T-shirt, brown suede jacket and a Bronco's ball cap, going for as nondescript as possible in the hopes that the suspect wouldn't recognize him if their paths happened to cross again.

He stood across the street, half a block up from the hotel, which gave him a clear view of the parking lot entrance and all points in between. He'd just bought a paper from a corner kiosk and tucked it under his arm, looking everywhere but directly at the cars exiting onto the street one by one.

There were so many windows, both inside and outside the hotel. The suspect could be in any one of them.

He eyed pedestrian and automotive traffic, thinking everyone he saw could be the suspect…including the woman with blond hair and large glasses.

He headed in the same direction as the convoy and took out his cell phone, pretending to answer a call and consult his watch.

He made out the sound of a siren.

While the sheriff's office was involved in the detail, they weren't supplying an official escort. So that meant whatever was going on didn't involve them.

He watched as a fire truck pulled into the intersection a block up.

Or did it involve them?

Shit.

He contacted Reece. "Looks like we've got a problem."

And he didn't think it was by accident…

GENEVA SAT AT THE DINER counter, her fingers wrapped around a coffee cup although she couldn't have swallowed if she tried. She was in a lull between customers, waiting for the local news to come on at noon in the hopes that they'd be covering Norman's visit.

She checked her cell phone: nothing.

Not that she expected anything. She knew Mace was busy. Doubly so since the rally was due to begin in a few short minutes.

Still, she'd hoped for something.

Of course, she could always text him. But she didn't want to seem needy. And after falling back to sleep for a while earlier, she'd wondered if she should have said something in response to his proclamation. At the very least, she should have acknowledged it. Had she said those same words and he not responded…

She turned her coffee cup in circle. Of course, Mace wasn't like her. And she didn't think he'd obsess the way she probably would have.

Of course, she wouldn't have guessed Mace to be the type to say those words, either…

Trudy turned the television up, pretending it was something she always did, but Geneva knew she'd done it for her as much as to satisfy her own interest. Talk around the diner was still all about what had gone down the other day. And the fact that Trudy and the crew knew Mace…well, it only made it infinitely more interesting.

"We're breaking into regular programming a couple of minutes early for the noon news update. There appears to be something unusual going on surrounding General Norman's rally today. If you'll remember, it was only two days ago that…"

Geneva tuned out the newscaster's voice. Her gaze was glued to the live footage being run. There was a fire truck blocking an intersection in downtown Denver a couple of blocks up from where the reporter said Norman was staying, and a five-car procession stopped while traffic was backed up, bumper to bumper, behind them.

She felt like she'd swallowed her coffee cup and it was stuck in her throat as she tried to spot Mace.

"What's going on?" Tiffany asked, coming up beside her.

Trudy was the one who answered from the other side of the counter, quickly explaining what they'd heard so far before hushing the waitress and everyone else. She grabbed the remote to turn the volume up even further.

"The guy's a stationary target now," Mel said, peeking his head through the service window.

"Looks like it's just a fire or something," Trudy said.

"Right," another male customer said, leaving his table to stand closer to the TV in the corner. "Looks like a setup to me."

Geneva felt suddenly dizzy at the thought that Mace was in one of those cars, an unwitting target of the man threatening Norman's life.

She took out her cell phone: still nothing.

"You okay?" Trudy asked, taking the stool next to her.

She nodded, but couldn't say anything as she continued staring at the television screen. She didn't dare blink for fear she'd miss something.

The reporter filled them all in on the details from the other day and footage from the event was run.

"Wait, hold on a minute," the reporter's voice broke in during his explanation. "Looks like something is starting to happen…"

The footage continued to run even as he spoke, nearly driving Geneva straight out of her skin as she willed the camera to switch back to live action.

"It appears the police department is clearing the street behind the procession…yes, yes, they are. Officers are directing traffic to side streets. The last of the procession cars is backing up."

Then, just like that, there was a flash of light and the camera went dead, cutting off the feed.

"Trent? Trent, are you still with us?"

The female news anchor held her hand to her ear as if listening through an earpiece when an image finally came back on. She appeared to realize she was back on the air and removed her hand, her expression one of shock.

Oh, God, no…

18

HOLY SHIT!

Mace watched as the second to last car exploded in a bright, yellow ball of flame. Broken glass and flying metal moldings hit surrounding buildings, taking out windows.

For a split second, he was back in Iraq and a convoy car had hit an IED.

Then he blinked and brought the current sight back into focus.

"Stay put!" he shouted into his mouthpiece. "Repeat, do *not* get out of the car!"

He suspected taking the last car out was an attempt to get everyone out and allow for an open shot on Norman.

All the cars were designed with just such a scenario in mind—essentially the vehicle portions housed safety pods engineered to withstand just such an attack. That meant the two security personnel in the subject car should be okay, with little more than a few cuts and bruises.

Norman himself wasn't in any of the cars. In fact, right about now he was arriving at the rally site in an unmarked, unrelated vehicle that had left the hotel ten minutes before the rest of them.

Had it been a car bomb? Seemed likely. Still, Mace

found himself eyeing the surrounding buildings. His gaze caught on a wisp of smoke coming from an open window some ten floors up. His first clue that this was the real deal was that the window was even open at all in a business structure where windows were required to be closed due to safety issues that had nothing to do with rally processions and controversial political figures.

Even as he listened to Reece ably direct the action on the ground, he rushed the door to the business building, mentally mapping out exits. He was going to get this guy, come hell or high water...

WHERE WAS HE?

Geneva didn't dare leave the support of the diner. Normally the lunch crowd was replaced by the dinner one, but today no one was leaving and the eatery was quickly filled to capacity by those watching the action being replayed on the local television station that had switched to live programming. It had been some time since Colorado Springs had seen this much activity and its residents were drawn together to experience it together.

Unfortunately, Geneva's connection was a little more direct.

Why didn't he call?

"Anything?" Trudy asked as she passed.

Geneva was standing in the middle of the diner floor, her arms filled with plates of burgers and fries even as she checked her cell phone. She shook her head, put her phone back in her apron pocket and continued on to Table Three.

Following the abrupt cut-off of live coverage earlier, the five-minute wait as a new connection was set up ranked up there as some of the longest of her life. The on-the-ground reporter and his cameraman were fine, it was explained, but their equipment had been taken out by the blast.

And what a blast it had been, too. At the first sight of the broken car sitting in the middle of a blackened circle on the downtown Denver street, Geneva had nearly projectile vomited, imagining Mace inside the vehicle.

That's when she began texting…

She told herself not to. That he was probably fine and that Mace had his hands full and the last thing on his mind would be her and her active imagination. But she hadn't been able to help herself.

Somewhere after the tenth panicked text, she'd forced herself to stop, even though her dread continued to grow.

It couldn't be good, his unresponsiveness.

So instead she'd watched coverage along with everyone else, both of the rally that the general had made it to safely even though all five cars in the procession remained at a standstill on a downtown street, blocked on one end by a fire truck that was now needed, and the disable vehicle. She'd gasped when firemen had gained access to the car, pulling out two men. Were either of them Mace? She'd run up to the television and stood directly underneath, not daring to blink as the reporter narrated events.

Ultimately, it was decided both men were fine…and neither of them was Mace.

At one point, she'd ordered herself to stop. Mace was a military pro and episodes of this nature were a regular part of his job.

But this wasn't Afghanistan: this was Colorado. And stuff like this wasn't supposed to happen.

After delivering the plates and refilling coffee cups, she caught herself standing in front of the television again, coffeepot in one hand, thumbnail of her other between her teeth. At this point, they were merely rehashing earlier events. There was no new information, no footage that included a shot of Mace.

It was just after five and while "Breaking News" was stamped in a special red icon in the upper right of the screen, the station had rolled into its usual pre-news hour.

She found it ironic that one of her basic reasons for never dating a man in the military had been because of the long separations that frequently found the object of a stateside lover's attention wandering. She'd never really considered the risk angle—the fact that the lover might wander off...permanently.

She'd turned her cell phone volume on high. It loudly chirped now.

Geneva fumbled to get it out of her apron pocket, nearly dropping it. Those aware of her connection to Mace stopped to stare at her.

A text.

From Mace.

Her relief was so complete, her knees nearly gave out.

She made it to the counter where she leaned against it for support as she accessed the text.

Running late. Meet you at the dance...

She stared, dumbfounded, reading it again.

He was okay.

The word swirled around and around her head.

He was okay.

"So?"

She looked to find Trudy hovering.

She blinked. "He says he'll meet me at the dance."

Dance?

She realized she'd completely forgotten about the dance.

"Girl, I need you here."

She nodded, then pressed the needed buttons to respond to Mace's text.

No way was she going to work overtime at the diner when she had a chance to see Mace.

She wrote, then rewrote the text. Finally, she settled on a simple Okay.

She sat for long moments, cell phone crushed in her hand, staring at the television screen, attempting to connect the surreal scene continuing to play out with the mind-blowingly normal one going on in her life.

"Running late. Meet you at the dance…"

His words as casual as if a meeting he was in was going long or he'd been caught in traffic.

Not that he'd been involved in a car-bombing incident that nearly took two men's lives.

"Table Five needs service," Trudy said, passing her.

Geneva looked at her blankly, her words taking a moment to register.

An hour. That's all she was going to give the diner. Then she was going home to stand in the shower until the water ran cold, or until her thoughts started to make sense. Whichever came first.

And then she was going to that dance.

19

HE SHOULD HAVE CANCELED.

Mace knew that.

Still, even though his mind was occupied with the day's event, he was late as hell and probably in hot water, the thought of seeing Geneva, even for a few minutes…well, it eclipsed everything else.

He straightened his Marine full-dress uniform jacket and scanned the good-sized crowd at the outdoor dance, his mind still going over the second attempt against Norman's life.

After pinpointing the position of the assailant, he'd rushed into the business building with backup on the way only to find the vacant office from which the rocket had been launched empty…although very recently occupied. The suspect had left behind items he probably hadn't intended to, which indicated Mace had just missed him. A scope bore a good fingerprint that Mace had immediately entered into the system. While nothing had come back yet, he had men out pulling samples from hotels and motels in the area hoping for a match and a further lead. He also had guys reviewing video from cameras in the area.

The two security men in the target car had suffered minor burns and concussions but thankfully, they were okay.

And General Norman had gone on to his rally as if nothing had happened, not learning the full extent of the second attempt until afterward.

It had been after seven before Mace realized what time it was…and remembered his promise to Geneva.

Now it was after nine.

The Harvest Dance was set on a farm outside Colorado Springs in a hulking old barn. A big band was set up in a corner among hay bales and there was a large dance area in front of the makeshift stage, while tables full of those taking advantage of the unseasonably warm night were set up both inside and outside the barn under large tents.

He didn't know how he was going to find Geneva. He hadn't heard anything from her after her simple "Okay."

Maybe he should call her.

Then he spotted her.

His stomach tightened in a way not all that different than it had in the wake of today's events, yet was entirely different. She was standing near the barn doors, a glass of what looked like wine in her hand though he guessed it was likely juice, her profile turned to him as she took in the scene. She had on a red high-waisted dress and heels, her hair swept back from her beautiful face, looking perfectly matched to the nostalgia-era setting.

He stood still, merely watching her when she seemed to sense his presence. Her chin went up and she turned her head, meeting his gaze.

Her smile erased everything that had happened that day. Nothing existed but her.

They met in the middle of the distance separating them and she hugged him. He happily hugged her back.

"Thank God you're okay," she whispered into his ear.

She smelled of gardenias and something spicy. It was all he could do not to press his lips against the long line of her neck. Damn, but she looked beautiful.

He hadn't thought about her worrying earlier. It wasn't until later he'd discovered the news about the car explosion had been pretty much broadcast live, which meant she'd probably seen it.

"I'm even better now," he whispered back, settling for brushing his lips against the shell of her ear as he pulled her slightly closer.

She smiled up at him.

As he smiled back, he couldn't help feeling as if he'd known her forever…yet as if they'd just met.

"You want something to drink?" she asked.

He watched her mouth say the words, but didn't immediately register them. The band had launched into a slow classic.

"What? Oh. No." He offered his arm. "But I would like to dance with you. Do me the honor?"

"The honor would be mine."

He took the glass from her hand, placed it on a nearby table, then walked her the short way to the dance floor. As he pulled her close, he couldn't help thinking there was nowhere else he'd rather be in that one moment. She fit just so against him, her soft sigh communicating she likely felt the same.

It had been a good long while since he'd danced with anyone. But Geneva wasn't just anyone. She was…she was…

He looked down at her.

She was beautiful. In every way.

"I was worried about you," she said softly.

"I know. I'm sorry. I should have called."

"I know you had more important matters to attend to."

Just then, he couldn't think what those could be. He was filled with the sweet scent of her, the feel…and wanted more. Oh, so much more.

"I was afraid you weren't going to make it tonight," she said.

"I was, too."

He smiled down at her and then held her closer still.

He closed his eyes, listening to the music, content to feel her heart beating against his, for now.

"About your text this morning…" she said so softly he nearly didn't hear her.

Had it really been only that morning since he'd texted those three words? Yes, he realized, it had been.

"Shh," he said into her ear. "Let's just enjoy the moment, okay?"

Her head nodded against his cheek.

He pressed his lips against her temple.

So much, so quickly. From one extreme to the next. Given the drastic swings, part of him wondered if his instincts and emotions could be trusted. But it was a small part, if only because this felt so right.

A tap on Mace's shoulder. "May I?"

He turned to look at Dustin.

He grimaced as he gazed into Geneva's surprised face. She looked back at him.

"Sorry. The lady's dance card is full," he said, experiencing a possessiveness with which he was unfamiliar.

Geneva gave Dustin an apologetic smile and then Mace danced her away from reality back into the dream…

A HALF HOUR LATER, Geneva reluctantly left Mace with some friends to go in search of Dustin. She'd much rather stick by Mace's side, get to know more about him and talk to his friends' dates and wives and girlfriends, but she needed to talk to the man who was making it his business to complicate her life in ways she didn't appreciate.

There. She found him talking to Tiffany from the diner near the open bar set up outside.

"May I speak to you for a moment?" she asked, after saying hello and telling Tiffany she looked great.

"Dance?" Dustin asked.

"Talk."

They both looked at Tiffany, who appeared curiously disappointed.

"Sure."

Geneva led the way and stopped on the fringe of the happy crowd.

"You've got to stop this, Dustin."

"Stop what?"

"You know what," she said. "You've got to stop acting like we're anything more than just friends."

His gaze dropped to her belly. "Oh? I'm thinking you need to stop acting like we're just friends."

"We're going to share parenting, but as for anything romantic…"

She watched as his expression darkened.

She touched his sleeve. "I'm sorry if this flies in the face of your basic instincts, Dustin. Really, I am. But…well, I just don't feel that way about you. And the days of marrying just for the sake of a baby have long since passed."

"But…"

"There really isn't a but."

Then it struck her. She suddenly realized because she spent so much of her time dodging his advances, she wasn't including him in a way that might allay some of his fears… and get him to accept a more fitting role.

"I have an ultrasound scheduled for next week," she said quietly.

His brows raised.

"Would you like to come with me?"

"Yes," he said. "I'd love to come with you."

She smiled at his quick answer.

"Will we learn the sex of the baby?"

She laughed. "No. Not yet. We're still a few weeks away from that, but you're welcome to be present then, as well."

He seemed to search her face long and hard.

"I'm not going to exclude you, Dustin. You are the baby's father. You're welcome to participate any way you'd like in that role."

"But nothing more."

"Friendship. You know, like what we shared before."

He nodded.

Thankfully, he appeared more thoughtful than genuinely hurt.

Had he really been afraid she'd cut him out?

"And Mace?" he asked.

"Mace?"

Then it struck her: Dustin wasn't only afraid of being cut out; he was concerned he might be replaced altogether.

"I don't know," she said truthfully.

While she hoped Mace might play a role in her future—and by extension in the future of her child—well…

"But whatever tomorrow holds," she said to Dustin, "you'll always be the baby's father."

He appeared satisfied with that. More than satisfied, he looked happy.

"Can I be there for the birth?"

Her eyes widened and she laughed. "How about we leave that decision for when we're closer to the birth?"

He grinned. "Fair enough."

She looked over his shoulder at the way Tiffany was watching them in a curious way.

She squinted.

Oh. Another light bulb moment.

Geneva cleared her throat. "Now that we've settled that, it looks like someone might like to dance with you."

"Who?"

She nodded in the other woman's direction.

"Tiffany?" he said incredulously. "We're just friends."

"So are Mace and I..." Geneva said. Then she smiled.

20

SHE DESERVED BETTER...

Mace hated parting ways with Geneva at the end of the dance, but he needed to hightail it back to Denver before the suspect trail grew cold. Now, hours later, all he could think about was her, all warm and sleeping in that big bed of hers, alone. And how much he'd like to crawl in behind her, draw her close, then lose himself in the touch, feel and taste of her.

He couldn't recall a time when a woman had captivated him to the degree where she was always on his mind. To where his every thought, every action, automatically extended to how it might affect her or them.

He'd never achieved that state of...consumption with Janine. In fact, every time he found a message waiting for him on his cell phone, which had thankfully trickled down to once a day instead of several, he was mildly surprised to find he'd forgotten about her.

"Match."

Reece's one word snapped his attention away from thoughts that might concern him if given further examination. He looked up from where the documentation on yesterday's reports from various team members was spread out on the conference room table before him.

Jon came over to where he sat. He placed a printout of the fingerprint found at the scene yesterday next to another. "Falcone lifted this from the front desk counter at a budget motel on the outskirts of town an hour ago."

They had their man.

Though if he was correct in that assumption, there was little chance their guy was still at the ratty motel on the edge of town. Especially if he'd spotted Dominic Falcone.

Still, it was a lead where previously there hadn't been one.

"Falcone still on the scene?"

"No. He's moved on."

With countless hotels and motels in the metro area to accommodate conventions, there was a lot of ground to cover, so it was anybody's guess where any of the men were at that given moment.

Mace pushed from his chair and grabbed his jacket. "Then let's go…"

GENEVA SAT AT THE DINER counter, the breakfast rush having slowed to a hushed trickle, proposals from her other job open before her in preparation for a meeting in an hour scheduled to take place at the eatery, since she wouldn't have time to go home and change and get back in time to meet her client.

Trudy plopped down on the stool next to her and sighed, slapping her morning paper onto the counter. "What a morning."

Geneva made a notation in the margin of the proposal. "Any luck replacing Cindy?"

Trudy made a sound that verified what Geneva had already suspected. "I haven't had time to interview much less hire anyone."

"You could always hire her back."

"I could…"

Geneva raised her brows. The usual Trudy response to such a suggestion would have been a snort and a dismissive scowl. Far be it from her to rehire someone who'd already proven herself unworthy. Her tolerance threshold was wide, but surpass it and there was no going back. Once you were out with her, you were out for good.

At least that had been the case before.

Although now…

Trudy opened the paper, pretending not to notice her open scrutiny although Geneva knew perfectly well she was aware of it; Trudy was aware of everything.

"Should I give her a call? You're going to be short-handed this weekend."

Trudy didn't respond, indicating the moment of Zen breakthrough had passed. At least for the time being.

Geneva returned to her proposal, figuring her suggestion was at least worth a shot. Truth was, considering how busy it had been lately, they needed an extra pair of hands. And while Cindy was known to call in sick once or twice a month without a hint of the sniffles, she was a good worker.

The idea of training someone new when there was already a well-trained waitress available was unthinkable.

And, according to Tiffany, Cindy was very much interested in having her old job back. Her new one at a nearby chain restaurant wasn't exactly working out the way she'd hoped.

"What are you doing next Tuesday?" Trudy asked.

Geneva glanced up from her proposal. Tuesday. Was it

really only four days from now? It seemed so far away…
yet so soon.

She hadn't taken much note of the time lately. She'd
been existing in an oddly enticing clockless bubble full
of emotion and sighs. But now that she was being asked,
she realized only two days remained of Mace's leave. Next
Tuesday…

Next Tuesday, he would be long gone.

Her heart stopped pumping.

"Geneva?"

She looked at Trudy, but didn't really see her.

"Did you hear me?"

"What? Oh. Yes. I heard you."

"It's not a complicated question."

Maybe not. But it did involve a complicated response.
Albeit one she would never dream of sharing with Trudy.

One she really didn't really care to explore her own response to, either.

"Why? What's going on?"

Trudy shrugged as if it was of no importance. "That
new Julia Roberts movie is out. I thought maybe you and
I could catch a matinee or something."

Geneva raised her brows.

While she considered her employer a dear friend, they'd
never really socialized outside the diner.

"Sure. Let's go. It's been a while since I've been to a
show."

"Me, too." Trudy stiffened. "I was thinking it was time
to change that."

Geneva smiled then returned to her proposal. It seemed
her friend was making a lot of changes lately.

It seemed both of them were.

Her hand went to her belly and she stared off into space.
The thought of Mace not playing a role in any of those

changes was so impossible to fathom, she couldn't bring herself to consider it. Not just now. Wherever she was, whatever she was doing, he was there, on the fringes of her thoughts, a presence that made her blood hum and her mouth smile. To consider otherwise...

No. She wasn't ready for that.

But she would have to be soon.

Whether she wanted to or not.

"Maybe we can do some shopping for baby clothes afterward," Trudy said.

Geneva's hand stopped and she smiled, grateful for the happy distraction. In just a few short months, the baby growing within her would be a separate human being with needs of his or her own. And as each day passed, that reality grew more and more. She couldn't wait to meet her child.

"Yes. Maybe we can," she said softly.

She glanced over at the stool of Dustin's choice, hopeful that after their conversation last night, he'd accept his role as father and let the rest fall aside.

"Wow!"

So seldom was it that Trudy was impressed with anything, it was worthy of note. Or, at the very least, her attention.

"What is it?"

Trudy turned the newspaper so Geneva could view the page she was reading. It took a moment to understand it wasn't a story her friend was sharing, but a photo. More specifically, a photo of her and Mace, taken last night.

Wow, was right.

With her in her retro forties dress and him in uniform, the big band behind them, the shot could have easily been taken decades ago. And the way Mace held her, looked at her...

She shivered.

"I hate to tell you this, sweetie, but he's going to break your heart."

She heard the words of warning, but paid them little mind as she caught on something under the caption. "Can I see that?"

"Sure."

Geneva opened the paper at the crease. "Local Hero to be Awarded Navy Cross."

Talk about wow...

When Mace had told her he wanted her to attend an awards ceremony with him, she'd had no idea he'd be the one getting the award. She'd assumed it was an event he was required to attend. And while the occasion certainly was that, well...

Wow!

"What?"

Trudy took the paper back and read the caption.

"That's our Mace, isn't it?"

She didn't miss the "our" as she nodded.

"Give that back."

Geneva did so blankly, unable to read the rest of the story.

"It says here that he rescued five of his fellow soldiers, carried one out on his shoulders. Holy cow. The one they're talking about is Darius Folsom." She showed her that page and Geneva barely registered the photo of Dari, the regular with whom Mace had been dining the night she met him, featured near the end of the story.

What kind of man didn't share something of that nature? Didn't tell her why they were attending a medals ceremony, what he had done?

She knew. The type of man who truly was a hero.

"I'm going to that."

"Going where? To Afghanistan?"

"No. To the ceremony."

"Tomorrow?"

She nodded again. "I'm his date."

She met Trudy's gaze, seeing in her eyes the same type of emotion ballooning in her: an acute mix of awe…and fear.

Awe that she had captured his attention.

Fear that Mace was undoubtedly going to break her heart…

21

LARGER THAN LIFE and twice as evasive.

Mace was beginning to really not like this guy. Not only had he made two attempts on General Norman's life, he was proving harder to find than a glass of water in the desert.

"Sorry. He checked out sometime before the maids hit the room at around noon yesterday," the motel owner said from behind the counter.

"Can we see the room?"

"There's another couple in there. They checked in late last night."

Mace pulled a hundred out of his wallet and placed it on the counter under his hand. "A call telling them the exterminator needs to get in there should help them decide to move to another room."

The owner didn't hesitate. He picked up the motel phone and dialed. A moment later he hung up.

"I'll have them moved in ten minutes."

Mace nodded then walked out of the office to join Reece where he stood under the entrance port.

"Anything?" he asked.

Reece shook his head and pocketed his cell phone. "The guy's off the grid."

The term meant the fingerprint hadn't turned up an ID. The guy they were after wasn't registered anywhere and had no arrest record that they knew of.

He watched the couple in Room 13 exit and the owner hurry out of the office to take them to another room on the other side of the complex.

But it was the sight of a baby carriage that caught his attention.

He stared at the simple blue fabric and then the baby within. The little guy couldn't be more than a couple of months old. And it was all too easy to imagine the pretty blonde pushing the stroller as Geneva.

His throat choked off air.

"They're clear," Reece remarked.

Mace coughed, forcing himself to look at the room and not the baby. "Okay, I'm going to go check it out. In the meantime, I want you to ask for access to the surveillance footage from the night before last when the owner gets back."

Reece nodded.

"See if you can get the names of the maids who cleaned the room and find out if they're on the premises, as well."

"Roger that. You want me to interview them."

He'd thought of doing it himself, but he was coming to trust Reece nearly as much. "Yeah. Go ahead. See if the guy said anything, or was carrying anything of note."

"Got it."

With that, he strode in the direction of Room 13. The owner met him at the entrance.

"I can give you ten minutes."

He didn't argue the point; he only needed five.

He stepped inside, blinking against the dimness after

being out in the bright daylight. He pulled the cord to open the curtains, careful to visually skim the floor under the window as he did so. The place smelled of baby powder. He tried to ignore it as he gave the room a walk through, then went around again, checking garbage pails. Baby wipes and empty formula bottles.

Damn.

He could have done without the reminder that Geneva was expecting…especially since he wasn't sure where he stood on the idea of children.

Simply, he hadn't given the idea much thought.

But to have the decision already made for you…

He dropped to one knee and checked under the first of two queen-size beds. He used the end of a pen to fish out a candy bar wrapper that was unnoteworthy along with a small slip of motel paper torn from a pad.

Now that was a little more interesting.

As he stared at the number written on it, he couldn't help thinking that he couldn't have gotten luckier had it said: "Answer here."

He pocketed the paper then sat down on the chair near the door, squinting at the room. But even as he tried to concentrate on his thoughts and where they were leading, his mind drifted back to Geneva and what the immediate future held for her.

What was he talking about? Long-term was more like it.

He ran his hands through his hair several times then drew in a deep breath.

What was he doing?

More accurately, what were they doing?

In two brief days, he shipped out…

He heard footsteps approach the door. He looked over his shoulder to meet Reece's gaze. If the other man found his sitting in the chair unusual, he didn't say anything.

"The owner's putting together a copy of the surveillance footage now," he said. "And the maid on duty yesterday is off today."

Mace got up. "Have him hold on to the footage for pickup later."

"You sure?"

"Yeah. We're heading to Lazarus."

Darius had gotten back into town that morning. He and his old friend needed to powwow…

"ASSIGNMENT IS DONE. Successful. We were even paid an unexpected bonus."

Mace walked through Lazarus headquarters with Darius, trading the offices for the outdoors. Recruits trained on the course but he paid them little heed. His attention was on his friend.

Dari looked at him when he didn't immediately respond. "The guy's still alive. That was our job. And we did it well."

"The suspect is still at large."

"It's not our problem."

Mace's footsteps slowed. It took Dari a moment to realize he wasn't keeping pace. Finally he stopped and turned back to him.

His friend grimaced. "Look, I understand how you feel about loose threads. But when we began Lazarus Security, I learned quickly that more often than not, it's best to cut them rather than follow them through to the end."

"Because there's no profit in it."

"Because there's no sense in it."

Mace stared out at the new recruits.

One of the biggest reasons he's signed up for the Corps was because it was the only thing that made sense to him in a world that made none. There was structure and discipline, a chain of command and a clear enemy. If working in the public sector meant the type of chaos Dari was suggesting, perhaps he'd be better off signing up for another stint, going pure career.

Dari slapped a hand onto his shoulder and gave a good squeeze. "You've got two days of leave left. Why not spend it doing something you'd enjoy doing?" He grinned. "Or someone?"

It was Mace's turn to grimace. Referencing Geneva that way was so off base, it was offensive.

"Aw, hell. Don't tell me you're still seeing that pregnant waitress?"

Now he was offended.

"Uh-oh. You are."

"And if I am?"

"If you are…"

Mace's cell phone rang.

He fished it out of his pocket even as his friend fished for words to complete his sentence.

Janine.

Damn.

He repocketed the phone, sending her to voice mail.

"That her?" Dari asked.

"No."

He began walking again and Dari followed suit. Silence reigned as they skirted the training area, the autumn sun beating down on them, the report of gunfire from the firing range cracking the only sounds.

"I've released Reece from his temporary contract," Dari said. "He's heading back to Arizona in a couple of hours."

Mace nodded. "Understood."

He felt Dari's visual scrutiny.

"Let it go, man," his friend finally said.

Mace squinted at him.

"Norman has moved on. Job is done."

He thought of the bit of paper he had in his pocket. The one that would sew everything up. He hadn't had the chance to tell Dari what he'd found because he'd been cut off at the pass before he had a chance to try.

Maybe Dari was right. Maybe he should just cut his losses and move on. Visit his parents. Take his grandfather out. It would be a good six months before he'd have the opportunity again.

"I'd also suggest you let Geneva go."

Mace stopped dead in his tracks.

Dari held his hands up. "Hey, I'm not saying anything any other friend wouldn't."

"You're out of line."

"Am I? Because I don't think so."

Mace turned and headed back toward the compound.

"Don't get me wrong. Geneva's a great girl."

Great didn't begin to cover it, but he kept his thoughts to himself.

"But…"

Dari drew in a deep breath. "But you're fresh out of one relationship, Mace. At a career crossroads. You don't know what's around the next corner much less five years from now. If you hook up with Geneva, your fate is sealed for the next eighteen years plus."

"That's a shitty way of looking at it."

"Maybe. And I sure don't like saying it. But Geneva's a package deal. You take her, you take her kid. Life and relationships are tough enough without that kind of baggage."

"She's not baggage."

"Yes, she is. Heavy baggage."

His back teeth locked together. Outside the choice of words, his friend wasn't saying anything that hadn't been hovering on the fringes of his thoughts for the past few days.

Still, hearing them come from Dari gave him a target to focus on.

"Continue seeing her and it'll only get more complicated."

He wanted to tell Dari about his and Geneva's temporary arrangement. Their ruse to pretend they were dating during the length of his leave. But somehow he felt doing so would be a betrayal.

Besides, they'd gone beyond pretend some time ago, hadn't they? What was developing between them now was very real, indeed.

"Look, I know what I'm talking about. Not that Megan's pregnant, I don't know if I'm ready to be a father. Frankly, the idea scares me spitless. And I went in with my eyes open."

Mace listened.

"Are you really prepared to take on the role with a woman you just met? Be a father to a child that isn't yours?"

His cell rang again, this time indicating a text.

Geneva.

Will I be seeing you tonight?

He put it back into his pocket without responding, feeling the slip of paper with the phone number on it as he did so.

"Just promise you'll think about it," Dari said as they continued walking back toward the main compound.

"Trust me, thinking is about all I'm capable of right now…"

22

THE SINKING SUN SET the autumn leaves of the trees opposite Geneva's living room window ablaze while a cold wind blew the ones that had fallen around the parking lot, signaling the change of seasons.

She wished she didn't fear the change of seasons wasn't the only thing the wind was blowing in.

She'd texted Mace hours ago asking if she might see him tonight. He had yet to respond.

He was probably busy.

He was probably avoiding her.

She attempted to warm herself with herbal tea and sorted through emotions as varied as the color of the leaves outside.

Even when Mace was busy, he managed to drop her a text, no matter how brief. And she knew General Norman had moved on. National news said the guy was now in Chicago. Which meant Lazarus Security was no longer needed.

So the only answer she had for his silence was that he was avoiding her.

Her chest ached in a way that made it difficult to breathe.

Heartache.

She didn't realize she'd come to expect so much from him in such a short amount of time.

She told herself it had been only a few hours since she'd heard anything. And she was likely allowing her imagination to run away with her. But given the limited amount of time they had left, well, every precious second counted.

She considered ways to distract herself. After all, it had only been a few hours. There was no need to think he wouldn't call or come over tonight.

Still, for reasons she was ill equipped to identity, she sensed that she wouldn't be seeing him before tomorrow.

Tomorrow…

Seeing how stirred up she was getting now, well, maybe she should cancel. After all, their original deal had outlived its purpose.

She closed her eyes. What an inappropriate way to refer to the bonds that had developed between them.

"I *love* you."

His words still filled her lungs like a breath full of sweet, autumn air.

Of course, he hadn't vocally said the words; he'd texted them. Still, in that one moment, he'd been experiencing the type of emotion that inspired the communication.

And she knew she loved him…

She was unsure when it had happened. She only understood that she did. Sometimes it seemed her body was incapable of containing the enormity of what she felt for him.

And the fear of losing him forever…

The battle raging within her stole her breath away as effectively as the wind.

She blinked to clear the moisture from her eyes. What did she know about battles? When compared to Mace…

The Navy Cross.

Wow.

The one word was still all she could manage when she thought of what he must have endured, what he'd done to earn the award. Not because she was surprised—far from it—but because he'd shared neither the importance of the award nor what acts had merited it.

Her cell phone chimed. She'd left it on her desktop to prevent herself from checking it every few seconds and now rushed to answer it.

"Hello?" she answered without checking the ID.

"Geneva?"

It was a woman. Not Mace.

She swallowed past the wad of sandpaper in her throat. "Yes."

"Hello, dear. I hope you don't mind my calling, but this is Mace's mom? Sharon?"

"Oh, yes, yes. How are you?"

While it wasn't Mace, she welcomed the distraction.

"I'm fine. How are you doing? And the baby?"

Geneva smiled, her hand automatically going to her belly. "We're both fine, thank you."

"Good. Good."

It dawned on her that she likely shouldn't welcome contact from Mace's mother. It would only make things more awkward when they parted ways.

Parted ways...

Her heart swelled painfully against her rib cage.

Not only the reality, but the inevitability of their parting after tomorrow hit her hard.

But she'd known the deal going in, hadn't she? She'd understood that what they had was only temporary.

Then what was she doing speaking to his mother? Surely she was only inviting disaster.

Especially since she didn't imagine Mace would appreciate her continuing any kind of connection with his family.

Then again, Sharon believed them only to be friends. So anything that did develop…well, would be between her and Sharon.

Right?

"I'm sorry if I'm interrupting something…"

"No, no." Geneva hadn't realized she'd gone silent until Sharon spoke again.

"I can try back again later if this is a bad time."

Geneva walked back to her spot in front of the window, telling herself it was to enjoy the fall foliage and had absolutely nothing to do with her hope she'd spot Mace pull up. "Now is just fine. How's Mike?"

"Oh, he's well. He's in the other room reading the paper. I just cleaned up the dinner dishes…"

And suddenly, the two of them settled into a pleasant conversation about nothing and everything.

Fifteen minutes in, Sharon circled back. "Anyway, the reason I called was to ask if you're attending the ceremony tomorrow?"

Geneva briefly bit her lip, wondering what her answer should be. While Mace hadn't retracted the invitation, his silence might be exactly that. She didn't know if it was a good idea to continue a ruse that had already snowballed into so much more.

"Yes," she said softly, unable to deny herself any chance of seeing him.

"Good! I was hoping you would be there. You see, I'd like very much for us to sit together…"

And just like that, Geneva found herself tumbling straight down the rabbit hole…

MACE SAT IN HIS RENTAL CAR outside Geneva's apartment building, staring up at her dark windows. It was after midnight and he'd spent the better half of an hour trying to figure out what he should do.

An hour? Try the past day.

His earlier conversation with Dari left a bad taste in his mouth.

Had he been irresponsible for getting involved with a mother-to-be?

Mother-to-be...

Such a narrow term to describe Geneva. She was so much more. But the fact that she would be a mother soon, very soon, should have played a larger role in his decision to see her. Strangely, it hadn't.

Then why was it such a big deal now?

He imagined her in the coming months growing plumper, rounder, softer, sexier. Saw her holding a tiny infant, smiling. But somehow he couldn't insert himself into that picture. When he envisioned her, her future, he saw only her.

He rubbed his face as if trying to rid himself of his skin.

Still, she deserved better than his silence.

He should have called her. He'd started to several times.

Tomorrow... Was it really his last day in Colorado Springs?

Yes. He left on the first transport out, first thing Sunday morning.

He knew such an acute sensation of...was it sadness? Yes, he suspected it was.

Never before had he not looked forward to heading out. Not because he wanted to escape anything, but because being a Marine was his job, what he did best. And that job required traveling to where he was needed.

And now?

Now the idea of stepping onto that plane left him feeling...reluctant.

Perhaps it was simply because he'd be leaving Geneva behind. There was so much change laying on her horizon that he wouldn't be a part of. Was that why he was feeling this way?

Whatever it was, he wanted to shake it off. Put on his sweats and run until he wasn't merely physically exhausted, but mentally, as well.

He should call her now.

He wanted to call her now.

What he really wanted to do was go up there, kiss her senseless then lose himself in a way no run would ever match.

But to do so would prolong the inevitable.

It would give her cause to hope there was going to be more.

Damn. When had something so simple grown so very complicated?

And what was he going to do about it?

His cell phone beeped.

He took it out of his pocket and stared at the text announcement, not realizing he was hoping it was Geneva maybe having spotted him, taking the decision out of his hands.

It wasn't.

It was Janine.

I'm at The Barracks. Meet me? We need to talk.

He sat for long moments after putting the phone back into pocket. Geneva's windows remained dark.

Janine.

Not a day went by since his return when she hadn't tried to contact him, talk to him. Their brief exchange at the bar the other night apparently hadn't been enough.

So much unfinished business.

He started the car and began backing out of the parking spot. Maybe Janine was just the distraction he needed right now. Meeting with her might help him decide one way or another where his path lay.

As he drove away, he looked up at Geneva's windows one last time. He couldn't be sure, but he thought he saw her bedroom light switch on, her silhouette against the glass.

He kept driving...

23

SHE STILL HADN'T HEARD from Mace.

Yet there she was, in a simple yellow dress and brown suede jacket and shoes, at the awards ceremony that had been his first "faux date" request.

The day was sunny and cool, frost on the grass at the site slowly melting off. Men and women in uniform wove easily through the crowd of civilians while those in higher command stayed closer to the stage. Geneva had never felt more out of place in her life.

She must have decided at least a dozen times not to come. Yet she ultimately had. If this was going to be the last time she saw Mace, well, she still wanted to see him. If only to say goodbye, congratulate him and wish him well.

"Geneva?"

It was a male voice.

She turned to find it wasn't the one she was hoping for. Instead, it was Darius Folsom and his wife, Megan, whom she had seen only a few times but knew on sight.

"Hi," she said. "I'm guessing you're here for the same reason I am?"

"In a manner of speaking," Dari replied. "I'm responsible for Mace getting that medal."

Megan elbowed him. "He's making it sound like he should be up there with him. What he means is that his is one of the many asses Mace saved." She smiled at her husband. "Something for which I am very grateful."

Geneva recognized several others she'd seen come into the diner with Dari, but couldn't ignore the fact that neither Dari nor Megan were inclined to introduce them, although she was certain they all had to also be Mace's friends.

Like she wasn't feeling awkward enough...

"Geneva!"

Once again, she found herself grateful for Mace's mom's interruption. She told the couple it was nice to see them, then turned to look for her.

Mrs. Harrison waved her hand, making her easily identifiable where she stood before a front row chair.

Front row.

Of course. Where else would she expect a medal honoree's family to sit?

Only she wasn't family. And her level of discomfort notched upward.

She considered merely waving back and choosing a seat closer to the back, but thought better of it. First of all, she wouldn't put it past Sharon to come get her. Second, the prospect of sitting near Dari and Mace's friends wasn't any more appealing.

Had Mace said something to them? Or had they said something to Mace?

She thought back to when she'd first discovered she was pregnant. She'd told Trudy, making it clear she had no intention of marrying the father, who she hadn't immediately revealed was Dustin. The salty diner owner had frowned at her and said, "You do know you're going to be the focus of gossip central for at least the next five years."

Geneva had laughed. "This isn't the fifties."

"Maybe not, but it might as well be. We women may have come a long way, baby, but in a lot of respects I'm afraid we'll never reach our destination."

Her next remark had helped erase a bit of the sting. "You're also never going to have your figure back."

Of course, Geneva had never really given Trudy's gossip warning any sort of weight. But as she made her way through the crowd with a weak smile, she couldn't help filing away Dari's expression as he'd spoken to her, which matched several of the other guys' in the group to which she hadn't been introduced. It had said: "Stay away from Mace. You have too much baggage."

She was somewhat relieved to note that Megan and the other women hadn't seemed to be wearing that same look.

She reached the front row and was enveloped in a hug by the sweet-smelling woman that was Mace's mom. She felt the breath she wasn't aware she was holding whoosh from her as a quiet sigh.

For a moment she was tempted to close her eyes, imagine the fear away and replace it with something much nicer. The embrace was so genuine, it would be all too easy.

Instead, she returned the hug then greeted Mace's father and grandfather, grateful that not a glimmer of the gossip shadow existed on either of their faces.

"You'll be sitting next to me, of course," Mace's grandfather said after kissing her cheek, his eyes sparkling suggestively.

For the first time, she felt slightly ill at ease, although at the lunch where she'd met them, she had been completely comfortable. The power of suggestion, she realized. If some people thought less of her, viewed her as unworthy, perhaps others might view her as loose and unfit for more than a romp.

She forced the thought away, refusing to allow anyone

to classify her as anything less than she was…including and especially herself.

"She most certainly will not," Sharon said. "You'll surely talk throughout the ceremony if she does. No, she'll be seated next to me."

Geneva found herself laughing at the light rebuke, happy to be rid of her concern, then turned to place her small purse on her chair…only to find herself staring straight into Mace's handsome face.

Mace.

Chills that had nothing to do with wind raised every tiny hair dotting her skin.

Mace…

DAMN. DAMN. Damn.

Geneva looked so incredible, everything else instantly faded away; she was a vividly clear figure against a blur of blurry colors.

Last night, he hadn't closed his eyes once. This morning, he'd felt every last minute of lost sleep, until now.

Now…

Now he felt like he could leap a tall building in a single bound.

"Hi," she said quietly.

He allowed his gaze to slide over her skin, taking in the sudden pinkness of her cheeks, the almost shy flash of her teeth, the curve of her long neck. The scent of her filled his every sense.

He'd missed her.

He told himself that was ridiculous. It had only been a day since he last saw her.

Still, he knew beyond anything that was tangible that he had missed her—on too many levels to count. He missed her laugh, her smell, her words, her body.

He'd missed her.

And if he could, in that one moment he'd take her hand and lead her away to someplace private where they could be alone. Make up for the lost time he'd so stupidly allowed to slip through his fingers.

Talk about stupid…

Against everything he knew was right, he'd gone to The Barracks last night and met up with Janine.

"Your mom called last night," Geneva said, hesitant in a way he'd never seen her before. "She invited me to sit with her."

He heard what she was saying but it took a moment for it to register. Did she think he needed an explanation? Obviously she did.

He berated himself for ever making her feel that way.

"Oh. Good." He looked to his mother whose own smile seemed a bit brighter than usual. But when he glanced back at Geneva, he could have sworn he glimpsed the same sadness he'd experienced last night in her eyes.

And his own sense of the dark emotion deepened.

The event organizer touched his elbow and quietly told him it was time to take his place with the others.

He nodded then met Geneva's gaze again. "I…"

He what?

He swallowed hard.

He had absolutely no idea what he was going to say, or where he went from here besides up on that stage to accept the award they insisted on giving him for simply doing what any other Marine would do.

"Good luck, honey," his mother said, stepping between them and kissing his cheek. "We're so very proud of you."

He blinked at her. He'd half expected her to say, "Marcus would be so very proud of you," as she'd said when he first shared the news.

His father followed suit along with his grandfather, no mention of his brother.

And then he and Geneva were alone in the gathering of others once again.

She smiled at him, but not in the way he'd come to look forward to. No, this one was tinged with melancholy and caution.

"You'd better go," she said quietly.

He looked over to find the organizer motioning to him.

"Yes, I guess I'd better."

She didn't move so he did…away from her and toward the others, his chest feeling heavier with each and every step.

PRIDE, SURE AND STRONG. That's what surged through Geneva as she watched Mace walk center stage in his full uniform, already covered with ribbons and medals, and accept the Navy Cross, the highest Marine honor.

If only he looked happier.

In the time she had known him, she'd never seen his handsome face set in such serious lines. He appeared to want to be anywhere but there. Why? And was that why he hadn't been more communicative about the importance of the day?

Did it have anything to do with his brother?

She didn't know. But she desperately wanted to find out. Not only for his sake, but for his parents and grandparent beaming so proudly next to her.

While she wouldn't ever expect him to jump for joy or boast about the occasion, or the experiences that had led to it…well, humbled would be preferable to grim.

The audience rose to its feet, applauding the day's honorees, the top one going to Mace. As Geneva followed suit, she realized she hadn't heard a single word. She'd been too busy scrutinizing his face, his demeanor, the shadows that clung to him that had nothing to do with the light.

Then she saw her—Janine.

Somehow she continued clapping, even as she met the gaze of Mace's tall, pretty ex-girlfriend back a row and halfway down the length. She looked…smug. Knowing.

The unwanted emotion cut into her, adding to the other uncomfortable feelings she was experiencing—Mace's silence, Dari's rejection, his grandfather's flirting—making it impossible to ignore. One on its own, a simple swallow and deep breath. Two, more concentration. Three…?

Undeniable.

"Geneva?"

Mace's mom was looking at her in concern.

She was unaware of the tear that had streaked down her cheek until she viewed Sharon's questioning gaze.

She quickly picked up her purse. "Tell Mace congratulations for me," she managed to choke out.

"You're not coming to the reception?"

Reception? She hadn't been told of any reception. Which meant she definitely wasn't going.

She was sure Janine would enjoy having Mace all to herself.

"No. I'm sorry," she whispered.

She turned to hurry away.

And ran directly into Mace.

24

MACE STEADIED GENEVA with his hands on her shoulders. Shoulders that seemed to suddenly bear the weight of the world. He feared they might not be equipped to handle it any longer.

He searched her face. Had she been crying?

No. She *was* crying.

The realization was like a blow to the gut, the medal with which he'd just been awarded like a stone he wanted to throw.

Still, she somehow managed to smile. "Congratulations. I'm honored to have been included. And so very proud."

Her voice caught on the last word. Before he could say anything, she threw her arms around him and squeezed tight, her chin resting on his shoulder.

"Thank you."

He squinted at her, barely able to hold her back before she wrenched away and nearly ran toward the aisle.

"Geneva, wait!"

He moved to give chase when a tree trunk placed itself between him and her in the shape of Darius.

"Let her go."

Mace grit his back teeth together. "If you know what's good for you, you'll move. Now."

"This isn't about her, Mace," Dari said quietly, his fingers digging in where he held his shoulder.

Mace was a breath away from decking him when Dari smiled at someone behind him.

"Hello, Mrs. Harrison." He removed his hand and reached around to shake his father's hand. "Congratulations, Mr. Harrison. Our boy done good, didn't he?"

Mace took advantage of the situation to look around, but found that Geneva was long gone, the lingering scent of her perfume where she'd hugged him the only proof that she'd been there at all…

GENEVA WISHED HERSELF one with the darkness when she sat in her apartment much later. She lay on the sofa staring at the ceiling, having cried a million tears and feeling another ten crowding her chest.

Mace…

The autumn wind howled outside, rustling the stubborn leaves that remained on the trees and rattling the windows. The same wind had blown Mace into her life…and now it was blowing him back out.

She didn't want his pity. And she was convinced that's what she'd viewed on his face when he'd caught her by the shoulders earlier.

Pity.

She'd run as fast as her heels could safely carry her, not stopping until she was inside her apartment where she locked herself away from the world…and him.

"…he's going to break your heart…"

Isn't that what Trudy had warned her against?

Isn't that exactly what was happening?

She told herself it had been worth it. The time she'd shared with Mace...

She bit hard on her bottom lip, swallowing the coppery blood that filled her mouth.

Her cell phone screen lit up where she had it laying face-up on her belly but was otherwise silent and still as per her settings. She knew it would be Mace again.

His last message had said he knew she was home since her car was in the lot; that he'd be waiting out there until she let him in.

She hadn't responded.

She also hadn't responded to his other ten voice mails and countless texts telling her he needed to see her, that they needed to talk.

Why? About what?

It was over.

That much was clear.

And while she might have preferred to spend this last night with him, well, that's not the way it had worked out.

She closed her eyes, ignoring the hot tears that seeped through her lashes.

Had she known... Had she guessed...

What?

What would she have done differently?

She didn't so much turn onto her side as she did fold, wrapping her arms around herself. So very much had happened in so brief a time. Was it really only three months ago she'd lost her mother? Wasn't it supposed to get easier?

She'd never missed her mom more than she did that moment.

She blinked at the wall, wondering if her mother was somewhere watching her right now. And if she was, what she made of the entire situation. Would she click her tongue as she'd been known to do, indicating Geneva had been a fool? Or would she merely hug her until she couldn't bear to be hugged any longer?

She didn't know. But, oh boy, she wished she did. She wished for the answers she couldn't seem to find anywhere.

Geneva caught the brightness of her cell phone screen again, the only source of light in the apartment. She blindly reached for where it had slid onto the couch next to her, blinking several times in an effort to clear her vision as she unlocked the phone and saw there were three text messages waiting.

She wiped her nose with the back of her hand and held the phone away from her until she could read the words of the first text.

I should have called you last night...

A sob wrenched from somewhere deep in her chest.

Yes, she silently responded to him. *You should have called last night.*

Perhaps if he had, none of this would have happened. She might be finding hot comfort in his arms instead of trying to hold herself together with her own.

Her eyes burned and her entire body ached. She hadn't eaten or slept since yesterday. This had to get better at some point. Right?

She rode out the wave then mopped her face with a wad of tissues she grabbed from a box near her head.

She accessed the next text message.

I miss you...

The words wended through her and back again.

"I miss you, too," she whispered.

Surely losing a limb wouldn't hurt this much. In that one moment, she'd gladly offer one up if she were promised this fathomless pain would stop.

Somewhere in the back of her mind, she understood that the heartache she was currently experiencing bled together with her grief over her mother's passing, but it was impossible to see where one left off and the other began so it became one massive ball of emotion threatening to suffocate her.

Only her mother was gone; and Mace was still here…

She absently ran the pad of her thumb over the keypad again, keeping the backlight on so she could read the three words.

Tomorrow, he would be on that transport out…

And she could begin healing.

Tonight… Well, tonight, knowing he was so close and wanted to see her…

She accessed the third text message.

I love you.

No fair…

She burst into tears and turned her head into the pillow, wishing the pain away, wishing the next month away, wishing him away…

MACE PACED BACK AND FORTH in front of his parked rental car outside Geneva's apartment building, checking his cell phone every five seconds and staring up at her dark windows. He was still in his dress blues, although he'd taken off the belt and unbuttoned the coat. The night was cold, the wind biting, but he was unaware of both as he moved, his mind on one thing and one thing only—Geneva.

All he could see was the image of her tear-filled eyes the last time he'd seen her.

Damn.

Damn, damn, damn.

The idea he'd hurt her ripped his guts to shreds.

She deserved better. Especially from him.

Still, he'd unwittingly caused her pain he was afraid he'd never be able to ease.

He restlessly checked his cell again. Nothing.

He rounded his car and stared at where hers was parked a few spots up on the opposite side of the lot. Had someone picked her up?

No.

She was there.

He was sure of it.

Then why wasn't she answering him?

He could only imagine what was going through her mind, what she must be thinking. About why he hadn't contacted her last night or this morning…

Still, there was no need for tears.

Was there?

Damn it. He hated not knowing what he'd done.

He hated even more that whatever he had done had caused her one iota of pain.

He rounded his car again and resumed pacing, his steps quick, his black dress shoes clicking against the asphalt.

What was he talking about? He was leaving tomorrow. And the minute he did, their agreement would reach an end.

He stopped. Is that what this was? Was she ending things early? Calling a halt before it went too far?

He thought of his last text.

Damn it all to hell. This had evolved into far more than a simple agreement.

How stupid was he? He should have known he wouldn't be able to keep his emotions out of it. Look how badly Janine had hurt him. And he'd gone into that with his eyes wide open.

And Geneva?

He imagined her tears again and felt like shouting, hitting something, anything to release the pressure threatening to turn him inside out.

Today had been one of the longest of his life. After absolutely no sleep, he'd gotten up and run ten miles before finally showering and attending a ceremony he had zero interest in participating in. Even now, the medal was sitting on his passenger seat, little more than a piece of tin to him.

Marcus…

He tilted his head up and closed his eyes. His brother was the hero—not him.

"Still running after me, little bro?" he could almost hear Marcus say.

The familiar hands—phantom digits that had curiously been missing the past few days—returned to their rightful place around his neck.

He had spent so much of his childhood trying to catch up with his older brother he lost his breath just thinking about it. Marcus was the one everyone looked up to, talked about, while he was the one they patted on the head and told him how lucky he was to have such a great brother.

No one had prepared him for what life would be like when his brother died.

If Marcus had been an ever-evasive shadow in life, in death…well, now he'd never be able to catch up.

He winced at the selfish thought.

Damn it. He hated feeling this way. He hated not being able to think of his brother without a deep sense that he was lacking, would never make the grade. He wanted to remember him with fondness.

It had taken meeting with Janine last night to remind him how deep his feelings went.

And to realize what she'd really been after.

He'd stepped into The Barracks to find the place still packed…and his ex-girlfriend sitting at the end of the bar staring at her cell phone. Waiting for a response from him? He didn't think so. Still, he'd gone and taken the stool next to her.

Her surprised expression had almost been worth the trouble.

Almost.

Janine Johnson had always been an attractive woman. Naturally platinum blond, tall, willowy. Problem was, she knew the value of her good looks…and that devalued them as she used them to push forward whatever objective she put her mind to, whether it was earning a promotion at her job as a sales associate, talking her way out of a speeding ticket…or seducing him out of looking a little too closely at her.

As closely as he was looking at her now.

They'd talked a bit about everything. He'd bought her another drink but had stuck to his one beer limit then asked to pay his tab.

Janine had cleared her throat. "So this medal thing tomorrow…"

He'd grimaced as he peeled off the money to cover his bill.

"What?" she'd said. "Tell me you aren't pleased."

"I'm not pleased."

"Why? It's a great honor. One I'm sure you earned."

He'd stared at her.

"Wait. Don't tell me. This is about Marcus, isn't it? Again."

"I've got to be going."

"Wait." She'd put her hand on his arm.

He'd stiffened, waiting to see what she'd do next.

She'd taken a deep breath and smiled. "I'm sorry. I really don't want to dig up old skeletons." She'd lightly rubbed his arm. "Partly because I have one or two of my own I'd prefer not to see again." She'd dropped her gaze. "Mostly because I'm hoping we can bury them for good and head out for new ground."

She'd blinked up at him.

Mace had found it incredible to think such tactics had worked on him before. But they had, hadn't they? Because he hadn't anything else with which to compare them? The image of Geneva's genuine smile and warmth loomed large in his mind.

Yeah, he was thinking that was the reason.

And now that he did have something, someone fundamentally more meaningful, well, Janine didn't measure up. Not just because of what she'd done, but because of who she was.

"I've got to go," he'd said.

"Come on," she'd said, an angry edge to her voice. "I deserve to be on your arm when you accept that award tomorrow, not that mousy waitress you've been hanging around with…"

He'd known such a moment of blind anger, it had been all he could do to remain speechless as he purposefully removed her hand from his arm, picked up his jacket and turned toward the door.

"You know what, Mace? You're right. You're never going to be as good as your brother. You never really knew what to do with a catch like me. But I bet he would have…"

The door had closed on her words, making them the final ones he ever intended to hear from her.

A car rolled up and a flashlight was focused on him, making him aware that he still stood below Geneva's apartment windows.

Geneva...

He couldn't ever envision her thinking the type of venomous words Janine had uttered—who had done who wrong, anyway?—much less saying them.

However, he did have Janine to thank for one thing: making him realize he was competing against a ghost.

He probably always had been.

"Can I help you?" a male voice asked abruptly.

Mace grimaced and looked back up at Geneva's windows, wondering if she was looking out one of them even as he spoke to the security guard.

"I'm waiting for a friend to let me up."

"And that friend would be...?"

"Geneva Davis."

"Ah. Yes."

The flashlight was removed and then just as quickly, it turned on him again.

"Hey, wait, that makes you Mace Harrison then."

Mace's jaw tightened. "Yeah."

He'd come across his fair share of information seekers in the wake of the Norman incident. Police and security officers tended to be some of the most annoying because they not only wanted details, they wanted to share how they would have handled the situation.

It looked like this guy fell solidly into that category.

And he had neither the time nor the patience for it right now.

He only wanted to talk to Geneva.

He checked his cell phone again.

Nothing.

The security guard was talking about having seen the two attempts on Norman's life on TV when Mace decided to walk to his car. He waved a hand and said, "Sorry, I must be wrong. She's not home. I'll try again later. Good night."

The officer blinked at him then offered a surprised greeting in return, backing up to allow him exit.

Mace took it, trying like hell to figure out what he should do. Or if, in fact, there was anything he could do…

His cell phone rang.

He nearly hit a parked vehicle in his rush to retrieve it from the passenger's seat where he'd tossed it.

"Hello, Geneva?"

"No. It's Dari, Mace. I've got some information you might be interested in knowing…"

25

6:00 A.M.

Geneva's cell alarm went off, loud enough to wake her. But she wasn't asleep. She still lay on the couch, in the dark, dawn still a ways away.

Mace even farther.

Right now he was on his transport out.

She hadn't heard from him after his final text last night. Those last three words would remain with her always. Words she felt and returned with all her heart.

I love you.

He was gone.

She'd expected the knowledge to somehow make her feel better; now the healing could begin. It didn't. Instead she felt oddly…numb. Empty. Not just like a gas tank that could be refilled, but hollow, the space gaping wide and exposed to the elements.

She looked down at where she rubbed her belly, issuing a silent apology to the life growing within her. She'd been impulsive and selfish and was now paying the price. It would have been fine had she been the only one affected. But she wasn't. Not anymore.

She told herself she should get up, eat something, make

an effort to rejoin the land of the living. But she couldn't seem to find the energy to do more than stare at the ceiling and hope the coming sunrise would help her do what she needed to do. Which was go on...

HE HAD HIS MAN...

Mace stood on the other side of the interrogation room watching as Thomas Michael Newsome sat back in the uncomfortable chair, looking a little too comfortable in his handcuffs and leg shackles.

Then again, he should, shouldn't he? Because this wasn't the first time Newsome had found himself in such a situation. And he didn't think it would be the last.

"Attorney," the twenty-nine-year-old with a covert military-op résumé as thick as Mace's penis said.

"9/11," Mace answered, meaning in the wake of the tragic event, local law enforcement could brand a suspect as a possible terrorist and hold him for as long as they wanted.

Despite Dari's recommendation to leave the Norman incidents behind and allow law enforcement to take it from there, he'd acted on the information he recovered from the motel room. Calls had been returned, more specifically, Lazarus partner and old friend Lincoln Williams had contacted Dari with the information he was looking for. Being connected with military intelligence and the FBI, Linc could tap into resources others couldn't.

In this case, the reason why Newsome's prints hadn't turned up on any nationwide criminal database wasn't because he'd never been arrested, but because he was a military gun for hire and some powers-that-be intended to keep his misdeeds covered so they could use him at will.

Only neither Newsome nor his contractors had anticipated he'd shoot the wrong gun at the wrong time.

Even if it had been at the right person.

The familiar phone number Mace had found at the motel had been the private contact number to Norman's head of security.

Meaning Newsome had been directly hired to perform a job. And if Mace was right, and he fully believed he was, Norman's men had arranged for the attempts against Norman. Why? Most likely to boost his national ratings and perhaps put him on the short list of presidential candidates for the next election.

Hell, for all he knew, Norman himself was behind the ruse.

Unfortunately for them, they'd done it under Mace's watch and two men were injured; he wasn't about to let this one slide. While he didn't expect to pin anything on Norman himself, Newsome's capture and the gossip that was sure to leak—he'd see to it—would be enough of a damaging bruise to give him a permanent limp when it came to any future political plans.

And Newsome himself would be out of commission. If not literally, figuratively, because he was now solidly on the radar, no longer operating in the shadows. And Mace intended to keep him that way.

He found himself checking his cell phone. Still nothing from Geneva.

He rubbed his face and nodded at where the police detective who'd allowed him access to the suspect held up three fingers, indicating his time was almost up. He hadn't fooled himself into believing for a second that he'd get Newsome to talk. Men like him were born without tongues. But it was enough for him to know he'd cracked the case, even if he hadn't been under any obligation to do so.

He was nobody's fool.

His cell phone vibrated. He took it out and checked it. He knew a spark of hope when he read he had a text from Geneva.

Take care of yourself...

A part of him stung at the obvious goodbye.

But a bigger part of him knew any contact at all was a good thing.

Even if she believed he was on that transport and couldn't follow up on it.

Especially because she believed he was on that transport.

Without another word, he passed Newsome and rapped on the security door.

He was done here.

THE ART OF MASS DISTRACTION.

Geneva hadn't mastered it. But it was proving to be helpful in at last getting her off the couch and at least appearing to be normal, although she felt anything but.

She'd considered calling in sick for the brunch crowd, but decided engaging in some sort of activity that didn't include a great deal of thinking would help.

Of course, she'd completely forgotten the smiling part.

That combined with her paleness, due to lack of sleep and eating, had garnered her more than a few unwelcome inquiries regarding her health and that of the baby.

But each had been easily avoided...or maybe it was her uncommunicativeness that had kept people at bay, no matter how well-meaning.

Now, nearly twelve hours later after a long, busy day, she felt sufficiently tired enough to sleep. And she'd forced herself to eat at least a little on two occasions.

The best thing was she hadn't cried.

Well, except for that one time when Trudy had shown her the photo of Mace accepting his Navy Cross that was featured in the local news section of the newspaper.

She'd rushed to the bathroom and stayed in a stall for fifteen minutes. After ten, Tiffany had surprised her by sticking a box of tissues under the door and asking if there was anything she could do. The demonstration of human kindness from someone who seemed to operate on a deficit of it had been enough to help her rebalance herself and get back to the diner floor.

Now, however, it was after ten and the last customer had finally departed, leaving her and Trudy and Mel. She bussed the final table then went back into the kitchen, saying something to Mel as she went. Only he wasn't there. And he appeared to have left entirely—his grill jacket hanging neatly on its wall hook—without saying goodbye.

That was odd.

She peered out the window looking for Trudy. "Everything okay with Mel?" she asked.

No answer.

She frowned, not finding Trudy either.

Doubly odd.

She leaned her hands against the counter and closed her eyes. They had probably said goodnight, but she was so out of it, she hadn't registered it.

She reached behind her to untie her apron when she heard the strains of a familiar song: B17.

She left her apron untied and rushed into the other room.

"Please, no, don't play that."

Her words trailed off as she found herself staring at the last person in the world she expected to see.

Mace…

"SHOULDN'T THAT BE 'Please, mister, please'?"

Mace's throat was so tight, his mouth so dry at the sight of Geneva looking pale but beautiful, being close enough to touch her again, he was surprised he could think the words much less say them.

She looked like she was caught between fight or flight, a delay likely brought on by her obvious tiredness, which Trudy had mentioned when he'd asked her to empty the place so he could talk to Geneva privately, promising to close up.

"Don't keep her too long. Girl needs some good, solid rest…and not just for herself," Trudy had said.

There had been more in her stern stare, but she'd kept any other advice to herself and agreed to do as he asked. He took that as a further good sign he was doing the right thing.

His gaze went to Geneva's still-flat belly and the way the open apron hung from her, giving the illusion of full-ness that hinted at what she might look like in the next few months…which was stunning. In the best possible way.

He was amazed he'd allowed fear to rule his actions, however briefly. But having a child in his life, well, it wasn't a contingency for which he'd ever prepared.

He only wished he could have muddled through it with Geneva rather than let it chase him away from her, cause her the pain he even now viewed as smudges under her unusually bright eyes.

He knew he only had a few more seconds before she fled. But the words he wanted to say to her scrambled like mice into the corner now that he was standing before her.

"I deserve to be taken to the woodshed and given a few good whacks," he said quietly even as the song played.

She remained silent.

The song ended and she looked toward the jukebox. He still had two additional selections to make.

"No," she said quietly. "Both of us are to blame."

Blame?

His stomach pitched five feet below floor level. Was there no hope of her forgiving him? Of grabbing what they were feeling and seeing where it took them?

Was she determined that they were over?

God, he hoped not.

"I prefer to think we're both to credit."

That brought her gaze back to him and he glimpsed a spark of hope in her eyes that nearly knocked him to his knees.

He couldn't resist going to her, enveloping her in his arms, a place he had feared he'd never have her again, a place he wanted to keep her forever.

"I've been so very, very stupid, Geneva," he whispered into her ear, breathing in the scent of her, absorbing her warmth and sweetness and wanting her so completely he ached with it. "I don't know what I was thinking. I'm sorry for ever having hurt you."

He made out her unwitting, soggy reply and drew back, holding her head still in his hands.

"Please, do you think you can ever find a way to forgive me?"

Thankfully she gazed back into his eyes rather than trying to avoid them.

"You…" he began, searching for words. No, he didn't have to search. They were all right there. It was choosing the right ones when there were really no wrong ones.

Damn. Why did this have to be so hard?

"You, Geneva, are incredible." She was that squared. "You're the most amazing woman, no, person I've ever met." He'd never uttered anything truer. "You're smart and funny, beautiful and thoughtful…" He swallowed hard. "And sexier than hell. Not a moment goes by that I don't want to make love with you, bury myself deep inside you…"

She cleared her throat. "That's sex. It'll pass…"

He slowly shook his head. "No, that's not sex. Sex we can get anywhere. This…" He rubbed his thumbs against her soft skin. "This is about so much more. And you know it."

"Do I? I'm not so sure…"

"If it was just about sex, you would have let me into your apartment last night so we could have some."

He glimpsed a shadow of a smile. "Maybe I was tired."

"Maybe you were hurting because of something stupid I said or did, which further demonstrates this is…"

"Shh…" She put her hand over his mouth, effectively hushing him.

When he remained silent, she moved her fingers to trail along his cheek.

"It appears I'm not the only one who got hurt…" she said.

He smiled sadly at that. "Yeah. Call me a coward, but I'd take a full-on assault from an entire enemy battalion over how I've felt the past two days. Any time."

Her eyes softened.

"Tell me, Geneva. Is that just sex?"

She didn't respond immediately. Finally, she shook her head.

He drew her close again and she sighed against him. He couldn't help feeling like the luckiest guy ever born. Not only because she was in his arms, but because she was giving him another chance. And he was determined not to blow it this time.

"Shouldn't you be somewhere in the Middle East right now?" she whispered, her hands trailing up and down his back, her cheek resting on his shoulder.

He took a deep breath. "Probably. But I figured if I had to accept that medal, well, I'd be damned if I didn't cash it in for something important."

She drew back to look at him. "What do you mean?"

He smoothed his hands over her hair then held her still as he leaned in for a kiss. She kissed him back.

"It means I'm not going anywhere. Not today…" He kissed her. "Not tomorrow." He kissed her again. "Not the day after that." He kissed her again. "I'm going to serve out my remaining six months here. Then I'm going to sign on with Darius at Lazarus…"

She looked confused. "I don't understand…"

Holding her gaze, he leaned in again for another kiss. "You will, Geneva. You will." He backed her up toward the jukebox and made his selection while maintaining his hold on her. Elvis's rendition of "Fools Rush In" began playing.

"Now," he whispered into her ear. "Tell me you love me."

He trapped her gasp in her mouth by kissing her.

"Tell me…"

He kissed her again until he felt her shiver and sigh against him.

"I love you…"

Her words were barely audible, but they were enough to make him feel like he'd been propelled into the stratosphere.

He smiled at her and her answering smile caused something monumental to shift within him.

"May I have this dance, Geneva Davis?"

"Yes, Mace Harrison, you may."

As he gently swayed with her close to him, his mind filling with doing much more, he hoped the dance lasted for a long, long time, indeed....

* * * * *

EVERY MOVE YOU MAKE

This one's for all our Texan friends!

Prologue

WHAT WAS SHE THINKING?

Jennifer Rodriquez Madison balanced the phone between her chin and shoulder while she wildly wrote notes with one hand and stuffed a cracker into her mouth with the other, trying like crazy to do the work of three people. She was afraid she was not only failing, but failing miserably. She eyed the agitated potential new client talking nonstop in front of her desk, then felt her heart squeeze as she glanced at her crying infant in the portable crib next to her.

When both Ralph Budnick and Roy Morales of Budnick and Morales Private Investigations retired, Jennifer saw their departure as an opportunity of a lifetime. Of course she'd taken the fact that she was newly married and about to have a baby completely for granted.

Now that the baby was three months old and Jen was back at the outside office, instead of working in the comfort of her home office, she was terrified that her decision to take on the company alone would be the death of her.

The cowbell on the front door clanged. Jennifer spared the latest visitor enough of a glance to notice he was tall, gorgeous and about as welcome at that moment as a deadly virus. "If you're here for an ongoing investigation, or looking to hire us for a new one," she told him, "I'm going to have to ask you to come back at another time."

She blindly found Annie's pacifier, where it was attached by a length of yarn to the front of her jumpsuit, and popped it into her mouth. Annie instantly spit it out and continued vying for the "most neglected baby of the year" award.

"So are you going to take my case or not?" the woman in front of her desk asked, tapping red fingernails against an alligator-skin purse Jennifer suspected was real. "A friend of mine recommended your agency to me." She looked around, disdain written on her well made-up face. "But seeing what I have so far, I can't imagine why."

Jennifer bristled and moved the silent receiver to her other ear, hoping the client she had on hold wouldn't hang up as she waited out someone else who had put her on hold. She absently realized that the tall stranger who had entered hadn't left. "You're right, Mrs. McCabe. Maybe we're not equipped to handle cases like you're describing. Have you ever thought of actually *asking* your husband if he's being unfaithful?"

"What kind of question is that?" Mrs. McCabe asked. Her carefully painted face had turned red.

She shrugged. "I don't know. A commonsense one? And definitely a step up from hiring an attractive, flirty woman to entrap him at a country club."

The woman scoffed.

The stranger moved out of Jennifer's eyeshot and almost instantly Annie quieted. Jennifer swiveled to find him hesitantly tickling the fussy infant. He gave Jennifer a sheepish grin that made her blink then began to pull his hand back. With a loud cry, Annie let her thoughts on the matter be known. Jennifer couldn't blame her daughter. She'd much rather have a great-looking guy tickling her, too.

"May I?" the stranger asked, indicating he'd like to pick Annie up.

Let's see, a choice between earsplitting screams and a happy baby? Jennifer gestured for him to go ahead. She watched as he awkwardly lifted her up and held her at arm's length, staring at her as curiously as Annie stared back. Jen opened her mouth to tell him to support her head, then the stranger awkwardly but successfully held Annie to his wide chest. He wore a coffee-colored suit that had Northerner written all over it, and he had the type of handsome good looks that would have turned her head before she had stumbled into Ryan's life for a case she was working on and had her own life turned upside down.

"Who are you and what do you want?" Jennifer asked him, thinking it a pretty good guess that he hadn't popped up out of the blue to help her with her unhappy daughter.

Maybe Ryan was right about what he had said that morning. He'd tried to convince her to keep working out of the house so that they could, um, pursue their personal interests as well as her business interests. He had also said she had bitten off a little more than she could chew. She sat up straighter, merely thinking the words making her feel combative. His overprotective tendencies both endeared him to her and irritated her. And those tendencies had quadrupled with the birth and his adoption of little Annie.

Of course Ryan was easily sidetracked if need be. A scrap of sexy lingerie and he was putty in her hands.

Jennifer's mind began to drift to all things sexy and hot but she forced herself to concentrate on the matter at hand.

"I'm Zach Letterman," the visitor said with a midwestern accent, a smile softening his striking features as he looked into Annie's face.

"Is there another agency you could recommend?" Mrs. McCabe was saying insistently, making no secret that she found the intrusion insulting. "Someone who can handle the type of case I'm proposing?"

Letterman, Letterman, Jennifer thought, trying to place the name.

Another telephone line rang, only adding to the general state of chaos. She sighed and rolled her eyes. "I'm sorry, Mrs. McCabe, but as you can see, I'm very busy right now. If you'd like to leave your card, I'll contact you later with any possibilities I come up with."

Jennifer's gaze was again pulled to the stranger.

He quietly cleared his throat. "Lily recommended me to you."

"Lily?"

"The job opening?" He grinned at her and she widened her eyes at the megawatt smile. "Looks like you could certainly use a hand around here."

"Oh. Oh!" Jennifer nearly pushed the package of crackers from her desk in her rush to shake his hand. "You're *that* Mr. Letterman. Lily's cousin from Indiana. I'm sorry. I wasn't expecting you until tomorrow." She checked her calendar. "Oh. Tomorrow is…well, today, isn't it?"

She recalled the phone conversation she'd had with Lily last week. Lily Garrett Bishop and her brother Dylan Garrett had established Finders Keepers out of San Antonio, Texas, in honor of their great-grandmother Isabella Trueblood. Aside from being a good friend, Lily regularly sent work Jennifer's way, doubling and sometimes tripling her workload. Her first case for Lily was also instrumental in her meeting and marrying her husband, Ryan. Lily had known Budnick and Morales Private Investigation desperately needed new blood and had recommended Zach Letterman to Jennifer.

And here he was now in the flesh…and what handsome flesh it was.

Mrs. McCabe slapped a postcard-sized piece of stiff paper filled with phone numbers onto the desk in front of Jennifer. "I expect to hear from you promptly with suggestions on who else I might consult."

Jennifer made a face and forced herself to be polite. "Mrs. Madison?"

The voice coming through the receiver nearly startled her, she'd been on hold for so long. Jennifer straightened the phone. "I'm still here."

"Sorry to have taken so long, but someone misplaced your test results and it took some doing to find them."

Jennifer waved her hand as she watched Mrs. McCabe huff through the front door. "And...?"

"And congratulations," her ob-gyn told her. "You and your husband are going to have a new addition to your family in about eight months."

Jennifer stared sightlessly at the blinking lights on the phone in front of her, and glanced at the man holding her infant baby. She and Ryan had talked of having several children. But so soon?

"Mrs. Madison? Jennifer? Are you still there?"

Jennifer was so distracted by the news she hung up the receiver without saying goodbye.

Then she turned toward Zach. "You're hired."

1

WELL, THINGS CERTAINLY WORKED differently down here, didn't they?

In the two days since Zach Letterman had traded Indianapolis, Indiana, for first San Antonio, then Midland, Texas, that was his most remarkable discovery. Things worked differently in the Lone Star State. Sure, he'd expected some differences—the sweltering summer heat, the manner of speaking, the types of food. But he'd been unprepared for the generosity of character, the easygoing nature that each Texan he'd so far encountered had displayed as proudly as he wore his custom-made suits. The most remarkable people so far being his cousins Lily Bishop and Dylan Garrett.

From the moment he'd contacted Lily and Dylan a month ago with his proposal, they'd treated him like part of the family. It hadn't mattered that he'd never seen them before. They'd accepted him as easily as if they'd had countless snowball fights in the backyard when they were kids. He glanced out the window at the Texas landscape, thinking maybe snowballs wouldn't have been an option. Playing cowboys and Indians probably would fit better.

The infant in his arms wriggled. Zach gazed down at

the bundle as if surprised to find he still held her. She was all pink and new and weighed next to nothing in his arms. He'd never held an infant before. Somehow he hadn't expected them to be so...light.

Zach carefully put the now sleeping infant back in her carrier then wiped at a spot of drool on the front of his suit.

"How soon can you start?" Jennifer Madison asked. "Oh! I can't believe I left Denton Gawlick on hold. Give me a minute."

"I have all the time in the world."

And he did. Zach crossed his arms over his chest as he watched Jennifer pick the phone receiver back up and punch at one of the red blinking lights. After ten years of grueling, twenty-hour days spent building up his tool and die company in Indianapolis, Indiana, he'd taken a good long look at his life and the way he was living it and decided it was time to make some changes. But it had taken his grandmother's death six months ago to compel him to implement those changes.

Of course, becoming a private investigator hadn't even been on the list of possibilities. He'd debated entering the Peace Corps, starting a charity to fight world hunger, traveling the world with little more than the clothes on his back, leaving his credit cards and tremendous cash resources at home. But losing his last, closest living relative, the woman who had raised him after his father disappeared and his mother died, had had a tremendous effect on him he was still trying to sort through. It had ignited in him a longing for family connections he no longer had. Stories Nana had told him as a kid sitting in front of the fireplace with her had come back to him, and he'd realized he'd absorbed every word and could probably recite them even now. And it had been the stories of his Texas relatives that had captured his imagination the most. And so had

Trueblood, Texas, the town that had been named after his
great-aunt Isabella Trueblood.

With Nana's death, he'd felt adrift, in need of more than
just the changes he'd wanted to make to his life that would
send him in a direction toward a more fulfilling career.
He'd needed to connect with someone. His family.

So he'd hired a local detective agency and found out that
his cousins Lily Bishop and Dylan Garrett had continued
on with the family legacy laid out by Isabella Trueblood
by opening their own agency, Finders Keepers, a detective
agency dedicated to reuniting family members and lost
loves. The rightness of their pursuit, and how it tied into
what he knew about Great-Aunt Isabella Trueblood, had
his mind start clicking in directions he would never have
considered before. And within two months of receiving
the background report on his Texas relatives, he'd made
contact and offered up a business proposal.

But meeting Lily and Dylan in the flesh had been less
business-oriented and much more personal than he could
have ever imagined. And fruitful in so many ways. After
spending a day with them and their blossoming families,
he'd gone into Finders Keepers and was immediately
hooked. After hearing their many success stories, he'd
known down to the bone that his decision was the right
one. That he was doing the right thing. The only problem
was that everyone in Trueblood knew who he was. There
weren't all that many true Truebloods left without creat-
ing a fuss in the small town. And that's when Lily came
up with the idea of sending him to Jennifer Madison to
learn the ropes incognito, the only ones knowing his true
identity being Jennifer and her husband, Ryan. He would
become a private investigator. Just as he'd worked from
the bottom rung of the ladder up in his tool and die busi-

ness, he would learn the art of private investigating in the same way.

And here he was, gazing at pretty Jennifer Madison, waiting for the next step of his life to begin.

Jennifer Madison was more than merely pretty; she was stunning in ways Zach couldn't begin to count. Lily had spoken highly of the young woman, and Zach could see why. Anyone would have been overwhelmed by the busyness of the office he'd seen so far. But Jennifer seemed to be managing, although barely. And the little one dozing next to her desk was a gem. Whoever Jennifer's husband was, he was one lucky guy.

Jennifer gave a deep sigh of relief, pulling Zach's gaze and attention back to her. "Mr. Gawlick. Good, good, you're still there. I'm sorry to have kept you on hold for so long…" She smiled. "Yes, of course, I understand that you want a spot person from our agency involved with your case." She eyed Zach. "In fact, I'm looking at just the person for the job as we speak."

Zach raised a brow.

"I understand the urgency. Yes. No. Very good, Mr. Gawlick. My associate should be there shortly."

She replaced the receiver and smiled at Zach.

He cleared his throat. "I take it you were talking about me?"

"Uh-huh." Jennifer reached down and tucked a blanket around the infant's tiny body. "Mr. Denton Gawlick, of the Odessa Gawlicks. He and his wife are renewing their wedding vows in a week. Only the dress Mrs. Gawlick was hoping to wear, well, it's been languishing somewhere in lost airline baggage hell for the past week."

Zach rubbed his chin and grinned. "The case of the missing wedding dress?" Definitely not Mickey Spillane material. Then again, it had its possibilities.

Jennifer laughed and tilted her head to look at him closely. "You're not licensed yet, right?"

Zach narrowed his gaze, hoping she wouldn't use his lack of experience as a reason to change her mind. "Right. I'm not just wet behind the ears, I'm soaked."

She opened a drawer and fingered through files before taking one out and handing it to him. "Then this should be a great case to break you in with." He must have registered the surprise on his face because she said, "Don't worry. It wasn't all that long ago that I was an accountant. You have Lily's highest recommendation, so you have my complete trust."

Zach eyed her, still not sure how to take this new way of operating. He didn't think he'd be half as generous if their positions were reversed. Referral or not, he'd have checked the applicant's references, asked a ton of questions and still would have been hesitant to trust the candidate.

Things really did work differently down here.

He swallowed. "Thank you, Mrs. Madison. I'll make sure your trust isn't misplaced."

"It's Jennifer," she said as if by rote, then paused while going through some papers and looked at him. "Are you staying in town?"

"Actually, I haven't checked into my hotel yet."

"Good. Because right after meeting the client, you'll have to head down to Houston and Clayborn Investigations. You see, I already farmed the case out to another agency to look into the dress down there since the flight the bag was scheduled to be on was bound for Hobby. But Mr. Gawlick wants someone from our agency to be hands-on, and so long as he's paying for it…"

"We're there."

Her smile widened. "Yes. We're there."

Zach couldn't help but grin back at her even as he mentally prepared a list of questions. What groundwork had been laid down on the case already? Was there any advice on how to handle Mr. Gawlick? How should he document his expenses? Was there some sort of ID he should use? But before he could ask a single question, the phone started ringing, the baby started crying and the few quiet moments they had just experienced vanished into a chaotic never-never land.

"Call if you need anything," Jennifer said as she propped the phone between chin and shoulder then reached for the wailing infant.

"Right." Zach hesitated. He supposed he'd have to find answers to his own questions, which, when you thought about it, was what being a private investigator was all about, right? He started toward the door, nodding at Jennifer's light wave as she adeptly handled both the caller and the baby. He stepped outside the office and into the warm Texas sun, then squinted at the file in his hands. His first case.

His first case.

He turned his face up to the sun and grinned.

THIS WAS THE LAST CASE she was going to take on from another agency.

"I'm sure everything will be fine," Mariah Clayborn said into the telephone. "I look forward to meeting your associate…" What had Jennifer Madison, the P.I. from Midland, said his name was?

"Zach Letterman," Jennifer said.

"Yes. Zach. Got it."

There was a pause on the other end of the line. She opened her mouth to end the call.

"Is everything all right?" Jennifer cut her off at the pass.

Mariah pushed back her thick dark hair then slumped

in her chair. Was her emotional state so apparent that a woman she didn't even know except via a couple phone calls could tell something was wrong?

"Everything's fine." Mariah forced a smile, even though Jennifer couldn't see it. "Thanks for asking." She cleared her throat. "I'll give you a call once Zach and I retrieve the piece of luggage with your client's dress in it."

"Good. Good."

After exchanging goodbyes, Mariah sat pole straight in her chair, her hand still on the receiver that rested in the cradle.

Oh, she supposed just a short time ago everything had been fine, just as she'd proclaimed. She'd been a woman in charge of her own life, with her own agenda, well down the road to convincing herself that she didn't need a man after her latest breakup.

Then this morning she'd come in to find a section of the office roof had finally given way under the most recent Texas deluge—surely the saying "when it rained, it poured" originated in Texas. Of course it wouldn't be just any section, but a stretch just above her desk, soaking piles of paperwork and the brand-new chair she'd finally given in to and splurged on a week ago.

But that wasn't what made today so bad. No. That reason had come while she was cleaning up the mess and her phone rang. She'd snatched it up to find on the line her least favorite person from Hoffland, the small town about forty miles southwest in which she was raised—gossipy Miss Twila Seidwick.

At first she'd been more than a little irritated that the woman was calling her at work. Then she'd been afraid that something had happened to her widowed father and Twila was calling with the news.

Thankfully her father was fine. Twila had been calling

to gloat over the fact that Mariah's third ex-boyfriend in two years had just gotten engaged within a week of breaking up with her.

Merely thinking about it made her brain go numb.

Normally Mariah would have said good riddance, and maybe even called up and offered her condolences to the blushing bride-to-be. But all three? Not one, not two, but all three of her ex-boyfriends had dumped her then become engaged within a week of breaking up with her.

It was enough to give a girl a complex.

She could see her headstone now. *She inspired men to want to get married. Just not to her.*

She leaned back in her chair, cringing when the sound of the plastic bag under her rear end mixed with the squishy sound of the water that still soaked the pad of her chair. Her brand-new chair. The chair she'd dropped two hundred dollars on because, well, she'd liked it. And now it was ruined.

"Good morning, Mar. My, don't you look pretty today."

Mariah made a face at her cousin as he came in the front door. For all intents and purposes, George was a pretty good guy. He had inherited the trademark Clayborn dark hair and pleasing features, but where they looked good on him, they made her look…well, tomboyish. She glanced at her watch. But the biggest difference between them lay in that she didn't know when to stop working, and her slightly younger cousin didn't know when to start. "You always tell me that," she murmured, glancing down at her old, faded jeans and T-shirt, then pushing at her thick hair again.

"And you never believe me."

"Yes, well, *you're* two hours late. Again."

George took the rebuke with his usual grinning charm as he made his way to the back where she'd put out the usual morning donuts and had made coffee.

Mariah sighed and returned to trying to make some sort of sense out of her ruined desktop. And if she could figure out what was going on with her life at the same time, well, so much the better.

Of course, it was only par for the course that George wouldn't even have noticed that the roof had caved in. She tried to remember a time when her cousin wasn't so careless, but came up with a blank. It probably explained why her Uncle Bubba, George's father, had left the P.I. agency of Clayborn Investigations to her when he finally kicked the proverbial bucket last year. Of course, the inheritance had been attached with the stipulation that George always have a job there so long as he wanted one and that he be paid a living wage, as well as be entitled to a percentage of the net income.

Not that Mariah would have fired her cousin. He was as much a fixture around the office as the coffeemaker. She only wished he was as productive as the machine. He made juggling her life between the office and the ranch a bit of a challenge. It wasn't so much that he didn't carry his own weight; it was that the weight he did try to carry on occasion she ended up having to take on herself. Especially now that her uncle was no longer there to help carry the load.

George leaned against his own squeaky-clean desk across from hers, took a bite of a sprinkle-covered donut, then chased it down with coffee from his Oilers mug. "Heard Justin is getting married."

Mariah stared at him, wishing at that one moment that she *could* fire him. "Boy, news sure does travel fast."

She pulled her garbage can out from under the desk and scooped into it the paperwork she couldn't salvage.

"That's the way it usually is with news. Bad news. Good

news." He finished off his donut. "Which category do you suppose this falls under?"

"Good news," she said. "Definitely good news."

Because it meant that *she* wouldn't be marrying Justin Johnson, also known as J.J.

Bad news because it meant that by the time she returned to the ranch by the end of the day, everyone and his brother in Oklahoma would have heard the news and be calling to commiserate.

"J.J. is a good man."

"J.J. is a jerk."

George grinned. "Well, then there's that."

"An awfully big 'that,' don't you think?"

George shrugged and rounded his desk to sit down. He immediately leaned back in his chair and crossed his cowboy boots on the desktop. "I don't know. He wasn't so bad." He shook his head. "You know, we all thought for sure this would be it for you—you'd finally take that long walk down the aisle."

Instead prissy Miss Heather Walker would be taking the walk.

Mariah stared at the opposite wall, not really registering the outdated dark paneling or the oil paintings of ranch scenes hung on it. Instead she thought about the girl who couldn't have been much out of high school, who wore pretty flowered dresses to church and whose only pair of jeans rode low, low on her boyish hips and were usually worn with clingy, belly-baring knit tops. She glanced down at her own regular uniform of classic Levi's and old T-shirt, clothing that varied only in the winter when she wore a denim shirt over them, and her scuffed brown cowboy boots, then pushed her hair back from her face again.

There had been a time not so long ago when she'd felt very comfortable in her own clothing, even in a place where the state motto seemed to be The Higher The Hair, The Closer To God. Wearing what she had on had allowed her membership into the exclusive all boys' club. It had permitted her to ride the range with her father and the ranch hands, and had, in essence, made her one of the guys. And, oh, how she'd always liked that. Barbie dolls had really never done it for her. Give her an ornery filly that needed breaking in any day and miles and miles of Texas earth, and she was a happy woman.

Oh, yeah? Then where was all that happiness now?

Somewhere down the line, the rules had changed— rules she hadn't even known existed but was seeing all too clearly now.

She grimaced then let loose a stream of inventive cuss words under her breath that left George chuckling. She glared at him and continued cleaning her desk.

Well, just who in the hell had gone and changed all the rules on her anyway? The ones that said that when she turned eighteen she would have to start acting like the Barbie dolls she'd never played with? That she'd miraculously know what to do with her hair, how to apply makeup and how to walk in a pair of heels? And just when, exactly, had meat and potatoes not been enough? Why had her father started mentioning on almost a daily basis all the exotic foods her mother used to make for him to eat—if you could count crepes as exotic? And why did he now talk about how delicate her mother had been?

Sure, Hallmark commercials made her blubber. But delicate was definitely not a word anyone would use to describe Mariah Clayborn, the only child of widower Hughie Clayborn and his late wife, Nadine. At five foot seven in stocking feet and with a solid build, she once took a great deal of pride in being able to better many of the boys. She could probably still get the better of them even now. But whenever a physical competition of any sort was mentioned with her as the opponent, the men merely grinned and held up their hands in a mock version of being gentlemen.

Gentlemen, her rear. She knew just how ungentlemanly all these guys could get. Had been privy to some of their more honest and graphic conversations on observations of the opposite sex. They might hold a door open for their latest lady of choice, light her cigarette and appear to bless the very ground she walked on, but it was all toward one end: getting that same "lady" into the backseat of their cars by night's end.

Unfortunately she, herself, had seen a back seat more times than she cared to count. But never had it come after a nice dinner out or dancing. No. Her handful of experiences had usually taken place on the back nine of her father's ranch after one of her boyfriends visited. And had lasted as long as the drive out, making her wonder just why so many girls were dying to get into the backseats of all those cars. Her? She didn't get it at all. Aside from being vastly uncomfortable, she'd always been left feeling...well, as if she'd missed something.

Of course, she knew what she had missed, but even thinking the word "orgasm" made her flush.

The telephone rang and she started, nearly jumping straight out of her skin at being caught thinking what she had.

"Do you want me to get that?" George asked.

"You could have just answered it, you know," she said, picking up the extension. She shot a look at George, who'd taken her jab in stride and simply turned the page in the magazine he was reading. "Clayborn Investigations."

"You got your man, Mariah."

She instantly sprang up and out of her chair. She didn't

need any more explanation than that. "Thanks, Joe." She hung up the receiver, slid her revolver into her hip holster, then pocketed her cell phone.

George didn't even look up from his magazine. "Word on Claude Ray?"

Mariah found cause for her first smile of the day. "Oh, yeah."

"Need some help roping him in?"

"Oh, no."

He turned a page. "Didn't think so."

Mariah headed for the door, her mood instantly lightening. She liked this part of the job. This is where she excelled. No matter what else was happening in her life, she always managed to get her man.

Her smile slipped.

Well, she always managed to get her man on the job, anyway. In her personal life...

She wasn't going to go there now.

She opened the door and darted outside––and ran straight into someone. A tall someone, who made her feel absolutely puny. A hard, nice-smelling someone who instantly grabbed her arms to steady her, sending a jolt of warmth over her skin.

"Excuse me," she said, finding her feet and stepping backward.

The man grinned, nearly sending her off balance all over again.

Whoa, cowboy.

"I think I'm the one who should be apologizing."

Okay, he wasn't a cowboy. His accent identified him as a Yankee. Mariah found herself tucking her hair behind her ears. And she never tucked her hair behind her ears.

She quickly fluffed her hair back out as if the move

alone could erase the nervous gesture. Instead she probably came off looking even more nervous.

"So long as neither of us is seriously injured," she said. "Pardon me again."

She began to skirt around him, surprised she was capable of any movement at all.

"Mariah?"

Her blood sizzled through her veins at the sound of her name rolling off the stranger's tongue. How did he know her name?

She turned slightly to face him.

"Are you Mariah Clayborn?" he asked.

"Um, yes. I am."

He grinned that grin again. "I'm Zach Letterman. I believe you're expecting me?"

Expecting him? In her dreams, maybe. Then his name sank in. Zach Letterman, Zach Letterman....

This was Zach Letterman? The P.I. Jennifer Madison had sent down to work with her? No, it couldn't be. He didn't look anything like a P.I. He looked more like he'd stepped straight from the pages of *GQ*. Not that she had ever read *Gentlemen's Quarterly,* but she was familiar with the comparison. And if anyone looked like he deserved to be on the cover of a gentlemen's magazine, it was this guy.

Whoa.

2

A PRIZE BULL UP FOR AUCTION, that's what Zach felt like. He stood stock-still under the blazing Texas sun and waited while Mariah Clayborn examined him as if she were considering making a bid. Then she seemed to realize what she was doing. Her large brown, almost black, eyes widened and she stared at him as if caught doing something she shouldn't. Zach grinned, suppressing the desire to ask her if he made the grade.

They stood outside a modest one-story building with Clayborn Investigations written in large block letters on the window. The four-lane boulevard behind him buzzed with traffic, and just over the rooftops of the other one-story buildings across the street lay the Houston skyline. But Zach paid attention to none of it as he gave the woman standing in front of him the same once-over she'd given him. He thought it fair that he not be the only one up on the auctioning block.

He absently rubbed his chin as he took her in. Her clothing of old jeans and T-shirt screamed tomboy through and through. He didn't think she had on a sweep of makeup, and her hair was naturally wavy, shining a warm cinnamon in the bright midday sunlight. But there was something…

very appealing that struck him straight off. An energy. Vitality. Freshness. An out-and-out sexiness that made him come away from his perusal feeling attracted to her in a way that puzzled him. A sleek, polished woman like Jennifer Madison was more his type. Still, he couldn't ignore the zing of attraction that sizzled along his nerve endings as he looked at Mariah Clayborn.

"Sorry," she finally said as she squared her feet and steadied herself under his gaze when other women might have fidgeted or struck a coy pose. "I wasn't expecting you so soon." She glanced at her watch—a simple Timex. "I only just talked to Jennifer an hour ago."

He remembered how busy the P.I. had been before he left. "It was probably the first chance she had to contact you."

"Mmm." Mariah licked her lips then glanced through the windows into the office. She appeared not to know whether to bid on him or pass and wait for the next lot up for auction. "The case of the missing wedding dress, right?"

He chuckled, mildly amused that she referred to the case the same way he had. "That would be it. Have you made any progress on it?"

"Not yet. I was waiting for you to arrive."

"Good."

"Yes. But unfortunately I have to see to the closure of another case first." She motioned toward the door. "If you'd like you could, um, wait in there. My cousin George will keep you company until I get back."

"And how long would that be?"

"About an hour or two."

"Would you mind if I accompany you?"

"You want to come with me?"

Her frown was so complete it was almost comical. "If

you don't mind. I've been on planes for the better part of the morning and would just as soon not do much sitting right now."

"You'd be sitting in the truck."

"Yes, but the truck would be moving." He glanced around. "Besides, I haven't had much of a chance to see Houston yet."

"My destination is about a half hour west of here. Outside the city."

He grinned. "Better yet."

She tucked her hair behind her ear again, appeared agitated that she had, then released a long sigh. "Okay. I suppose it wouldn't hurt to bring you along." She started in the direction of the street.

Zach picked up his single suitcase and followed her, his gaze drawn to the back of her faded jeans. The old denim fit just so across her lush, rounded bottom. While Mariah Clayborn's clothes shouted tomboy, the body that lay underneath murmured one hundred percent woman.

"You can put that in the bed."

"Pardon me?" he asked, blinking at where she was opening the door of a beat-up old blue Ford.

"Your suitcase. You can put it in the back."

He eyed the truck bed, which held a rusty gas container, a partial bale of hay and an old gray-and-red wool blanket. He put the suitcase on top of the blanket then climbed into the truck cab, the door protesting against the movement and letting rip a loud squeak.

"Sorry," she said, starting the ignition. "I don't usually have much company in the truck."

She put the truck into gear then gathered together countless fast-food wrappers littering the floor at his feet. She didn't appear to know what to do with them. She finally tossed them back behind the bench seat.

"I can see why."

She glanced at him for a long moment, then seemed to come to some sort of decision as she smiled. "A guy with a sense of humor. I like that." She gestured toward the door. "You may, um, want to buckle up. Nelly rides a little rough."

Nelly. She'd named her truck. He fastened his safety belt and quickly found out just how bumpy the ride was going to be as the truck lurched forward.

"You can't say I didn't warn you," she said over the roar of the engine.

Zach grinned at her, wondering just how much of a ride he was in for....

ZACH LETTERMAN WAS definitely not your normal, run-of-the-mill thorn in the side. Mariah sneaked another glance at him and his cool, clean looks, and the admirable way he looked. He appeared relaxed as her truck bumped and rutted over the dirt road leading to Claude Ray's place, which was little more than a shack tucked away on a corner of someone else's land. It had been that someone else, namely Joe Carter, who had called to tip her off about Claude's return.

"What's the case about?" Zach Letterman asked.

Mariah pulled her gaze from where she'd been staring at his thick, long-fingered hands and looked into his face. The gleam of recognition in his moss-green eyes made her skin heat up. "Pardon me?"

"This case you have to close. What's it regarding?"

She gripped the steering wheel tighter when she hit a particularly nasty pothole. "Horse thief."

Zach's eyebrows shot up high on his smooth forehead. "Horse thief?"

"Yeah." She slowed down a bit so the engine didn't roar

too loudly. Claude wouldn't be going anywhere without her seeing him anyway, seeing as this was the only road leading in or out of the place. "A nearby breeder had two of his prime studs come up missing day before yesterday. Maybe you recognize the names? Gentle As Rain won the Kentucky Derby last year and Black Thunderfoot won the Triple Crown three years ago."

He slowly shook his head. "Sorry. Don't follow racing."

"Oh. Well, anyway, those are the studs that came up missing. Carter charges twenty-five grand a pop for stud fees."

"That much?"

She smiled. "Yes. Funny, isn't it? Kind of like male prostitution of the animal variety." She waved her hand toward the west. "Anyway, when Carter called me to look into the matter, I knew immediately who was behind the theft. A guy by the name of Claude Ray. He's a local of sorts who sweeps into town every now and again, leaving a trail of illegal activities in his wake. He usually shows up again when the fuss dies down and the local authorities have moved on to bigger and better things." She hit a nasty bump and would have catapulted from the seat if not for her own safety belt. "I heard Claude showed up again about a week or so ago."

"Is this something P.I.s usually handle around here?" he asked, raising his voice to be heard. "Isn't this something for the authorities?"

"Usually, yes. But Carter's spread borders my daddy's ranch and our families go way back. My uncle Bubba—the P.I. business was his before he kicked, er, before he passed on last year—always saw to these kinds of favors for friends."

Zach turned his head to look out the window at the passing landscape. Long stretches of open plains extended as far as the eye could see.

Mariah took a deep breath, finding a deep satisfaction being near the place where she'd grown up. There was something about the Texas plains that crawled right up under your skin and stayed there, much as the soil did when it got under your fingernails. She glanced at Zach to find him shrugging out of his suit jacket then tossing it over the back of the seat. His shirt was white and crisp and covered him to the wrists. Well, at least until he popped the buttons at the cuff and rolled the material up to the top of his forearms. Mariah swallowed. And what forearms they were, too. While his hands looked much softer than she was used to—hell, they looked softer than hers—his forearms were nothing but thick, corded muscles, his skin dotted with soft almost black hair. And he had the kind of wrists she doubted she could get the fingers of one hand around.

Oh, the man next to her might be a Northern city boy, but she suspected he was as strong as any man who had spent his life on the range.

"You're from out here?" Zach asked, pulling her attention back to his face.

She nodded and pointed to the west again. "Daddy's cattle ranch is about five miles that way."

His gaze on her face was softly probing. "How did you end up a P.I.?"

Mariah stared determinedly ahead. Now there was a question you didn't want to have to answer when you least expected it. "Long story."

"I'm not exactly going anywhere," he said with a grin.

She cleared her throat, thankful it couldn't be heard over the roar of the engine as she sped up again. "Let's just say it was serendipity along with a healthy dose of nepotism."

While that was true, she didn't want to delve into the fact that there had come a point a couple years back when she felt her presence at the ranch wasn't welcome anymore. "A distraction," that's what her father had called her. A woman doing a man's job is how she interpreted his explanation. It seemed that overnight she had moved from a valued member of the ranch to unwanted company. The ranch hands went silent when she joined them for dinner. Her father scowled whenever she came back from a run. And she'd been relegated to menial tasks a two-hundred-year-old woman could have done.

She blessed the day when her uncle Bubba had offered her a one-time only assignment that included tracking down the very man she was tracking now: Claude Ray. He'd stolen some of her father's cattle back then, rebranded them, and was selling them at auction in the next county. The idiot.

Conniving, Ray definitely was. Smart, he was not.

But the one-time assignment had quickly turned into a full-time job. And it had basically become her mission in life since she couldn't work at the ranch.

"How about you?" she asked him.

Zach stared at her as if she were speaking a foreign language. And she supposed in some way maybe she was. It usually took Yanks a bit of an adjustment period before they got used to the easy cadence of Texas speak. And she had the impression that he'd definitely just gotten off the boat. Or plane.

He shrugged and squinted against the sun as he stared out the window. "You could say I came about it much the same way."

Mariah smiled. So he didn't want to share his reasons any more than she did. Good. That was just fine with her. More than fine. Because it meant he wouldn't hound her.

She turned her attention back to the road. They were maybe a half a mile up from the shack where Claude Ray sometimes hung his hat. And there it was. She could see the smear of weathered gray boards against the horizon. And behind the shack she made out horses. Two of them. Exactly the number she suspected Claude had stolen from the Carter ranch.

She stepped on the gas, then noticed a spot of red dart from the shack and make a run for a white pickup nearby.

"Oh, no, you don't," Mariah muttered under her breath.

Finally she elicited a physical reaction to her driving from Zach as he gripped the dusty dashboard. "I, um, take it this is the part where I should hold on?"

"If you value your life." Mariah smiled at him, feeling a rush of adrenaline that warmed her entire body.

She told herself the rush had nothing to do with the man next to her. She got a rush from tracking someone down, especially someone like Claude Ray, who was a regular. And who gave good chase.

She spared Zach another glance as she bore down on Claude. There was no way Claude was going anywhere anyway. Not with this being the only road out. "You okay?" she asked.

Zach grinned at her in a way that made her stomach leap higher than it should have. "Great."

"Good. Hold on."

Ten yards away from Claude's white truck she stood on the brakes and pulled the steering wheel to the left, sending her own truck careening to a stop and blocking the road.

"Here." Mariah slid her revolver from her holster and tossed the firearm to the seat next to Zach. "If he comes running back this way without me, shoot him."

The expression on his face was priceless. "Shoot him?"

"By shoot him, I don't mean execute him. A simple nick to the arm should do the trick."

His expression didn't change.

Mariah opened her mouth to ask if he knew how to use a gun, but caught sight of Claude making a run for it.

The question could wait for later. She had a horse thief to catch.

HOLY SHIT.

Zach stared at the firearm in his hand then at Mariah Clayborn's retreating back. He'd never held a gun before, much less fired one. Okay, sure, he'd had a cap gun and a BB gun when he was a teenager. But this was no pea-shooter. This was a full octane Colt that weighed at least two pounds if not more.

The longer he held it, the warmer the metal grew against his skin. He swallowed, excitement ricocheting through his bloodstream. Before he knew it he was grinning like a kid on Christmas morning. He had to shoulder the door to get it to open and he stood on the hard-packed dirt outside, squinting against the dust that remained from Mariah's daredevil maneuvers. He lifted a hand to shield his eyes. There she was behind the shack. His brows rose. She was grabbing the mane of a sleek dark stallion and hauling herself up onto the horse's bare back. He shifted a little to the right to find Claude Ray doing the same with less success some couple yards away, his caramel-colored stallion in a full run while Ray tried to pull himself up on top, completely graceless.

Mariah, on the other hand, was as fluid as the animal she commandeered. The horse seemed immediately to sense she was the boss and held still while she hauled herself up, waiting until her toned thighs straddled him and her boot heels gently nudged his sides before shooting out after Ray. Mariah's dark hair blew out behind her, her back straight, her fingers tangled in the horse's dark mane as she bent over the back of his neck, using the power of her thighs to stay astride.

Holy shit. Things did work differently down here.

Sure, like most Americans, he was well-versed on the stories of Texas and the Southwest, cowboys and Indians and Clint Eastwood movies. But he'd never thought that that kind of stuff still went on down here.

The two riders galloped out of sight. Zach stared at the truck with the tricky gearshift and scanned the landscape. The road ran out beside the shed. There was no way he could follow in the ancient vehicle.

Instead, he undid the top couple of buttons on his shirt and leaned against the door to get just a bit out of the unrelenting sun. He grinned. He'd never met anyone quite like Mariah Clayborn before. He'd bet dollars to donuts that she ran Clayborn Investigations. And if what he'd seen so far was any indication, he suspected she was very good at what she did.

He tried to tuck the gun into the waist of his dark slacks. The shear weight of the firearm bent the material back, nearly sending the weapon to the dirt at his feet. He fumbled for the gun then laid it on the hood of the truck instead, his gaze watchful, as if he was afraid the revolver would take on a life of its own.

He rubbed the back of his neck. Okay, so he hadn't given the gun part of the job that much thought before. He hadn't thought there would be a reason to, what with the focus of Finders Keepers being the recovery of lost loved ones, rather than dangerous horse thieves. But while Finders Keepers knew Jennifer Madison because they subcontracted work from her, it didn't mean Jennifer Madison's agency was strictly a low-risk venture. And, so it appeared, neither was Mariah's.

He did have to admit to feeling a thrill as the truck hurled over the dirt road toward their quarry, though. And the gun…

He heard the clump-clump of hooves hitting the earth before he spotted the horse. Given his thoughts on Mariah, he expected the rider to be her. Instead the caramel-colored horse shot out of the brush and straight by him.

Shit. Shit, shit, shit.

Zach fumbled for the gun, although he wasn't entirely certain what he was going to do with it. He eyed the back of the horse, the gun, then aimed the muzzle skyward and pulled the trigger. Nothing.

"The safety!" Mariah called, shooting past him moments after Claude. "Release the safety!"

The safety. Zach hurriedly eyed the metal in his hands and pushed a button. The clip slid out and dropped onto the ground.

Not the safety.

Damn.

Not that it mattered. He shielded his eyes and watched as Mariah caught up with Claude and yanked on the back of his shirt, pulling him from his horse and plopping him into the middle of a particularly prickly looking bush. Within minutes, Mariah shoved Claude in the direction of the truck, his hands bound behind his back with some sort of plastic tie, while the horses followed behind her.

Zach smoothed down the front of his shirt. He'd never before witnessed such a sight. But given the high color in Mariah's cheeks, the bounce to her gait, she was not only used to such events, she thrived on them. And Zach couldn't take his eyes off her.

Mariah paused in front of him and picked up the clip still on the ground. "Drop something?"

Zach grimaced and accepted the ammunition pack, then stepped aside to let Mariah put Claude inside the cab of the truck.

Claude spit on the ground near her boots. "Don't think this is over, Clayborn. Because it's not. Not by a long shot."

Mariah closed the truck door then pulled a cell phone out of her front pocket and placed two calls—one to the authorities to pick up Ray, another to what he thought must be the horse owner to pick up his animals.

She clapped the phone closed and turned to look at him. "Handle a gun often, cowboy?"

Zach grinned. "Not often."

"We'll have to fix that if we're going to work together."

The prospect of working with Mariah Clayborn took on a whole different sheen. Zach watched her round the truck and take a couple of leather leads from the bed, wondering what else the fiery Texas lass would have in store for him. And wondering how quickly he could see if she performed as well in bed as she did on the back of a horse.

3

NOW THAT'S MORE LIKE IT.

Mariah drove back to the office feeling psyched and energized, mentally ready to deal with anything and everything, even the news about her latest ex and his wedding plans. Well, mostly ready, anyway. If the handsome man next to her made her think of hot and heavy honeymoons, it was solely because his case involved a missing wedding dress. And her reluctance to feel in any way attracted to him had nothing to do with his lack of skill with a gun in a state where it was almost a requirement that a person know how to handle one, and own at least one or two…or ten or twelve. Her reluctance was because, let's face it, he was as far away from her type as it was for a man to get.

If a little part of her mind reminded her that what she thought was her type appeared not to be her type…well, she was ignoring it.

"Anything happen while I was away?" Mariah glided into the office on triumphant wings, holding the door open for Zach behind her.

George looked up from where he was idly playing a game of Spider Solitaire on his computer, appearing not to have budged more than an inch since she'd left him a couple of hours ago. "Nope."

Mariah looked to their visitor, feeling her stomach bottom out again, like it did every time she glanced his way. She figured it was probably the effect he had on most women, simply because of his tremendous looks. "Zach Letterman, meet my cousin George Clayborn. George, Zach."

Zach crossed the office and offered his hand. George glanced at it, raised his brows then got to his feet to give Zach's hand a shake. "How do you do?" George said.

Zach appeared not to know how to respond, and didn't.

Mariah rounded her desk, happy to find most of the damage from the morning's drenching of her chair had dried out. Still, she repositioned the plastic bag she'd laid across it earlier before sitting down.

"Did Buckley come over to take a look at the roof?"

George nodded. "Yeah. Said he'd come by with the materials in a couple of hours and patch it up."

"Did you get an estimate on what it would take to redo the entire roof?"

"He said he couldn't get to a job that big for two months anyway, so the patch is all he can swing now."

She noticed Zach eyeing the hole above her desk. He grinned at her. "Do something to anger the gods?"

The gods? "I figure if I had, I'd be toast right now."

He chuckled then pulled a nearby chair closer to the front of her desk.

"Did you get Ray?" George asked.

"Of course. Don't I always?"

"Oh." Her cousin looked around on top of his desk and lifted his clean blotter. "Justin called. He wants you to call him back at this number."

ZACH HAD NEVER SEEN anyone go so pale. Where moments before Mariah's face had been full of color and her eyes had danced with excitement, now she looked as if someone had just hit her in the stomach.

"A client?" Zach asked, referring to the caller.

"An ex."

The way she said it made it sound as if she had a whole battalion of exes. Zach squinted at her.

"He, um, just got engaged."

"Ah," he said, as if that explained everything. "To you?"

"No," she said a little too curtly. "Not to me. The word never even came up while we were dating."

"And that was?"

"Five days ago."

Zach lifted his brows. "Fast worker, your ex."

"Fast workers, all three of my exes. Only not with me."

She made busy with her hands as he watched.

Zach silently pondered the striking woman not three feet from him. If he bought what she was trying to sell him, he'd think it didn't bother her one iota that her latest ex was engaged to someone else. In all honesty, he couldn't say it bothered her in the way one might expect. She didn't appear heartbroken, on the verge of tears or particularly sad that the man she had dated was about to bite the big one.

She did, however, appear highly agitated. As if she could go after another four Claude Rays, on foot if necessary, to expend the energy that radiated from her. An energy that intrigued him, drew him in, made it impossible for him to look anywhere but at Mariah Clayborn. The woman was fascinating.

He absently rubbed the back of his neck. What was he thinking? He was supposed to be focusing on the case. His first case. And here he was entertaining ideas of how he and Mariah might expend some of that primo energy she exuded.

"So, the case," he said slowly.

She blinked at him as if having forgotten he was there. "The case? Oh. Yes." Talk about your grimaces. Mariah wore one that could go up against the best of them. "The case of the missing wedding dress."

He leaned forward and rested his forearms on his knees. "Where should we start? A trip to Hobby Airport?"

She picked up the telephone receiver, dialed information, then dialed the airport, consulting a fax that resembled the fact sheet he had folded in his front shirt pocket.

Zach looked over at George, noticing the way he tuned in to the goings-on without really appearing to. George glanced at him and Zach grinned.

"It's not there," Mariah stated.

Zach turned toward her. "What's not where?"

"The bag with the dress in it. It never made it to Hobby."

"Are you sure?"

"Uh-huh." She handed him a notepad in which she had written an address in Alabama. "But it may be here."

"Here, as in…?"

"Here as in the Unclaimed Baggage Center in Scottsboro, Alabama. According to the airline supervisor I talked to, that's where all the lost luggage in the universe piles up until it's either claimed or auctioned or sold off after ninety days."

Zach scratched his chin, thinking a couple of pieces of his own luggage probably had ended up there over the years. "A kind of graveyard for dead baggage."

Mariah smiled. "Yes. Something like that."

"So when do we go?"

Her soft brows lifted. "How do you mean?"

He glanced at his watch. "My client renews his vows in

less than a week. He's willing to pay us whatever it takes to retrieve the dress posthaste."

"Us?"

"He's covering all expenses."

"Ah."

Zach grinned. "Unless, of course, you want to sign off on the case."

"No, no. Of course not."

Zach could tell that's exactly what she wanted to do. And it surprised him how much he wished she wouldn't. He was highly attracted to her and he'd like to see what it would be like to kiss that saucy mouth of hers. He couldn't do that if she sent him packing.

The telephone at her elbow rang. She glanced at the display showing the number of the caller, the ashen color returning to her face.

She reached back and picked up what looked like a duffel bag. "Let's say we go now."

"Just like that?"

She nodded, barely looking at him as she headed for the door. "Just like that."

MARIAH SECURED both her tray and her seat in the upright and locked position then rubbed her arms.

"Cold?"

She glanced at where Zach Letterman seemed to take up the air of half the plane, his knees jammed against the seat in front of him, his shoulders nearly topping the back of the chair.

She cleared her throat. "Um, yes. A little. But we'll be landing soon, so it doesn't matter."

"Here." He gestured to a nearby flight attendant, who immediately stepped to him, a solicitous smile on her pretty face.

Mariah grimaced and watched as Zach Letterman charmed another willing female. The strange thing about it was that he didn't even appear to be trying. He looked a woman's way and she was all smiles and readiness. She'd witnessed it first at the airport when the desk clerk had practically drooled on the counter separating her from Zach. Then she'd seen it at the airport coffee shop, where he'd stopped off for some caffeine and the *Wall Street Journal*.

"No, it's not for me," Zach told the pretty blonde.

The blonde definitely looked disappointed, not that Mariah could blame her. To have the perfect excuse to touch Zach ripped out from under you…well, that would be enough to make anyone frown.

"Thank you," Zach said, accepting the plastic-wrapped blue blanket.

Mariah watched the flight attendant reluctantly make her way back to the front of the plane.

She cleared her throat. "Thanks, Zach, but no, really, that's okay…"

Mariah's words trailed off as she watched him make quick work of the plastic then begin to cover her with the nappy cotton. The back of his fingers skimmed her bare arm, making her feel like the plane had hit an air pocket as her stomach bottomed out. "I…um, can do it."

His eyes scanned her face, making a whole different sort of goose bumps dot her flesh.

"Thanks," she said.

She'd never seen a guy grin with his eyes before. But if anyone could, Zach Letterman was the man. A pure knowing seemed to lurk in the meadow-green depths, inviting her in, robbing her of both breath and words.

"You're welcome," he murmured, then he returned his attention to the *Wall Street Journal*.

Mariah puffed out a long breath and settled the blanket over the upper part of her body. She turned to look out the window. Why was it that whenever he looked at her she found it suddenly impossible to breathe?

She shifted and made a face. P.I., her butt. If the man next to her was a private investigator then her name was Cindy Crawford. She surreptitiously watched him turn the page of his newspaper, her gaze lingering on his long, thick fingers and the springy dark hair that dotted the backs. He struck her as a man used to traveling. He barely looked at the flight attendant who offered a drink and a snack, while she had spotted the attendant the instant he began serving the passengers fifteen rows up. She never took her eyes from him for fear that he would miss her. Okay, so she wasn't a frequent flier. This was her third time on an airplane and, admittedly, she didn't much like being so far up off the ground. There was something... unnatural about it.

But it was more than Zach's comfort with airplane travel that fueled her suspicions. Take the gun incident. Investigation training usually required the investigator to take at least one course in the art of using a firearm. She knew things worked differently up North, but she didn't think they worked that differently. Then he had avoided answering her question on what had led him to be a P.I.

She made a face. Okay, so she hadn't shared her reasons, either, but that didn't mean she wasn't a licensed P.I. She was.

Maybe he just didn't get out in the field much.

Still, a niggling part of her suspected that Zach Letterman knew as much about being a P.I. as she knew about weeding a flower garden, which was basically limited to whatever she saw when she tuned in to Martha Stewart. And that wasn't all that often.

Her gaze slowly slid back to Zach's handsome profile. While he lacked experience in the private detecting arena, she'd guess he had a whole lot of experience in other more intimate arenas. He was the type of male who would know exactly what a woman wanted from a man. And would be able to give it to her.

Zach folded his newspaper and slid it into the pocket in the seat in front of him. His gaze met hers and, as usual, her stomach bottomed out—especially when his eyes darkened, an unmistakable attraction lurking in the green depths. In fact, for a moment she thought he might even kiss her. She caught herself licking her lips in preparation.

"So what do we do once we get there?" he asked.

"Hmm?" Mariah slowly blinked, his words taking even longer to register. "Oh. We rent a car and drive the forty miles from Huntsville to Scottsboro to visit the Unclaimed Baggage Center."

The gleam in his eyes turned into a grin, making Mariah's own mouth suddenly go dry. "I'd gathered that. I meant, will we be checking into a hotel?"

Checking into a hotel? With what had to be the most attractive guy she'd come across since she used to pin up pictures of rodeo stars on her bedroom walls?

"No. No, I don't think a hotel will be necessary." She swallowed hard and wished she could pull the little blue blanket up over her head. "If luck is on our side, we'll find the bag and be on the next flight back to Houston."

"And if luck isn't on our side?"

"Then we should be able to ascertain that the bag isn't in Scottsboro, and be on the next flight back to Houston."

He glanced at his watch, making her crane her neck to look at the sleek crystal as well, completely forgetting that she wore a watch of her own. "Well, then, we'd better make quick work of getting to the center, because the last flight out to Houston is at six."

Mariah's eyebrows shot up.

He seemed to notice the move. "I asked back at Hobby."

"Oh. Good. Good."

That was a P.I. move, wasn't it? Either that or he was a man used to being prepared.

The question was, prepared for what?

Okay, what was it with her today? Her thoughts seemed to bounce all over the universe and back again. Then she remembered Justin's announcement and collapsed against the chair and frowned. So, this was what being a reject did to you. It made you look, feel and act like a fool.

Or maybe being a fool was exactly the reason she couldn't land a forever guy to begin with.

So MARIAH CLAYBORN WASN'T the chatty type. As Zach watched her climb out of the rental car outside the Unclaimed Baggage Center, he told himself he should be thankful. He wasn't much for small talk himself. In fact, he told himself he should be glad she wasn't asking him too many questions. He'd decided early on that he was going to keep his real reason for being in Texas, and working for Jennifer Madison, to himself. Yes, while the entire P.I. business intrigued him, he had no intention of making a living as a P.I. He reminded himself that he was down here strictly to get the feel for the territory so that when he returned to Indiana he'd be prepared for the task of opening satellite offices of Finders Keepers.

He was, however, used to letting other people do the talking. Ask a couple of questions, and most people went off on long tangents that usually left him knowing more than he'd like.

But with Mariah, he found he didn't know nearly

enough. She'd been quiet ever since they'd left her office in Houston. Throughout the drive to the airport, the plane ride, then the drive to Scottsboro, the few questions he had asked had received little more than one-word answers.

Zach rubbed the back of his neck as he closed the cab door, watching Mariah lead the way to the door of what looked like a retail store about as big as a city block. While he didn't consider himself a ladies' man, he certainly thought he knew a whole lot about women. And one of those things was that they loved to talk. All you had to do was find the key word. Shopping usually did the trick. But he'd tried no fewer than ten of the regular conversation words on Mariah and she hadn't bitten on one of them. Not even politics had gotten more than a small smile from her.

He shrugged and followed after her. Okay, so she wasn't interested in idle conversation. It was a new one for him, but Zach could handle it. Well, he could if there wasn't the whole P.I. angle to think about. He'd like to get to know more about the business. And he'd like to get to know a whole lot more about Mariah Clayborn.

They talked to a clerk who told them that the type of baggage they were talking about wouldn't be on the sales floor yet, but back in the warehouse behind the store. She made a phone call then walked them back to a large door. "Go on in. You're expected. You'll find James somewhere in the piles."

Piles? Zach scanned the countless objects for sale, the place looking like a garage sale lover's paradise, then stepped through the door the clerk held open. He immediately saw what she was talking about. Everywhere he looked were mountains of luggage. Big pieces, small pieces, expensive pieces, cheap pieces. All things that belonged to somebody somewhere and held cherished memories from their trips.

"Oh, boy," Mariah said, next to him.

"You can say that again."

"Oh, boy."

Zach jerked to look at her and grinned. "I meant figuratively."

She smiled back. "I know. I thought it deserved two."

"Ah."

Zach couldn't quite put his finger on why, but whenever Mariah smiled, he either grinned or grinned wider, and an inexplicable heat slinked through his abdomen, making him want to touch her. It didn't matter where. To tuck her wild hair behind her ear. To run his finger down the smooth column of her throat. To circle her right breast where the soft cotton of her T-shirt draped enticingly over the small mound.

"Hello!"

Zach heard the greeting, but was at a loss as to where it had come from.

"I take it you're Miss Clayborn?"

It seemed to take Mariah a great effort to tear her gaze away from him. The heat he felt sizzled, knowing that she was as compelled by him as he was by her.

"Um, yes, that would be me," she said finally.

A middle-aged guy with thick glasses popped up from behind a pile of suitcases nearest to them. Zach raised his brows.

"James, at your service," he said, wiping his hands against his striped, short-sleeved shirt, then offering his hand. "Would either of you like some Starbucks?"

"No, thank you," Zach said.

Mariah shook James's hand. "You're the one I talked to?"

"No. That would be Sally. I don't sound like a woman to you, do I?"

Zach suppressed a chuckle. The guy in front of them definitely didn't look like a woman.

Mariah cleared her throat. "Sorry. I was calling from the Houston airport so I really couldn't make out much about the voice with all the background noise."

"Airports. Hate 'em," James said, offering his hand to Zach.

Zach nodded in complete agreement as he gave James's hand a brief shake.

"So you all are looking for a wedding dress." James pushed up his glasses again and peered around him. "Someone else here on the same errand. You'd be surprised how many of those things end up here."

"Wedding dresses?"

"No, people looking for them."

"Ah."

"Found one the other day." He kicked a suitcase out of the path and called out to another guy nearby, telling him to keep the pathways clear. "Wouldn't be able to find your way out without the pathways," James explained.

"By 'found,' do you mean people or wedding dresses?"

"Wedding dresses, of course."

Zach tuned in on where Mariah was going. "And by the other day, which day, exactly, do you mean?"

"Two days ago."

The right timeframe.

"Where is it? The dress, I mean?"

James motioned toward the far corner of the room. "Right where I directed the other guy who got here about twenty minutes ago looking for a dress, too."

"Ah," Zach said again, barely hiding his amusement.

Mariah laughed.

James stared at them both, having missed out on the joke.

"Sorry," Mariah said. "I was just wondering if, you know, the guy looking for the dress actually plans on wearing it."

James's brows hovered above the dark rims of his glasses. "You don't mean…you aren't saying…" He let out a deep breath. "Oh Lord, I hope not. Either way, I don't care, though. I'm a firm believer in the don't ask, don't tell policy. But now that you've said that, it's put…well, an image in my head, you know? And that's one image I could do without."

"You and me both," Zach said.

Zach took Mariah's elbow and steered her toward where James was leading the way down one of the paths he'd mentioned. Little more than two feet wide, the path wound around mountains of varying sizes and colors. A Louis Vuitton here, a knockoff there. A khaki duffel bag in the way of the path, a package of skis at shoulder level, ready to decapitate anyone who wasn't watching where they were going. How did all of this stuff come to be lost?

"James, what happens to all this?"

He shrugged. "Well, the airline does extensive tracking for ninety days. Sometimes the owners themselves find their way here, but not often. If they do, or the airline matches up the bag with the passenger, they regain their things. Otherwise, we sell the stuff in the front room. We also hold auctions. We wouldn't have room otherwise. We have a website, you know. Sell stuff there, too."

The older man stopped and scratched his chin, considering the piles in front of him when they came to a fork in the path. He looked one way, then the other, then pointed to the right. "This way, I think. Yes, yes. This way."

Zach gazed down at Mariah, who was looking at the

baggage with as much curiosity as he. "Lose anything recently?" he asked her.

She shook her head. "No. But it looks to me as though it wasn't for lack of the airline trying."

"I've lost no fewer than three bags over the years."

"Do a lot of traveling, do you?"

"Yes."

"Work related?"

Zach rubbed his chin. P.I.s traveled, didn't they? Sure they did. "Yes. Don't you?"

"This was my third time on a plane. And, this trip aside, my travels have been strictly personal. I haven't had much call to travel out of Texas yet, you know, for the job."

"Personal? That one trip wouldn't have had anything to do with your exes, would it?"

She winced, making him wish he hadn't said anything. "No. It was for my mother's funeral. I was eight."

Zach felt lower than the bottom of his shoes. "I'm sorry."

She shrugged, obviously trying to pull off a nonchalance he was sure she didn't feel. "That's all right."

He cleared his throat. "My mother died when I was nine."

Her big brown eyes widened. "Your father?"

"Out of the picture. I don't even know where he is. Not that it matters. He wasn't around long enough to make an impression."

Zach grimaced. He wasn't entirely sure why he'd volunteered the information. He didn't think he'd told anyone in his adult life how old he'd been when he'd lost his mother. Yet here he had known this woman for only a few hours and he'd shared the information with her as easily as he did the time.

"I guess it's my turn to say I'm sorry."

He mimicked her moves and shrugged his shoulders,

knowing the casualness he was going for fell far short of the mark. "That's all right."

His response brought a warm smile to her face. He discovered again he liked it when she smiled. He liked it a lot.

"Here we are," James said, coming to a halt and breaking the quiet moment. The older man scratched the top of his head. "At least this is where I think it is." He looked around. "But where's the other guy?"

Fifteen or so jumbo suitcases were stacked behind Mariah. Zach squinted, trying to make out whether or not one of them had just moved. Then suddenly the entire stack began to teeter precariously.

He calmly reached out and touched her arm. She blinked up at him, her tongue darting out to moisten her bottom lip. Then he yanked her into his arms, away from where she'd been standing, where the cases were now hitting the floor one at a time.

"Dang nab it!" James shouted.

Zach had never actually heard a person say the words in the flesh and, despite what had just happened, he fought a smile.

"If I've told the kid once, I've told him a thousand times, you've got to stack these bags carefully." He eyed where Mariah had curled her hands into the front of Zach's shirt, the side of her head resting against his chest.

Zach could hear the *thump-thump* of his own heartbeat. He wondered if Mariah could hear it, too. The soft smell of sunshine—Texas sunshine—filled his nose, and the feel of one-hundred-percent Mariah Clayborn filled his arms. The heat that had earlier taken up residence in his abdomen dropped to his groin. His condition was not helped any by the shifting of Mariah's hips.

"You okay?" James asked her.

Zach looked down to find her staring at the man as if

just realizing he was there. She pushed away from Zach so fast she nearly toppled them both over. Zach caught her and chuckled.

"I'm fine," Mariah said, squaring her shoulders and looking everywhere but at Zach. "Where did you say this damn suitcase was?"

4

WHOA, COWBOY.

Mariah could swear she was shaking. She eyed the avalanche of suitcases, then Zach Letterman's wide, hard chest, and swallowed hard. The problem was she wasn't sure what bothered her most-that a few measly suitcases were to blame for her shaken demeanor, or Zach Letterman.

Definitely Zach Letterman.

She covertly lifted her hand. Definitely shaking. She smacked the hand back to her side and made a fist.

Okay, so for those few moments it had felt good to be pressed against his hard male length as if she was a damsel in distress and he the brave hero. Even if he'd only been protecting her from suitcases. She'd breathed in the crisp scent of his shirt, felt his large hands pressing against her back, and felt...different somehow. At least different from the way she'd felt with any other guy. She was used to the smell of chewing tobacco and sweat. But somehow she got the impression that when Zach sweated, he smelled like cologne.

It didn't make any sense, really. All her life she'd been around real cowboys. Men who hiked up their pants and puffed out their chests and made it their mission in life to play the role of heroes. Yet whenever any of them had tried to help her, she'd shunned them. Felt insulted. Had even broken her leg in three places once in her haste to show she could take care of herself. Her horse had rolled and caught her underneath.

Yet let a few bags fall to the floor and she was hopping into a Yankee's arms and batting her lashes as if she wasn't capable of tying her shoes right.

"I'll be darned," James said, breaking into her mental musings.

Zach moved up next to the man and Mariah moved to the other side. Before them sat no fewer than fifteen suitcases, all hanging open and gutted, their contents mixing with the next.

"I take it this isn't the way to go about searching for bags," Zach said dryly.

"Heck no, it ain't." James kicked a few steps forward. "All the stuff gets mixed up then." He threw his hands in the air.

Zach looked down at something he'd taken out of his front pocket. "Blue canvas suitcase with blue leather straps."

Mariah noted that all the suitcases that had been opened matched that description.

"The guy," James said.

"The guy? What guy?"

He waved his hand. "You know, the one who got here just before you looking for a wedding dress." He looked around and Mariah followed his gaze, finding no other person in sight. At the far end of the warehouse, a door clanged. She couldn't say for sure, but she'd have chanced a guess that the man in question had just left the building.

Zach frowned and glanced at her. "I don't have a very good feeling about all of this."

Mariah had to admit she felt the same way, but she wasn't about to admit that to him. It reeked too much of the damsel-in-distress situation. "We're talking about a wedding dress here."

"A wedding dress our client is paying through the nose to locate."

James wasn't paying attention to them. Instead he was stepping through the small piles of clothing. A moment later he said, "Forgot one."

Zach leaned closer. "If the dress is in there, that means the guy who got here before left without it."

"Maybe he found the dress he was looking for."

"Only one dress in this lot," James said.

James unzipped the bag then flopped the lid open.

Sitting in the middle of wads of balled up tissue paper sat the wedding dress in question.

"Coincidence," Mariah said.

"Fact," Zach countered.

"WE'RE BEING FOLLOWED."

Zach stared in the rearview mirror through the back window of the rental car, watching another sedan shadow their moves. He didn't miss Mariah's exasperated roll of her eyes.

"We're not being followed. Maybe the driver is going to the same hotel we are. Have you thought about that?"

Zach sat forward and straightened his suit jacket. Ever since discovering that they were too late to catch the last flight out to Houston, Mariah had been a tad bit cranky. When he'd asked why, she'd said something about not having her toothbrush. Zach told her he always carried an extra and she was more than welcome to have it. He'd barely heard her murmur, "What kind of P.I. carries an extra toothbrush?"

Okay, so since Jennifer had first given him the case this morning, he'd felt a little let down that it had been something so menial, so unexciting. His meeting with Denton Gawlick and his wife had gone smoothly, no red bells. They were renewing their wedding vows next week and needed to have the dress, simple as that.

Then they'd arrived at the Unclaimed Baggage Center to discover someone else was looking for a wedding dress in a suitcase similar to the suitcase in which they'd found their dress. That is the *client*'s dress.

Zach pulled at his tie, which had grown a little tight around his neck. The mere mention of a "their" in the same sentence with "wedding dress" was enough to choke off air.

Hey, he was just as willing as the next guy to stand in front of an altar, only he intended to be ready for it when it happened. Of course his longtime girlfriend Kym had found out the hard way that he wasn't anywhere near ready for it now. After two years of dating, of mingling their lives, she'd come out and asked him to marry her. That the proposal had come on the heels of his explaining to her what he planned to do, namely pass over control of his tool and die business and pursue what she subsequently called this "P.I. thing" hadn't helped matters. That he didn't want to get married had been his response. Kym hadn't given him a chance to add the "yet" he was sure had been about to come out of his mouth. She'd up and walked out on him, never to be heard from again. Well, except for a voice-mail message telling him not to bother retrieving anything from her apartment because there was no longer anything there to retrieve. The whir of what he'd suspected was her garbage disposal on the other end of the line hadn't sounded good.

"You'd think the rental car companies would make sure their vehicles had air-conditioning, wouldn't you?" Zach said.

"That's okay," Mariah said, closing her eyes against the hot breeze wafting in the open window. "I don't like air-conditioning anyway."

Zach gazed at her. At the warm stains of color on her smooth cheekbones. The dots of moisture on her forehead and long, long neck. The way her damp T-shirt clung to her small breasts. Of course she'd say that. She was used to the heat south of the Mason-Dixon line. Dealt with it on a daily basis.

He settled back against the seat but he couldn't say it was comfortable. The truth was, looking at Mariah Clayborn made him think of crisp sheets and sweaty bodies. Namely his and hers. Entangled together. Beads of moisture sliding down her elegant neck and over the crest of a breast and pausing there, waiting to be licked off.

"Are you okay?"

Mariah's voice surprised him out of his reverie. "Yes, I'm fine." If you counted being in a high state of arousal fine.

It wasn't like him to be so…obsessed with the idea of sleeping with somebody. Of imagining how her thighs would look pressing against his hips instead of a horse's back. Or how her mouth would purse just so as she fought to catch her breath.

Zach wiped the sweat from his brow.

"You don't seriously think someone's still following us, do you?"

Zach blinked at Mariah. She'd obviously tuned into his

distracted state. But just as obviously she didn't appear to have a clue as to the nature of his distraction.

"I don't know," he said.

He judged the hotel to be another mile or so down the road. Good. Because he didn't think he could last another minute in a car alone with Mariah without either spontaneously combusting...or doing something a professional man shouldn't be thinking about doing with a colleague, no matter how temporary that working relationship would be.

IF YOU TAKE ZACH LETTERMAN out in public, they will come.
As Mariah unpacked the entire inventory of her travel necessities—the toothbrush Zach had given her—she stared at herself in the dimly lit hotel bathroom mirror and sighed. Okay, so he *was* a striking man. Tall, lean with an air of self-confidence that could equal any rodeo cowboy's. But Mariah couldn't remember being around a man who attracted so much female attention. From the flight attendant hoping to be totally at his service, to the hotel clerk who had thrown in room amenities Mariah hadn't known existed, Zach Letterman seemed to be a walking, talking billboard for male sexuality. Sure, she'd tuned into it the instant they'd met. But to be a victim of it, and having to witness how it affected others were two completely different things.

She ran her fingers through her hair, piling it up on top of her head then considering the results. Not that Zach seemed any the wiser for the attention. He had spoken to the clerk and the flight attendant the same way as he had to James, the flighty baggage caretaker. But she wasn't entirely convinced that his being oblivious to his effect on women was any better than him knowing.

Of course it didn't help at all that the women barely spared her a glance before writing her out of the picture altogether. No competition. She didn't even have to see it written on their pretty faces. Their attitudes spoke volumes.

She sighed again and released her hair so it hung around her face again in thick, unruly waves. Not that being no sexual competition was anything new to her. She may have grown up competing with the males, but the females… Well, at first she hadn't been interested in competing with them. Then there had come the time when she was so far behind in the imaginary competition she'd had to drop out of the race altogether.

Recently a confusing kind of restlessness had begun to coat her insides. A strange kind of itchy sensation, only it was under her skin, not on top where she could get at it. She caught herself scratching her arm and stopped. Had her exes found her sexy? Desirable? She figured they had, considering their physical attentions. But if that was so, where did that leave her in the sex appeal race? Did she have a minute amount that allowed her to go only so far, but just short of the altar?

Not that she was all that experienced. Sure, she'd been intimately involved with three men. Well, two. The first didn't count because they'd never really had intercourse. Heavy breathing was about as far as things had gone with him, then he'd been in a hurry to drive her back to the ranch. She'd always thought it was because at the last minute he'd decided he hadn't wanted to have sex with her.

And the other two…

Well, she didn't want to think about them right now. She couldn't change them. But she could change herself. She leaned forward and studied what looked like an oncoming zit on her cheek. She made a face then eyed the travel-sized toothpaste tube. One of her cousins had put a dab on a pimple when they were teenagers. Personally, she had thought the action pretty gross. But now that she thought about it, she couldn't remember Jolene ever really having a full-blown zit.

The mirror reflected the bed in the other room and the open suitcase sitting on top of it. Seeing the old lacy off-white dress lying there in clouds of tissue paper made her heart pitch to her feet. Justin Johnson was getting married. Tom Brewer had gotten married six months ago. And Jackson Pyle two years before that. And none of the three had ever mentioned the word *marriage* around her.

Mariah strode out into the other room, her intention to close the suitcase so she wouldn't have to see the dress inside. Instead she stood in front of it, staring down at the lace with reluctant fascination.

The only other wedding dress she'd ever seen up close had been her mother's. It had been tucked away in a box in the attic. The day after her mother's funeral, she and her father had flown back from Amarillo, where her mother's family was from and where her father had decided it was best she be buried. After they'd returned home, Mariah had hidden out in the old, dusty attic to get away from the nonstop stream of well-wishers and old women bearing casserole dishes. Up in the attic their voices had faded to an incomprehensible hum, and she'd looked out onto the stables, wishing she could be there instead. She'd leaned against a box only to have it collapse against her weight. She'd opened it up and, sitting on top of some old clothes, was the dress she'd seen her mother wearing in her wedding pictures. It had looked so tiny, so perfect. Just like her mother. And so unlike Mariah.

Three hours later, her father had found her sleeping in that same spot, an imprint from her mother's dress on her cheek.

Mariah had found the dress again last year while clearing out the attic to make room for a home office for her father. When she'd opened the box, she found the dress looked no less perfect…and no less small. As she'd held the delicate fabric in front of her, she wondered if even at eight she'd been small enough to wear it.

Mariah reached out and rubbed the lace of the wedding dress between her thumb and index finger. She wasn't sure of this dress's history, but she was sure it had one. Although she knew that making new things look old was an art these days, she didn't think anyone would want a dress to look this old. It appeared to be held together by sheer will alone.

What made a woman a woman? she wondered. What did they do that made men want them? Not just for short-term relationships but for the whole nine yards?

There was a soft knock at her door. Her heart shot up from the vicinity of her feet and she quickly closed the suitcase and stuffed it under the king-size bed, almost as if being seen in the same room with it would make her come up wanting even more. Then she crossed the room to open the door.

"Hi," Zach said, seeming to fill the entire width of the hallway from where he stood her outside her door.

"Hi, yourself."

"You ready to grab a bite?"

Mariah glanced back at her hotel room, thinking that the somber, empty appearance mirrored exactly how she was feeling right now. "Um, actually, I'm beat. I thought I'd, you know, just order something up from room service."

In all honesty, she didn't think she could weather another round of "Ooh, it's a handsome guy" sure to come from the waitresses at any restaurant they went to.

"They have anything good?"

He walked into the room, leaving Mariah clutching the

door handle tightly in her hand. "I don't know. I haven't looked yet. I thought I'd catch a shower first."

A lie, to be sure. But right now she just wanted to be alone. Being around a man as strikingly attractive as Zach not only made her feel inadequate, he made her feel hot.

"Okay, then. How about I order from my room, you take your shower, then by the time you come over, the food will probably already be there?"

Didn't the guy know how to take no for an answer?

Mariah rubbed her temple, feeling the thud-thud of her pulse pick up speed at the mere thought of spending more time around him. "Okay, sure. Why don't you do that."

Zach smiled at her and a strange longing filled her stomach. "Is there any food I should avoid ordering for you?"

"A burger and fries should be a pretty safe bet."

"The works?"

Despite her misgivings, Mariah found herself smiling back. "Even the onions."

Zach seemed to linger longer than was necessary for the simple exchange. Mariah tilted her head to stare at him. Finally he cleared his throat. "See you in twenty minutes then."

"Twenty minutes."

Mariah closed the door after him then collapsed against it, her breath catching in her throat. She wouldn't fool herself into thinking that Zach had hesitated because he was attracted to her. That he felt even the tiniest fraction of the hectic emotions rolling through her. The thought was too difficult to contemplate.

"Time for a shower, Mariah. A cold one."

ZACH COULDN'T exactly put his finger on it, but Mariah's go-get-it demeanor had taken a nosedive since their drive to the hotel. He pulled his tie off and tossed it across the bed then rolled up his shirtsleeves, the air conditioner just beginning to cool the room to a livable temperature. Maybe it was as she said, that she was simply tired, but somehow he got the impression that the day's activities weren't nearly enough to tap into her reservoir of energy.

His gaze slipped to the king-size bed, then to the window where the sun was just sinking below the horizon. He couldn't help thinking that her weariness was emotional rather than physical. The engaged ex? Probably so. He couldn't imagine being on the other side of that equation.

Well, actually, yes, he could. Because a week after Kym had given him her marriage ultimatum, she'd been going out with someone else. And, it was rumored they would be making an engagement announcement soon.

How did he feel about that? Zach absently rubbed his neck. He really couldn't say one way or another. He supposed a part of him was sad that Kym was no longer in his life. But he didn't regret not agreeing to her demands. So much of his life was unsettled right now. He knew what he wanted, but there was a ways to go before he actually achieved it. And the thought of Kym with another man bothered him not at all.

Which should strike him as odd, shouldn't it? You're with a woman for two years and she's seeing someone else. Shouldn't that make him at least a little jealous? The thought of her being intimate with another man?

Odd that it didn't.

Of course, Kym could never understand his need for family ties. Yes, she might be an only child, and her parents were divorced, but there was a big difference between her situation and his, where essentially every last member of the family he'd known was lost to him. His mother. His grandmother. His father.

No, his father wasn't dead. Or maybe he was. He

couldn't say. When his dad had run out on him and his mother when he was four, he'd been rated as good as dead.

His gaze drifted as if on its own accord back to the large, empty bed, and his thoughts slid to the woman in the room next door. Mariah Clayborn. Now there was a woman he was completely unprepared for. Fresh. Vibrant. Her sexiness was innate, something woven in with her bones, not something worn or fussed with or made up. She was earthy and sassy and so downright sexy he couldn't stop imagining laying his hands all over her compact body. Of kissing her kissable mouth and thrusting his fingers into all that thick, dark hair, tugging it back to allow him access to her delectable neck. A neck so elegant not even a T-shirt could hide it.

A knock at the door. Probably room service. He pulled the barrier open, but instead of a waiter he found Mariah looking him squarely in the face.

"You're not really a P.I., are you?"

Zach blinked at her several times to make sure he'd heard correctly. "Hello to you, too. Why don't you come on in?"

She eyed him almost warily, making him want to laugh, then swept past him into the room, leaving the subtle scent of hotel soap in her wake. She turned to face him, but before she could repeat her question, room service did appear. In the few minutes it took the waiter to set up the tray and for Zach to sign off on the check, he considered how he might respond to Mariah's question.

Finally they were once again alone. Zach crossed his arms over his chest and grinned at her. "What gave me away? My lack of experience with a gun? Or that I don't wear a gray overcoat?"

"None and both of the above."

"Ah."

A smile played at the corners of her unpainted mouth.

"You're right," he said, sitting at the desk table and indicating she should take the seat across from him. "I'm not a P.I. At least not yet, anyway."

Mariah hesitantly sat down across from him but didn't touch her food. "Then what are you?"

"Right now? Unemployed."

Her eyes narrowed.

How much did he tell her? He had yet to get used to the idea of franchising Finders Keepers. And it wasn't so long ago that he'd flubbed up his explanation to Kym.

"Jennifer Madison knows this?"

"About my being unlicensed." He nodded. "Yes." He gestured to her food. "Eat before it gets cold."

"I'm used to cold food."

"Well, I'm not."

"Ah." She smiled around a bite of pickle.

Zach lifted a French fry to his own mouth and nearly choked on his own saliva as he watched the unaffected way she first sucked then bit the pickle in half.

Good God.

"Where are you from?"

Zach lifted his brows. "What if I said Texas?"

"Then I'd have to call you a liar."

"Not very polite."

She shrugged. "Not one of my qualities."

"Indiana."

"Indiana," she repeated.

"Uh-huh. You know, the state between Illinois and Ohio?"

"I know where Indiana is."

"I thought you might."

Her brown eyes twinkled as she picked up her burger. "So you're in Texas for a job then?"

"In a manner of speaking, yes."

"In a manner of speaking?"

"That's what I said." He put down his own burger and wiped his hands. "Tell you what. You tell me the story behind your becoming a P.I. and I'll tell you why I want to become one."

He knew he had her there. He'd sensed a real hesitation earlier when he'd asked her how she came about the job.

"Never mind." She wiped her own mouth.

"That's what I thought."

She squinted at him, as if trying to follow his train of thought.

Zach twisted his lips. "Okay, Mariah. It's obvious you've got something on your mind. So why don't you just come out and say it?"

"All right, then," she said quietly, her face draining of all emotion. "I have a proposition for you."

"Hmm. A proposition. Sounds interesting." He gestured with his hand as he took another bite of burger. "Go on."

"I'll teach you everything I know about being a P.I."

He nodded. Sounded good so far.

"If you teach me everything I need to know about becoming a desirable woman."

Zach froze, wondering if part of Mariah's training included the Heimlich maneuver.

5

MARIAH SAT STONE STILL, waiting for Zach to respond. Well, respond in a way that didn't include him keeling over face first into his dinner from cardiac arrest.

In all honesty, she hadn't known she was going to make the offer until it was out of her mouth. Sure, she'd all but guessed that Zach wasn't a P.I. Not yet, anyway. But the other part...well, the other part was born out of desperation. Having one boyfriend jump ship and marry someone else was one thing. Three definitely indicated there was a problem. And that it originated with her was also clear.

She sat with her hands spread flat on her thighs. How long was too long in terms of a response? Whatever it was, she was sure Zach had gone over it.

She cleared her throat. "By, um, teach, I mean...verbally instruct me." Her face burned so hot she was afraid her skin might melt off. "As I, um, will verbally instruct you, as well."

"Verbally instruct..." he repeated, as if unable to wrap his mind around the words.

"Yes. Seeing that we only have these few hours tonight, I don't really think there's time for much else. We go back to Houston in the morning, you deliver the dress to your client, case closed."

He remained silent, although he had begun chewing the food in his mouth again. A good sign, no?

"Right?" she prompted.

He swallowed then coughed a couple times. "Right."

He took a long swallow of water then sat back in his chair, his gaze plastered to her face. Mariah had never felt so uncomfortable in her life, so under the microscope. Was he even now thinking of pointers to give her on her appearance? She lifted a hand to her hair then tucked it behind her ear.

"So is it a deal?"

His eyes twinkled at her. Great. He was laughing at her. That's just what she needed.

"Deal," he said.

Mariah let out a long breath. "Really?"

He nodded. "Really."

The heat of embarrassment she'd felt mere moments before was replaced by an entirely different heat. A sizzling awareness that wound around and around her body then snaked inside, filling her stomach with liquid warmth.

She shifted uncomfortably. Of course his agreement was only because he wanted to be tutored in the art of private investigation—not because he wanted her. As long as she kept that straight, she'd be safe.

"So who should start?" she asked quietly, her voice barely audible to her own ears.

He slowly got up, rounded the desk, then held out his hand for her to take. She blinked up into his eyes, unsure what he was going to do.

"I say I start," he said. "But in order to do so, I need you to stand for me."

Mariah swallowed hard. Okay, so she was going to get

a lecture on her poor posture. It wasn't as if she'd hadn't heard it before. George often cracked that she walked like a guy. She considered Zach's hand, thought about not taking it, then forced herself to put her fingers in his. She was completely unprepared for the jolt that zinged through her, further heightening her awareness of the man gazing at her. Her tutor in all things sexy.

She stood on shaky legs and faced him, holding her shoulders rigid, chest out, just like one of her girlfriends had schooled her.

But Zach didn't tell her to stand differently. In fact, he wasn't paying attention to her posture at all. He was staring directly into her eyes, holding her captive. Then he trailed his fingers over her jaw then into her hair, leaned in and kissed her.

EVEN ZACH KNEW the meaning of the saying, "Never look a gift horse in the mouth." He'd read somewhere that it had something to do with rotting teeth, but that's not how he was interpreting it just then.

Mariah's lips were soft and irresistibly sweet. He brushed his mouth against them once, twice, then pressed against them more insistently.

One minute he had been wondering how to get her into the bed—so close but so empty—the next she was offering herself up to him.

Oh, yeah. He knew this wasn't what she had in mind. Her idea probably included makeshift chalkboards and longhand notes. But something in him had responded to her softly made request on a fundamental level he wasn't sure he wanted to explore just then. He only knew a need to kiss her, to show her how desirable she truly was. And now that he was doing that, he wanted more. Much more.

At first Mariah didn't appear to know how to respond

to the unexpected attention. Her lips were unmoving, her chocolate-brown eyes wide. Zach dipped his tongue inside the corner of her mouth and she made a strangled little sound that seemed to come from somewhere deep within. Then she leaned against him as if unable to stand without his support and her tongue made a few furtive moves of its own.

Good God, but the woman had no idea how incredibly wanted she already was. He slid his hand to rest at the back of her neck, finding her skin hot, her hair soft, as he deepened the kiss, stroking her tongue with his, exploring all the textures and tastes until his own breathing came in ragged gasps.

There was a directness about Mariah that was undeniable. The moment she registered what he had in mind, she pressed her hands flat against his shirtfront, plainly exploring the muscles beyond, boldly exploring the planes of his abdomen, then skimming back up and over his shoulders and arms. Each pass felt like a flame flicking along his nerve endings, making him want her more with each second that passed.

He felt her fingers on his pants front and drew in a quick breath. He trapped her hand with his and smiled down at her. The shadow of sudden uncertainty on her face made him want to groan. She genuinely didn't get it, how much he wanted her. Just a single move or gesture and she questioned it, then processed it as a rejection.

"I'm hesitating because I want to make sure this is what you want," he said quietly.

Her gaze moved from one of his eyes to the other, a playful smile tugging at her lips. "Do I strike you as the type of girl to do something she doesn't want to?"

He chuckled softly. "Oh, no, Mariah. You strike me as many things, but definitely not that."

She tugged his shirt out of his pants and rubbed her fingertips over his skin. His breath hissed out between his teeth.

"So hush up and let's continue our lesson."

She edged him toward the bed, then pushed him to lie across it, leaving him to wonder just who was supposed to be tutoring whom. From where he stood—or lay—Mariah didn't need any help in the sex department. She straddled him, then up and off went her T-shirt, revealing a plain white bra underneath. Then that scrap of material was gone, as well, revealing breasts that were more nipples than flesh. A groan wound through his groin then exited out his throat as he caught the stiff peaks between his fingers. She gasped and caught his hands, pressing them harder against her sweet flesh.

Mariah felt as though his palms were branding her, claiming her. She shifted her hips until she cradled his erection between her thighs, a shudder beginning somewhere down around her toes and winding up and up until she was positive her very hair shivered.

The combination of her doubts about him wanting her and the proof of his desire made her head swim with conflicting emotions. Emotions she wanted to clarify. To challenge until all that remained was pure human need. She fumbled for his belt buckle and pushed his shirt up. Her movements were erratic and anxious as the back of her fingers skimmed the skin of his chest and his abdomen, then lower to tug down his zipper.

In one smooth move Zach rolled her onto her back until she found herself trapped between him and the mattress. He kissed her deeply, then ran his tongue along the column of her neck. "I've been fantasizing about having you on top of me since watching you ride that horse," he whispered, then kissed her ear lobe. "But I'm afraid I don't have the patience for that right now."

She marveled at his words. He wanted her. Now. The knowledge was more powerful than any touch and filled her with such wanton longing she nearly cried out from the intensity of it. He quickly shed his shirt and his pants. With her eyes, she devoured every inch of him, from his well-developed biceps and six-pack abs to his narrow hips. She wondered if all Yanks were built as well as Zach Letterman without having spent an hour on a ranch. Then he shed his briefs and she saw the very proof of his want of her, thick and long and pulsing as he rolled a condom over the turgid flesh. Her breath caught in her throat and she restlessly wet her lips as she reached for him.

"Good God," he said between clenched teeth as he sank, inch by glorious inch, into her slick flesh.

Mariah's back arched off the bed and her hands grasped his hips. Otherwise she was rendered completely immobile. She could do little more than wonder at the scorching heat swirling inside her. She felt the contrasting sensations of being utterly filled yet hungry for an unnamable something hovering just beyond her reach.

A long, deep thrust brought her so much closer she nearly cried out. She dug her fingers into his firm rear and ground up against him.

Zach cursed against her neck then kissed her again, long and hard. "I don't know how long I'm going to be able to last, Mariah."

"Shush up, cowboy, and make love to me."

And he did. Sweat trickling from his handsome brow, his straight white teeth gnashing against each other, he lifted himself from her then rocked into her, his arms straining, every sculpted muscle standing out in relief. Mariah gasped for air and touched his biceps, fascinated with the size of them…the size of him as he surged inward again. She threw her head back and moaned, then heard a long, almost reluctant groan from him.

No, no, no, she wanted to cry out. Not yet.

But even as she thought the words, she knew it was too late. Zach grew rigid above her, driving deep and hard as he rode out his own climax. Mariah swallowed hard, biting back frustration and grasping his hips tightly to hers, seeking but knowing the moment was out of her reach for good.

Zach buried his face against her neck, his damp chest heaving against her bare breasts. Mariah blinked back sudden, hot tears as she drew her hands up and over his arms and back, her feet locked around his calves. She pressed a kiss to his shoulder, resisting the urge to bite into the salty flesh.

Long moments later, he drew back, his eyes intense and probing.

She smiled at him and kissed him, hoping to erase the curious look from his face. "Hmm…I'd say as first lessons go, that was a good one, Dr. Letterman."

A slight grin from him, but still the watchful shadow in his green eyes. "Nice try, Mariah." He propped himself on one elbow then drew a finger along the curve of her jawline, sending little shivers everywhere. "You didn't come, did you?"

Whoa. Okay, Mariah guessed there was a first time for everything. And that definitely applied here. She'd never been asked if she'd achieved orgasm before. Of course, she never had. Not during intercourse, anyway. But no one knew that except her.

"I, um…" She stumbled over the words.

He kissed her long and hard, his flesh still filling her to overflowing. "You're tense."

"I'm tired," she disagreed.

He squinted at her, as if the different way of looking at her would reveal something else. "Uh-huh."

He slipped a hand between them, the back of his fingers skimming her stomach. She drew in a quick breath, then gasped altogether when his fingertips sought and found the bit of flesh at the apex of her thighs. He gave a gentle tug then squeezed. Mariah's back came up off the bed and the chaos that had filled her moments before returned tenfold, swirling around and around, twisting and turning, until she was rendered breathless and tense. Then it exploded, chaos, rushing through her bloodstream at the speed of light, her muscles convulsing and quivering.

Sweet, long minutes later, she cracked her eyes open and stared at the man who hadn't moved but for his hand, his fingers still stroking her swollen flesh.

"How…how did you do that?"

He grinned, making her heart hiccup. "You don't really want me to answer that question, do you?"

She smiled. "No."

"I didn't think so."

He slowly slid his hand out from between them. Mariah braced herself for him to roll off her. Only he didn't. "Guess what happened while you were off having fun all by yourself?"

Mariah restlessly licked her lips. "What?"

He surged into her, chasing the air from her lungs.

"You don't really want me to answer that question, do you?"

Mariah moaned as he rocked into her again. "I, um, think you just did."

ZACH LAY BACK and watched Mariah sleep, holding her to his chest with one arm, his other hand supporting the back of his head. A complicated woman, this Mariah Clayborn.

He ran his fingertips along her arm and watched her nipples pucker and harden. One moment she'd been all hot and bothered, unable to get his pants off fast enough, the next minute she had tensed up on him so thoroughly that the sensation of her slick muscles squeezing him had inadvertently toppled him over the edge. Then the rapidness of her climax when he touched her told him there was a mental battle going on inside that pretty head of hers that he couldn't hope to understand. Not unless he could convince her to voluntarily share it. The problem was he didn't think she knew it was there, or have a clue how deep it went.

They'd continued having hot and steamy sex, and having had his first climax, he was able to sustain later bouts, but in order for Mariah to achieve orgasm he'd had to rely on other skills. Later on he'd used his probing fingers in conjunction with intercourse and had instantly blown apart when the tactic worked. But he felt a deep-rooted desire to have her reach her climax at the same time he did and for the same reason.

It was a desire he feared might be as deeply rooted as his need to change career paths and get a nationwide chain of Finders Keepers off the ground.

Zach frowned, taken aback by the comparison. Surely he wasn't comparing something as weighty as his need to do something more meaningful with his life with something as seemingly meaningless as sex with a woman he'd known for less than twenty-four hours? But as Mariah murmured in her sleep and sought closer contact with him, he knew that, indeed, he was.

But there was only so much a guy could do in the short time they had left together. In a few short hours they'd be on their way to Houston, where he'd probably say goodbye to her at the airport, then be on his way back to Midland to give Gawlick the wedding dress.

Zach removed the hand from behind his neck then rubbed his face, remembering the sensation earlier that they were being followed. Of course, if they were being followed, it was connected to the wedding dress. And once the dress was back in his client's hands, that would be over, too, wouldn't it?

He stared at the plain ceiling unblinkingly. One week ago everything had loomed simple. Difficult, maybe. Life altering, certainly. But simple. Now simple was turning into complicated. If Mariah could so easily unearth his lack of expertise in the art of private investigating, then surely others would, too. Fine, Jennifer knew he wasn't licensed yet, but she couldn't know how truly green he was.

He glanced at Mariah's sleeping face again, hearing a silent clock ticking in his head. She'd offered to show him the ropes. He'd agreed to show her how to be sexy. He swallowed hard. The only problem was, she'd send him into cardiac arrest if she were any sexier.

He trailed his fingers down over her hip. She shivered in her sleep, bringing a smile to his face as he edged his fingers over her hipbone toward the soft fleece between her thighs. Her breathing grew shallower. With the tip of his finger, he burrowed through her hair, seeking her fleshy core. Mariah moaned and lay back, her sweet thighs instantly opening to him.

Good God, but she was beautiful.

With her no longer lying across his chest, he carefully repositioned himself until he was down between her legs. They might not have much time, but he intended to make every minute count....

MARIAH SLOWLY AWAKENED, aware of the shallowness of her breath, of the scorching heat filling her stomach, and the heat that coursed through her veins, making her feel wonderfully, gloriously alive. And as much unlike herself as it was possible to be. ·

Something wet touched her between her legs and she moaned, half surprised to hear the sound rip from her throat and half amazed that Zach was positioned between her thighs, visually drinking in her swollen, pulsing womanhood. She licked her lips and tried to reposition herself.

"Shh," he told her, gently stilling her with a hand on her hip.

Truth was, she didn't think she could move if she tried. A languid peace and awareness swirled around and around in her. She was aware of the rasp of the soft sheets against her bare back, the cool air sweeping over her skin from a vent on the ceiling, and of Zach's fingers as he parted her then dipped his tongue inside. Mariah threw her head back and moaned, louder this time, her hands curling in the sheets on either side of her.

She couldn't remember a time when she'd felt this...hot. This...outside herself. Her desire seemed to be centered directly inside her chest, pulsing fire to the rest of her body. She seemed to float in some kind of parallel universe, not quite real, not quite asleep. She pulled in deep breaths, but they didn't seem enough to feed the fire raging out of control within her. Zach ran his tongue lengthwise over her clit. Her hips bucked from the mattress and her entire body tensed in climax. But before she could topple over the edge, Zach's tongue was gone. She restlessly licked her lips and cracked open her eyelids wide enough to see Zach's face mere millimeters from hers. Then he was filling her. Oh, how he was filling her. Every nerve ending shivered and her stomach quaked. Zach threw back his own head and groaned then drove all the way home and the thin piece of glass separating her from the rest of the world cracked and shattered altogether, giving her the most phenomenal climax she'd ever had in her life.

6

THE FOLLOWING MORNING back in her own hotel room, Mariah felt…well, different somehow. She seemed to be able to count off every spray of the shower on her sensitive skin. Could smell the subtle scent of chlorine in the water. And her body seemed to be in a constant state of arousal, her nipples pebbled, her womanhood pulsing, her stomach completely bottomless, as if hungry to be filled. And the desire had nothing to do with food, but rather the man in the other room, one incredible Zach Letterman.

She shut off the shower and reached for a towel, wondering at the thick terry and rubbing it languorously against her neck then down over her tingling breasts. Where she'd usually rush through the process of drying off, now she took her time.

Who knew sex could be this good? She certainly hadn't. Of course, she'd never actually spent the night with anyone before either. And, in retrospect, she probably shouldn't have fallen asleep in Zach's room either. But she'd been so emotionally and physically sated she'd drifted off without a second thought, only to wake up with his hot mouth pressed against her and then found out it got better yet…

Mariah shivered with remembrance as she wrapped

the towel around her and padded into the other room. She had an hour before they had to leave for the airport, yet it felt like she'd need at least two before she was ready. Not because she had anything to do. Rather she felt like doing nothing. She wanted to loll around on top of the bed and relive what she and Zach had shared.

She sat down on the mattress and gave in to the urge to lie back, even though she kept her feet on the floor. Why hadn't she spent the night with anyone before? While her father's ranch—where she lived—was out, all three of her boyfriends had had their own places. But she'd never drifted off to sleep in any of their beds. She idly fingered the terry of the robe, pulling the material more tightly across her breasts. And she'd certainly never walked around in this state of mind after any of her previous intimate encounters, seemingly in a dream, not caring what was happening at the office just then, what trouble George was getting himself into now, or what people might think if they found out she'd slept with Zach.

Okay, maybe the last one she was a little concerned about. But she wasn't even in the mood to tackle that point either right now.

She heard a sigh and realized it was her own. She giggled. *Giggled.* She'd never known herself to giggle before. And a tiny part was appalled that she was doing so now. But that part was easy to ignore.

She began swinging her feet back and forth, then forward and back. Zach. Heat rushed over her skin all over again and she turned her head against the bedspread, just a little embarrassed by all that she'd said and done last night, even though there was no one around to see her.

When she'd woken up this morning with her cheek plastered against Zach's wide chest, she half expected to be horrified by what they'd done. Instead she'd cuddled

up to him further, pressing herself against him. She had
looked up to find a smoldering expression on his face
as he watched her. She hadn't even been aghast to realize he'd been watching her sleep. She'd merely closed her
eyes again, smiled, and rubbed her cheek against the fine
hair on his chest.

Okay, so she was a no-good hootchie. She laughed
and rolled to her side. Her. Mariah Clayborn. A no-good
hootchie mama. Not only had she slept with a man she
barely knew, she'd done it again...and again...and again.

Her swinging foot hit something under the bed. She
continued to hit it until it dawned on her what it was.
Namely the suitcase holding the missing, no *found,* wedding dress.

Summoning a tad of energy, she lifted herself to a sitting position, then bent to pull the suitcase out, laying it on
the bed next to her. She sat staring at it for long minutes,
waiting to feel something other than completely blissed
out. Nothing. She smiled and popped the suitcase locks
then opened the top, staring down at the lovely wedding
dress inside.

She supposed it probably wouldn't hurt if she tried it on
just once. No one need know about it. And she was clean,
so she wouldn't stink it up or anything. If it even looked
like it wouldn't fit, she'd immediately put it back.

Stretching to her feet, she gently picked the delicate
garment up and held it to her naked front. The hem hit
the top of her feet. Measuring the lace to her sides and
waist, she thought it just might fit. She slowly undid the
buttons all the way down the back then carefully slipped
the ultra feminine material over her damp head. It slipped
over her nude body with the quietest of whispers, draping
where it was supposed to drape. She shivered again then
turned toward the full-size mirror, the image reflected

back at her taking her breath away. The dress made her look like she had a waist. She absently reached behind her and fastened the buttons she could reach, then turned to first one side, then the other, admiring the way the lace complemented her body, making her look like a woman through and through. If a quiet voice whispered to her that she was insane trying on a wedding dress, she made a concerted effort to ignore it. It wasn't her dress, after all. And since no one would know, she wasn't breaking any rules or anything.

She smoothed her hair back several times then twisted it into a loose knot on the top of her head. An image of her mother flashed through her mind, an old photo Mariah had on her bedroom night table. While she knew she was taller than her mother had been, and at least thirty pounds heavier, the resemblance was strong.

A crisp knock sounded at the door.

Mariah froze, her eyes growing round as she stared into the mirror.

"Mariah? I thought you might want to catch breakfast before we left."

Zach.

Not only was she trying on his client's wedding dress, she was going to get caught by Zach. Her pulse kicked up and she jerkily reached for the buttons on the back of the dress.

"Slowly, slowly," she whispered.

"Mariah?"

"Be right there," she called out.

She wove one way, then the other, trying to get a grip on the slippery pearl buttons, but her hands were damp and growing damper by the minute. She nearly wiped her palms on the lace, then caught herself and used the towel instead. Something poked her arm from the sleeve of the dress. She stared at it, spotting something shiny peeking out from the other side of the lace. It looked like a... She slid her fingers up the sleeve until she could tug the bracelet out. She stared at the piece of jewelry. Silver chain links with a polished silver heart that had Priscilla London engraved on it.

A chuckle from the hall.

"You know, you don't have to, uh, bother getting dressed, if that's the problem," Zach said through the door.

No, her problem lay in getting undressed, which was definitely a first for her.

She tucked the bracelet into the pocket of her jeans, which lay across the bed, and continued her battle with the dress.

"Mariah?"

She opened her mouth to tell him she didn't want breakfast, that she'd meet him downstairs in an hour. Only she was deathly afraid she might still be wearing the dress even then.

She dropped her hands to her sides and let out a long, frustrated breath then attacked the buttons again, hoping to enlist the mirror as an ally. No such luck.

Finally she swung open the door and stared defiantly at Zach's grinning face. His smile faded, though it remained in his rich green eyes.

"Is there something you'd like to tell me, Mariah?"

DAMN, BUT SHE LOOKED GOOD in the dress.

Zach knew just how sexy the woman in front of him was, both inside and out, but he hadn't been prepared for the sucker punch to the gut that seeing her in all that white lace would have on him. She looked...magical. Feminine. Utterly sexy.

"No, there's nothing I need to tell you," she said, looking flustered. "But I do have a question."

"Uh-huh."

She turned her back on him. "Could you get me out of this thing?"

Zach couldn't help chuckling as he followed her into the room, allowing the door to close behind him.

"Is this it? The dress?"

He knew it had to be, but there was a big difference between seeing a dress lying in a suitcase and seeing it on Mariah's subtle curves.

"Yeah, I, um…"

Zach's gaze drifted over the puffy shoulders, peeked at the skin between the upper part of the dress that she hadn't buttoned, then down over her sweet bottom.

"You…?" he prompted.

She sighed heavily. "I don't know what I was thinking, really. One minute I was looking at the stupid thing, the next thing I had it on."

"And now you can't get it off."

"That's all I needed. Someone to state the obvious."

Zach's grin widened. They'd said very little when they'd woken up this morning. In fact, Mariah had been notably quiet, though very happy, if the flush to her skin were any indication. And his ego was just big enough to allow him to think that. But in the half hour since she'd left his room, she had found her voice again and then some.

"Stop wiggling," he murmured into her ear.

She shivered. "I don't wiggle."

He rubbed his freshly shaved chin against the outer edge of her ear. "You definitely wiggle."

He licked her neck and kissed the damp area. She caught her breath. It was all Zach could do to remember that the dress she had on was his client's. He didn't think Denton Gawlick would appreciate his having sex with Mariah while she was in it, no matter how tempting the thought was of tugging up the long hem and seeing what she had on underneath.

"Zach, would you just please get me out of this thing?"

He rubbed his temple against her fresh-smelling hair. "I thought you'd never ask."

He found the tiny pearl buttons near her waist and started popping them loose, revealing her pink skin inch by inch. And revealing that she wore absolutely nothing underneath.

Dear God...

She had a pair of dimples at the top curve of her bottom that just begged to be licked and explored. And that was saying nothing about the shallow crevice between her firm, rounded flesh. He finished with the buttons, then slid his hand inside the lacy material and skimmed his palm along the curve of the warm flesh.

"Are you...done?" Mariah softly asked.

"I'm just getting started."

She stepped away from him, her face full of need and desire. "I meant with the buttons."

"Oh. Yes. I'm done."

And, oh boy, was he. And ready to move to the next step. Bursting with need to take the woman disrobing in front of him into his arms. He idly scratched his chin as she turned from him, presenting him with her bare bottom as she slid out of the dress then slipped into a pair of panties, her jeans, a bra and T-shirt. Zach couldn't help feeling a sting of disappointment. Or a wash of surprise.

Sure, he'd had relationships based on pure sex before. But he couldn't remember ever being this sex obsessed for this long a period before. Half of what he and Mariah did the night before would have sufficed usually. Now as he stood there watching her fold the dress, he feared that a weekful of last nights wouldn't be enough.

The problem was he didn't have a week with her. They'd get on that plane in an hour and a half, be in Houston an hour later and that would be all, she wrote. No more Mariah.

"Here," he said, watching as she folded then refolded the dress, her hands shaking. He took the dress from her. It was plain she was humiliated by having been caught wearing it and that she was more than a little distracted.

Her gaze slammed into his and she quickly licked her lips. "Okay. I'll, um, just go finish getting ready."

Zach opened his mouth to tell her she looked ready enough to him, but she had already zipped out of view.

He glanced at his watch, then the dress, a grin spread across his face. What would happen if they were to discover the dress had one carefully placed tear? It would have to be repaired before he could get it back to the client, right? He glanced toward the closed bathroom door and examined the material, his attention drawn to the hem where any damage and subsequent repair work would be the least noticeable. Okay, so ripping the dress would be devious at best, but he couldn't shake the niggling sensation that there was more going on here than a simple wedding dress recovery.

Besides, being around the delectable Mariah Clayborn a little longer wouldn't exactly be hell on earth.

He smiled wryly as the material gave way easily in his hands. *Mariah, forgive me...*

MARIAH CLOSED the bathroom door behind her, then leaned her hands against the counter. All she wanted to do was fill the sink with water and drown herself.

God, could she have been any more...pathetic? Trying

on another woman's dress. What was she thinking? She didn't even like to shop, because it usually entailed trying the clothes on before buying them, except when it came to jeans and T-shirts. Which explained why she had drawers full of the same, while her closet held nothing but nicer clothes she'd grown out of ten years ago.

"Mariah?"

Zach again.

She groaned.

Well, what had she thought? That he'd put the dress back in the suitcase and just leave?

She cracked open the door. "What?"

His face was very obviously minus his usual grin. He held up the dress, showing her a part of the hem. "Was this here before you tried the dress on?"

She carefully examined the material. A tear in the delicate lace. About three inches long and right in the front. She gently sifted through the material, hoping against hope that it was a trick of the light, that she'd shift back to where the tear was to find it gone.

No such luck.

There was very definitely a rip. And she had been the one who had ripped it.

"Oh, my God." She raised her eyes to stare into Zach's face. "I am so, so sorry. Had I even thought I would damage it, I would never have "

An inexplicable shadow crossed his face. "Maybe the tear was already there before you tried the dress on," he said, his gaze flicking over her features. "At any rate, I wouldn't worry too much about it." He walked back to the suitcase and she followed him out. "But I will, you know, need your help before I can return this to my client."

"Help?"

"Repairing it."

"You mean like sewing?"

He finished packing the dress and closed and locked the suitcase. "I mean like finding a professional to repair it."

She twisted her lips. "I know how to sew."

"An old wedding dress?"

"Socks."

"Ah."

She couldn't help the smile that threatened. Okay, so she wasn't exactly the domestic type. But she knew how to round up cattle with the best of them. And if you ever needed to catch a horse thief, well, she was your gal.

"Do you know of anyone in Houston?" Zach asked.

She blinked at him.

"You know, a qualified seamstress."

She thought about it a minute. "I, um, no."

He frowned.

"Oh, wait! I know someone. Only not in Houston. In Hoffland. That would be Miss Winona McFarland. Some say she used to be a fashion designer before she married Walt, who died a couple of years back. I hear tell that she takes in some sewing on the side to supplement her income."

"You think she might be able to repair this?"

Mariah shrugged. "I don't see why not."

He looked skeptical.

"If she can't, then she could probably recommend someone who can."

He finally nodded. "Good. Good." He picked up the suitcase. "I'll go put this in my room while you finish up. Meet you in the hall, say, in five minutes?"

She nodded. She'd only need two.

"You KNOW, I've never done anything like that before," Mariah said for the tenth time since she'd met up with

Zach again outside her room. "I don't know what got into me. I am so, so sorry."

Zach followed her outside the hotel restaurant. "No harm done."

Only they both knew that harm had been done. Namely to the dress, not to mention to Mariah's self-esteem.

Every time she thought about having to ask Zach to unzip her out of his client's wedding dress, she cringed straight down to her toes, and the little she'd managed to eat churned in her stomach.

Still, above and beyond all that, she couldn't help but be happy that she and Zach wouldn't be parting at the Houston airport.

Then again, maybe they would be.

She looked at him as he opened the passenger door to the rental car for the forty-mile drive to the airport in Huntsville. "Um, so I guess I'll take the dress at Hobby and have it couriered to you when it's repaired?" she asked.

He handed her into the car. "No. I'll be staying with the dress, if it's all the same to you."

"At Miss Winona's?"

"No. In Houston."

"You know, you could always stay at the ranch with Papa and me."

When she realized what she'd said, Mariah wanted to crawl under the car seat and die right then.

Okay, so it was the Texan way, being neighborly. But one did not invite a man she'd known for only a day to stay at the ranch along with her father.

She could only imagine how it looked to Zach.

Hootchie. That's what she was. A through and through hootchie.

"Why, thank you," Zach said. "I'll put the bags in the trunk."

Zach rounded the back of the car and opened the trunk.

Mariah closed her eyes and banged the back of her head against the seat. How was she going to get out of this one? She supposed she could make some sort of excuse when they reached Houston. Tell Zach she'd forgotten that her father had a cousin over, or was sick, or something equally lame. But wriggling out of the invite was even worse than the invite itself.

She felt for the bracelet she'd found snagged on the dress in her jeans pocket and sighed. Well, at least some extended time together would give her a chance to tell him about it. Not that she thought it made any difference. While she knew his client's name was Denton Gawlick, that didn't mean his wife hadn't kept her maiden name. But was it Priscilla London?

She twisted her lips in contemplation. At any rate, someone named Priscilla London would never have ripped a beautiful dress like that. Priscilla London would be pretty and ultrafeminine and would know just what to do with a man like Zach Letterman.

She peeked through the back window and watched as Zach hoisted his suitcase into the trunk, then lifted the recovered one. Movement caught her eye to the left. She craned her neck to see a suspicious guy dressed in a black long-sleeved shirt and pants and a knit ski mask quickly approaching the car.

"Zach!" she called out, blindly reaching for the door handle, her gaze fastened on to the two men at the back of the car. "Look out!"

Zach raised his head, a puzzled expression on his handsome face as the masked man drew close and grabbed the case.

"What the hell?" Zach refused to release his grip on the bag.

Mariah was outside in a second, but by the time she reached the back of the car, the thief was gone and Zach was flat on his rear on the asphalt, rubbing his chin.

"Are you okay?" she asked, helping to him to his feet.

"Fine, except for the dent to my ego." His grimace was as attractive as his grin. "Not only do you know I don't know how to handle a gun, it appears I'm not good at sparring either."

She smiled and checked his jaw. A fist-wide red splotch marred his smooth skin. "You would have wanted to trip him, not hit him."

"Would that be Lesson One?"

She laughed. "If you'd like." Her eyes widened. "Oh, no! The dress."

Mariah visually searched the area for the thief, then started in the most likely direction.

Zach caught her. "The dress is fine."

"What do you mean the dress is fine? Someone just stole it."

He shook his head and reached inside the truck. "No, someone just thinks they stole it." He popped opened the top of his suitcase. Inside lay the dress, the seed pearls sparkling in the sunlight. "I switched bags upstairs."

"Oh." She lifted her gaze to his handsome face. "Oh!"

He put the bag back inside and closed the trunk. "So, now will you believe that someone was following us last night?"

She twisted her lips and got into the car, waiting until he slid into the driver's seat beside her. "If that's the case, then the guy looking for a wedding dress at the Unclaimed Baggage Center wasn't a coincidence, either."

"Not if he knew which suitcase to take."

"Hmm," Mariah agreed. "The question is, who would want to steal it and why?"

"Jilted boyfriend?"

"Didn't you say your clients were *renewing* their vows?"

"Jilted lover?"

She curved her fingers around his arm then lay her head against his shoulder. "I hope Miss Winona's going to need some time to fix that dress, because you, Mr. Letterman, are going to need an awful lot of training in the art of private investigating."

"Hey, I switched the bags."

She smiled up at him. "Yeah, that you did, didn't you?"

He curved his other hand over hers, sending a jolt of awareness rippling through her bloodstream.

What went unsaid was the rest of the agreement they'd made last night. That in return for her helping him to become a P.I., he was going to train her on how to be sexy.

Just thinking about it made Mariah hot all over.

7

"YOU REALLY SHOULD have reported your bag stolen," Mariah was saying from where she took the seat behind her desk. Zach noticed the way she checked it for dampness, then glanced at the ceiling. The hole that had been there the previous morning was now patched up, the plaster whiter against the remainder of the ceiling. She frowned and sat down.

"To whom should I have reported the incident?" he asked. "The police? We would have missed our flight. The hotel? They would have claimed no responsibility."

At any rate, he didn't have anything in the bag that wasn't replaceable. Two changes of clothes, underwear, his toothbrush and an array of books on private investigating. The rest of his things were in his house in Indiana. As soon as he found a temporary apartment in Midland, he planned to fly back to Indiana to retrieve more of his personal items and clothing to see him through his stretch in Texas.

"They might have caught the thief," Mariah pointed out.

"If we're right in our assumptions, then the thief wasn't from there, anyway. In fact, he may have been on the same flight back to Houston as us."

Mariah grimaced. "Yeah, I thought about that, too. You think it was the old geezer in 15B?"

"I'd put my money on the blonde in 25C."

That got a smile from her, which was a rare occurrence since he'd caught her wearing the Gawlick wedding dress earlier that morning. The change in her demeanor made him feel guiltier than hell for having torn the dress and allowed her to believe she had done it. He hadn't intended for things to go down that way. Still, somehow she seemed more preoccupied than just mildly embarrassed, a state that seemed to increase after her impromptu invitation to stay at her father's ranch. Presumably with her.

The mere thought of spending more private time with her was enough to make him almost uncomfortably aroused.

If she did regret the hasty invitation, he wasn't going to make it easy for her to back out. The truth was, he wanted to be around Mariah Clayborn for as much as time as he could shake out of the deal. Yes, it was the sex. But there was something else there. Something that emerged as a mystery to him, a mystery he wanted to solve. Not just about the sexy woman herself, but his inexplicably insatiable desire for her. And it was something that left him just wanting to be in her company whether they had sex or not. He wanted to unlock all of her secrets. Find out the name of her first-grade teacher. Know what her favorite color was.

Mariah frowned then blinked up at him, her cheeks instantly coloring. "What's Gawlick's wife's name?"

Zach raised his brows. "Why?"

She averted his gaze and shrugged. "Just curious."

"Peggy Sue."

She looked thoughtful for a moment. "Peggy wouldn't happen to be short for Priscilla, would it?"

"I'd say no." He squinted at her, sensing she wasn't telling him something. "May I use your phone?" He indicated the empty desk across from her.

"Oh. Sure, go ahead. Nobody else is using it." She took a deep breath and attacked some papers on top of her desk. "Where in the blue blazes is George anyway?"

"Lunch?"

"Is it that late already?" She glanced at her watch. "Of course. Lunch. How could I forget? Lord forbid George should arrange to eat something here while I was away."

Zach chuckled then picked up the receiver on George's desk and dialed Jennifer Madison's number in Midland. When she picked up, it sounded as if things hadn't let up any since he'd left. He explained the situation to her, promised to call Gawlick to keep him informed, then broke the connection, his mind still on Mariah's curious questions moments before.

When he'd driven out to Denton Gawlick's impressive estate in Odessa, he'd done so without reservations and with the sole purpose of making contact with the client and reassuring him he would get the job done. Since the dress was wanted for vow renewal, he hadn't been surprised to find Denton and his wife in their fifties. He would have been surprised if they were in their twenties. But once he'd gotten a look at the dress itself, alarm bells went off.

He turned and watched Mariah balance the telephone receiver between her chin and shoulder and rifle through some papers. Her brow was creased in concentration and a smile was nowhere to be found, but he still found her completely irresistible. He scratched his chin, trying to recall what Gawlick had told him.

"Peggy Sue found the dress in Boston and just had to have it. She won't go through with the ceremony without it. Do you know how much cash I have buried in that ceremony?"

Peggy Sue had a sweetly polite disposition…and she was too large to fit into the dress.

On the other hand, the dress had fit Mariah to perfection.

He leaned on the corner of the desk and crossed his arms over his chest, wondering just where in the hell that thought had come from. It seemed the ongoing case of the missing wedding dress was making him hear wedding bells all over the place. Bells he had no intention of heeding.

Mariah finished her call, then scribbled something down on a notepad. The telephone rang again. She automatically moved her hand to pick it up, then glanced at the caller display. Her hand froze before she snatched it back and used it to smooth down the soft cotton of her T-shirt over her flat abs.

The ex. Zach didn't have any doubt that's who she was avoiding.

He considered the puzzle that was Mariah. Yesterday he'd guessed that she was more embarrassed than upset that her ex-boyfriend had become engaged to someone else mere days after they'd stopped seeing each other. Yet in Alabama she'd tried on the Gawlick wedding dress. Could it be that she had hoped to marry the ex? The thought was unsettling. Especially coming as it did on the heels of their explosive night together.

The thought of Mariah carrying a torch for someone else ignited other feelings in him, as well. Jealousy being front and center. That thought shocked him solely because he couldn't recall ever being jealous of any of the women he'd dated. Not that he and Mariah were dating. Was that why the big, green-eyed monster was paying him a visit now?

"You want to catch some lunch?" he asked, breaking the silence that ensued after the phone had stopped ringing.

She blinked at him. "We just got here."

He grinned. "Yes, I know. But we *are* here. And I was hoping you'd show me some of Houston's eateries. Then we could take the dress in for repair."

She blinked at him again, appearing not to know how to respond. As if of its on accord, her gaze skimmed him from the tips of his toes to the top of his head. If the deepening of her flush was anything to go by, he'd guess that food was the farthest thing from her mind just then—making it the same with him. Need snaked through his groin until he virtually throbbed with it. He looked through the same door she had earlier, seeing that the back room was empty and had lots of tabletops they could make use of.

But that wouldn't serve his purpose. Because he wanted to go on a date with Mariah Clayborn.

Lunch.

Mariah swallowed hard, thinking that after the morning's, not to mention last night's, events, she wanted to find a little space to come to terms with everything. She wanted familiarity. To put everything back in order.

Unfortunately she had the feeling that nothing would be normal again. And since gaining space would mean sending Zach to a hotel, she wasn't willing to go that far, either.

She rubbed her forehead, then pushed her bangs back. She felt so…sizzlingly aware of the man standing across from her looking like temptation incarnate. So confused. So damn…conflicted.

A desperate part of her wanted to send him on his way. Tell him to go shopping to replace the items that were stolen from him. At the same time she was thinking that he was about the same height as George, though wider through the shoulders and chest, and George could probably lend him a couple pairs of jeans or something until he flew back to Midland.

She was filled with the sudden desire to bang her forehead against the desk in the hope that it would shake her thoughts straight.

"After that large breakfast, I'm not very hungry right now," she said quietly.

His eyes twinkled at her as if he was aware of everything she'd just been thinking.

Mariah fidgeted, nearly sighing in relief when George came through the front door, a takeout bag from a Tex-Mex place up the street in his hand.

"You're back," he said to Mariah. "Nice to see you again, Zach."

"Same here," Zach said.

Mariah looked at her cousin. She'd been in the office for at least twenty minutes. It didn't take twenty minutes to pick up takeout. "Anything interesting happen while I was in Alabama?"

"Nope." George rounded his desk and sat down.

"No one called with leads on the Thompson case?"

"Nope."

"No new clients?"

He seemed to hesitate. "Nope."

Mariah supposed she should be glad. Had a new client dropped in, or one of her feelers come back, George probably would have mucked it up anyway.

She scanned the paperwork on her desk, none of it looking particularly urgent, and none of it capable of grabbing her attention. She noted Zach was watching her with one of those strikingly handsome half grins on his face. She suddenly had difficulty swallowing.

She grabbed her purse and got up. "George, hold the

fort down for me, will you? I'm going to take Zach out to the ranch."

"The ranch?" George said, his brows rising as he looked between her and Zach.

"Yeah, he's going to be staying with Papa and me for a day or two." She didn't think it necessary to go into detail about how she'd nearly destroyed a client's property and that was the reason Zach was stuck in town. "Oh, and you wouldn't happen to have any clothes you could let Zach borrow, would you? Someone lifted his bag in Alabama."

"Sure. I'll bring something by the ranch later."

"Good."

She avoided meeting her cousin's gaze again, not wanting to see the speculative gleam in his eyes. Let him think what he wanted. Only she had to know that she'd never invited anyone to stay out at the ranch with her. The men she had dated before had already known her father, so there had been no need for introductions.

Oh boy, what was she getting herself into?

"You ready?"

Zach's grin told her he was. Only it seemed to indicate he was ready for much more than she was willing to consider in present company. In fact, it would be a good idea if she just avoided the whole topic altogether since they were going out to the ranch. Her father probably wouldn't appreciate her learning the finer points of great sex under his roof.

She opened the door and Zach followed her out.

Not that she was going to tell Zach that.

She climbed into Nelly, then reached over to unlock the door for him. Why she continued to lock the moving pile of rust was beyond her, but she figured it was a good habit. After all, she wouldn't want anyone stealing all her fast-food wrappers.

Speaking of which, she pulled out a couple of stubborn ones that had wedged into the crack of the seat, before Zach got in, then smiled at him as if he hadn't just seen what she'd done.

"I, um, have to warn you, my father's a pretty gruff guy."

"I can do gruff."

"Yeah, I bet you can."

She had the feeling he could charm the skin off a snake with just one grin if he put his mind to it.

"Fasten your seat belt," she reminded him. "This is going to be a bumpy ride."

"ARE YOU RIGHT-HANDED or left?" Mariah asked him.

Zach squinted against the early afternoon sun to where she stood a foot away from him in a fresh pair of jeans and another T-shirt. Purple this time, with the name of a footwear company emblazoned across the front. "Right."

"Okay then." She slid her gun out of the back of her jeans then swiveled him to face an old wood slat fence some twenty feet away. Cans lined the top. Empty, he hoped. "You'll want to hold the gun in your right hand, then use your left to help balance the weight and steady it."

He held the gun out in his right and closed one eye to aim. "I can handle it pretty well with one hand."

"You say that now." She stepped behind him and pushed up his other hand, forcing him to hold the gun with both. "Why don't you get used to the kick before you go around one-handed, okay?"

Kick. Now that was a word. Because, right now, feeling her soft front pressed against his back made a lot of things kick into gear. His pulse, for one, and his arousal, for two.

"Feet shoulder-width apart," she said, positioning her

booted foot between his legs and nudging his feet to the side.

Damn. He supposed he wasn't the first guy to get turned on by a woman teaching him how to shoot a gun, but he was pretty sure he should be focusing on what she was telling him rather than how he wished the hand that rested on his hip would move a little to the right and south.

He hadn't known what he'd expected when Mariah had brought him out to the ranch she shared her with her father. Probably that his high state of awareness would lessen a bit. But when they'd pulled up in front of the long, one-story ranch house, there hadn't been a soul in sight. Mariah had said they'd all probably be back by five or so, but that they usually took their meals out at the ranch house where Red, a retired cowboy who now looked after the others, would have fixed dinner. When he'd asked if that's where she ate, she'd avoided his gaze. Judging by the number of fast-food wrappers littering the inside of her truck, he'd chance a no.

The house was simple but clean, the furniture old but not ratty. There wasn't a single plant in sight, though, and there was a silence about the place that made him want to lower his voice when he spoke. Pictures of a woman, Mariah's mother, he guessed, were hung and set all over the house, a ghost of sorts whose eyes followed you wherever you went. He had tried to imagine a young girl in this environment and couldn't quite capture it. While newspapers and magazines were stacked on the coffee table, they had looked out-of-date. And the only dish in the dish rack was a coffee cup. Sure, Mariah had been out of town that morning, but he'd guessed that the only addition with her presence would be another coffee cup.

"You're not paying attention," Mariah accused, looking over his shoulder.

"You're right, I'm not." He repositioned his feet the way she had suggested. "It's a bit hard to concentrate when you're up against me like that."

He'd half expected her to move away from him. But for a long, lingering moment she stayed put. Even pressed more suggestively against him.

"Mariah, it's a good thing the gun's pointing the other way or we'd both be in trouble."

Her husky laugh teased his ear. "Don't worry, cowboy. I won't let anything happen to you." Her hand seemed to brand his hip where she'd splayed her fingers flat and lightly stroked him. "Not anything bad anyway."

Then her heat was gone, leaving him standing with the warm Texas wind whipping around him.

"See if you can hit the can on the far left," she said.

"I'll be lucky to hit a can at all," he murmured.

Judging by her quiet laugh, she must have heard him.

He squeezed off a round, unprepared for the kick that she'd mentioned earlier. His hands jerked up and the bullet went some twenty feet above the target.

"Whoa," he said, breathing in the sharp scent of gunpowder. "This baby packs a punch."

"Yeah, and it'll put a hole in you the size of a pizza. Extra large." She came to stand behind him again. "Aim lower this time, allowing for the kick." She skimmed her hands over his outer arms then steadied his hands. Zach could swear he could feel her nipples spear him from under her T-shirt and through his shirt. He heard her lick her lips as she removed her hands. "Try again."

He did, with only moderately better results.

"At this rate I'll be lucky to hit the fence." He dropped the gun to his side and looked at her. "Dare I ask how long it took you to hit the cans?"

"Second try. I was seven and my father gave me a .22."

"Seven, huh?" he asked, raising his brows.

She smiled. "Things are different down here in Texas."

"I'll say. Have many drive-bys?"

"Drive-bys?"

"Never mind."

With everyone and their brother armed in Texas, he figured a drive-by shooting would be akin to launching World War III.

"Oh, damn." She looked at her watch. "It's my night to cook dinner."

"For the ranch hands?"

She shook her head as she looked out on the plains. "No. For my father." She'd pulled her hair into a ponytail before they'd come out, but the wind had torn a good deal of it out, leaving wisps blowing across her pretty face.

He checked the gun, making sure to slip the safety into place.

"That's okay. You go on ahead and practice. I'll just be inside in the kitchen." She gestured toward the large window overlooking the back.

"I'd much rather watch you cook dinner."

She grimaced. "Trust me, it's an experience you'll enjoy missing." She squinted her eyes. "Besides, the next time we run into trouble, I want to be reasonably sure you're capable of protecting me."

Why all of the sudden did Zach feel his chest puff out and his shoulders widen? "Oh, yeah?"

Her teasing smile lit her whole face. "Yeah."

MARIAH WASN'T SURE why she'd said that, about Zach's protecting her, considering that she wouldn't allow a ranch hand to help her up if she were drowning in quicksand, but somehow it had seemed the right thing to say at the time. And it had felt right.

She peeled a couple of Spanish onions in the sink and watched him squeeze off another round, his shots getting closer and closer to the targets. If there was any irony in the fact that she'd picked the one man probably the most incapable of protecting her to say the words to, well, that wasn't lost on her. Her father had always told her she had to do things the hard way or no way at all.

She brushed a few stray strands of hair with the back of her hand and sighed. Of course, since she was talking about Zach, she had to admit that he soon wouldn't be around to protect anyone, much less her.

On the drive out they'd stopped by Miss Winona's cute little clapboard house about five miles east of the ranch. Yes, she'd told them, she could fix the dress. But it would probably take her a day or two to find the right texture and color of thread to do the job. She was going to call them later tonight at the ranch to report on her progress. Zach had been generous in paying her in advance, but it hadn't made a difference in Miss Winona's time estimate.

One more day, maybe two days tops, and Zach would be on a plane for Midland. Mariah turned from the sink and cut the onion, wiping her eyes as she did so. God, she hated cutting onions.

"Those aren't for me, are they?"

Mariah blinked to find Zach standing in the kitchen doorway, taking a close inventory of her.

"What, the tears? Ha. I never cry. Ask anybody."

He washed his hands then came to stand next to her. She swore she could feel his heat penetrate her jeans and T-shirt, despite the few inches that separated them. "I'm not asking anybody. I'm asking you," he said quietly.

She glanced at him. "I never cry," she answered.

His gaze flicked over her face as she finished cutting the onions then wiped her eyes on the sleeves of her shirt.

"Well, except when I'm cutting onions. Useless act, crying. It never solves anything."

"It doesn't bring anyone back either," he said quietly.

"No," she said after a long moment. "No, it doesn't."

They didn't have to clarify that they were talking about death. They'd both lost their mothers at a young age, so she knew what he was referring to. And, yes, she had cried after her mother had died. For days. But rather than helping to fill the hole that gaped inside her, it instead seemed to widen it. Everything she did, everything she said, seemed to emphasis the loss of her mother. It even got to the point where she and her father barely spoke at dinner for months because she was afraid she'd say something that would remind them both of Nadine Clayborn.

"What are you making?" he asked, taking the other onion, then picking up another knife that lay nearby.

"Meat loaf." She frowned and looked inside the large metal bowl where she'd put ground beef and the onion.

He adjusted his motions so that he cut smaller pieces. "You'll want to cut them like this. You want to taste the onions, but not see them."

She lifted her gaze to his face. "You cook?"

"You didn't live with my grandmother without learning how to cook." He smiled. "She used to test me."

"She didn't!"

"Oh, yeah. Every Saturday I would be in charge of dinner, from the grocery shopping to the temperature of the oven. She wouldn't be in the kitchen while I cooked, but I'll be damned if she didn't know I had the burner on high instead of simmer."

"I never knew any of my grandparents," Mariah said. "How old is she, your grandmother?"

His hands slowed. "She died last year."

"I'm sorry."

"Don't be. She was ninety-two. And probably damn happy to be over with it." He cleared his throat. "She was pretty sick there near the end."

Mariah opened her mouth to say she was sorry again, then snapped it shut and nodded her understanding instead.

"Do you have any breadcrumbs?" he asked.

Mariah blinked at him. "Oh. The meat loaf. I, um, just usually crumble whatever bread we have lying around." She grabbed a loaf and took out a couple of pieces.

He eyed them. "Next time try leaving a couple of pieces out in the morning and let them get stale. It affects the consistency."

Mariah couldn't help laughing. "Okay. Thanks."

Silence reigned as the two of them put their heads together to fix the meal. Finally Zach put the loaf into the oven, had some sort of sweet tomato mustard sauce ready to pour over the top later in the cooking time, and washed his hands. Mariah was cleaning up the mess they'd made, but somewhere between washing the metal bowl and running the trash disposal, she became acutely aware of Zach's gaze on her. Her skin grew hot as she moved around the kitchen. If she presented him with her front, her nipples grew hard under his visual perusal. If she turned her back, shivers ran up and down her spine, making her very aware of her bottom and the way she moved it.

"You know," he said quietly, his voice stroking her like a caress. "We could always push forward with the other part of our deal."

Mariah anxiously licked her lips, the words "push forward" making her damp. "You have some advice you'd like to give on my appearance?"

His eyes twinkled seductively. "Uh-huh. I'd like to have you out of those clothes. Now."

Her breath caught in her throat. "And what would you like me to put on instead?"

"Me."

She laughed, but the sound wasn't in the least bit funny. The truth was, she wanted to put him on that instant. Yearned to stretch out on top of the butcher-block island and have him continue where they'd left off early that morning. Fit his arousal against her slick heat then enter her to the hilt. Feel his hands on her bottom, squeezing possessively as he madly thrust into her. Feel the sensation of his tongue lapping her breasts, his thumb rubbing her ultra-sensitive bud.

She gasped, realizing she'd come awfully near to climaxing just thinking about what they could be doing right then. She, who could count the number of climaxes she'd had prior to meeting Zach with one hand.

Mariah took in his heated gaze then tugged the hem of her T-shirt out of jeans. "Just remember later that you asked for this."

8

ZACH DIDN'T THINK he'd ever seen anything more beautiful than Mariah stripping in the middle of the kitchen with the late-afternoon sunlight slanting through the window. Despite the time she must spend outside, her skin was like fine white chocolate and his mouth watered with the desire to taste each inch of glorious skin she bared. Her T-shirt came off. Next her boots and jeans, until she stood clad only in a plain bra that had anything but a plain effect, and white cotton panties.

Damn. He'd never seen anything sexier in his life. She touched him in a powerful way without even laying a finger on him. His gaze drifted to where she'd hooked her thumbs in the waist of her panties. She drew the material down, then slowly back up again. He looked into her face to find her wearing a teasing closemouthed smile.

Oh, she didn't need any cues on how to become sexier. The woman was already more than any two men could handle.

"Zach?" she said softly. "I'm getting cold." She skimmed one hand up to her mouth, moistened the tip, then dipped it inside the front of her left cup. He could see her nipple harden further through the material. "See," she whispered.

Oh, yeah. He saw a lot.

"Come here," he said, crooking his finger at her.

She slowly shook her head, causing her dark hair to sway in front of her face then back again, a strand catching on her bottom lip. He nearly groaned.

"No. You come here."

He did. Faster than she apparently expected, because she gasped when he hauled her into his arms, his hands diving for her lush bottom, his right leg parting hers so that his thigh rubbed enticingly against her heated core.

"Mmm," she moaned, grasping his shoulders as if for balance. "That's nice."

Nice wasn't exactly what he was going for. He wanted wild. Out of control. White-light insanity. He ran his fingers along her bottom then slid them under the elastic of one leg, not stopping until the tips found the shallow crevice he sought. With infinite care, he parted her. She gasped and he kissed her, then slid his index finger inside.

Her low moan was nearly his undoing. Damn, but the woman seemed to control him as easily as a light switch. He hitched her leg up over his hip then pressed himself against her softness, continuing his intimate stroking. She began rocking her hips in time with his thrusts, shifting her head this way and that as the tempo of their kiss increased. She tasted of mint toothpaste and Texas summer and he wanted to devour her whole.

"Mar, you back yet?"

Zach froze, hearing the words before he'd registered that the back door behind him had opened.

Mariah gasped again, but this time for an altogether different reason. She tugged her leg free and stared into Zach's face, desperation written all over her flushed features.

Zach quickly turned, hiding the unclothed Mariah behind him. Just inside the door stood a hulking chunk of a man as tall as Zach but twice as wide, his face a map of how many years he'd spent out on the range. Stubble dotted his dark skin and his blue eyes were piercing where they'd caught and held on the couple in the middle of his kitchen.

"Daddy!" Mariah said softly. "You're...early."

The older man cocked a salt-and-pepper brow. "And you, my dear girl, are naked."

"I'm not...naked."

Zach fought a grin. Not yet, she wasn't. But if they'd had a couple of moments more she would have been. So would he have been, for that matter.

He spotted Mariah's jeans in front of him. He stretched out his foot and scooted them to her.

"Thanks," she mumbled.

"Don't mention it."

Having somewhat recovered from his shock, the elder Clayborn took off his weathered cowboy hat and hung it near the door, then faced Zach again.

"Do I know you, boy?"

"No, sir, you don't." Zach started to move to offer to shake his hand, but stopped when Mariah made a small, strangled sound in her throat. "I'm Zach Letterman. It's a pleasure to meet you."

If Zach wasn't mistaken, that was amusement lighting the older man's eyes. "More like it's a pleasure to meet my daughter." He stepped to the sink and started to wash up. "You ain't from around these parts, are you, son?"

"No, I'm not." Mariah finally finished putting herself together, all but for her boots, and stepped up to Zach's side. "I'm from Indiana."

"Yes, well, if you know what's good for you, that's exactly where you'd be heading before I turn back around."

"Daddy!" Mariah said, clearly astounded. "That's no way to talk to our guest."

"Guest?" Hughie turned around.

"Yes, guest." Mariah bent to pick up her boots. "Zach and I are working on a case together and he didn't have anywhere to stay so I invited him to bunk with us for a day or two."

"No place to stay? What? Is the man homeless?"

Zach chuckled. "In a manner of speaking, sir."

Mariah leaned closer and whispered, "Don't call him *sir*. It'll go to his head."

"So explain yourself, then."

"I'm resettling in Midland, but am following up on a case here in Houston. That's how Mariah and I met."

"And that's how you came to be caught going at it like rabbits in my kitchen, then?"

Mariah rolled her eyes. "We were not going at it like rabbits."

"That's the way it looked to me." Hughie narrowed his eyes on his daughter. "This the guy you stayed with in Alabama?"

Mariah stepped to the refrigerator and took out a milk carton, then to a cupboard where she collected a glass. "Here, drink your milk and shush up about this, will you?"

Zach didn't know what to expect from the older man, but was surprised when he roared with laughter. He accepted the glass then pointed a finger at Mariah. "I knew you had it in you somewhere, girl. I guess it was just a matter of the proper timing, wasn't it?"

Mariah turned brighter than her T-shirt.

Hughie drank down his milk then rinsed the glass. "Zach, you don't know how I worried about this girl. Never caught her playing doctor in the closet with one of the neighbor boys, or spin the bottle at a pajama party. Hell, she didn't even go to the prom."

"Daddy," Mariah said in warning.

"What? You don't want me talking to our guest?"

"Not if it's me you're talking about."

"Well, hell, what would you have us discuss then?"

She whacked a rolled-up newspaper into his stomach. The older man groaned and caught it. "How about the weather?"

"It's summer, it's hot. Now what?"

Mariah rolled her eyes to stare at the ceiling, then pushed her father toward the door. "Go catch a shower, old man. Dinner will be ready in a half hour."

MARIAH HAD NEVER been so embarrassed in her life. At twenty-six years old caught making out with a stranger in her underwear in her father's kitchen. She hadn't even kissed any of the other guys she'd dated inside the house and here she had nearly had sex with Zach right there in the middle of the floor.

She leaned her hands against the island to stop them from trembling. She jumped when she felt Zach's fingers on her shoulders.

"Wow, you're wound up tighter than a ball of string."

"You would be, too, if you knew my father a little better."

He kneaded her muscles, but she battled against relaxing into his touch, a battle she found herself quickly losing.

"Oh. I don't think he's such a bad guy." He leaned against her, his arousal indicating that he'd been affected not at all by the interruption. "At least he didn't go for the shotgun."

She laughed. "You've been watching too many movies."

"I don't know. So far, much of what I've seen about

Texas is a lot like the movies." His hands smoothed down over her arms then back up again, leaving goose bumps in their wake. "Except for you, of course."

She turned in his arms and gazed up at him. "Why? Because I'm not movie material?"

He hooked his finger under her chin. "No, because this reality is too much like fantasy to be real."

Mariah's heart hiccuped in her chest. She didn't think anyone had ever said anything so nice to her. She dropped her lashes and stared at the crisp whiteness of Zach's shirt, though he still held her chin up with his finger. "You know, I have to say that I don't think you're fulfilling your end of the bargain."

"Oh," he said, and she could hear the smile in his voice. "How so?"

She shrugged and he released her chin, although he didn't move from where he had her pinned against the counter. "You haven't said one thing about how you'd really like to see me dressed—what I should say, how I should do my hair."

"Is that what you want me to do?"

She made a face. "I don't know. I suppose I want you to tell me what you think makes a woman sexy."

"Dinner ready yet?" Hughie boomed as he came back into the room. "I'm starving."

Mariah rolled her eyes to stare at the ceiling, not daring to look at Zach's face for fear of what she'd see there. Afraid her words would make him take a closer look at her and find her lacking. Find her as plain and as unappealing as her exes apparently had.

Finally she was forced to look at him in order to convey the importance that he let her go now that her father was back in the room. What she saw in his eyes made her knees go weak. Desire was there, yes. But also a heat that had little to do with sex and a lot to do with her.

"Hey, Letterman, you going to let my daughter get me some grub or what?"

"Actually, I thought I'd do the honors tonight, if you don't mind."

Mariah stared at him as if he'd gone insane.

"You know, by way of thanking you for having me while I'm in town."

"Hell, boy, the words are enough." Hughie took a seat at the table. "Come over here and sit down with me and tell me about yourself. I figure you owe me that much considering I caught you making out with my daughter in my kitchen."

"Dad…"

Zach laid a finger across her lips. "That's okay. I'll get this one."

Mariah swallowed with difficulty. She'd never had anyone offer to help her with dinner before, much less with her father.

Zach swiveled her around and sat her down in the chair next to her father, who looked at them both with raised brows.

"Why don't I let Mariah tell you about Claude Ray and we can all talk while I serve?"

HUGHIE CLAYBORN WAS LAUGHING so hard he was crying. "So the clip dropped to the dirt?"

Mariah smiled as she took a sip of her coffee while Zach watched them both with growing admiration.

It wasn't often that he got a look at other families up close and personal. And the only thing he had to compare Mariah and Hughie's relationship to was his own with his grandmother.

"A Northerner like me doesn't have much use for guns," Zach offered up a mock protest.

"A Yank like you wouldn't last a week by himself here," Hughie said, wiping the dampness from the corner of his eyes with the heel of his large, callused hand.

"You make it sound like gunfights are a daily event for us in Texas, Dad," Mariah said. "Life in the big cities here—Dallas, Houston—is just like life in other cities."

Hughie shrugged. "Maybe so. But I'm saying a man isn't worth his salt if he can't survive on the brushlands."

"You mean catching cattle rustlers?" Zach asked.

Both Hughie and Mariah looked at him as if he'd gone soft in the head.

Hughie sighed, all amusement gone from his face. "I mean putting a cow out of her misery after she's gotten herself tangled hopelessly in a length of wire fence. Or shooting rattlesnakes. Or chasing off coyotes. Or riding all day in the Texas heat and discovering you drank your last bit of water an hour ago and knowing it's going to be another two before you see a drop of the precious resource. Or steering your cattle to a pasture where they can graze if the sun hasn't scorched the land. Now that's what being a rancher is really about."

Zach pondered what the big man had said.

A good three hours had passed since Zach had served dinner and the threesome was still seated around the table. Conversation had flowed easily, blending with the sound of the first crickets outside the open kitchen window. Zach glanced out now, surprised to find the sky filled with red clouds set against a dark azure sky, the sun saying its final farewell until the morning.

Hughie broke into his thoughts. "Of course, there's always a way for you to find out firsthand what being a Texan is really about."

"Dad, I don't think Zach has the time or the inclination," Mariah said, collecting their empty dessert plates and coffee cups and carrying them to the sink.

Zach met the old man's gaze, noting the challenge in them. "Oh, I don't know. When did you say Miss Winona would be done, Mariah?"

"She said she'd be getting the thread tomorrow afternoon…" She turned to face them. "Oh, no."

Zach leaned back in his chair and shrugged. "Why not? I don't think I'm going to get another offer like this in my lifetime."

Mariah put her hands flat on the counter. "Trust me, you'll regret having gotten this one if you take him up on it."

Hughie crossed his arms over his barrel chest. "What's wrong with inviting the guy to ride with me, Mar?"

She stalked over to the table. "I'll tell you what's wrong with it. I know you, that's what. You'll go out of your way to make sure everything that can go wrong with his experience will go wrong."

Zach's gaze drifted to Mariah's face. Her color was high. Her dark eyes were throwing sparks. And he suspected she'd just revealed an important part of her upbringing without meaning to.

Had Mariah wanted to be a cowboy so bad she could taste it? Had her father invited her out for a similar ride? And had he thrown up every roadblock to try to keep his daughter from achieving her dream, simply because it wasn't his dream for her?

Hughie chuckled softly then cleared his throat. "Considering Letterman's first experience with a gun yesterday, I don't think I'll have to do any of that."

"Dad…"

"No, it's okay," Zach said, wondering what Hughie,

himself, would reveal once they were alone. And if it took a day on the plains to do that, well, then so be it.

"You're on," he told her father.

Mariah rolled her eyes to stare at the ceiling and let out a long breath. "I was wrong. Life is the same now as it was back in the old days. Only now you use your lousy heads instead of pistols to duel it out."

She made a beeline for the door. "I'm calling it a night. Zach, you're in the last bedroom to the left." She trailed back to her father and kissed him on the cheek. "Night, Daddy."

"Night, sweetheart."

Zach lifted his chin as if he expected a kiss, too. Mariah turned on her heels and left him hanging. Hughie chuckled. "Letterman, why don't you go over to that cupboard there and get out a real man's drink…."

THE ONE THING FEMININE about Mariah had always been her bedroom. And then only because her mother had decorated it and she didn't have the heart to change the decor, even though the twin-size white canopy bed was a little too narrow and the lacy coverlet and curtains were old and faded. She lay back in bed now, her arm artlessly draped across her forehead, her feet sticking out of the bottom of the pink top sheet, searching for answers from the canopy overhead. She'd left the kitchen in frustration some three hours ago, and listened as George had stopped by to drop off some clothes for Zach, then Zach and her father continue on together, laughter drifting from the kitchen window to her bedroom window, even though she couldn't make out their words. Another hot southern Texas night, but it wasn't the external heat that got to her. Rather, it was the internal, twisting, skin-itching awareness just knowing Zach was not only staying under the same roof, but the very roof she had grown up under. About a half hour ago she'd listened as the door down the hall from hers had closed, indicating her father had finally called it a night. But she hadn't heard any movement in the guest room next to hers.

Mariah rolled over and gave a strangled little cry, hoping her pillow was enough to muffle the sound.

Never in her life could she remember mooning over a guy the way she was with Zach. Yes, he played her body like a fine instrument, but it was more than just the sex. Something else had come into play over the past couple of days, may have been in play since the moment she met him. Something that seemed to seep into her very bones the more time she spent around him.

Of course, she told herself that their time together had a clock ticking on it. As soon as the wedding dress was repaired, Zach would be on the first plane to Midland. She reminded herself of that ceaselessly. And her want of him increased exponentially.

And maybe that's what made him different from the other guys she'd dated. She'd known that Justin, Jackson and Tom would live no more than a five-minute drive away for the rest of their lives, while Zach…well, she knew very little about him, didn't she? She knew he was determined to be a P.I. And that he was from Indiana. But why Texas? And what had he done before?

Mariah rolled over onto her back and pressed her pillow to her face, her head spinning with questions and possible answers, and her body just wanting him, period.

It was natural to be emotionally interested in the first man to give you an earth-shattering climax, wasn't it? Earth-shattering? That she'd had one at all during sex was a major milestone. But was he to credit for it? Or was she?

In his attempts to make her more "feminine," her father had brought home one of those chic women's magazines from the store one day. After letting it lie on the coffee table gathering dust for weeks, she'd finally picked it up. Shout lines like "You're in Charge of Your Own Body," and "Ten Ways to Drive Him Wild" had been splashed across the front cover along with a scantily clad woman who could have posed for Anorexics R Us. The articles suggested that she was to blame for her own sexual dissatisfaction. That she should tell the guy what she wanted and how she wanted it and how often. But the last part hadn't been what caught her attention. Rather the first part had lodged in her brain and stayed there. She was guilty for not achieving orgasm. It was simple as that.

So she'd tried harder after that. But the more aggressive she became in her quest for orgasm, the faster her boyfriends finished, leaving her even more frustrated than before she started.

Although Zach had been the only one to ask her whether she was satisfied, she sensed that if she'd pretended otherwise, he would have known she was lying. And would have made sure she came anyway.

Was this a Southerner-Yankee thing, she idly wondered? No. She recognized this was strictly an individual issue.

"Get to Know Your Own Body." The headline from another of the magazine articles rang out in her head. Even though it was dark, and she was alone, she could feel her cheeks burning. To listen to the pastor at church, you burned in hell for even thinking about masturbation. Touching oneself was the work of the devil and would only lead to decadence and ruin. Then heap on top of all that, God hovering over you, watching you as you…pleasured yourself and, well, Mariah had rarely dared scratch herself down there when she itched.

And, oh boy, did she ever itch now.

Her throat grew thick as she turned over again. Where

was Zach now? Still in the kitchen? Or had he gone into the guest room without her being aware of it? She caught herself pressing her pelvis into the mattress, ultra aware of the hardness of her nipples, the molten heat filling her body. She closed her eyes and gave a soft sigh, then slid her hand under her body near her hip. Not too close to the area she longed to touch, but close enough to make her shudder. She splayed her fingers against her stomach through her nightshirt, surprised by the growing tension down there, under her skin. Right at that moment, burning in hell didn't seem as important as easing the pressure that made her breathing shallower and her thighs damp. She edged her fingertips down, feeling where her nightshirt had ridden up during all her tossing and turning so that she touched the thin cotton of her underpants.

Whoa.

Her hips seemed to buck involuntarily, pressing further against the mattress, trapping her hand against her stomach. She was so hot, she was afraid she'd spontaneously combust. And the only person around to extinguish the fire was her.

She closed her eyes tightly and tucked her fingers inside the top elastic of her pants, then down, down even farther until they tunneled through the tangle of hair between her legs. The instant her fingertips made contact with the core of her chaos, she flew apart, a small cry ripping from her mouth.

For long moments she rode out the wave of the self-induced orgasm, her muscles clenching, her breathing coming in rapid gasps. She sagged against the mattress, waiting for guilt to assault her. But it didn't. Instead, she smiled softly into her pillow, feeling giddy at the guilty little pleasure she'd just experienced.

Mariah wasn't sure what alerted her to the change in

climate in the room. But when she turned her head, she wasn't surprised to see Zach standing just inside the closed door, the light of the moon illuminating his glorious body clothed only in jeans, his eyes seeming to burn a path straight to her.

"Please, don't stop on account of me," he whispered.

9

ONE OF THE HARDEST THINGS Zach had done was stand completely still and watch Mariah Clayborn hesitantly coax herself to climax without any help from him. He didn't have to wonder whether or not she'd done it before. Her tentativeness was a clear indicator that she hadn't. And knowing that lent even more encouragement to his already painful erection.

He watched as she rolled over, then sat up, pulling the sheet tighter around her compact body. "I didn't hear you come in."

"I'm glad. Or I wouldn't have witnessed what I just did."

She turned her face away from him, but even in the dim light he could see the small smile she wore. "You know my dad is just two doors away?"

Zach dared take a step closer to the bed, quelling the desire to launch himself across the narrow mattress and find out for himself how hot she really was. "I think Hughie is pretty convinced that I wouldn't dare try anything with him under the same roof."

She laughed quietly and moved over on the bed to make room for him. It wasn't much, but Zach made do. The box springs gave a telltale squeak that made him cringe.

"You ever consider getting a new mattress?"

Mariah giggled and tucked her hair behind her ear. "Not until just now."

"I think you should see to it first thing in the morning."

He could feel her probing gaze on him in the dark and looked back.

Yes, while he'd enjoyed the male bonding session in the kitchen with Hughie, all he could think about was sneaking into this very room and, with any luck, into Mariah's bed.

Now that he was there, he didn't know quite what to do.

"Dad went to bed?"

"Yeah."

Mariah was quiet. "You know he's going to run you through the ringer, don't you?"

"I wouldn't expect anything less."

She shifted until she squeezed her sheet-covered knees to her chest. "Just don't say I didn't warn you."

Zach reached out and smoothed her hair back. "Oh, I think I've been warned enough. Your father strikes me as the type of man to give any guy near his only daughter a hard time."

She made a small sound. "He's doing it because you're a Yank. An outsider."

"He's doing it because I'm interested in you."

She fell silent.

Zach wished he knew what was going on in that beautiful head of hers. Did she really think that Hughie was only interested in besting him, putting him through the ringer because of his outsider status? He bent his knee and leaned in closer. Having been an observer for so much of his life, he believed he'd come to know people pretty well. It wasn't because he yearned for his idealized version of what life and family should be like to be true. But being raised by his grandmother, with no other family around to interact with, he'd been insatiably curious about the inner workings of the families around him. The next-door neighbors. The families of the friends he'd made in school. The dynamics of a one-parent household versus two. The shyness sometimes found in only children and the confidence of those who had been raised in a house full of children. He'd often lain in bed deep into the night running what he'd seen over and over in his mind. And if he sometimes indulged in thoughts of what it might be like if he could construct a different family environment for himself, wondered what might have happened if his father had stuck around...well, that was between him and his pillow.

But what he'd seen over dinner that night was a crusty old man who loved his daughter very much. You had but to see the way Hughie looked at Mariah to know that. His generous mouth tipped up in a proud smile, his blue eyes glistened with adoration.

And it didn't take a psychologist to see that Mariah didn't have a clue how her father felt about her. She interpreted his teasing as criticism. Saw his sharing her childhood stories as a way of undermining her. And she ultimately believed she fell way short of the mark in her father's eyes.

Unfortunately, he didn't think telling her that she could do no wrong in Hughie's eyes was going to help matters any. Besides, he'd only passed a few hours in the household they had spent their lifetimes in. He didn't feel completely comfortable telling them both they needed to talk.

"I didn't know if you would come," Mariah whispered. "You know, to my room."

A part of him was glad she'd thought that, because he wouldn't have viewed what he had otherwise. Another was disappointed that she questioned his need for her.

He untangled one of her arms from around her knees

then pressed her hand against his pulsing erection through his jeans. "Then you don't know me very well."

She explored the thick ridge through the denim. "I was just thinking that I don't know you at all."

Zach fought a long groan as she squeezed the knob of his arousal. "I think you know all that matters."

He heard her lick her lips in the dark and longed to have that saucy mouth of hers on him, all over him. "You think?"

"Mmm-hmm."

He heard the pop of the button on his jeans before he realized she was freeing him from the tight fabric prison, only to be ensconced in the warm sheath of her hand. She wrapped her fingers around his hard heat then slowly moved down, then up again. Then she bent toward him.

Zach caught her before she could touch her mouth to him. "I don't think that's such a good idea."

He heard rather than saw her smile. "Why not?"

"Because it'll be over before you've begun."

She slowly moved her hand over him again, causing him to groan. "Then tell me about yourself while I'm... well, otherwise occupied."

He chuckled and threaded his fingers through the hair over her right ear. "What's say we move to the floor where I can be inside you—where I've wanted to be all night?"

She shook her head. "Why don't you start by telling me what you used to do before you decided to become a P.I.?"

She pressed a kiss to the very end of his erection. He finger-combed her hair back, straining to watch by the moonlight streaming in through the window behind her bed. She dipped her tongue out, tentatively tasting him. Appearing to like what she found, she pressed another kiss to his hypersensitive skin, this time openmouthed, swirling her tongue around him before pulling back again.

Good God, there was something about watching her forge ahead with a plan. He didn't have to ask if she'd performed oral sex before. It was obvious in her sweet hesitancy that she hadn't.

She slid her hot, wet mouth down over his arousal and he nearly came right then and there.

She removed her mouth. "You're not talking."

He swallowed hard. "Talking? You expect me to do this and carry on a conversation?"

She laughed quietly. "No. I expect you to perform a monologue. I, um, plan to be busy with other things."

She squeezed him in her fingers.

"Ah," he murmured. "Okay. What did I do before I decided to become a P.I.," he repeated, using the tactic every kid learned in school when forced to speak on a subject. Only his mind blanked the instant she moved her mouth over him again, this time applying suction.

"I, um, used to own an, um, tool and die company." He sucked in his breath with a low hiss, fire burning a trail over his skin as she continued her efforts. "Actually, I still do own it. I just don't run it on a day-to-day basis anymore."

She paused as if taking in his words, giving him a moment to regroup. Sweat coated his brow with the effort it was taking to hold back.

He felt her tongue again and groaned.

How much did he tell her? Houston was far from San Antonio and Trueblood, Texas. Did she know about Finders Keepers? Did she know about his great-grandmother Isabella Trueblood? Would she care?

She moved her mouth down until she nearly had his entire length in her mouth. No small task. His hips automatically bucked and he was forced to remove his hand from her hair so he could hold on to the bed to keep himself from toppling over the edge, both figuratively and literally.

"My maternal grandmother died last year, the last of my Indiana blood relatives. I, um, knew I had family in Texas, and decided to look them up. My cousins own a P.I. agency and, well, I decided to see if I had what it took to make it in the family business."

White-hot heat flooded his brain, making it almost impossible to think. "So my cousins arranged for me to work, incognito, for Jennifer Madison until I get my P.I. legs under me."

Amazing how quickly Mariah dropped all hesitation and surged ahead with the instincts of a pro. She sucked and licked and worked her hand until he felt like every ounce of blood in his body might explode into her sweet, hot mouth.

Where was he? Oh, yeah. Coming to Madison. He gritted his teeth. Better not to think of the word "coming."

"Then, I…" It was getting harder and harder to concentrate, to hold on to the sentences in his head. "My first case, I was assigned to work with this beautiful, smart, incredibly sexy woman I haven't been able to stop thinking about making love to since."

Mariah slowed her movements. Zach panted, the only sounds in the room her mouth and tongue and his breathing. He vaguely wondered what he'd said to make her pause. Did she still doubt that he found her irresistibly attractive? Or was it—Mariah moved her mouth down almost all the way, which meant he'd have to be at the back of her throat.

All coherent thought scattered and the liquid fire that had been building in his balls exploded in one long stream. Mariah lifted her head and continued stroking him with her hand, prolonging his crisis as she watched, fascinated, his desire flow down over her fingers.

When the flood abated, she leaned down and ran her tongue across the tip of his erection, tasting his desire.

Zach's entire body shuddered again. Then he urged her back onto the mattress and pinned her under his weight.

"I hope your father's a heavy sleeper. Because squeaky springs or not, you and I are going to give this old bed a workout."

Mariah smiled. "Bring it on, cowboy...."

ZACH AWOKE before dawn the next morning, Mariah spooned against his front, his arm asleep from the awkward positioning required for them both to fit in the narrow twin-size bed. He pressed the button to illuminate his watch then gently retracted his arm from under Mariah's sleeping head. She murmured something in her sleep and wriggled her bottom against him. His physical reaction was full and immediate, despite the hours they'd gone at it the night before. He briefly splayed his fingers across her hips and pressed her more fully to him, earning another low sound from Mariah. Then he sighed and quietly slipped out of bed.

Considering the noise they'd made last night, between the squeaky bedsprings and Mariah's soft cries, it didn't matter how soundly Hughie slept, he had undoubtedly heard what was going on in his daughter's room. And Zach wanted to soften whatever reaction he was sure to receive by getting into the kitchen first and fixing breakfast.

He slid into his jeans, then realized he would have to go back to the guest room for the remainder of his things. Damn. He listened for noises on the other side of the door, then opened it. The coast was clear. He closed the door after himself then crept down the hall…and ran smack-dab into Hughie Clayborn coming from the opposite direction.

Aw, hell.

"Morning," Zach said quietly.

"Morning yourself," Hughie said just as quietly, then cleared his throat.

Zach squinted at the older man in the dim light. If he wasn't mistaken, Hughie was wearing the same clothes he had the night before. And the undeniable scent of a woman's perfume filled Zach's nose.

He raised his brows, realizing that Hughie hadn't caught him coming from Mariah's room. Rather, Zach had caught Hughie sneaking back in after a midnight rendezvous of his own.

Here he and Mariah had been afraid of making too much noise, of waking Hughie up, and Hughie had been out of the house all along, likely using the excuse of calling it an early night to do some midnight creeping of his own.

Zach started to chuckle, then rubbed his fingers over the stubble covering his jaw. "I, was, just heading for the bathroom."

"Go on ahead." Hughie pointed toward a door down the hall. "I'll, uh, meet you in the kitchen in a few minutes."

Zach nodded and began to pass him.

"Oh, and Letterman?"

Zach glanced at him.

"What you've seen…this stays between us, ya hear?"

Zach was certainly in no position to censure the other man for his behavior, because he'd behaved just as badly if not worse. "Does Mariah know?"

Hughie cursed under his breath. "No. Why in the hell do you think I just asked you to keep quiet?"

Zach grinned and headed for the bathroom.

MARIAH AWOKE to sunlight streaming across her bed. She closed her eyes again and stretched, feeling muscles she couldn't remember having. Then the bedsprings squeaked and she bolted upright, everything from the night before rushing back.

Oh, God, her dad…

She closed her eyes and covered them with her hands. Oh, God, oh God, oh God. Sure, she and Zach had tried to keep quiet, but it had been virtually impossible on the old bed…and Zach had urged her so far outside herself that she'd been incapable of not crying out.

She'd never had anyone stay the night before, not even a girlfriend when she was younger. The first houseguest they had who wasn't a ranch hand or family, and she turned into a sexual hellcat.

A hellcat? Heck, she didn't even recognize herself anymore. The Mariah from three days ago would never have done anything like she had over the past two. She'd shamelessly pleasured herself while Zach watched. Okay, she hadn't known he was there, but that hadn't stopped her from feeling hot all over again just thinking about him quietly standing in the dark, his gaze on her while she reached climax by herself.

In fact, ever since meeting Zach, her body seemed to hum in some sort of high state of awareness. Her thighs were always damp. Her pulse thrummed thickly. And her breasts were always tight, her nipples puckered, as if longing for the touch of Zach's talented mouth.

That just wasn't like her. She didn't go around thinking about sex twenty-four/seven. The only time she used to think about sex was when she was having it. Now when she was having it, she was incapable of thinking about anything else, and when she wasn't having it, she wanted to be having it. Everything else came a very distant second.

She peeked at the clock on her bedside table and catapulted from the bed. After ten. Her heart raced and her gaze leaped from here to there as if she'd been caught sleeping on the job. She hadn't slept that late since...well, since she couldn't remember when. She had a business to run. A guest to look after. A case to finish. And here she was lolling about in bed as if she hadn't a care in the world. As if all she wanted to do was stay in the bed that smelled like her and Zach and long hours of making love and wait until they could take up where they'd left off.

What was she thinking?

She stared at the bed, thinking she should change the sheets. But somehow she couldn't bring herself to. Instead, she hastily straightened the coverlet, gathered her things for a shower, then paused next to the nightstand and picked up the cordless phone there, dialing the office with her thumb.

"George?"

"Yo, Mar."

Yo? When had he started saying "yo"? She sighed, telling herself she should be thankful he'd picked up the phone at all, much less on the second ring.

She glanced out the window, wondering what time Zach had left with her father and when they would be getting back. She didn't kid herself into thinking Zach would last the whole day. But did that mean she should put her day on hold and wait for him?

She decided that, no, it didn't. She'd warned him against going out on the range with her father. Now he would have to pay the price.

"George, I just wanted to tell you that I'll be in a little late this morning."

"A little?"

"Okay, a lot." For a guy who was perpetually late, he

was awfully judgmental this morning. "I've been busy...
following up on some leads."

"Mmm."

Mariah felt her face burn. George knew exactly what
she'd been doing, that the only leads she'd been following
up on had been attached to Zach Letterman.

"Anything happen this morning?"

A shuffling of paper on the other end of the line. Mariah
imagined him putting aside a magazine. "Yes, Justin called
again."

A sharp pain stabbed Mariah behind the eyes.

"You know you really should talk to him, Mar. The guy
sounds desperate."

"That's because he is desperate. Desperately dim-
witted." She blew out a long breath. "Okay, maybe I'll
stop off at the Triple S and see what he wants."

"Good."

"Any developments on our current cases?"

Silence.

"George?"

"Nope. Not a one."

"Okay. Oh, and thanks for bringing the clothes out yesterday. I appreciate it."

"Don't mention it."

"I just did."

She could tell he was working to control himself.

"Oh, George?"

"Hmm?"

Mariah twisted her lips and looked out the window at
the range again. "I was hoping you could do something
for me."

He seemed instantly alert. "What is it?"

Mariah raised her brows. "Run a check on Zach Letterman of Indianapolis, Indiana. Just your typical check."

"Why?"

Why, indeed?

"I'm just a little curious about the guy I'm...working with, that's all."

She'd nearly said "sleeping" with, and was glad she'd caught herself in time.

"You got it. I take it you want this on the Q.T.?"

"Like if you see Zach it wouldn't be a good idea to mention it to him? Yeah."

"You don't think he's an ax murderer or anything, do you?"

Mariah laughed. "Just run the check, George."

"Gotcha."

Mariah pressed the disconnect button and stood for long moments clutching her clothes to her chest and staring out the window. She told herself that she wasn't betraying any kind of trust by checking into Zach's background. She was just curious.

And if it were true that curiosity had killed the cat... well, she'd deal with that if it happened. She had something in mind that she didn't think Zach would agree with, but she felt compelled to do it anyway. But first she had to figure out if she could do it at all.

10

No service.

Zach closed his cell phone and ran his hand across his brow to stanch the flow of sweat pouring out from under his hat. Satan, the black stallion he'd been given to ride that morning, neighed and stepped from here to there, never having stood still since the moment he'd climbed into the saddle at six that morning.

Hughie glanced back at him from where he rode some ten yards ahead, his expression as self-satisfied as they came. Zach gently nudged the horse onward to catch up to the man who had set out to make his life a living hell this morning, and was succeeding quite admirably.

"How's it going, Letterman?"

"It's going," he muttered under his breath.

"Ready to call it quits yet?"

Hughie had asked him that every hour on the hour. The first few Zach had merely smiled back at the old man and shook his head. Now...well, now he was an inch away from throwing in the towel and heading back to the ranch house.

Oh, he'd known Texas was hot. But he hadn't known it would loom doubly so out on the plain, where it was humid as hell but dry as an abandoned well. On a normal day he'd experience the heat for no more than a few minutes at a time, as long as it took to get from one air-conditioned place to the next. Not because that's what he set out to do, but because that's the way it worked.

But here, riding in the sun for hours on end, keeping constantly shifting cattle moving in a straight line, he was beginning to wonder if he'd ever feel cool again.

He supposed he should be glad that he was a little familiar with horses. No, he had never ridden one bareback as Mariah had. And, no, he'd never ridden one for longer than an hour. But he had ridden for a year in his early teens when his grandmother splurged on lessons because his mother had loved horses and he, well, he had loved anything his mother had loved if only because it made him feel that much closer to her. If he hadn't known horses, no doubt the aptly named Satan would have thrown him within the first five minutes and generally set the tone for the day instead of the other way around. While he didn't kid himself into thinking he had complete control over the animal, he did have his respect. And that went a long way toward a tolerable ride.

He checked to make sure his cell phone hadn't bounced out of his front pocket. He'd hoped to take care of some business while he was riding with Hughie and the eight other ranch hands that worked for him. But he had yet to get a line out in the middle of this no-man's-land.

He tipped back his borrowed hat and squinted at the sun. He had put a call in to Denton Gawlick yesterday afternoon, just after he and Mariah had returned from Alabama, but a check of his voice mail had yet to yield a return call. He wanted to know if Gawlick had any idea of who might want the wedding dress as much as he did. Did Peggy Sue have any ex-lovers who might want to stop the couple from renewing their wedding vows? And what was the reason for the renewal ceremony in the first place? Had they separated and recently reconciled, wanting a fresh start with a new exchange of vows? Or, alternatively, did Gawlick have business enemies that might want to interfere with his plans?

He pulled the hat back down over his eyes and reached for his water bottle. Maybe taking Hughie up on this he-man challenge hadn't been the brightest idea now that he thought about it. He had a case to solve, a dress to repair and a career to continue getting off the ground.

The water bottle was empty.

Hughie chuckled next to him. Zach grimaced at him.

"There's another bottle in your saddlebag. I thought you might be needing it."

Zach squinted at the crusty old man. "What, making things easy on the Yank, Hughie?"

"No. Just looking out after the only man my daughter's found fit enough to bring home."

Zach hesitated from where he was retrieving the fresh bottle from the bag. "You understand that I'm staying at the ranch because we're working on a case together."

Hughie's blue eyes sparkled knowingly. "Uh-huh. That's the way I hear it told."

Zach took a long pull of the lukewarm water. "And the woman you sneaked out to see last night?"

The twinkle left, replaced by a scowl. Hughie looked around them to make sure none of the other men had heard what he'd said.

Zach put the bottle back into his bag. "Trust me, if this has been going on for a while, Hughie, they already know all about it."

The old man sat up higher in his saddle and sighed. "Yeah, I suppose you're right."

"So has it been going on for a while?"

Hughie looked at him long and hard. "Anyone ever tell you you ask too many questions?"

"No. But I'll take that as a compliment if it's all the same to you."

Hughie didn't have to spell it out for Zach to know that the older man wasn't ready to spill the beans about his midnight run. And if he were, Zach highly doubted it would be to him.

Hughie pulled the reins so that his horse stepped closer to Satan. "You know why I really brought you out here, don't you?"

"To prove that Texans are better than Yanks?"

"Yeah, well, there's that, too. But no. I invited you to ride so that you and I could have a little talk."

"Does it include a shotgun?"

Hughie threw back his head and roared with laughter.

Zach kept his gaze on the other man.

"No." He pointed a thick, callused finger at him. "But that wouldn't have been such a bad idea."

His horse got a little antsy and he made soft sounds to calm him. "No, I just want to tell you not to hurt my little girl."

Zach stiffened his shoulders.

"You know what's been happening lately, don't you?"

Zach nodded. "A little. You're talking about her ex becoming engaged to someone else?"

Hughie spit on the other side of his horse. "And the two exes before that one."

They rode quietly for a few minutes, then Hughie took off to chase a straggling cow back into line and rejoining Zach when a collie took up where he left off, barking on the cow's hooves.

Hughie cleared his throat. "She's had a tough time of it, Mariah has. Not that she'd tell you that. But I can see it. Ever since her momma died…well, let's just say that I don't think I've handled things all that well."

"All things considered, I'd say you've handled things admirably," Zach said, aiming his gaze forward. "You have a wonderful daughter, a successful ranch—" he slid him a glance "—and a woman on the side who sees to your other needs."

"You're not going to let me live that one down, are you, boy?"

"I don't know. I might consider it. You know, if you stop calling me boy."

"What would you have me call you? Yank?"

"Zach," he said, meeting his eyes. "Zach will do just fine."

He ran the back of his wrist across his brow again. "Now what do you say we give up the ghost and head back to the ranch house, old man?"

MARIAH SAT AT HER DESK and examined the engagement announcement in the *Boston Globe* for one Priscilla London. The faxed copy of the black-and-white newspaper was grainy at best, but she could definitely make out the date and the people in the photo. Dated five months ago, it revealed the wedding would have taken place two weeks ago from today.

She weighed the silver bracelet she'd found in the sleeve of the wedding dress in her hand, then picked up the phone to call the Boston newspaper office again. If the wedding had taken place two weeks ago, then surely there should be a wedding picture. A couple didn't place an engagement announcement then not follow up with a wedding picture.

Mariah put the bracelet back in her pocket and noted that George was working on something at his computer. Probably playing a game. She sighed. She'd been in the office for two hours, but she couldn't seem to drum up the enthusiasm to do more than the bare minimum. She'd placed a couple of calls to follow up on leads she had on two other cases, then received another call from Joe Carter, telling her that Claude Ray had given the county sheriff the slip in the middle of the night by feigning the stomach flu then beaning the young deputy on duty with the toilet plunger. Mariah shook her head and fought a smile. The guy would probably never live that one down. Not in that neck of the woods. But at least no one had been seriously hurt.

However Claude Ray was at large again. Of course, all that law enforcement officials had to do was wait for another crime to happen and they'd know right where to find Claude. Or, more likely, this latest brush with the law had sent Claude out of state for another stretch until tempers cooled down a bit. Then he'd come back and start all over again.

But none of that included Mariah in the hunt until someone hired her, no matter how much she itched to apprehend Ray, this time for good.

The telephone on her desk rang. She snatched it up when she didn't recognize the number on the display. "Clayborn Investigations."

Silence.

Mariah frowned into the phone. "Hello?"

"May I talk to George, please?" a small female voice asked.

George? Mariah looked at the man in question across from her. A casual glance might have shown him uninterested, but she caught the way his shoulders squared when he looked at the caller ID.

"May I ask who's calling, please?"

"Sure. It's Janette Pratt."

"Just a moment, please."

Mariah put the call on hold, but didn't immediately say anything to George. She opened a file on her desk, waiting for him to say something.

She knew George dated frequently, usually Houston girls who worked as secretaries for some large company. But none of them ever lasted more than a couple weeks. And none of them had ever called the office.

"Who's that?" George finally gave in and asked.

Mariah shrugged. "You tell me. She called asking for you." George moved to pick up his extension. "Whoa there, George. You're not conducting personal business during work hours, are you?"

George looked at her.

Mariah sighed and waved at him. "Go ahead. Pick it up."

He turned from her as he said hello to the woman on hold. Mariah narrowed her eyes at him. Odd. Was this girl serious?

She shrugged her shoulders then turned back to the open file in front of her, her gaze trailing again to her wristwatch. She silently berated herself, realizing she was ticking off the minutes until she could make a smooth departure and get back out to the ranch…and Zach.

She absently rubbed the side of her neck, trying to banish the shivers there. Merely thinking about Zach, about his hands on her, him being deep inside her, made her breathing grow shallow and her breasts perk up. She glanced down at the area in question under the thick white sports T-shirt she wore. Well, what little of them she had anyway.

She reached for the phone to call Miss Winona to check on the status of the wedding dress, then slowly returned her hand to her lap. The truth was, she didn't want to know when the dress would be done. She figured the longer she put it off, the longer Zach would be in town.

And that kind of manipulative behavior, no matter how harmless, was not her at all.

She was renowned for shooting straight from the hip. Telling it like it is. No coy smiles or eye batting from her. Yet, strangely, for the first time she wanted to do both with Zach Letterman.

What struck her as stranger still was that neither of them had really fulfilled the terms of her original proposal. Sure, she might have showed him the basics on how to shoot a gun, but she hadn't pursued the other areas of private investigation. The countless resources you could tap into for information from credit agencies, public record archives, newspaper headquarters, libraries, the census bureau, divorce records, private and public property records. Then there was the art of the chase itself. The pounding of the pavement to piece together clues and get a picture of the entire puzzle. Or the connections you made or developed that kept you working, like the one she'd made with area ranchers in regards to Claude Ray.

She swallowed with difficulty. Then, of course, there was the whole sex issue....

While, undoubtedly, she *felt* sexier—which sounded infinitely better than calling herself an insatiable hootchie—she hadn't changed one iota in becoming outwardly sexier. She still had on her worn-out jeans, T-shirts and boots. Her hair still hung combed but not styled around her shoulders. And while she occasionally fingered through the jewelry box she'd inherited from her mother, as she had that very morning, she'd never worn any of the delicate jewels.

Realizing she hadn't read a single word of the file in front of her, she slapped it closed and turned her attention to George again. He was still talking on the phone, his back half to her, his voice lowered.

Curiouser and curiouser…

Mariah entered the name Janette Pratt on her computer just as George ended his call and the cowbell above the door clanged. Deciding to let George see to the visitor, she stared at the computer screen and waited for something to come back on the search of the main computer hard drive.

"Hmm…have you done something different to your hair?"

A full-blown shudder eased from her neck down her spine at the words Zach whispered near her ear.

Her hands shaking, she blanked her computer screen, then slowly swiveled to face him.

Whoa, cowboy.

And this time the greeting fit him through and through. The faded jeans he wore fit him like a second skin, his blue-and-white checked shirt hugged all the right muscle groups. His boots were scuffed and dust covered, his tanned face showed the results of hours in the hot Texas sun, and the hat on his handsome city-boy head was tilted at a cocky angle.

But it was the grin, with or without the cowboy garb, that made every moment of last night come drifting back… and made her want to do it all again. Twice.

"It's funny you should say that." Mariah cleared her tight throat. "People have been asking me that all morning."

George perked up. "I said the same thing when she came in."

"Hi, George," Zach said. "Thanks for letting me borrow the clothes."

"Don't mention it."

Mariah noticed the fine hairs on her arm were standing on end. She absently smoothed them down and tried to look past him. "Where's my dad?"

"Probably back out on the range." Zach leaned a hip against her desk and crossed his arms over that enormous chest. "I borrowed his truck to buy some clothes."

Mariah's heart dipped low in her chest.

"And to come in to see you." Zach's grin widened. "I've been thinking of you all morning."

Her mouth went completely dry. "You have?"

The ringing of the phone reminded Mariah that they weren't alone, that George was watching them without a trace of decency. After the third ring he seemed to figure out that he should get the phone and answered.

Mariah got up, grabbed Zach by the hand, then led him to the back room. Once inside, she closed the door then backed Zach up against it, licking her lips before she kissed him.

Long minutes later, she finally pulled away, her breathing ragged, her heart pounding. "God, I've been wanting to do that all day."

Zach pushed aside a strand of her hair. "Not as much as I have."

On the other side of the door, Mariah heard George talking to someone, presumably on the phone since she didn't hear any other voices. She clamped her eyes closed, realizing he'd probably heard them. She forced herself to peel her hands away from where they were splayed across Zach's wide chest, then retreated until her bottom hit the supply table. She boosted herself up to sit on top of it.

"So?" she said, licking the taste of him from her lips.

Zach's gaze followed the movement, his eyes growing darker. "So what?"

"So how did it go? The lesson on what it's like to be a Texas cowboy?"

"Rough."

She cracked a smile.

"It would have gone much better if you'd been out there with me." The sides of his mouth turned up suggestively. "You know, we could have pulled away from the group and this cowboy could have done a bit of exploring with his cowgirl...."

GOOD GOD, but she looked better and better every time he saw her. Zach's gaze took in the vee of her jeans and the swollen flesh hidden beyond the thick denim. The points of her breasts beneath the soft cotton of her T-shirt just begged for attention. Then he lifted his eyes to her face to find her staring at her hands as if they were more interesting than what he'd just said.

"I would have come, but I don't think Dad would have liked my being there."

Zach lifted his brows. "You can't be serious."

She leaned back on her arms, thrusting her breasts out, then began swinging her legs as though the revelation didn't bother her in the least. "Completely." She shrugged, pulling the cotton more tightly across her pert nipples. "Dad made it clear to me over a year ago that he'd prefer if I didn't ride with them anymore. Said I was a distraction."

Zach rubbed his fingers across his chin, feeling the slight stubble there. She was being serious. "That's funny, because at every turn all he could do was talk about you. About how you could best any of his ranch hands. That when you rode with him, nothing went wrong, because you could spot trouble in the making a mile away."

She looked unconvinced, but he did see a flash of hope in her eyes.

She squeezed the edge of the table with her fingers. "You know, I was just thinking about how neither one of us has been living up to our end of the bargain as far as my proposal goes."

"Are you questioning my skills as a lover?"

Her face turned the most attractive shade of pink. "No. I'm questioning your skills as a private investigator."

He stepped toward her until her knees rested on either side of his hips and he stood directly between her legs, not touching her, but wanting to, dearly. "Back to the lover part…"

He moved a little closer, now a hairbreadth away from pressing his arousal against her softness. "That's not where I was heading with this."

He shook his head. "No, it's not. You're questioning my skill in teaching you how to be sexy."

She dropped her eyelashes and bit her bottom lip. Her slight nod told him that's exactly what she was referring to.

He placed his hands on her thighs, pressing his thumbs into the soft flesh.

"Well, you know, I'm glad you brought that up. Because I've been doing some thinking on that very matter myself."

She blinked to stare at him.

"Oh, yeah. You see, I was questioning whether or not you were getting what you needed from me."

If the sudden catch of her breath was any indication, the double entendre had hit its mark.

He placed one of his hands against her neck and slid it under her thick, silky hair. "That's why I think you should tell me what you expect from me."

Her pupils dilated, making her brown eyes look black. "I guess I was thinking about, you know, suggestions for lingerie. On what I might do with my hair. I've never, um, been able to walk in heels, but I think with some help I might learn."

Zach probed her provocative face. "Is that what you think makes a woman sexy?"

"I think it's what makes a man want to marry a woman."

"Ah." They had finally gotten to the crux of the problem.

She moved to wipe her hands on her jeans and ran into his hand, where it still rested on her thigh. She began to pull back, then changed tactics and instead laid her fingers over his.

"I don't know. It's stupid, really. This obsessing I've been doing over my exes. It's not that I want any of them back. I don't."

He smiled.

"It's just that, you know, one or two dumping you then becoming engaged to someone else...well, it's not easy, but you can explain it away. But when it happens a third time..."

"Then it happens a third time," Zach said quietly. "Tell me, Mariah, do you think your appearance is what is scaring these guys off?"

She shrugged, refusing to meet his gaze.

He hooked his finger under her chin and lifted her face up. But she still refused to meet his gaze.

Zach chuckled softly. As stubborn as her father, he couldn't hope to ever win in a contest against her. But if he could make her think, make her take a good, long look at herself, see how utterly sexy she was and how any man would count himself lucky to have her...well, then he would have more than done what she'd asked of him.

He flipped his hand over so that he was gripping hers. "Come on."

"What?" She blinked at him, obviously surprised by his sudden change in demeanor.

"I said come on. I think it's long past time you and I went shopping."

She made a face. "I hate shopping," she said, but slid from the table anyway.

He smoothed his hand down over her firm bottom then kissed her exposed neck. "You won't after I get done with you."

11

MARIAH STILL HATED SHOPPING. With a passion. All those delicate boutiques. All that pink and lace. It all made her itch something terrible. She caught herself where she was scratching her arm then picked up Zach in the rearview mirror. He was following her in her father's later-model four-door pickup. She smiled as she realized she was doing eighty and he was keeping up without any problem.

The smile quickly vanished as she realized all the fast-food wrappers had been replaced by shopping bags. The only time she'd come near to having a good time was when she and Zach hit the menswear section of Neiman's. Now that was an area she could identify with. Not a splash of pink to be seen. Well, okay, maybe there was one shirt here and there, but she'd bet that in Texas they'd sit on the rack until someone either sent them back to the manufacturer or some poor slob got suckered into wearing one because his pink-loving wife thought it cute.

But when she'd started browsing through the sportswear section, Zach had caught her and steered her toward the women's department. He hadn't even let her buy the T-shirt she'd picked up.

She released a long sigh. She supposed she'd asked for that, given what she'd said to him at the office.

Okay, so maybe she liked a few of the items in some of the bags. Especially the stuff she'd sneaked into the piles Zach had collected for her. She could practically hear her savings account groan from here, but as Zach had told her, if there was anything she didn't like she could always return it.

She was of a mind to think he already knew she wouldn't set foot in a few of those places again if dragged kicking and screaming. Especially the froufrou shop where Zach had made her buy a pink silk robe and matching nightgown.

Hmm…maybe she could give it to Justin's fiancée as a wedding present. The ensemble struck her as something Heather would wear to accept a package from the UPS delivery guy.

Realizing she was coming up quicker than she thought to the turnoff, she eased off the gas and watched as Zach had to stand on his brakes to keep from plowing into her backside. She gave him an apologetic wave, though she could tell by his expression he was more amused than upset by her reckless maneuver. She flicked on her blinker and turned onto the road leading to Miss Winona's two-story farmhouse. She didn't know if the dress would be done, but she'd been short of excuses why they shouldn't stop on their way out to the ranch.

Something dark and leaden slowly coated her stomach. And she knew why. The repair of the dress would also do away with any remaining reasons Zach had to stay.

Minutes later she pulled to a stop in Miss Winona's driveway and got out of the truck, then stood and waited as Zach pulled up to park next to her.

"Dangerous move you made there, Miss Clayborn," Zach said, climbing from the truck cab and closing the door.

Mariah uncrossed her legs where she leaned against the truck. "Sorry, I was preoccupied with all that…pink stuff you made me buy today."

He chuckled then came to stand in front of her. His cowboy hat blocked the late afternoon sunlight, casting his eyes in shadow while highlighting the rest of his face.

He leaned closer to her. "I can't wait to see you in them."

"All of it?"

He nodded, a devilish glint shining from his eyes. "Every last piece."

"All at once?"

He chuckled. "Come on, let's get this over with."

She covertly looked at him as they walked up to Miss Winona's side door. If she wasn't mistaken, he didn't like picking up the dress any more than she did.

But that was ridiculous. There wasn't any reason he would want to stay in Houston.

Zach knocked briefly on the door then stood back out of the way.

No answer.

Mariah frowned, and knocked herself.

Tires chewing up gravel sounded. They turned to find the sheriff pulling up into the driveway behind their trucks just as the door opened.

"Oh, thank God he's here," Miss Winona said.

A HALF HOUR LATER Zach was still trying to process everything that had happened. He noticed that everything that had been in place yesterday when he and Mariah had dropped off the damaged wedding dress was…well, out of place. More specifically, moved, turned over or broken altogether.

It didn't take a veteran P.I. to know the place had been ransacked. What remained was what the thief or thieves had been looking for, because it was obvious they were looking for something in particular. Miss Winona's silver set hadn't been touched, nor had any of her jewelry upstairs, apart from a diamond pendant the thief probably had taken a liking to, but which held no real worth. Not when compared to the countless items that had been passed up.

Miss Winona hadn't been home at the time. She'd returned ten minutes before Mariah and Zach had arrived to find her house in its present squalor.

A familiar flowery scent filled Zach's nose. He turned to find Miss Winona walking behind him. But the reason the scent was familiar eluded him.

Sheriff Crump closed his notepad and scratched his head. "Are you sure you didn't see any suspicious characters lurking around lately, Miss Winona?"

"Positive. You know how I am about those sorts of things, sheriff. A stray dog comes into my yard and I'm on the phone to your office."

The man's grimace told Zach that was true.

Mariah picked up an old figurine that even Zach recognized as a Remington piece. Or a reproduction.

"You don't think Claude Ray could have done this, do you?" Zach asked her.

All three of them looked at him as if surprised he'd voiced the question. Not because it was stupid, but because he was an outsider.

Mariah put the figurine down. "No. This doesn't fit Ray's M.O. at all. He left too much stuff behind for it to have been him."

"Still, it might warrant some looking into," the sheriff said, sighing. "Can't imagine what anyone would want way out here. Why, we haven't had a house burglary in these parts since the Thompson twins terrorized the town back in '76."

Zach frowned. Weren't the Thompson Twins an eighties musical trio? He shook his head to clear it of the image of the English performers ransacking Miss Winona's farmhouse.

The sheriff directed his attention to Mariah. "What are you doing out this way anyway, Mariah?"

"Zach and I came by to pick up a wedding dress." She looked at Miss Winona, completely oblivious to the way the sheriff was staring bug-eyed, first at Mariah, then Zach. Zach merely shrugged, not about to dispel any strange ideas running through the guy's mind. "Speaking of which, is it done?"

Miss Winona nodded and passed behind Zach again, giving him another whiff of her perfume. No, no, not perfume. It smelled liked powder. The scented kind.

And exactly the scent Hughie Clayborn had been wearing that morning.

Zach chuckled softly, then cleared his throat when Mariah looked at him strangely.

So Hughie was having a go at it with Miss Winona. He rubbed the back of his neck and ducked his head to hide his face from Mariah, then turned around altogether to get a good look at the fifty-something widow looking prim and proper in her flower dress and neat little bun.

"I took it to the weekly sewing bee with me. You know, the local girls and I get together once a week to sew quilts and the like, but since there was such a rush on this, I decided I'd work on it rather than the quilt Twila's making for Justin and…"

She gave Mariah an apologetic look. Zach suspected that this Justin was Mariah's ex.

The sheriff hiked up his pants. "Why the rush on the

wedding dress, Mariah? Something going on we don't know about?"

Mariah wasn't paying attention to him. And neither was Zach for that matter.

"You mean the wedding dress wasn't here during the break-in?" Zach asked as Mariah accepted the dress. He mentally made a note to himself to check into whether or not Miss Winona had insurance. If not, he'd arrange for some compensation to help out with repairs.

"That's what I said. I had it with me." She carefully folded back the material and showed her handiwork. "There. You can't even tell there was a tear."

Mariah nodded, but Zach could tell her mind was clicking away on the possibilities. She met his gaze. He nodded.

"Thanks, Miss Winona," Zach said. "How much did you say this would be?"

OKAY, SO ZACH WAS RIGHT. Someone was after the wedding dress. But who? And why?

Mariah mixed the flour and lard in a bowl at the kitchen counter as Zach had shown her and worked through the questions ticking off in her head.

The wedding photo of Priscilla London's important event had come through. As Mariah had expected, featured prominently in the picture was the wedding dress sitting in a box on the kitchen table.

She pushed her hair away from her face with the back of her hand and attacked the mixture with a fork again until it looked like a bunch of white peas. "Are you sure this is how it's supposed to look?" she asked Zach, where he stood browning chicken breasts at the stove.

"Trust me, will you?" He stepped to the sink and half filled a coffee mug with water then took a large spoon from the drawer. "Now add three to four tablespoons of water, one at a time, mixing well after each addition."

Mariah sighed. "Okay, but I still think this isn't going to be fit for anything but the garbage can."

She smiled, not doubting his expertise in the kitchen, but questioning her own abilities beyond making mashed potatoes and semi-edible fried chicken. She'd watched in fascination as he'd hammered out chicken breasts with a meat mallet that she'd seen in the drawer but never used except to bang on a stubborn jar that wouldn't open. Then he'd covered each with a piece of ham and chunks of Swiss cheese and rolled them up and was now browning them.

She looked down at what she was doing and was surprised to discover that the mixture was coming to resemble dough.

"I'll be darned…"

Zach came up behind her, running his hands the length of her arms then into the bowl with hers. "That's enough water. Now, roll it up into a ball. There you go. Scatter some flour on the counter. Mmm."

He nuzzled her neck where she'd pulled her hair back into a ponytail. "Would you stop." She nudged him with her shoulder. "I want to learn how to do this."

"You can't learn while I'm nibbling on your neck?"

"Uh, no."

"Ah."

Mariah firmly landed her elbow in his stomach and his breath came out in a loud whoosh. "Okay, okay," he said, covering his abdomen with his hands and standing next to her. "I give up."

She glanced at him and flattened the ball out on top of the flour. "Like this?"

"Yeah. Now do you have a rolling pin?"

Mariah completely blanked. Did they have a rolling pin?

She remembered her mother using one years and years ago, but she couldn't recall having ever seen it outside of her mother's hands.

She stared at Zach.

He scratched his chin then walked to the utility closet and pulled out a couple of brooms. He chose one with a wood handle and broke it over his bent leg.

"Hey! That was a perfectly good broom."

He took the length of handle to the sink and scrubbed it with steel wool. "Yes, well, now it's a perfectly good rolling pin."

Mariah watched him thoroughly clean and dry it. He sprinkled flour over it and went to work on the blob of dough, rolling it out neatly this way and that, turning it over, then rolling it again.

This time she couldn't resist coming up behind him. "Hmm, I like a resourceful man."

A chuckle resonated in his chest, where she had her arms wrapped around it. "That's not what you said a few minutes ago."

"That was before you took over for me."

He moved to the side and slapped the makeshift rolling pin into her hands. "Here. Put it into the pie pan and smooth all the air bubbles out between the dough and the pan."

"Yes, sir."

His grin looked especially dangerous. "You just made me think of those leather panties you bought."

Mariah's throat threatened to close up at the thought.

"You, those leather panties and a subservient disposition. Has possibilities."

The back door opened, letting in her father.

"Hey, you two. Dinner cooking yet?"

Something was cooking, but it definitely wasn't dinner.

Mariah cleared her throat and exchanged a few pleasantries with her father then waved at him as he left the room to go clean up.

She deflated the instant he was out of sight. "God, what am I going to say if he mentions anything about last night?"

"What about last night?" Zach asked.

"Well...you know."

"He didn't hear us."

"How could he not have?"

Zach looked away then shrugged. "He didn't say a word to me this morning about having heard us. Don't you think he would have said something otherwise?"

Mariah narrowed her gaze. "How are you in the liar department?"

"Pardon me?" he asked with raised brows.

"You know. Did you use to forge your grandmother's signature on report cards? Tell your teacher the dog peed on your homework. Stuff like that?"

He shook his head as the sun slid farther south outside the window, spotlighting him in a yellow glow. All he'd need was a halo and the image would be complete.

"Nope."

"That's what I thought."

He finished up whatever he was doing at the stove and moved to the table, where the sunlight seemed to highlight the wedding dress there. Mariah finished the dough, wiped her hands and turned to watch him.

"What are you thinking?" she asked.

"Oh, I don't know. That the guy who stole my suitcase in Alabama is that same guy who broke into Miss Winona's house."

Mariah shook her head. "Too big a coincidence."

"Not if the guy's been following us."

She twisted her lips. "Have you and the client touched base yet?"

Zach sighed. "Yes. He said he doesn't have a clue who would want the dress other than him."

"Did he tell you where he got it?"

Zach looked at her. "No. Why do you ask?"

She shrugged. "Just thinking aloud."

Something flashed in the light as Zach slightly raised the front of the dress.

"Hold it," she whispered.

"What?"

She repositioned herself, her eyes glued to the bust of the dress. "Pull it out a little bit more. Yes, that's it. Now move it around a bit."

She'd noticed the tiny seed pearls sewn across the front of the dress before. But something had caught her eye this time around with the sun reflecting off the semiprecious jewels. It almost looked like a— "Map of some sort," Zach said at the same time she thought the words.

She crossed to stand in front of him. "But a map of what?"

Zach ran his free hand through his hair. "It could be of anything, anywhere. The dress got lost on a flight from Boston. But I don't know if that's where it originated. For all we know it could have been flown in from Europe somewhere."

Mariah ran her fingers over what could have been roads across the delicate lace of the dress. "Boston is where it originated."

"How can you be so sure?"

She took the bracelet from her pocket. "Because I found

this snagged on the inside sleeve of the dress when I tried it on."

Zach turned the bracelet over and read the name. "What's this got to do with Boston?"

"Priscilla London got married in Boston two weeks ago." She pressed her finger against the dress. "Wearing this."

"Ah."

Ah, indeed.

She felt Zach's probing gaze on her. "And when were you going to share this with me?"

She shrugged. "Tonight, most likely. I placed a call to the London family and talked to a servant. The dress came up missing a week after the ceremony."

Zach turned his attention back to the dress. "So you think this is a map of something in Boston?"

"I don't know." She ran her fingers around one curvy line, then followed another. It seemed the majority of them originated at the lace rose at the neckline. "This looks like it's a point of reference."

"It looks like a rose to me," Zach said.

Mariah frowned at him.

Hughie stepped into the kitchen, looked over their shoulders and said, "That ain't no rose. That's Bisbane's Bluff."

"BISBANE'S BLUFF?" Zach said, after dinner had been served, and the peach pie he and Mariah had made had cooled enough to cut. He served it and Mariah scooped out vanilla ice cream. She mounded it next to the pieces and they carried the plates to the table.

"It's a rock formation about sixty miles to the northwest of here," Hughie said in answer to Zach's question.

"Old Man Jock Bisbane owned the land so they called it Bisbane's Bluff."

Zach looked at Mariah. She shrugged, indicating she wasn't familiar with the story.

"You make this pie, Mar?"

Zach watched her cheeks turn pink. "With help from Zach."

"Good Lord, girl, I haven't had peach pie since your mother used to make it for me."

"I remembered that it was your favorite."

Hughie seemed thoughtful as he looked at his daughter. "Yours, too."

Mariah nodded but didn't say anything.

Zach wanted to shake his head at two of the most stubborn people he'd ever met in his life. Instead he took a bite of pie and concentrated on the dress. "How can you be sure the flower designates the bluff?"

Hughie stretched his neck to swallow the extra large bite of pie he'd just put into his mouth. He used his fork to point to the lower left-hand corner of the bust, well enough away from the dress not to risk touching it. "See that there? The grouping that looks like an arrowhead? That's Fontaine Point." He moved the fork to the other side. "And that there, where the white things come together in an oval is Josiah's Loop."

Zach noticed that Mariah had stopped eating, her expression indicating she was somewhere far away as she stared unseeingly at the dress. Hughie finished his pie, as did Zach, yet Mariah still sat as if mesmerized. Hughie's silverware clanked against the side of his plate and he patted his belly. "Best damn peach pie I've had in a pig's life, Mariah. Thank you."

That finally seemed to snap her out of her trance, though she didn't appear to have heard her father's words. "Jock

Bisbane... You wouldn't happen to be referring to Jock of the Jock and Ellie story, would you?"

Zach frowned. "Weren't Jock and Ellie J.R.'s parents on *Dallas?*"

The twosome stared at him in a way that made him feel as if he'd never get it.

Mariah piled the plates up, hers on top. "You know the saying that there's a little truth behind every work of fiction? Well, we're all convinced the writer of the show must have taken the names from the legend of Jock and Ellie."

"Oil people?"

Mariah nodded. "Yes, but not what you saw on *Dallas*. Jock was a third-generation Texan who worked the land and accidentally struck oil when he was twenty-five. The find allowed him the resources and the courage to ask the woman he'd loved for years, but hadn't dared court, to marry him."

"Ellie."

"Yes. Ellie was from a wealthy family that had moved here some years before from Virginia, I think. Anyway, it's said that the night before they were to be married Ellie took ill. She was dead by dawn."

Zach raised his brows.

"Those types of things happened back then," Hughie said. "Now we know it was probably food poisoning or some kind of poisoning, accidental or otherwise. But back then sudden deaths were just accepted as a freak of nature."

"How long ago are we talking about?" Zach asked.

"A hundred years, easy."

All eyes shifted to stare at the dress.

"You don't think this is the dress Ellie was to wear?" he asked.

Mariah's face was full of wonder and fascination. "It couldn't be."

"It sure as hell is," Hughie disagreed. "The story doesn't end with Ellie's death. It's said that Jock had this dress made up special for Ellie, and somewhere on it was a map of something called Jock's Treasure."

Mariah waved her hand. "I never bought that part…." she said, then trailed off as she continued fixating on the dress.

"Yes, but you can't deny the rest of the story," Hughie said. "The fact that shortly after Ellie's death, Jock disappeared. And so did his fortune."

"Myth," Mariah said softly, as if trying to convince herself. "Something the locals tell themselves in the winter when the sun sets early and the family's gathered around the fire."

While the other two focused on the dress, Zach gazed solely at Mariah. God, she was beautiful. He wondered what he would do if she ever, Lord forbid, fell ill.

He caught himself and blinked several times, astounded by the thought.

"Could you find this place?" he asked when the silence stretched on.

Two pairs of eyes shifted to look at him.

"Bisbane's Bluff. This tiny X on the map. Can you find it?"

Mariah nodded and a smile slowly spread until it nearly swallowed her face. "Oh, yeah. Why?"

"Why, because he intends to find it, Mar," Hughie said, scratching his chin. "But it's going to take some doing. Something that's been buried for over a hundred years… well, it tends to stay buried."

Silence reigned as the three of them considered what Hughie had said.

"Well, a little checking around never hurt anybody, did it?" Zach asked.

Mariah's eyes sparkled. "Nope."

Hughie was already moving for the phone. "Let me see what help I can scare up."

12

MARIAH STOOD ALONE in the middle of her bedroom wearing one of the more comfortable ensembles Zach had insisted she buy earlier that afternoon. The lights were off, and she could barely make out her silhouette in the full-length mirror on the inside of her closet door, but she didn't need to see herself to know how she felt. Hot as molten lava.

She heard Hughie's hearty laugh come from the direction of the living room, where the three of them had moved after the Jock and Ellie conversation. She smoothed her hands over the silky material covering her stomach and sucked in a breath. Could it be true? Could the dress she'd left on the kitchen table be the one Ellie was to have worn on her wedding day? The dress Jock was rumored to have a map to his fortune laid out on?

She shook her head. It couldn't be true. While there were different variations on the story, one of them was that Jock had taken the dress with him wherever he'd gone and that it was lost forever.

Another story said that Ellie had actually been buried in the dress.

But what had her wondering was the one that said the dress had been left with Ellie's family, and the family was so distraught over the loss of their only child that they'd given the dress to a wealthy family visiting from up north—more specifically, the New England area....

No. It couldn't be true. Mariah didn't believe in fairy tales, and she certainly didn't believe in stories old ranch hands told in saloons near closing time when they all were good and sloshed.

Still, it wouldn't hurt to check it out, would it? Especially with what had happened so far, the dress's connection to the Northeast, and what could very well be a map sewn across the delicate lace of the bust.

She and Zach had agreed to look into it first thing the following morning. She swallowed hard, reminding herself that several hours separated now from then.

She sighed gustily. At some point she really should get a peek at how she looked in her new underwear, no matter how reluctant she was to do so. It didn't matter that she was afraid her breasts would look too small, her waist too wide, and her thighs like mounds of cottage cheese.

Bracing herself for the nightmare, she reached over and flipped the light switch near the door that illuminated the lamps on either side of her bed behind her.

And she lost her breath.

There was no way...it couldn't possibly be...she couldn't believe it. The woman looking back at her from the mirror...it wasn't her.

She lifted her hand to her chest, watching as the creamy skin heaved under her shaky fingers. Breasts. She had breasts. She covered her mouth to stop the giggle that threatened. Okay, so maybe the bra she'd bought only made it look like she had breasts. But there, staring back at her, were two creamy mounds made all the whiter by the black of the push-up lace cups.

Her gaze ventured lower to where the black lace contin-

ued down over her abdomen, cinching her in at the waist,
the high cut of the matching panties giving the appearance
of legs. Long, shapely legs whose imperfections were covered by black fishnet stockings.

Whoa....

Mariah swallowed with some difficulty. Okay, so maybe
the reflection staring in fascination back at her did look
a little familiar. The hair. The wide eyes. The unpainted
mouth. She sucked her bottom lip between her teeth, then
scrambled to her dresser drawer where she'd stashed the
makeup she'd bought some six months ago but had never
worn. She'd even asked the woman at the department store
counter for help, so she was reasonably sure the colors
she'd bought wouldn't look too bizarre against her skin
and coloring. Burnt umbers and rich reds jumped out at
her. Palming several of the cosmetics and a plain black hair
band, she hurried back to the mirror as fast as she could
in the low-heeled mules pinching her toes. First went on
the eyeliner. Then some blush. Then next came the va-va-
voom red lipstick. She nearly hiccuped as she scrutinized
the results that looked right at home with the sexy lingerie.

She allowed her attention to wander downward again,
to where the underwear disappeared between her legs.
Soft tendrils of pubic hair curled up over the edge of the
narrow scrap of material. She swallowed hard. Should she
shave? She dropped a finger down to touch the downy curls
and decided that, no, she wasn't going to shave. Instead,
she tucked the wayward curls inside the crotch, gasping
when her fingertip slid easily between the slick, soft folds
of flesh there.

Whoa...

Now in a hurry to finish the effect, she pulled back her
hair. She secured it into her usual ponytail and smoothed
back the top. Too dominatrix. She tugged the band until

it sat nearer to the top of her head, causing the strands to cascade like a fountain, first up, then down over the top of her head.

"Good God."

Mariah jumped, dropping the tube of lipstick onto the carpet at her feet. She was almost afraid to look. To see the man who was undoubtedly standing in the doorway looking at her.

"Where's my father?" she whispered.

"He went out back to check on the ranch hands."

Good. Mariah didn't think she'd said the word, but it didn't matter. She began to turn toward the door.

"Don't move," Zach murmured throatily.

The click of the door closing and locking sounded, then the thud of his footfalls as he moved to stand behind her.

Mariah lost all ability to breathe when she saw him over her right shoulder, his expression dark, his eyes so full of passion she nearly wet herself right then and there.

"You look...you are...incredible," he whispered, his eyes holding hers in the mirror.

Mariah began to turn toward him, but he stayed her with a hand on her shoulders. "No, don't. I want..." He seemed to be having a little trouble breathing himself. "I want you to look at yourself, Mariah. Really look at yourself."

He moved to stand closer, mere millimeters separating them, his heat arcing between them like static electricity. He slid his hands between her arms and waist, sliding them up to where her breasts heaved, threatening to pop out of the push-up cups. "Look at this. Have you ever seen a pair of breasts so perky?" He curved his fingers up to cover the cups, then over the small half globes. "My mouth's watering just wanting to suckle them."

Mariah nearly lost her footing. He pulled her to him so

that her back rested against his front, supplying the support she had suddenly lost.

"Look at your waist," he murmured, his breath hot on her ear.

Mariah did, her eyes moving to where his hands rested on the stiff material at her midsection, then dropped lower still, to the patch between her legs. She tried to drag air into her lungs, but failed, anticipating the moment he would come in contact with the swollen flesh waiting for his touch. Instead, he swept his hands out to her hips then down her outer thighs, causing her to gasp for air.

"I knew you had long legs under those jeans," he murmured, his lips teasing her ear yet not really touching her. "Wow. Fills a guy with all sorts of decadent thoughts."

Mariah restlessly licked her lips, tasting the lipstick there. "And a guy saying that makes a girl wish he would act on those thoughts."

She looked at him in the mirror, finding a naughty grin on that handsome face of his. "In time, darling. In time. Good things come to—"

"Those who wait, my ass," she whispered, trying to turn in his arms again.

He held tight. "Uh-uh. I'm not done yet."

Mariah was so hot she was afraid she might burst into flames. But she forced herself to stand still. Apparently convinced that she would, Zach moved his hands from her legs to her outer arms, caressing the skin there. Mariah shivered, her hard nipples very near to popping out of her bustier.

"Zach…"

"Shh," he murmured, covering the back of her hands with his.

Mariah blinked, watching as he bent her arms at the elbows and guided her hands to rest against her stomach just below her breasts. "You know," he said, running his tongue along the shell of her ear. "There are few things that turn men on more than a woman who not only knows the beauty of her own body, but appreciates it, as well."

He was calling her beautiful. The heat sizzling outside Mariah swirled inside.

"Show me how much you love your body, Mariah."

He guided her hands to rest over her breasts.

Mariah's heart stopped. She'd never touched herself in such an overt way. But somehow, seeing her fingers resting against her breasts, she was filled with a desire to try, as much for Zach's sake as for her own growing desire to explore uncharted territory.

Zach's hands dropped to her wrists, presumably to prevent her from stopping, and to encourage her to go on.

And Mariah did.

She squeezed her breasts through the black lace, watching as the top of the mounds grew. Her right nipple popped up and out of the lacy cup. She stared at the dark tip, which was as thick as a pencil eraser, surprised that she didn't want to tuck it back inside. Instead, she ran the palm of her hand over it, then pinched the puckered end between her fingers. Zach groaned, pressing his hard arousal against her barely clad backside.

"That's it," he whispered hoarsely. "Touch yourself, Mariah. Touch yourself as you imagine you'd like me to touch you."

And she did. With her other hand, she freed her other nipple, then pinched and rolled the tips of both breasts in her fingers, tugged and pulled and pushed until her breathing came in rapid gasps.

Zach cursed under his breath and caught her hands again. "Now for the grand prize..."

Mariah's throat grew thick as he covered her fingers with his and pointed them in the direction of her crotch.

Already she could feel the wetness dampening the inside of her thighs. But as Zach edged her hands down her waist, she knew a moment of hesitation. To indulge in self-gratification when she hadn't known he was watching was one thing. To do it with him not only watching, but watching him watching...

She nearly came right then and there.

"Shh," he said in her ear. "Not yet, baby. Oh, not yet."

Then her fingers were skimming over her throbbing flesh, down between her legs, undoing the snap there. The material sprang upward, revealing her pink folds glistening with her own moisture, the core of her need peeking through her dark curls, thick, pulsing evidence of her high state of arousal.

"Yes," Zach said. "Oh, God, Mariah, you are so, so beautiful..."

Where he had moved his hands to her wrists and allowed her to move to her own rhythm before, now he gripped her hands harder, keeping the control as he pressed her fingers against either fold then gently parted her so that she could see her most intimate parts. Then he was guiding her fingertips toward her molten center.

The instant that finger met flesh, Mariah threw her head back and moaned, her climax assaulting her from every angle, every muscle convulsing and churning and jerking. She collapsed against Zach as she rode out the storm, moaning again when he slid one of her own fingers up into her dripping wetness, moving it in and out, in and out.

"Oh, Mariah. Oh, yes, baby, that's it. Come for me...."

Mariah blinked open her sleepy eyes near the end of her climax, watching the wanton woman in the mirror, the one with her nipples shamelessly peeking out of the top of her bustier, the snap on her crotch undone, and her own finger dipping in and out of herself. She cried out and instantly came again.

Behind her, Zach cursed and removed his hands from hers. Mariah brazenly kept up the rhythm of her own finger, then added two, until she saw Zach bend at the knees and his condom-covered erection appear between her thighs. She took out her fingers and guided the hot, thick velvet-covered steel to rest between her slick folds. At this angle, he couldn't enter her. Instead he moved his penis back and forth, and back and forth.

Mariah knew a need so powerful, so overwhelming, that she nearly cried out from the enormity of it. When Zach pressed her back until she was bent over, she willingly went, keeping her eyes glued to him on the mirror. She arched her back and tilted her bare bottom even farther up in the air. He groaned and entered her with one long, soul-filling stroke, his face awash with pure ecstasy.

Mariah cried out, bracing herself against her knees as he moved his hands to her hips and slowly withdrew, only to rock up into her again. Then again. And again and again and again, until Mariah knew nothing but the feel of him deep inside her, his needy groans filling her ears, his engorged flesh filling hers.

She knew the instant he was near climax. Could sense it in the trembling of his legs, his almost painful expression. Surprising even herself, she reached between their legs and took his soft, hair-covered testicles in her hand and rubbed them.

Zach stiffened and threw his head back, his neck mapped with popping veins as he gave himself over to climax. Just watching him launch into the land of white-hot light and exquisite sensation, and knowing she was the one responsible for it, nearly sent her over the edge.

Her breath caught. Correction, it did send her over the edge.

ONE OF THE HARDEST THINGS Zach had ever done was leave Mariah alone in the bed they had spent so many mind-blowing moments in. But if they were going to do this thing, search for hidden treasure, there probably were some things he should see to. Investing in a metal detector might not be a bad idea. If there was treasure, it had been buried for a century.

He steered the truck with one hand and rubbed his neck with the other. The truth was, even after Mariah had slipped into an exhausted sleep, he hadn't been able to close his eyes. All he could think about was that he was quickly running out of reasons for staying in Hoffland, remaining in her bed. In the back of his mind a clock was ticking away the precious moments of their time together. And no matter how hard he tried, he couldn't come up with another reason for him to stay.

It was more than that he had a client waiting in Midland. Or even that he was working with Jennifer Madison. What loomed above him was a dream he'd been working toward for the past six months. A goal that had consumed him and continued to consume: his need to learn the business then return to Indiana to implement his plans to franchise Finders Keepers. Family was so very important in a man's life. He saw it when he sat with Hughie and Mariah. Had longed for it after he lost his grandmother. And now that it was within his reach to offer services to others to have the same, he wasn't about to back away from it.

Then there was Mariah.

Dear, witty, smart, sexy Mariah with her big brown eyes

and her passion for life and everything in it. She'd lived all her life in the same house. Had admitted that their plane trip had been her first time outside Texas. Relied on her father as much as Hughie relied on her, even though both of them were far too stubborn to admit it.

The Houston skyline loomed ahead of him, seeming unfocused in the early morning smog. He could never ask her to leave. Would never even consider asking her to give up everything she was familiar with, everything she knew, to go to Midland with him, then on to Indiana. She belonged in Texas. And he belonged in Indiana.

The only certainty he could see was that he would leave. As soon as they found out whether Jock's Treasure was a myth or reality, he would pack up and head back to Midland and Jennifer Madison's agency. Or maybe not. Perhaps he'd head straight back to Indiana. Because if he'd learned anything in the past few days, it was that he didn't have what it took to be a private investigator. But he did know enough to spot someone who did have what it takes. And that had been his objective all along. With his cousins Lily and Dylan's help, he could get his plans off the ground quicker than he'd anticipated. Instead of taking him a year to open up several satellite offices in secondary cities, he might be able to do it in six months.

He sought solace in the knowledge but found none.

RAW...SORE. That's how Mariah felt the following morning. Barely daring to move, she tucked her nose into her pillow, breathing in Zach's unique scene, then she gingerly slid her hand between her thighs, finding her labia swollen and blood filled. She winced but couldn't resist dragging her fingertip along the jagged crevice, finding herself wet and still hungry for the one thing only Zach could give her, despite how sensitive she was.

Whoa.

She swallowed deeply. Just when she thought things couldn't possibly get any better, Zach proved her wrong. But it wasn't that Zach had done anything differently. It was that he had coaxed her to look at herself differently. And in doing so had unleashed an insatiable sexual monster that wanted him even now.

She carefully rolled over. So long as she kept her legs slightly spread, she was fine. She pushed her hair from her eyes, finding the band she'd held it back with the night before still holding a couple of strands of hair on the top of her head. She tugged it off and tossed it to the nightstand. Blinking, she saw something green resting against the white-painted wood. She squinted then reached to pick up the notepaper.

"Gone to pick a few things up. Back soon."

It was signed simply "Z."

Mariah smiled and held the note to her chest. Her own personal Zorro. But rather than slaying arch enemies, he was conquering her inhibitions one by one, until she was at the complete mercy of him and her own spiraling needs.

She glanced across the room to where Zach had positioned her closet door so that everything that happened on the bed was reflected in the full-length mirror secured there. She gasped. Here she'd thought her hair was her only concern. Sure, she'd expected the puffy eyes, but not the black rings from the eyeliner, or the lipstick smeared against one cheek, making her look like a circus clown on steroids.

If anything was capable of chasing her out of bed, that was. She ventured closer, completely oblivious to her nakedness in a way she'd never been before, and stared at her face in the mirror. Yikes! She supposed she should be glad that Zach had shut off the lights at some point. She caught herself smiling. Of course, her appearance might have been the reason for his sudden need for darkness.

Okay, she needed to shop for stuff that stayed put. Waterproof eyeliner and mascara and lipstick.

She reached for her old, ratty terry robe in the closet, only to find it gone, replaced with the short sexy pink number. Zach, the devil. The silk whispered up her arms and brushed against her sensitive nipples as she tied the belt at her waist. She shivered. Okay, so maybe there was something to be said for pink. Almost immediately she felt pretty and feminine and supersexy.

Gathering fresh panties, she hesitantly opened the door and looked both ways down the hall, just in case her father was lurking around somewhere. The door to his bedroom was open, and just inside she could see the bed was made. She frowned and stepped absently out of her room. That was odd. Her father never made his bed. Before she realized that was where her feet were carrying her, she was standing in the doorway of her father's bedroom. After a long moment, she sighed. Oh, well. Maybe he figured she'd have enough on her plate today. She squinted, noticing the neat corners, the smooth surface of the comforter. Only, even when Hughie did occasionally make his own bed, he never made it that neatly.

Strange. It almost looked as if he hadn't slept there the night before. She glanced down the empty hall behind her. Could he have suspected what was going to happen between her and Zach and bunked with the ranch hands for the night?

Her face burned with embarrassment. What kind of hussy chased her father out to the bunkhouse so she could sleep with her lover?

Not up to answering the question, she headed for the bathroom, only too happy to leave her thoughts behind in exchange for a hot shower. When she finally emerged, she found her muscles were more limber, relaxed, and walking was much easier. She combed her hair and made sure there were no traces of makeup left on her face, though she was certain nothing could have survived the scrubbing she'd given herself.

She heard a sound out in the hall. Her father? No, she didn't think so. Whether he'd stayed in the bunkhouse or not, he rarely if ever came back in the middle of the morning.

Zach.

She smiled, checked herself a final time in the mirror, then opened the door. But the person standing on the other side of the door wasn't Zach. Nor was it anyone she had expected or wanted to see.

"You!"

13

MARIAH STRUGGLED against the duct tape wound around her wrists and ankles and tried to shout in frustration, the tape across her mouth muffling it to the point of nonexistence.

She collapsed against the kitchen island and sighed. There were few things more humiliating than being tied up in your own house without a soul around to find you.

She knocked the back of her head against the tile of the island and groaned. The last person she'd expected to see when she'd pulled open the bathroom door was Claude Ray. But there he had stood, looking grimy, as if he hadn't had a bath for days, his face full of malice and ill intention. She'd known in that one moment that she would pay for every time she'd caught up with him and dragged his no-good carcass back to jail.

And, oh, had she been right. Before she could collect her wits, he'd wrapped a rope around her midsection, pinning her arms to her sides, then wound it around her upper legs so that she was virtually a Barbie doll, with no moving parts.

"Like the robe, Mar," he said, his gaze raking her barely clothed body, his leer indicating he liked more than the robe.

Thankfully he hadn't acted on the interest. She didn't know what she would have done if he had. Instead he'd hauled her to the kitchen where he'd found the duct tape in the utility drawer and secured her hands behind her back and her ankles straight out in front of her. And that's where she'd been forced to sit, watching him ransack the ranch with the thoroughness of an experienced thief, her only weapon her mouth. She'd alternately cursed him, then tried to engage him in conversation only to resort to cursing him again. Well, at least until he'd shouted in agitation and taped her mouth shut, too.

Mariah closed her eyes and swallowed deeply. God, she didn't think she'd been so humiliated in her entire life. She, Mariah Jane Clayborn, had been hog-tied.

Claude had left a half hour earlier, but the unforgiving tile under her bottom made it feel like longer. She shifted awkwardly, trying to see if she could gain a foothold and move herself to one of the kitchen chairs. No go. She slumped against the island again, only perking up when she heard the familiar sound of her truck engine in the driveway.

Zach!

She heard the front door open and close, then there he stood, in all his tall, strikingly handsome glory, in the kitchen doorway.

ZACH'S HEART POUNDED in his chest as he released the last of the tape binding Mariah's hands and feet together. He rose to help her to her feet only find her already standing next to him.

"God, I can't believe I let that happen," she said, looking angry enough to spit nails.

Zach rubbed the back of his neck, trying to shake the uneasiness that had settled over him when he'd come into the house to find Mariah tied up and alone. "Are you sure it was Claude Ray?"

Her brows shot up so high they were almost lost in her hairline. "You're joking, right? Of course I'm sure it was Claude Ray. I saw the idiot with my own two eyes." She hurried to the table where the box that had held the wedding dress gaped empty. "Damn." She stomped her bare foot against the tile. "Damn, damn, damn. I should have known he would take it. 'Are these real pearls?' he asked. Like I could answer him with my mouth taped shut."

"Claude took the dress?"

"It looks that way, doesn't it?"

"Do you think he knows what it is?"

"What? That it was Ellie's dress? That it has a map sewn into the bodice that might lead to a virtual treasure? No." She twisted her lips. "At least I don't think so."

She ran her hands through her hair again and again, looking at her wits' end and utterly kissable. His gaze skimmed her neat figure under the silk of the robe, and a desire to put his hand inside the flap and cup a small breast was almost irresistible. Almost.

"What are we going to do?" She puffed out a long breath, her brown eyes wide. "The map is on that dress. And I…and I…" She gestured with her hand. "I have no idea where he might fence a wedding dress. Horses, yes. Horses are pretty difficult to hide. But a wedding dress?"

"Do you think he's getting married?"

She let out a short laugh. "No. Just about every other man in my life might be getting married, but not Claude. Besides, who would have him?"

"Oh, I don't know. A woman as desperate to get married as he is?"

She laughed, then fell silent, her eyes planted on Zach's face as if trying to figure out the reason for his saying that.

He allowed his gaze to drift down to the front of her robe, to the deep vee, then lower still to where the hem rested against her magnificent thighs. "Mariah?"

He looked up to see her lick her lips in the telltale way that said her mind was rolling down the same track as his. "Yes?"

"I think it would be a good idea if you got dressed just now."

"Why?"

He forced his attention to remain her face. "Because we have a treasure to find."

"LET ME GET THIS STRAIGHT," Mariah said from the driver's seat of her old truck. "While I was playing dress-up in my bedroom, you and Dad were tracing the map on the dress?"

Zach smoothed out a piece of notepaper on his lap. "Call us stupid, but we didn't think it would be such a good idea to run around holding that old wedding dress trying to find X."

"Delicate."

He squinted against the morning sun slanting through the driver's window. "What?"

She squeezed the steering wheel more tightly as they bumped and rutted over the old country road. "The dress is delicate. Antique. It's not just…old."

She watched the corners of his delectable mouth turn up in a smile. "Ah."

She made a face and pretended to concentrate on the road.

"Hughie's going to meet us out there with the prospector." He refolded the map and checked his watch. "They're probably getting underway now, so we should pretty much reach there at the same time."

"Prospector," Mariah said under her breath. "Clooney is

an old coot at best, a walking cadaver at worst, who hasn't said a coherent word in over twenty years." She couldn't believe her father was bringing the bony old man who was a hundred if he was a year. "He's known for coming in after everyone else has done all the work, pointing a gnarled finger and running away with the credit for finding something that would have been found anyway."

"That's not the way your father tells it."

"Yeah, well, my father's an old fool."

Zach's quiet chuckle skated over her nerve endings, making all sorts of naughty memories glide through her mind.

She tucked her hair behind her ear, then berated herself for the nervous gesture. Okay, so maybe Claude Ray, and her father bringing in Old Man Clooney, weren't really bothering her. Sure, both incidents combined would be enough to buck anyone off the saddle. But as the miles disappeared under Mariah's truck tires, so too did the distance between now and the moment Zach disappeared from her life.

She shifted uncomfortably on the bench seat. No, going in, she hadn't been looking for anything serious. She would have to be insane if that had been her purpose for making her proposal. What she'd been looking for was someone to give her the answer to the question that had been haunting her for the past four years, namely why the men she'd dated had dumped her in favor of marrying someone else. She'd wanted to know what it was about her that they not only ran away from, but ran to someone else to escape. She'd thought it was the sexiness issue. Or her lack of sexuality. Only instead of getting an answer, Zach had posed even more questions she was ill equipped to address.

And in a short time he, too, would leave her alone to deal with them.

She grimaced. No, it wasn't fair to compare Zach to her previous three exes. Not in the least. They'd both gotten involved for the sake of their individual agendas. To discuss marriage, or anything lasting, would have been ridiculous. She was a Texan, he was a Yank. No, no. It went well beyond that shallow factor, although the tags did play a role. Their lives were completely different. Their goals, ambitions. While she enjoyed running after Claude Ray on horseback, Zach's P.I. skills would probably be focused on something on a grander scale. Cases dealing with big money that he could wear a business suit to solve. Or rather direct other more qualified investigators to look into.

She didn't get it. The night before last he'd told her he owned a tool and die company in Indiana. But how did that tie into private investigating? Why would a man who probably had more money than God want to become a private dick?

It didn't make any sense. And given the limit on their time together, she was afraid it might never make sense.

"There," Zach said, pointing out the windshield. "Is that Bisbane's Bluff?"

Mariah squinted against the sunlight reflecting off the hood of the truck. A half a mile up the road to the left loomed a rocky outcropping in the middle of Texas prairie land. "I think so. It's been a long time since I've been out this way."

Zach nodded and opened a professional road map where he'd traced Jock's map on top of it. "Okay, judging by the map, we need to make a left up here."

"Where?" she asked, not seeing any crossroads.

"There!" Zach pointed to a narrow unpaved opening in the road.

Mariah put on the brakes and backed up to make the turn. The truck kicked up dust. Trying to decide between slowing down or rolling up the windows, Mariah rolled up her window and indicated Zach do the same. The quicker this was over with, the faster she could get to solving the mysteries of her life.

"Another left coming up here," Zach said. "There."

Another dirt road that was more like ruts than a genuine road. Mariah tapped the dashboard. "Hang in there, Nelly."

She turned to find Zach watching her with a close-mouthed grin. "What?" she asked sharply.

He shook his head. "Nothing."

She blew a long breath through her lips, hating that she sounded snappy. She never sounded snappy. She was good ol' Mariah Clayborn who could handle anything. Had a difficult case to solve? Contact Mariah. Needed to sow some oats before marrying someone else? Contact Mariah. Needed the satisfaction of stomping all over someone's heart? Mariah was the girl for the job.

She was surprised by the way her heart responded to her thoughts. It seemed to double in size and press against her rib cage uncomfortably. She absently rubbed the area.

It seemed strange somehow that she was admitting that her exes' desertions had been more than mere irritations. They had hurt. Badly. And the admission made the pain all the more acute. The back of her eyes stung and she caught herself making a wringing motion with her hands against the steering wheel.

She was not going to cry. She was not. Mariah Clayborn didn't cry.

Her throat thickened. Yes, well, while that may have been true of the old Mariah—the chin-up, shoulders-squared Mariah who knew that everything would be okay so long as she acted like it was—the new Mariah—the one who had fallen in love with Zach Letterman—realized that all she had been doing was putting off the inevitable. That what bothered her didn't really go away, it merely camped out in a quiet corner waiting to overwhelm her when she least expected it.

She laughed without humor and turned her head to hide the tears she suddenly had to blink away. And now was the single most unexpected, not to mention inopportune, moment. They were on a treasure hunt, for Pete's sake, not going out for some carefree Sunday picnic.

"Mariah?"

She took a deep breath and squinted through the window. "What?"

"Is everything all right?"

She didn't dare look at Zach for fear that all the emotions bubbling just below the surface would come pouring out. "Fine." She lifted her chin. "Some dust just got into my eye, that's all."

"Both of them?"

"Yes, both of them." She stared at him. "You have a problem with that?"

She cringed at the strident tone of her voice, but noted that Zach didn't react one way or another to her short burst of anger. Rather he was looking at her with concern, with banked desire, and with another emotion marking his handsome face that she couldn't quite put her finger on.

A car horn sounded.

Mariah looked around them until she spotted where her father was parked off to the side a short ways back.

Great. She'd completely missed the spot because she'd been too busy trying to read something into Zach's expression that wasn't there.

She stepped on the brakes then jammed the truck into Reverse, silently counting backward from ten as she did. The action not only helped calm her nerves, it reminded her of the limits set on her and Zach's relationship. Limits that would not be altered by her professing her true love.

ZACH GLANCED at where Mariah rolled her eyes, kicked at the dusty ground, then walked away mumbling something under her breath.

"Where you reckon this is?" Hughie asked Zach.

Zach looked over the older man's shoulder. "I'd say you're target on. But given what I know about maps, I wouldn't put any money on it."

Hughie chuckled then stepped over to Old Man Clooney, who appeared to be checking wind direction with a wet finger. What wind direction had to do with treasure was anyone's guess. But despite Mariah's skepticism, and his own lack of knowledge in the area, the man who looked like little more than weathered skin stretched over a skeleton fascinated Zach. If Clooney should tell him that he was going to make the Red Sea appear, then part it, Zach would probably half expect it to happen. He shook his head. Looked like age didn't have anything to do with being a fool.

Cupping a hand over his eyes, he scanned the desolate area. Not a house or a building or another person in sight. The sound of the summer wind whipping over the plains was almost eerie.

Hughie had told him all this land belonged to the state now. What with Bisbane disappearing and no blood relatives left to claim his land, the state had stepped in to claim it. That meant anything found on the land would also belong to the state.

He frowned, trying to compile all the information that had gathered in his mind over the past twenty-four hours. There was the thief who had showed up first at the Unclaimed Baggage Center in Alabama looking for the same suitcase they were. Presumably it was the same thief who had snatched the bag when he and Mariah were on their way to the airport.

Then there was the whole issue of Peggy Sue having to drop fifty pounds in the next three days if she hoped to fit into the dress in question in time for the renewal ceremony.

And what of the details Mariah had gathered? That the dress had been worn by a Boston socialite at her wedding a mere two weeks ago? Would a new bride sell her wedding dress?

He absently rubbed the back of his neck and sighed. Throw on top of that the whole Claude Ray fiasco and you had yourself a mighty fine mess.

He watched Mariah, who was crouched down close to the earth, smoothing her hand over the soil. To say she'd been quiet during the ride out would be an understatement. Sure, he supposed that Claude Ray's tying her up and leaving her alone in the kitchen for him to find would ruin anyone's day. But he suspected her dour disposition was a little more complicated than that.

He squinted his eyes. And why shouldn't it be? Everything else was turning out to be complicated as hell. Why should whatever was happening between him and Mariah be any different?

"Find anything?" he asked as he stepped to stand next to her.

"No, I was just thinking."

"That could be dangerous."

She swatted at his leg then stood to her full height. "Very funny. No, I was just considering everything that has happened on this simple case of the missing wedding dress so far."

"I was just thinking the same thing myself."

She wiped her hands on her jeans. "Okay, so there's

this guy in Odessa who's been married God knows how long, and he and his wife decide to renew their vows, you know, because a number of years have passed and, well, maybe they forgot them."

Zach watched her begin to pace back and forth in front of him.

"So he, or his wife, who knows which one, finds the perfect dress to do it in—"

"A dress that wouldn't fit if she had a body-sized shoe-horn," he interjected.

Mariah blinked at him. "You didn't tell me that."

He shrugged. "You didn't tell me about the bracelet."

She made a face and resumed pacing. "Okay, so this couple find the perfect wedding dress, whether it fits or not is immaterial…" She paused. "Only the bag the dress is in gets lost in lost baggage hell." She stopped again. "Did they tell you where they got the dress?"

He shook his head. "Irrelevant information."

"Yes, of course, because being in a bag on its way to them already denotes ownership, right?"

"Are you saying the Gawlicks stole the dress to begin with?"

"I'm saying that the Gawlicks had someone steal the dress. The same someone who showed up in Alabama Unclaimed Baggage Center, then stole the suitcase—sans dress—from you outside the hotel."

"Go on," he said.

"This same someone, well, if he's working for Gawlick, then it's safe to assume that he knows who you are, because Gawlick hired you. Which makes you an easy target to follow."

"Yes, but why try to essentially steal the bag from himself? Seeing as Gawlick hired me to retrieve the dress and get it to him, then that's what you're saying he was doing."

"Because…" She trailed off, obviously thinking.

Zach looked out on the prairie again, noticing that a vehicle was kicking up dust about a mile or so away. "State land."

Mariah stared at him. "What?"

Zach pointed a finger at her. "Let's say for the sake of argument that Gawlick did steal the dress. If that's the case, then he did it not because his wife refused to wear anything else, even if she could fit into it. No. He did it because—"

"Because he knew about the map on it."

"Which means that he was—"

"On a treasure hunt."

He nodded. "Only if the hunt were fruitful, then he just spent a whole lot of resources giving the state of Texas a lot of money."

Mariah frowned. "I don't follow you."

Zach stomped his foot against the ground. "This land became the property of Texas when Bisbane died, bit the dust, disappeared, whatever."

"Uh-huh."

"So anything found on the land also belongs to the state of Texas."

"When the bag was lost, Gawlick hired Jennifer Madison's agency as a front to find the dress," she continued, understanding dawning on her face.

"Then he hired another man, or ordered the thief who was already in his employ, to steal the dress from us. When that happened, so far as we would know, the dress would be lost forever."

"And Gawlick would go on to secretly claim the treasure, there would be no renewal ceremony and no one would be any the wiser."

They stared at each other for a long moment without saying anything.

"Awfully complicated."

"Oh, no, it's quite simple, really. The circumstances are what make it complicated."

A couple yards away, the old prospector made an odd, throaty sound more animal than human. Zach lifted his brows and he and Mariah simultaneously shifted their gazes to watch the old man lift his arms as if giving praise to some unseen entity, his mouth moving, his skinny barrel chest vibrating.

Hughie moved to stand next to Zach, cupping a hand over his mouth. "It's something, watching him work."

"Is he Native American?" Zach asked.

"Nah. Never even been around 'em. Says this is how he's always worked."

"Ah."

On the other side of him, Mariah stifled a laugh.

The old man suddenly dropped his arms, startling the threesome where they stood watching. They all laughed uneasily as Clooney crouched down in a position Zach was half afraid he wouldn't be able to get back up from, then started hopping on each foot, swooping side to side like an airborne eagle with his feet stuck on the ground.

Mariah released a long breath next to him. "We probably could have found something quicker with the metal detector."

"Assuming the item we're looking for includes metal," Zach whispered.

Another loud sound issued from Clooney and Zach cleared his throat, determining to keep quiet from here on out…after he asked one more question.

He leaned closer to Hughie. "How long does this usually take?"

Hughie blinked at him. "How am I supposed to know? It takes what it takes."

"You mean you haven't worked with him before?"

Mariah leaned against Zach's side. "Remember, it's a legend."

Oh, great. Here they were standing out in the middle of nowhere watching an old coot imitate something he probably saw on TV, waiting for some sort of divine intervention to find the treasure of a man who had been dead for over a hundred years and who had traced a map of seed pearls onto his ill-fated bride's wedding dress.

It suddenly struck him how…bizarre this all was.

"Where are you going?" Mariah asked, grabbing his sleeve.

"To get the metal detector and a shovel. You with me?"

Hughie grabbed his other arm. "Wait. I think he found something."

Sure enough, Clooney was bent over at the waist, appearing to stare at the ground with unerring intensity.

"I think he threw his back out," Mariah whispered.

"Here," Clooney said, pointing a finger at the earth and surprising them all by uttering something intelligible. "It's here."

Zach blinked once, twice, then rubbed the back of his neck again.

The spot Clooney had pointed to was at least twenty feet from where they had reckoned the X on the map was. Did they start where Clooney indicated? Or where common sense and math dictated?

Mariah grabbed Zach's shirtsleeve. She stared at something in the distance. A truck. Black, silver-tinted windows, appearing to emerge from the dust, and rolling up quickly.

Clooney turned toward Hughie and held out his palm. "That'll be twenty bucks."

14

"WHAT IN THE HELL is Gawlick doing here?"

Mariah blinked at Zach's words as the truck bearing down on them drew to a stop mere feet away and two men climbed out from either side. One was Gawlick and the other looked oddly familiar. Then he realized where he had seen him. In Alabama. More specifically, holding the suitcase he'd taken from him as he ran away.

Mariah blew out a long breath next to him. "How much can happen in one day?" she whispered, then leaned closer to Zach. "I think he's about to prove our hypothesis."

"What in the hell is going on here?" Hughie asked.

Having collected his twenty, Clooney walked in the other direction, away from the threesome and away from the vehicles. Zach frowned. What was he planning to do, walk all the way back to town?

"Letterman," Denton Gawlick said, coming to stand in front of him.

"Gawlick," Zach said back, squinting against the late-morning sun that rested over the other man's shoulder.

"Do you mind explaining to me what you're doing out here, boy?"

Okay, so the man was twenty years Zach's senior, but

he didn't much like anyone calling him *boy,* as his conversation with Hughie the other night attested to. Especially someone he figured had set him up as a patsy.

Zach took in the man with Gawlick. At somewhere around six feet, he equaled Zach's height, but had at least thirty pounds on him—in raw muscle if the tight shirt was anything to go by. Zach tried to penetrate the mirrored glasses the dark-haired guy wore, but to no avail. He'd have to go with his unsmiling demeanor and set jaw to read his mood, which didn't look to be too good.

"Actually, Gawlick," Zach said, returning his attention to his client, "I was just about to ask the same of you."

Denton gestured toward his friend. "I had Allan tail you."

Mariah crossed her arms over her chest, drawing Zach's gaze there. "I would have known if we were followed."

Gawlick grinned at her. Zach didn't like the way he did it. "There is more than one way to tail someone, Miss Clayborn."

Hughie puffed out his chest, apparently not liking their visitors any more than Zach and Mariah did. "Just who in the hell are you two and what do you want?"

Zach grimaced and rubbed the back of his neck. "Hughie Clayborn, this is my client, Denton Gawlick."

The two men stared at each other, but it was Hughie who spoke first. "You mean the guy who paid you to find Ellie's dress."

"So you know then," Gawlick said, looking around the barren location, "though I probably should have figured that out given your location." He squinted off into the distance. "Bisbane's Bluff?"

"How did you know?" Mariah asked.

Gawlick chuckled. "Everyone knows about Bisbane's Bluff, my dear. It's the exact location of Jock's treasure I was unsure about. Considering that the old man had over two hundred thousand acres, that's a lot of land to cover without any guarantees." He stared at Zach. "Give me my dress, Letterman."

"Don't you mean you'd like to have your wife's dress?"

Gawlick scratched his chin, his head bobbing as he laughed. "You didn't really think I'd spend a dime to re-marry that old bag, did you? Hell no. I want the money Jock buried so I can leave the battle-ax and move on." He clasped his hands behind his back then rocked on his heels. "You know all the wealth you saw when you came out to my estate? Well, it's hers. From her family."

"After thirty years of marriage you're still entitled to half," Mariah said.

"Doesn't matter. All that money wouldn't be worth anything to me in what it would cost my reputation."

"What? For taking your part of the family money?"

"No, for taking her part of the family money."

Zach stared at the man as if he'd gone insane. "Okay, so let me see if I can get this straight. You arranged to steal Ellie's wedding dress from an unsuspecting bride in Boston…"

Gawlick shrugged. "She was done with it. How do you think I found the damn thing? The last proof of its exis-tence was from a wedding over twenty years ago. Again, in Boston. I knew if I waited long enough, searched dili-gently enough, it would pop up again."

"You've been waiting for twenty years?" Hughie asked, obviously incredulous. "Damn, man, ain't no woman worth that much if you can't stand to live with her."

Gawlick's face contorted. "You haven't seen the way I've grown accustomed to living."

"I repeat," Hughie said, spitting tobacco juice near

Gawlick's shiny Italian shoes. "Ain't no woman worth that much if you can't stand to live with her."

Gawlick's jaw tightened. He turned his attention to Zach. "Where's the dress?"

"Gone."

"What do you mean gone?"

"Gone, as in taken. Stolen. Pinched."

Gawlick looked immediately to his cohort, who shrugged his shoulders and said, "It wasn't me. If it were, we wouldn't be way out here in no-man's-land."

Gawlick cursed then paced away and stood with his back to them.

"Is this guy dangerous?" Mariah asked quietly.

Zach looked at her, an overwhelming sensation of wanting to protect her hitting him straight in the solar plexus. "I don't know, Mar."

Hughie lowered his voice and pretended an interest in the ground and the spit he was covering with dirt with his boot. "The old man might not be, but I'm not too sure about his friend there."

Zach had to admit that Hughie had a point. While Gawlick was short and pudgy and didn't look capable of lifting a stool in a bar fight much less surviving one, his stooge looked like he ate bar stools for breakfast.

He slanted a gaze to where Hughie was strapped, a mean-looking firearm gleaming from a shoulder holster. The sight didn't reassure him since Gawlick's goon sported an even bigger one. Surprisingly, Mariah wasn't packing. It was the first time he'd seen her go anywhere without her firearm. And now that she might need it...

He caught himself up short. What was he thinking about? There was no reason for him to think anyone was going to get hurt.

Gawlick seemed to regain his bearings and strode quickly back to them.

"You copied the map, didn't you?" he said, his face freshly animated. "Let me see it."

Zach narrowed his gaze. "We're going by memory."

"My ass," Gawlick growled. "Search him."

The ape stepped up and grabbed Zach by the arms. Zach instantly shrugged him off, his palms itching to clock the guy just for having touched him.

Mariah stepped up and slipped the map out of Zach's front pocket. "Here. Enjoy."

Hughie nodded. "If you don't mind, we'll be leaving now."

Gawlick stared at the map as if comparing it to what he knew about the dress.

Zach couldn't believe they were actually just going to walk out of there. Since Hughie's truck was a little farther than Mariah's truck, they all headed for Mariah's together, Zach bringing up the rear.

"Just a minute."

Zach grimaced, knowing it was too good to be true.

"We're going to need someone to dig this thing up."

SWEAT DRENCHED MARIAH where she sat in the relative shade of the side of her truck, her hands tied behind her back for the second time that day. But unlike earlier, this time Hughie was tied up right alongside her, both of them watching as Zach drove a shovel into the hard Texas earth and tossed it aside, the mound next to his target growing higher while the hole grew deeper.

She squinted up at the sun. She judged it to be afternoon, but she couldn't be sure given that she couldn't see her watch. But the sun was always a good indicator.

"Hey, Gawlick, even slaves need water," Hughie called

out. "Give the kid something to drink before he shrivels up and blows away with the wind."

Gawlick said something to the dark man at his side.

Zach stood up, his bare chest glistening as he wiped sweat from his brow. He'd taken off his shirt and used it to protect his head against the harsh summer rays, but that left the rest of him at the sun's ruthless mercy. "There's some water in the back of the truck. Give it to them," Zach called out to Gawlick.

Mariah blinked at him. She and Hughie weren't in need of water. He was.

The goon reached into the back of her truck and found the insulated packs. He held out a bottle to Mariah. She glared at him. "What am I supposed to hold it with? My breasts?"

The stranger's eyes drifted to the area in question, then he leered at her.

Hughie chuckled next to her. "I used to wonder where you got that mouth of yours. Then I woke up one day and realized it was me. Not that I figured it out on my own, mind you. It took Miss Winona pointing it out to me. 'Hughie,' she said to me, 'if you had been born with breasts, you'd have been Mariah.'" He shook his head.

Mariah stared at him. Miss Winona? When had her father spoken to Winona McFarland?

"Untie his hands," Mariah said, indicating her father. "You've already taken his gun. What are you afraid he's going to do?"

She was guessing that the goon wouldn't think her father capable of tackling a five-year-old. Of course, he had no idea Hughie spent his days on the range.

"She's right, you know," Hughie said to Mariah. "Miss Winona. You're me all over again, you know?"

The goon motioned for Hughie to lean forward. He then

crouched down to cut the plastic tie he'd fastened around his wrists, then stepped back and handed him the bottle of water. Satisfied that neither of them were going anywhere, the goon walked back to the growing hole and stood holding his gun to his chest while he watched Zach.

Hughie cracked open the water and started holding it out for her. She shook her head. "You drink some then toss it to Zach."

"God, you're as stubborn as I ever was," Hughie said. "Drink, girl. Now."

Mariah glared at him then took the tiniest sip on record. He forced her to take more by refusing to remove the bottle until she did.

"Talk about stubborn," she murmured, absolutely no malice in the response.

He was right, she realized. All these years she'd been so preoccupied with how unlike her mother she was that she hadn't noticed she was so much like her father. She looked into his weathered face and knew instantly it was true. The fact made her...happy somehow. Content.

The truth was, she'd spent so much time counting off who and what she was not, that she hadn't really paid attention to who and what she was. She focused on the powerful muscles in Zach's back as he heaved, dug, then heaved again. And it had taken a Yankee to do that for her.

She'd asked him to teach her how to be sexy, instead he'd showed her sexy wasn't just what you wore or how you acted, but was a state of mind. And damned if she didn't feel sexy.

She swallowed hard. Or was her new sensuality a direct result of the man himself instead of something he'd awakened in her? She couldn't be sure. All she knew was that she seemed to hear the very humming of blood through her veins whenever he was around. Aware of every sweet nuance of life and sex…and love.

She leaned against the side of the truck. Hell of a time to come to that realization. Oh, she'd long suspected that things were more serious for her than she'd ever dared let on. She'd had three whole relationships in her life before meeting Zach. But she'd been so distracted by the fact that her exes soon became engaged to other women that she'd missed all the warning signs. And it could have been that very distraction that had allowed it to happen.

God, this was so confusing. Everything. From the case of the missing wedding dress to hidden treasure. To a casual agreement with Zach Letterman that had turned into something much more intense.

Then there was her father…

She looked at Hughie Clayborn, who appeared to be holding up better than she was. He sat up straight, his eyes alert, undoubtedly formulating a plan to get them out of the mess they were in.

He was a loyal man. A handsome one. And she'd been so very selfish to ignore that he might want to move on after her mother's death. Find someone else to love. Perhaps even marry.

The thought took her breath away.

Wasn't anything in her life the way it had been a week ago?

Heave, dig…heave, dig. Mariah concentrated on the simple action, wishing she could take turns with Zach.

Then the shovel hit something obviously metallic, and even the wind seemed to stop blowing.

EVERY MUSCLE in Zach's back was jarred from the impact of his shovel hitting something hard and yielding.

"Get it out, get it out!" Gawlick yelled, leaping from his

car where he'd been sitting with the air-conditioning on. He ran to the side of the site. "It's the treasure."

Zach grimaced, the thought of handing his ex-client a grain of dirt disgusting to him. "It's a rock."

Gawlick stared at him then motioned to the other guy positioned somewhere behind Zach. He felt the cold muzzle of a gun pressed against the back of his neck. "Get it out."

Anger filled Zach to overflowing as he stood still, staring at Gawlick and the goon's reflection in his sunglasses. He'd been prepared for just this moment. He moved the shovel over a couple of inches and overturned a shoebox-sized rock that he'd dug around instead of uncovering the metal he'd hit.

"A rock," Gawlick said numbly.

Zach wanted to hit him in the head with the shovel, only he was a millimeter too far away. Probably by design.

"Drop it."

Zach stiffened, recognizing Hughie's voice, then a telltale metallic click.

"Next time you take a man's gun from him, you might want to check to make sure he doesn't have another one."

Zach slightly turned his head. Mariah was struggling to her feet with her hands still bound behind her back. "Stay where you are, Mar."

She glared at him. He could see how much it was eating away at her not being able to help.

The gunman behind him moved, looking at Mar, as well.

Zach swung around hard with the shovel, catching him on the hand, whacking it and the gun he held away just as he squeezed the trigger. A shot spit up dirt a couple of feet to Zach's left. Zach dropped the shovel then caught the guy in the mouth with what had to be the sucker punch of a lifetime. The goon stumbled backward, forcing Hughie to move.

"Whoa there, bud. You don't want to fall on me."

And he did fall, straight to his knees.

Zach climbed out of the hole and advanced on the man, pulling him to his feet by the front of his shirt. He jerked him closer so he wouldn't have to speak in more than a whisper. "Touch my girl again and you'll regret the day you were born."

A HALF HOUR LATER Mariah sat brushing the last of the dirt off the oblong metal container that looked like a regular run-of-the-mill toolbox.

The instant Zach and her father had turned the tables on Gawlick and his hired muscle, everything had changed. Instead of her and Hughie being tied up, the other guys were. She eyed where the sun was beginning to edge around her truck to where they sat. Gawlick moved his legs as if he'd been burned by the sunlight slanting against his legs.

"Well, don't just sit there," Hughie said from behind her. "Open the damn thing."

She did. With a swift flick of her hand, she released the two rusty latches and popped open the lid. Beside her, Zach went still and she could hear her father drawing a deep breath behind her.

Sitting at the bottom of the box was a handful of pictures and a small velvet bag. Mariah reached for the pictures. Zach picked up the bag.

"This must be Ellie," she whispered, very gently handling the sepia shots of a woman in various poses. There were maybe ten of them all told, none larger than the palm of her hand. But it was the last one that captured her attention. While Ellie had been pretty in all the pictures, in this one she stood smiling up at a man. Jock? She turned the photo over to find the back blank, no indication of who the man was. She stared at the couple again. It had to be Jock. The way Ellie was looking at him, it couldn't be anyone else.

Zach emptied the contents of the small velvet bag into his open hand. But it wasn't the items Mariah was so much interested in as the man himself. Was the way Ellie had looked at Jock the way she looked at Zach? Oh, sure, she had pictures of herself. The odd shot over the years at school graduations and birthday parties. A few of her with her former boyfriends. But in none of them had she looked particularly happy. She appeared more interested in figuring out a way to either duck the camera or break it altogether.

She carefully put the photos back into the box.

"What's in the bag?" Hughie asked, supporting his weight with his hands on his knees as he peered over Zach's shoulder.

"Wedding rings."

Mariah gazed at the two perfect pieces of gold shining in his palm and reached out a shaky hand to touch them. They seemed a richer shade of gold than she'd ever seen. Thick and unpolished and the most beautiful things she'd ever seen. She picked up the larger of the two bands. Inscribed inside was "Ellie-7-2-1899." She tilted the other where it still rested in Zach's hand. It read "Jock," with the same date.

She rocked back on her heels, staring out at the vast land surrounding them.

"Jock's Treasure," Zach murmured.

Jock's Treasure hadn't been bars of gold, or bags of diamonds, or deeds to land. Jock's true treasure had been Ellie.

"WHAT ARE YOU DOING?" Mariah whispered.

It was near dusk, usually her favorite time of the day, when the sky turned into a living copy of the watercolors displayed in the window of the store next to the P.I. office. Tonight the sky was especially beautiful with smears of purple and orange tingeing the wispy clouds on the horizon.

She stood in the gravel driveway of the ranch house watching as Zach closed the bed of her truck. They'd returned there shortly after they'd retrieved Jock's Treasure and the county sheriff had arrived on the scene to take over custody of Denton Gawlick and his hired help. The metal box was in the kitchen, her father looking for false bottoms and secret compartments, unconvinced that a story that had survived for so many years had yielded nothing but a couple of unused wedding bands and a handful of old photographs.

Zach slid his hands into his jeans pockets. "I thought you and I might go for a ride."

Mariah raised her brows. "A ride? Haven't we done enough traveling already today?"

She stepped toward the truck bed and he sidestepped her, preventing her from seeing what he'd been doing inside. "Nope." He gestured toward the house with a nod of his head. "I figure I couldn't wait until Hughie, um, went to bed."

She frowned. "Hughie hasn't been going to bed for at least the past couple of nights. Hughie has been sneaking out to meet Miss Winona."

Zach's brows rose high on his forehead. "How did you find out?"

"You mean you knew?"

"Yeah. I ran into him that first morning outside your room. I thought he was just getting up and that there was going to be hell to pay, but it turned out he was just getting in."

Mariah silently considered him. "Why didn't you tell me?"

"I thought you said you knew."

"Yeah. I figured it out. This morning."

"Oh." He took one hand out of his pocket and rubbed the back of his neck. "I promised I wouldn't say anything to you, or to anyone else for that matter."

"Don't you think I had a right to know?"

"I think it was important that I honor my word."

Honor his word. Mariah's heart beat loudly in her chest.

"So what do you say? Are you up for a ride?"

Mariah swallowed thickly and faced the horizon. Any excuse to stay outside and watch the remainder of the sunset was a good one. That this was Zach's last night in Hoffland, that she would be driving him to Hobby first thing in the morning...well, she refused to think about that for fear she might cry.

Her. Mariah Clayborn. Cry. But she wouldn't just cry. The emotion dammed up in her chest felt suspiciously like a deluge just waiting to happen whenever she thought of Zach's leaving. She had a feeling if she gave herself up to tears she'd end up bawling.

She blinked and looked over her shoulder toward the house.

"Hughie already knows about my plans."

"Oh? Seems like you and Hughie are sharing an awful lot lately."

Zach grinned. "Does that bother you?"

"No." Yes.

But she wasn't about to launch into all the reasons that made sense. Not right now. Not when her chariot in the shape of her rusty old pickup truck awaited. So what if it would turn back into old Nelly at midnight? That her prince would disappear without even leaving a glass shoe behind in the morning?

She frowned, wondering just where all these strange thoughts were coming from. She wasn't the "and they lived happily ever after" type. She preferred action flicks over romantic comedies. And yes, while she admitted to tearing up during the occasional Hallmark commercial, well, that was between her and the TV.

Besides, she had but to remember her three exes and their quicksilver engagements to other women to know that she wasn't the only one who didn't look at her as Cinderella material. Obviously neither did men. She was little sister or friend material, not lover or wife.

She rolled her eyes to stare at the sky above her. God, was she really setting up all the makings of a pity party? Oh, poor Mariah Clayborn. She'll never find herself a man to settle down with.

So what?

She was happy with her life. Happy with who she was. More importantly, she couldn't change if she'd wanted to. Twenty-six years had gone into making the package that was her. And she was proud of every one of them.

She eyed Zach in a new light. He hadn't moved from the position he'd been in when he'd blocked her passage. The light evening breeze brought his scent to her. Of fresh lime and one-hundred-percent pure Zach Letterman.

She smiled, wanting this last night more than anything. "Bring it on, cowboy."

15

Zach pulled to a stop only a couple of miles behind the ranch. He'd had to drive carefully since he'd covered this ground on the back of a horse the day before when he'd been out with Hughie. He'd spotted an area that was perfect for what he had in mind. A tall oak tree rose out from the ground on a small rise. Mariah looked at the scene now, and the waning sunset behind them, unusually quiet on the ride out, though she had sat smack-dab next to him, her side pressed to his, her arm entwined with his, her hand resting none too innocently on his jean-clad thigh.

He switched off the engine, silence wrapping them in an immediate intimacy.

Mariah cleared her throat. "I, um, hope you didn't come all this way hoping to do something in the truck."

He cocked a brow. "Oh?"

She twisted her lips. "Let's just say that I've been there, and, well, it's not fun."

He opened the door. She attempted to free herself to climb out the other side, but he held on to her hand, hauling her out after him on the driver's side instead. She gasped and he caught her up in his arms, then allowed her to slide slowly down the length of his body, letting her in on the fact that he was already partially aroused.

She smiled up at him. "You're a sneaky devil."

"And you're beautiful."

Mariah dropped her gaze and he forced her attention back up to him.

"You still don't get it, do you?" he asked.

"Get, um, what?"

Zach considered telling her, but decided it would probably be better to show her. "Come on."

"Zach, I…" She gasped again when he tugged her hand, dragging her after him. He stopped at the bed gate and opened it.

"I hope you're not planning on doing anything in there, either," she whispered.

"Picky tonight, aren't we?"

She shrugged but refused to meet his gaze.

"Here." He handed her a wicker basket that was a little on the heavy side. She had to think fast or risk dropping it. "I was thinking we could find a spot under the tree over there."

He waited to see if she'd object to that, complain of dripping sap or something equally lame, but she didn't. He inwardly breathed a sigh of relief, took out a thick wool blanket and a small cooler, then followed after her.

Silently she helped him stretch out the blanket then position the items they'd carried within arm's length. He kicked off his shoes and sat down on the blanket. After a long pause, she followed suit.

Zach leaned back, supporting himself on his elbows as he took in the sunset. "Ah. I knew the view would be incredible from here."

Mariah appeared to finally notice which way they were facing and her face brightened as she stretched out next to him. The sun was just sinking down over the horizon, leaving myriad colors in its wake. "Incredible."

The instant she was captivated by nature's display, Zach allowed himself to become captivated with her. "Mmm, it is."

She slowly turned her head, his voice likely tipping her off to what he'd been referring to. "You're a charmer."

"And you don't know how to take a compliment."

"Maybe it's because I haven't gotten a whole lot of them."

He gently tucked a stray strand of hair back from her face. "I don't believe that."

"You wouldn't."

He chuckled softly then turned his attention back to the sky.

Mariah was tenser than he'd ever seen her. He wanted more than anything to stretch out on top of her, to take advantage of every last minute they had together. But he sensed that she wasn't ready yet. And even accepted that maybe she wouldn't be tonight.

And he knew why. Like him, her mind was on tomorrow morning.

He absently rubbed his chin. He had yet to tell her that he'd already asked Hughie to drive him to the airport. After tonight...well, he didn't think he'd be able to handle a long drive in the truck with her. Not and still get on the plane. And he had to get on that plane.

Of course, it would only be minimally better riding with Hughie. He'd come to care about the big guy; he'd never bonded with another man like that. In a way he'd never had a chance to bond with his own father. And Hughie hadn't been nearly as successful at hiding his disappointment at Zach's leaving as Mariah was.

"What in the hell do you mean, you're leaving?" he

said when Zach had quietly asked him to drive him to the airport. "I was just getting used to having you around the place. Thought you might like to stick around for a while. Like forever."

Subtle Hughie was not. But that's part of what made Hughie Hughie.

As for the forever part, that had taken him aback like few things he'd encountered in his life. Forever right now was a bunch of plans on a chalkboard. He'd mentally prepared himself for the changes necessary to adapting to life in Texas, but for a *fixed* period of time. He'd had no idea something would happen to him, more specifically *someone,* who would make him want to stay.

"You know," he said to Mariah, who hadn't budged an inch next to him. They weren't touching physically, but he felt her presence as fully as if she were under his skin. "I'd really love to crawl inside your head right now and see what's going on."

Mariah kept her eyes focused on the horizon as the colors faded slowly to black, the bright quarter moon rising from the east not strong enough to light the sky yet. "It would be a pretty dull visit because there's nothing going on," she said.

"Bull. I can hear the click-click of your thoughts from here."

"Oh?" That got her attention. She rolled onto her side and propped her head on her hand. "So tell me, Letterman, what am I thinking?"

She was reverting to calling him by his family name. Not a good sign. "You're probably thinking about what happened today. About Gawlick. Jock and Ellie. Claude Ray might rate a second or two, as well."

Mariah focused on the wool blanket. "I'm just thankful they found the wedding dress, undamaged and unsold at the downtown pawnshop." She made a face. "I can't believe it was sold for twenty-five bucks."

"Oh, I don't know. I hear it told that Jock's Treasure was a complete bust."

Finally, a smile from her. "Yeah, it was, wasn't it?"

"Oh, I don't know."

Her gaze snapped to his face. "What do you mean? The only things in the box were the pictures and the rings."

"Mmm-hmm. The thing is the box wasn't all that was down there."

She scrambled to sit up. "What are you talking about?"

Zach leaned forward and took something out of the wicker basket. Mariah blinked at it, saying nothing for a long moment. "A rock?"

"But is it just a rock?" Zach murmured, using every ounce of restraint he had to keep from tackling her to the blanket and kissing the skeptical expression from her face. He handed it to her. "Awfully light, don't you think? For a rock of that size."

Mariah frowned, weighing the rock in her hands. As he knew she would, she turned it over, immediately locating the piece he'd worked loose when he'd noticed the rock was a little on the light side. She took out the U.S. savings bonds dating back to the late 1800s, gasping as she shuffled through the thick pile.

"A veritable fortune," he said when she blinked at him.

"You weren't...I mean..."

"Planning to keep it? No. I just thought you'd like to see it before I hand it over to the authorities."

She was quiet for a long moment. "Maybe some kind of memorial could be built with the money. You know, to commemorate Jock's love for Ellie."

Zach's heart contracted so tightly it took his breath away. *Mariah* took his breath away.

He put the rock back in the basket, then leaned forward for a chaste kiss to her nose that turned out to be anything but chaste. Mainly because Mariah tilted her head, her lashes fluttering closed against her cheeks, her mouth budding open to accept the attention meant for her nose.

Zach groaned, his self-control flying out the window. He moved the rock out of the way and hauled her against his length. Well, there were no windows out here in the middle of the Texas plains, and that knowledge made his restraint flee, leaving him with a truckload of lust and one incredible woman capable of handling it.

Mariah sighed and melted against him, soft against his hard. This moment, when they first kissed, when the simple action was full of promise but no pressure, was one of the few times when Mariah shed her Texas cowgirl bravado, seemingly content to be just herself, not who she thought she should be, or who she thought she was.

Zach slipped a hand up to trap a tight-tipped breast in his palm, drinking in her soft moan as she pressed her pelvis more insistently against his growing arousal.

Things quickly escalated from there. Hands caressed and stroked and probed, limbs entwined, and breathing grew ragged. Damn, but she was the most incredible woman he'd ever met. She embodied everything that was appealing in the opposite sex without any of the props that usually detracted from that appeal. She was salt of the earth with eyes and hair the color of rich Texas soil, skin the color of golden sunshine and a smile that could make a blind man shield his eyes. But it was her heart, her zest for life, her tentativeness and her boldness, her confidence with a gun and skill with a horse, and her passionate responsiveness to him that absolutely took his breath away.

Zach could have continued kissing her for hours. Stroking her, touching her, feeling her. But she gently pulled back, her husky, quiet laugh filling his ears.

"Whoa," she whispered.

With the sun's rays no longer competing with the moon, the crescent burned bright in the big sky, bathing Mariah's features in soft light.

Zach smiled at her, his hand caressing her bare arm just below the sleeve of her T-shirt. "Yes, I'd say that about covers it."

She restlessly licked her lips then tangled her hand in the front of his shirt. "You know, I still have a beef with you."

He examined her face, feature by feature. From her full, unpainted, irresistibly ripe lips, to her strong yet so delicately formed chin, then up to her dark, dark eyes fringed with lashes that needed no mascara. "What's that?"

"Our deal."

"Mmm," he responded. "You mean the part where you wanted me to school you in sexiness."

She nodded almost imperceptibly, her attention on where her hand was fisted in the front of his shirt.

He kissed first one side of her mouth, then the other. "Mariah, if you were any sexier, you'd be the death of me."

Her deep brown eyes shifted until she was staring at him. "Then why are you leaving?"

Good God. Zach felt as if someone had poured mercury down his throat. It coated and pooled in his stomach, making him feel ill and hot at the same time.

They hadn't discussed that particular topic, his leaving. He presumed it was because they both had known that he would, no matter how much he wished things were different.

He threaded his fingers through the hair above her ear and held tight, then rested his forehead against hers. Too close to see her, he closed his eyes, breathing deeply of her scent.

Damn it, this type of thing just didn't happen. You didn't meet someone one day, then want to abandon everything you'd worked for, planned for, the next. It didn't make any sense. It was too reckless. Too untrustworthy. Too fast.

But he and Mariah, well, they didn't have the luxury of time. He'd barely gotten any sleep the night before, thinking about everything. Thinking about her. Thinking about his feelings for her. He'd toyed with the idea of asking her to come back to Indiana with him. Or to consider making a go at a long-distance relationship. He could fly down to Houston every other weekend, and she could fly up to Indiana on alternating weeks.

But even that idea had seemed impossible to him.

He heard her deep swallow. "Never mind. Forget I said that," she whispered.

He opened his eyes and pulled back just enough to see her close her eyes.

"God, I couldn't sound more desperate, could I?" she moaned.

He smoothed her hair back with gentle passes of his hands, then held her face in his palms. "Oh, Mariah. You don't have a clue, do you? You have no idea what you've done to me. What you're still doing to me."

Her eyes loomed full of hope and longing.

"Do you want to know why I haven't taken the initiative to teach you how to be sexy? Because you're already sexier than any ten women combined. Hell, Mar, I'm coming to think that your exes didn't leave you because you weren't enough for them. They left because you were too much."

A frown marred her soft brow.

"I want you so much I hurt with it," he whispered urgently, needing her to understand. "And at the same time a small voice is telling me that I don't deserve you. The problem is, I don't know if there is a man out there alive who deserves you. Hell, just thinking of you with someone else who might be more deserving ties my stomach into knots."

She tried to wriggle from his grasp, but he refused her the freedom.

"In fact, I've been tied into knots ever since I first met you. You're honest. Gentle. *Real.*" He dropped his hands to her shoulders and held her fast. "And you're the sexiest damn woman I've ever met in my life."

Her bottom lip began to tremble. Zach groaned and leaned forward to kiss her.

"And you don't believe a single thing I'm saying, do you?"

She didn't answer with words. Rather she put her arms around his neck and launched a sensual assault on him, filling his senses with everything that was wild, wonderful Mariah Clayborn.

Her tongue dove and darted and dueled as she restlessly moved her head from side to side, her breathing quickly growing ragged. Her hands fluttered against his chest, his stomach. Then she boldly grasped his erection, first through his jeans, then when that appeared not to be enough, she fumbled with his zipper, not giving in until the night air caressed his pulsing arousal along with her fingers.

Zach tugged on the hem of her T-shirt, forcing her to stop her attentions briefly while he pulled it over her head. Next came her bra and jeans and panties, leaving her gloriously bare under the loving rays of the moon.

She moved to tug his jeans down his hips.

"Shh," he said, although she hadn't said anything. Rather he meant to halt her for a moment, just long enough for him to visually drink his fill of her. "I want to look at you."

He half expected her to try to cover herself, for the inhibited part of her that had played hide-and-seek over the past few days to peek out. He trailed his fingertips down over the curve of her neck, her collarbone, then around and over one large-tipped breast, then the other. His mouth watered with the need to taste her there and he did, limiting it to a brief pull deep into the depths of his mouth before drawing back again. He moved his fingers onward, over her toned belly, over one hip and down one outer thigh then following with the other. She had the figure of a goddess. Lean and powerful and stunning.

He touched the top of the wedge of dark curls between her legs and hesitated, wondering if she'd close up on him.

One heartbeat…two…

Mariah opened her thighs, spreading them wide so that the core of her essence was bare and unprotected under his gaze.

"God help me," he whispered, heat searing his veins as he possessively moved his hand to her core. She shuddered and made a strangled sound. Afraid he'd hurt her, he started to release his grip.

She immediately grabbed his wrist and held him tight. "No," she said, licking her lips. "Don't stop."

Zach groaned, only too happy to oblige. He drew his finger through her dripping channel, purposely avoiding contact with those areas she wanted touched the most. She moaned and her hips bucked from the blanket as if trying to force the contact. His temperature gauge shot up past the danger zone at the look of raw need on her face.

Her lashes fluttered down and her elegant throat worked around a swallow.

Within moments he'd completely stripped and sheathed himself, then none too soon found himself nudging her thighs farther apart with his knees.

"Please," Mariah whimpered, rubbing her wet curls against his erection.

"Please what, Mariah?" he whispered, tilting his hips to rub against her without entering.

Her eyes blinked open. "Please love me."

And he did. In every way it was possible for a man to love a woman.

Zach fit himself against her tight opening then surged into her to the hilt, causing her to cry out, her back arching off the ground, her hands desperately gripping the blanket. Her slick muscles contracted and convulsed and shivered, pushing him precariously toward the edge. But he held on to the cliff through shear will, nothing more beautiful to him than watching Mariah soar to climax, with no more incentive needed than having his body inside hers. He'd done this. He'd coaxed and charmed and eased his way past her defenses until finally he was rewarded with watching her achieve a violently intense orgasm with one, long stroke.

Her spasms slowly diminished and she fought to catch her breath. Zach stayed painfully still, waiting for the moment when she opened her eyes and stared up at him in wonder.

God, how he loved this woman. Loved her ability to trust. To jump into any situation with both feet, consequences be damned.

He loved her, period.

And leaving her was going to be the single most difficult thing he'd ever have to do in his life.

But there were ten hours between now and the time his plane departed. And he intended to make every moment count.

16

IF THREE STRIKES MEANT you were out, what did four strikes mean?

Mariah covered her ears, as much to block out the sound of the workers replacing the roof on the agency as to quell the sound of her answer. No matter, the part of herself that refused to stay silent answered, "It means you're a Texas-sized fool." How else could you explain the loss of man number four?

Even up to the very last minute, Mariah had held out some hope that Zach would stay. That he would realize that what he felt for her was much more than lust and that they could forge a life together in her hometown. Live in the house she'd grown up in and which had played so much of a role in their blossoming relationship. Have the white picket fence and 2.5 kids.

Then seven days ago a lightbulb went off...or rather the sun had risen, and there she'd stood outside the ranch house, Hughie waiting with his truck engine running in the driveway, and her staring at Zach with what she was sure had to be her heart beating in her eyes.

He'd gripped her shoulders as if he might never let her

go, hauled her to him and kissed her until she felt her legs go weak.

Then he'd walked away from her without saying another word.

"Fool, fool, fool."

"Did you say something?"

Mariah blinked George into focus where he sat across from her.

She shook her head. How could she possibly explain to her cousin what had happened? She'd merely told him Zach had gone back home, then clammed up.

She tuned in to the lack of sounds from the roof.

"What happened to the workers?"

"It's lunchtime, Mar." George put the magazine he was reading down and took his feet off his desk. "Speaking of which, I could go for something. Can I get you anything?"

She shook her head and took a lunch bag from her desk drawer. "I'm good. Thanks."

George put on his hat and walked through the door. She stared after him, then at the bag she held. What was wrong with her? She never packed her lunch. But somehow, after Zach left, she'd been able to walk into the kitchen without feeling uneasy, the mystery gone and plain common sense taking its place. She was learning how to wield a pan with the best of them. Well, okay, maybe not the best, but she was growing braver, venturing beyond the ordinary staples and sampling other recipes. Some solely by trial and error, others from her mother's old cookbook that she'd unearthed from the attic along with a lot of other things that had been stowed away up there, presumably for safekeeping, though Mariah was coming to believe it was because neither father nor daughter had been able to deal with the reminders.

It was nice that that was no longer the case.

Instead she had to deal with the fact that with every breath she took she felt Zach's loss like a sharp knife to the chest.

The telephone at her elbow rang and she automatically snatched up the receiver, relieved for the interruption. "Clayborn Investigations."

"Mariah?"

Mariah resisted the urge to anxiously hang up the receiver and crawl under her desk, cursing herself for not checking the caller display before picking up. On the line was none other than strike three, Justin Johnson.

"God, woman, what's going on over there? I've been trying to contact you forever."

Mariah blew out a long breath. "Had it ever crossed your mind that maybe I didn't want to talk to you?"

"No."

Of course it hadn't. J.J. called a woman, the woman picked up. "Look, J.J., I'm busy," she said. "What do you want?"

"To apologize."

Mariah's brows drew together. "For what?"

"For getting engaged to Heather so soon after, well, you know…"

"After we broke up?"

"Yes."

"Don't worry about it. Water under the bridge and all that." She tucked her hair behind her ear. "Anyway, what does it matter if you got engaged a week after or six months?"

"The last name of the baby Heather's going to have."

Mariah's mind went blank. "Oh." That would mean that he and Heather were together while she was dating J.J.

"And no, I did not sleep with Heather while we were going out, if that's what you're thinking."

"Funny, that's exactly what I was thinking."

"Mariah, Heather is six months along."

"What?" She did the mental calculations. That meant that he would have been with Heather before Mariah had ever said yes to his request for a first date. Which meant that, in essence, Justin had dumped Heather for her.

She frowned. Somehow, in the scheme of things, that didn't make her feel any better. Well, not much anyway.

"I see," she finally said.

Justin's sigh filled the earpiece. "Anyway, mum's the word on the pregnancy thing. She's managed to keep it a secret until now—don't ask me how—but we're going to announce it the day we get back from our honeymoon."

Mariah didn't know what else to say, so she didn't say anything.

Justin cleared his throat. "Anyway, I was thinking…if you ever need anything…you know, if you ever get any urges you need taken care of…"

"You'd be the last person I called, J.J." Mariah stared at the extension with repulsion.

"Oh. Okay. I just thought, you know, that it wouldn't hurt to ask."

Mariah caught herself smiling slightly. "Anyway, congratulations, J.J. And thanks, you know, for telling me what you did."

A few moments later she hung up the phone and sat staring at the same stretch of space that had occupied so much of her time that morning.

Heather was pregnant…had gotten that way before Mariah and J.J. started dating.

She shook her head, unsure what, exactly, the information meant except that J.J. pretty much *had* to break up with her, and *had* to marry Heather.

Okay, so the information made her feel better. It was nice to know she hadn't been to blame for the breakup.

The bell over the front door rang. She looked up as she blindly put her lunch bag back in her drawer.

A young woman maybe a year or two her junior stood looking around.

"Can I help you?" Mariah asked.

"Is...is George here?"

Mariah instantly recognized the voice, and the hesitancy in it. This was George's female caller.

"He just went out to lunch." She gestured toward his desk. "You can wait if you'd like. He shouldn't be more than a few minutes."

The woman looked at her as if something just dawned on her. "Are you Mariah? Mariah Clayborn, George's cousin?"

Mariah knew a moment of pause. Only because the young woman looked almost awestruck. "Um, yes, I am."

"Oh, my God, it is you!" She rushed across the space separating them and thrust her ultrafeminine hand toward Mariah. "I can't believe I'm talking to you live and in the flesh."

Okay, so maybe there had been a bit of press on the Jock and Ellie story and her and Zach's involvement in helping find Jock's Treasure. Plans had been announced to build a small museumlike memorial near Bisbane's Bluff. In it would be the wedding dress, the pictures reproduced, enlarged and framed, the wedding bands, and the story of the star-crossed lovers and the conclusion to the story written in script on the walls. The savings bonds the bogus rock had held would be used to finance it. And the existence of the museum would serve as a reminder to anyone who thought there might still be something buried out there.

As for Denton Gawlick, his wife was backing him

with her considerable financial resources. Meaning that he would probably get off without so much as a slap across the wrist. She seemed to be completely oblivious to what he'd really intended to do with the booty, apparently buying into what he was telling the press, that he'd planned to propose to his wife all over again and had bought the dress for her and then the rest just happened by accident. Gawlick's lackey had disappeared the instant he was let out on bail.

At any rate, the first couple of days after the story broke, Mariah had had to beat reporters away from the door.

And now she was facing a starry-eyed young woman who thought she walked on water.

"Yes, I am," she said, managing a smile, telling herself it wasn't the woman's fault.

"I'm Janette Pratt. Oh, I'm so happy to finally meet you," she said, animatedly pumping Mariah's hand. "George has told me so very much about you."

"I'll bet."

Mariah managed to salvage her hand.

"I'm so glad you and I could have a moment alone together. I know George asked me not to, but I need to thank you for all you and George have done to help find my little sister."

Mariah blinked once, twice.

Apparently she'd been way off base. With more things than one.

George chose that moment to saunter back into the office, whistling as he did. He froze in his tracks the instant he spotted Janette standing in front of Mariah's desk.

Mariah smiled at the young woman. "You'll excuse us a moment, won't you?"

She rounded her desk and asked George to join her in

the back room. Moments later, after he spoke briefly with Janette, he came into the room. Mariah closed the door.

"Her little sister?"

George's grimace was as handsome as any of his grins. "Yeah. While you were, you know, otherwise occupied, Janette came in and asked for help looking for her younger sibling. They were, um, split apart ten years ago after their parents died and she hadn't seen her since." He shrugged. "So I helped her out."

"You...helped...her...out."

Mariah stared at the man before her as if she didn't know him at all. Not only had he accepted a case in her absence, he'd seen it through to the end.

"Yeah. Felt pretty good, too," he said, the grimace turning into a grin.

Mariah found herself smiling. "That wouldn't happen to have anything to do with the pretty young woman standing in the other room, would it?"

"Yes, I suppose it has something to do with it. But more...well, I've been meaning to talk to you. You see, I've wanted to take on a bigger load around here for a long time now."

"Bigger load?"

"Uh-huh."

Mariah didn't know quite how to react. She threw her arms around her cousin and kissed him loudly on the cheek, laughing when he turned a brilliant shade of red.

"Well, what did you go and do that for?"

"By way of congratulations," she smiled at him, "on becoming a man."

LATER THAT NIGHT dinner hadn't come out exactly the way Mariah had planned. She'd taken chicken breasts out of the freezer earlier in the day, but by the time she'd gotten home, she'd been too preoccupied to remember everything Zach had done with them while he was here.

She stood staring at the mess she'd removed from the oven, poking one of the stuffed breasts with a fork. The prongs stuck and it took some doing to get them back out again. The chicken was drier than dust and harder than the summer ground before a rainstorm.

She sighed and leaned her hips against the counter. Spaghetti it was, then. A few minutes found water on to boil and a store-bought can of sauce on to simmer.

She distractedly rubbed her forehead. Hughie should be coming in a few minutes and she hadn't even thought about what she was going to make for dessert.

Oh, the heck with it. Canned fruit had done all right before that handsome Yankee's shadow had ever darkened their doorstep.

Hughie came in from the living room instead of the back door, startling her.

"What's the matter with you, girl?" he asked with a chuckle.

Mariah swallowed hard, wondering how long it would take before she didn't jump at the occasional odd sound. Out there somewhere Claude Ray roamed, waiting to strike again. And until he surfaced, and she caught him, she wouldn't feel entirely comfortable.

"I didn't know you were in already."

"Yep. Just finished a shower." He crossed to stand in front of the stove. "I came home earlier hoping to catch you. You know, to tell you not to go to any trouble with dinner on account of me."

She caught a whiff of cologne and made a face. "Oh?"

"Yes. Now that the cat's out of the bag, Miss Winona has invited me over for dinner, you know, during the day when God and everyone can see us." He eyed what she was making. "It looks like you're not going to any trouble anyway."

Mariah switched off both burners and dumped the pot of water into the sink with a bang.

"Now why did you go and do that for?"

"Because now that you've criticized my cooking, I'm not going to sit around here alone and eat it!" she bellowed.

Hughie's bushy brows rose to his hairline.

Mariah paced slightly away, then lightly tapped the heel of her hand against her forehead. "I'm sorry. That was uncalled-for."

"No harm done," Hughie said quietly.

Great, now her father was looking at her as if she had a screw or two loose. That's all she needed right now. She had been doing so well skimming past any mention of Zach and acting as if everything was okay. Now in one burst of rarely displayed anger, she'd revealed all.

Hughie cleared his throat. "I think I have time for a cup of coffee before I go."

When Mariah moved to pour him a mug, he caught her hands. "No, I'll get it. You go sit down."

She collected a bag of cookies and plate on her way then poured the cookies onto the plate, the action about as domestic as she felt right then.

Hughie joined her, putting a cup in front of her, as well. Mint tea. Her favorite.

She blinked at him, wondering at this new attentiveness.

"You know, I knew there had to be more in there that you weren't sharing," he said. "I guess Zach was right in that there's much more to you than meets the eye."

She made a face. "I don't want to talk about Zach."

"I didn't realize we were."

Mariah searched her father's eyes.

"Anyway, I've been doing some thinking," he said,

in much the same way George had at the office earlier. Mariah braced herself, thinking there was far too much thinking going on for her liking.

"I want you to come back and work the ranch with me."

Mariah could have sworn she was hearing things. "What?" she whispered.

Hughie shifted, apparently uncomfortable. "Okay, you want me to do the whole bit, don't you? Apologize for saying the things I did, telling you that you were nothing more than a distraction, making you feel that…well, that I didn't appreciate you as you are. My daughter. The precious child I created with the first woman I ever loved, your mother."

"Oh, God." Mariah pushed from the table, finding tears closer to the surface than she felt comfortable with.

For long, silent moments she stood at the preparation island, battling back the pesky dampness, attempting to regulate her breathing, and trying like hell to figure out what was going on with everyone lately.

She nearly jumped when she felt Hughie's beefy hand rest against her shoulder. "Are you all right?"

Mariah closed her eyes tightly and nodded.

"Good. But I don't think it would hurt to tell you something I haven't said in a good long time." He squeezed her shoulder. "I love you, baby. More than any other person walking this earth."

Mariah gripped the countertop tightly. Oh, God.

Finally she gave in to the battle raging within her and threw herself into Hughie's big ol' arms. It had been a long, long time since she'd done that. Lost herself in the feel of her father's hug. Given herself permission to be his daughter instead of the stoic little girl, then independent woman, who didn't want to cause him any more heartache. The girl then woman who had barricaded her own heart against that same pain.

If you didn't love, then you couldn't hurt. At least that had been the reasoning.

And it turned out she'd been right.

Only she'd never stopped loving her father. And now she loved Zach.

"Aw, sugar," Hughie said gruffly, awkwardly patting her hair. "All these years I was afraid I had lost you." He kissed the side of her head. "Welcome back, baby. Welcome back."

17

IT WASN'T WORKING.

Zach hung up the phone from where he'd been talking to a Detroit P.I. about setting up a meeting next week in the Motor City. He sat back in his chair and stared at the modest Indianapolis skyline outside his top-floor office window.

Oh, his plans to franchise Finders Keepers were going off without a hitch. It was the…other part that wasn't working. Namely, his plan to edge Mariah Clayborn from his mind.

Zach dry-washed his face with his hands, taking minimal comfort in the rasp of skin against skin. Only the sound reminded him of running his hands over Mariah's silky, pliant flesh. Hell, everything he did reminded him of the maddening woman. He opened the refrigerator, there was a miniature Mariah, her boots shoulder-width apart, her arms crossed and that jaunty smile on her face standing right next to the bottle of orange juice. He opened the shower curtain and there she was again, turning her face into the spray, the water sluicing down her incredible body. He looked out at the Indianapolis skyline and he saw not buildings but the endless Texas plains and there on the horizon was Mariah, her hair flying around her enchanting face as she rode a horse bareback.

"You're losing it, Letterman."

Zach sighed and closed his eyes. When he'd left Mariah standing alone in her driveway ten days ago, her heart in her remarkable brown eyes, he'd thought he was doing the right thing. Not just for himself, but for her. And he kept telling himself that during his four-day stay in Midland until Jennifer hired on more help, then throughout his trip back home and succeeding days, hoping that time and distance would help him.

Instead time and distance made the ache in his chest even more acute.

He eyed the telephone. Would she welcome a call from him? More than anything, he wanted to share with her the progress of his plans. Tell her what he'd been doing. Then ask her to get on the next plane up so that they could take up where they left off.

But they really wouldn't be taking up where they left off, would they? There was no telling what effect his departure and subsequent absence had had on her. Did she hate him? Had she corralled him in with the previous men in her life, just another guy who had loved her and left her?

God, what had he done?

"Zach?" His assistant's voice rang out over the intercom. "Call for you on line one. They wouldn't say who it was but said it was important."

Important?

He stared at the blinking light, his mouth going dry. Mariah? He hadn't left her any contact information, but finding out where he was would be a piece of cake for Mariah the P.I.

"Thanks, Jan."

He hesitantly picked up the receiver and held it to his ear before pushing the button.

"Letterman here," he said in the strongest voice he could muster.

A long pause.

He frowned.

"Hello?"

An awkward male chuckle, then the caller cleared his throat. "Well, how do you like that?" an unfamiliar voice said. "There's a Letterman on the other end of the line, as well."

Zach's stomach bottomed out. He swiveled his chair, trying to counteract the feeling of the room spinning around him. There was only one other Letterman that he knew personally. His father. And he hadn't talked to him in over twenty-five years. Not since his dad had left him and his mother and headed off for parts unknown.

"Zachary?"

A deep breath didn't come near to providing him the oxygen he sought. Unable to think of anything else to say, he murmured, "How did you find me?"

There was a rustling of papers on the other end of the line. "Actually, someone found *me*. She said…"

Zach's mind whirled, leaving him completely incapable of registering the rest of his father's words. Someone had found him. A she.

Mariah.

"Zachary?"

"This she…did she give you her name?"

"Yes. Yes, she did." More paper rustling. "Clayborn. Mariah Clayborn."

Zach's stomach bottomed out and he suddenly felt hot. All he could see was her pain-filled face when he'd kissed her goodbye. He'd been too big of a coward to actually say the words. But they'd been there nonetheless.

He'd hurt her.

Yet she'd helped him by finding his father for him.

He realized the line had gone silent, then a quiet, awkward voice filled his ear. "I know how you feel. I went through pretty much the same thing when Miss Clayborn called me at home last night at an unlisted number." Another lengthy pause. "You don't have to say anything now, Zachary. I understand. A lot of water has rushed under the proverbial bridge. I...I just wanted to let you know that I'd like to establish contact with you. How far, how involved that contact will be...I'll leave up to you, son. But I'd love to see you. To talk to you. To try to explain what happened all those years ago. Tell you how big of a coward I was for not seeking you out before Miss Clayborn called me."

Zach rubbed the back of his neck. He knew the role of coward. He'd been playing a big one for the past ten days. Much longer, if the truth be known. But it was only now that he was coming to see just how big a yellow-bellied coward he'd been.

"I'd like that," Zach finally managed to force through his tight throat. "Where should I meet you?"

He took down his father's contact information in Tacoma, Washington, and gave him the rest of his contact information, since Mariah had only given Barry Letterman Zach's business number. After a few more minutes of awkward conversation he slowly hung up the phone, staring off into space as if an alien force had just zapped him with a beam, turning everything he'd thought he'd known on its ear. Changing white to black. And right to so very, very wrong.

"Oh, one more thing," his father had said before hanging up. "Miss Clayborn asked me to pass on a message when I spoke to you."

Zach had gripped the phone so tightly he thought he might break it.

"She said to tell you that a joint business venture might have some possibilities...."

Zach said his good-byes, then tossed down the receiver, snatched his jacket from the back of his chair and rushed out the door.

"Mr. Letterman?" his assistant asked, getting to her feet as he breezed by her desk.

"Jan, hold all calls," he told her, pushing the button for the elevator.

"For how long?"

"Forever."

It was Saturday and for the first time in two weeks, Mariah found herself without a single thing to do.

She sighed and flipped the page of the morning paper, her hand blindly reaching for her coffee cup on the kitchen table. Ever since George had established that he wanted more work to do, she'd found her caseload suddenly cut in half. Not only was her cousin making good on his word, he was doing a damn good job to boot. And that left her with a little more time on her hands that she'd prefer not to have.

She glanced toward the open kitchen door and the plains beyond. Maybe she would take her father up on riding the range with him a couple of times a week. Lord knows she missed the feel of a horse between her thighs, the Texas sun on her back, the smell of the earth filling her senses.

And maybe it would help her forget one certain Mr. Zach Letterman.

She propped her head on her hand and sighed. Well, so much for getting through the day without thinking of his name. It was eight o'clock, she'd been up for no longer than twenty minutes and, bam, there he was again, haunting her dreams, shadowing her every step.

The doorbell rang.

Mariah looked up from the paper and frowned. Who could that be this early on a Saturday morning? Hughie had spent the night at Miss Winona's, so she was the only one around to answer the door. The only one without a life and no sign of getting another anytime soon.

She opened the door to a deliveryman in a brown uniform.

"Morning, ma'am. Delivery for you."

He handed her a clipboard, and she noticed the certified status of the package, then signed her name.

"Thank you," she said absently, accepting the oblong-shaped box then closing the door. Her name and address were written across the front of it. She began to walk back toward the kitchen. That's odd. She couldn't remember ordering anything.

She put the box down on the table and reseated herself, grabbing her mug with both hands as she turned her attention back to the newspaper.

She was searching for any sign of suspicious crimes in the area. Any tip-off that Claude Ray was still around where she might nab him. No, not because anyone had hired her to do it, but simply because she owed him this personal debt. She turned the page again and mumbled under her breath. Tying her up in her own kitchen, indeed. Oh, she owed him big time.

A piece on one of the horses Ray had stolen from Carter, which had won some sort of prize, no doubt increasing his stud fees…a Houston businessman was throwing a charity gala for a hospital's burn unit…the newly formed Bisbane

Foundation had approved a request from a private citizen to borrow Ellie's dress…

Mariah's eyes widened as she read the last headline. Who would want to borrow Ellie's dress? She rubbed her forehead then read the piece three times. It didn't give any names, citing that the individual wished to keep his or her identity a secret.

Mariah twisted her lips. She hoped it wasn't another fortune hunter convinced there was more out there to be found.

She closed the paper and leaned back in her chair, wondering what she should do with the rest of her day. She remembered the delivery box. Could Hughie have ordered something for her? She reached out and pulled it to sit directly in front of her. There was no return address. She checked the paperwork, noting a company name but not recognizing it. A mail-order catalog? She grimaced. She certainly hoped not. The last time Hughie had ordered anything for her she'd been sixteen and the stretch of pink ruffles that was supposed to be a dress had been more suited to a six-year-old. The offensive piece of clothing was still stuck in the back of her closet somewhere, never worn.

She tilted the box one way, then another. God, opening these things was like solving a crossword puzzle. Pull here while pushing there—oh, and don't forget to turn the box a quarter way to the east.

She heard the sound of an approaching car engine. Hughie returning from his night out. She looked up, wondering what would happen when he finally proposed to Miss Winona. Would Miss Winona move to the ranch? Or would Hughie move to her frilly little house a few miles up the road?

She gave up on the box then picked up her coffee mug and stepped to the sink to wash it out.

"Hello, Mariah."

Her heart did a funny little dip in her chest. Zach? She frowned, thinking it a trick of the running water. Still, she found it curious that she was hesitant to shut off the water.

A familiar hand snaked around her and shut the water off for her. Definitely not Hughie's hand. And definitely not Hughie's body brushing up against her backside, setting every inch of her skin ablaze.

"Is that any way to treat a guest?" Zach whispered into her ear.

Emotion swelled up in Mariah's throat, blocking the passage of air. She stood frozen to the spot, trying to figure out how to regain control of her body. Trying to figure out how to respond.

"Turn around and look at me, Mariah."

Hot hands on her shoulders did the job for her, gently swiveling her until she leaned against the sink and stood staring at the last man she expected to see standing in her kitchen this Saturday morning.

"Zach," she whispered.

She stared into his eyes as his gaze swept from the toes of her boots to the top of her head. "Were you expecting someone else?"

"No, I, um…I wasn't expecting anyone."

Mariah told herself she should play it cool. Act like, yes, she was surprised to see him, but that his impromptu visit affected her not at all. He was no more, no less than a friend stopping by to say hello.

Only she'd never really mastered the art of playing it cool. And Zach Letterman was so much more than a friend. And his standing there, looking at her as if he wanted to devour her, moved her down to her toes.

She anxiously licked her lips. "In the neighborhood, were you?" she asked.

That grin made her knees lock together and a rush of heat dampen her thighs. "Something like that. It took me three planes, a car rental and a helluva drive, but, yes, I was very definitely in the neighborhood." He lifted a finger to smooth back a strand of her hair, but he stopped midway through, instead rubbing it between his thumb and forefinger as if the simple gesture mesmerized him. "You see, there's someone I had to thank."

"Ah," she said.

His gaze slammed into hers at the use of the response voiced so many times during their whirlwind affair.

Affair. It seemed such an inappropriate word for what had happened between them. What they had shared.

Zach considered her through hooded eyes. "Yes, you see, there's this friend…a really good friend, who did a favor for me. A favor I didn't ask for. But one that I wanted without really knowing that I wanted it. And this friend, well, somehow during the brief time that I knew her, she figured this out."

Mariah caught her breath as his hand dropped to her hip.

"I'm talking about you contacting my father, Mariah."

She nodded, knowing that was the answer. Ever since he'd shared with her in an offhanded way that he didn't know where his father was, she'd wanted to find him for Zach. If only to give him the chance to achieve some kind of closure. To perhaps get answers to questions that she knew had to be shadowing his every adult step. She'd begun her search with the check on Zach's background, which turned up the name of his father, and had branched out from there. And when Zach had left…well, she'd continued the search to gain some closure for herself.

Closure Zach was ripping open all over again.

"Thank you," he said quietly.

She nodded, not knowing quite how to respond. "So everything worked out okay, then?"

"We've talked on the phone and agreed we'd like to see each other."

"Good."

He smiled. "Yes, very good." He tugged on her hips until she was flush against his very apparent arousal. Need and longing swept through her so intensely she was dizzy with it.

"But you see, before I can do that, there's this other thing I had to see to."

"Other thing?" Mariah's gaze was plastered to his mouth. His full, well-defined ultimately delectable mouth that she wished would stop talking and kiss her.

"Mmm-hmm." His hand slid down over her bottom, pressing him more tightly against her. A sound rumbled in his chest, a groan. "It's about that possibility of pursuing a business venture...." He blinked as if trying to remember something. Then his eyes cleared. "Did you get the box?"

"Box?" She stared at him as if he were speaking a foreign language, fixated on her need for him to kiss her. *Now.* She didn't care that he'd been gone. That he'd left her standing alone in front of the house without so much as a goodbye. She didn't even care how long he planned to stay. Just so long as he was there for the next five minutes, time enough for her to feel him buried deep with her slick flesh, that's all that mattered to her.

"Oh, the box," she whispered, his words finally penetrating her distracted state. She looked over his shoulder. "It's over there. On the kitchen table."

He released her and she wanted to object. Instead she brushed by him on her way across the room, feeling him even when he wasn't touching her, as if he'd worked his way under her skin and would be there always.

She picked up the box. "Are you talking about this?"

He nodded and came to stand on the other side of the island. "Open it."

She really didn't want to. She didn't know what she would do if it was some exotic piece of lingerie, or worse, a dress or something equally feminine. Over the past two weeks she'd gotten comfortable with herself. She no longer felt the need to change, to alter who she was in order to grab herself a man.

She took a deep breath and went to work on the box. It took her a good five minutes and an attack with her pocketknife before she finally opened it. She put it down on the table and peeled back the white tissue paper.

She gasped.

Nestled in the box was a dress. Only it wasn't just any dress. It was Ellie's wedding dress.

She lifted a trembling hand to her mouth. "Oh, my God."

She turned to face where Zach was leaning against the island, his arms crossed over his chest, warmth shining from his gorgeous face. "Marry me, Mariah."

She didn't know what to say. Didn't even know if she was capable of speech.

"The moment I first saw you in that dress, how right you looked in it, I knew there was something different about you. About what was happening between us." His thick throat worked around a swallow. "And, damn it, it seems like I've been fighting fate ever since."

"Fate?"

"That business venture you proposed? Well, I think we'd make a great team getting the Finders Keepers satellite offices off the ground. But it comes with a price attached. It has to be a full personal venture as well as a business one." Then he breathed in deeply. "And you haven't answered my question."

Mariah looked from him, to the dress, and back again. "I can't...leave Texas, Zach."

"You won't have to."

She stared at him.

"If your answer is what I hope it will be, I thought there'd be enough room for me right here." Zach groaned. "God, woman, you don't know how much I want to touch you right now."

"Then why don't you?" she whispered, wanting that more than anything in the world, as well.

"Because I want you to be able to think when you give me your answer. And we don't seem to do a whole helluva lot of thinking when we touch."

Mariah realized in that one moment that you didn't have to be a Texan to have a Texas-sized heart. Tears pricked the back of her eyes. But rather than turn away from Zach, hide the emotion, she lifted her chin and stared straight into Zach's eyes, aware that moisture swam in hers. "Yes. Oh, yes, I'll marry you, Zach Letterman."

She thought he would come to her then. Sweep her into his arms. Satisfy the desire in her to have his arms wrapped around her again.

Instead she watched as he tightly gripped the counter with both hands. "Strip for me, Mariah."

Flames flicked through her veins, threatening to consume her and the provocatively whispered request. She remembered when he'd asked her the same thing such a very short time ago. And she all too readily remembered her response. It had been the same one she was going to give him now.

She slowly peeled off her T-shirt, kicked off her boots, wriggled out of her jeans and panties, then popped the clasp on her bra. Before it hit the floor Zach was hauling her to him, burying his hands in her hair, plundering her mouth with his.

"Oh, how I love you, Mariah Clayborn," he murmured, his breath coming in ragged gasps, his hands branding her hypersensitive skin as he ran them over her back and her bottom, then up again. "I was such a fool for leaving. For staying away so long. Can you ever forgive me?"

Mariah kissed him back, fumbling with first the buttons of his shirt, then abandoning them for the buttons on his jeans and the ultimate prize just beyond. "I'm marrying you, aren't I?"

The back door opened.

Mariah froze, staring into Zach's widened eyes. "Don't tell me," he whispered.

"Okay," she said, swallowing hard. "I won't. But that doesn't make it any less true. It, um, looks like this is a complete replay of that other time. Hughie—"

"Included," her father finished for her.

Zach turned and faced the older man, allowing Mariah the coverage she needed to get dressed again.

"Damn good to see you, son!" Hughie boomed.

Epilogue

"ARE YOU GOING TO BE all right?"

Jennifer Madison took in her husband Ryan's concerned expression from where she stood holding their four-month-old daughter, Annie. At two months' pregnant, she had already experienced some of the worst morning sickness of her life. And she had seven months yet to go.

"I don't know," Jennifer admitted, trying to calm the ominous churning in her stomach.

Ryan took Annie from her. "Go on. You can probably make it to the bathroom before the wedding starts."

"But I'm Mariah's matron of honor."

"Better to do it now than risk tossing your cookies all over Mariah's wedding dress."

Jennifer held up a single finger. "Good point. Wait here."

"Forever."

Jennifer rolled her eyes then made a dash for the ranch house some twenty feet behind her, leaving behind the white tent with its neat rows of chairs, countless flower arrangements and dozens of brightly dressed guests.

No one could have been more surprised than she when Mariah Clayborn had called her up out of the blue a couple of weeks ago and asked her to be her matron of honor. But, Mariah had explained, it was due to Jennifer that she'd met Zach Letterman at all.

Bathroom...bathroom.

There. She spotted the door with a small group of women already lined up outside it.

"Pregnant woman about to heave!" she called out.

Gasps, then the group parted like the Red Sea, leaving Jennifer with a direct line to the bathroom.

She opened the door then quickly closed it behind her, skirting the person standing in front of the sink so she could access the toilet. She pushed up the seat and bent over. Only nothing came.

She took a few deep breaths just to make sure, then slowly straightened. She glanced at the woman still in there with her and smiled. "False alarm." She realized she was looking at the bride. "Oh, Mariah! You're beautiful."

She supposed that Mariah looked a lot like any bride did mere minutes before the ceremony. She plucked nervously at her hair, looked as if she could use a half a tube of blush to make up for the color that had drained from her face, and appeared a breath away from doing what Jennifer had nearly done moments before. But all that aside, she was absolutely stunning.

"Are you sure the dress is okay?" Mariah asked.

Jennifer had never laid eyes on the other woman until that morning when she and Ryan and the baby had arrived at the ranch house for the ceremony, but the instant she had, she'd felt a kinship with her. Mariah reminded her so much of herself. Not in looks, but in pure tenacity. She was a woman making it work not only in a man's world, but in a man's profession.

"'Okay'?" Jennifer looked over the antique dress, knowing its history, and bits and pieces of what had happened a month ago during the simple case of the missing wedding dress that Jennifer now wore. "No. Okay is definitely not the word I'd use." She smiled at Mariah's panicked expression. "It's perfect."

Jennifer automatically reached to fluff out the back of the dress. "You know, there are reporters out there. I don't know how they got word, but they're scouring the place, looking to get a snapshot of you in Ellie's dress."

Mariah groaned and Jennifer questioned having shared the news.

"Don't worry about it," she said quietly, giving Mariah's shoulder a reassuring squeeze. "I'm sure they just want to share this moment with you. To see everything come full circle. You know, the dress that Ellie never wore being worn at the wedding of the local woman who found Jock's Treasure."

A smile played around Mariah's lips. "Yes, it does sound romantic, doesn't it?"

"Yes." Jennifer's smile widened. "It does."

There was an urgent knock at the door. "Are you about done in there?"

Jennifer cocked a brow.

Mariah took a deep breath then nodded. "Let's do this."

THE FALSE ALARM three hours behind her, Jennifer had been able to fully enjoy the traditional ceremony alongside Ryan. A while before, she'd reluctantly handed over a sleeping Annie to a woman named Miss Winona, who was watching over a couple of other infants in a spare bedroom in the house. She checked her portable baby monitor, hearing what was presumably Miss Winona softly singing a lullaby, then tucked her hand into Ryan's arm. He grinned down at her.

"It reminds me of our wedding at your parents'."

Jennifer visually sought out the bride and the groom and the way they looked at each other, dancing as if no one else existed, the physical chemistry between them seeming to raise the temperature at least another ten degrees. Mariah's father cut in on Zach, leaving the groom to sit out the rest of the dance. After watching his new wife for a moment, he came to stand next to Jen and Ryan. They exchanged some small talk about the ceremony, then Zach asked how everything was going with the agency in Midland.

"Things are going very well," Jennifer responded as Ryan put his arm around her waist, the heat of his hand causing shivers to run over her skin. "In fact, I'm thinking of expanding the agency."

Ryan cleared his throat. "Someone put an idea into her head about offering entrapment services."

Jen laughed. "It's not entrapment." She looked at Zach. "I'm thinking that offering up forbidden fruit and seeing whether or not a client's husband or wife bites is an affordable way to find out if an extramarital affair is a possibility. There's nothing wrong with that."

"It's still entrapment," Ryan said.

Jen rolled her eyes. "Good thing I don't have anything to worry about, isn't it?"

Ryan kissed her soundly, his eyes sparkling with attraction. "We could be seventy and I still couldn't get enough of you."

Zach quietly cleared his throat. Jen shifted her attention to him. "Anyway, enough about me, how are your plans to franchise Finders Keepers going?" she asked.

"Two satellite offices are set to open in St. Louis and Detroit next month," he said, pride evident on his handsome face. But as evident as the emotion was, it didn't come near matching his expression whenever he gazed at his bride.

Mariah had stopped dancing with her father and was now chatting with another couple across the tent from them.

"Uh-oh."

Jen blinked at Zach. His expression had changed as he looked at a man who had entered the side of the tent in jeans and a denim shirt.

"What is it?" Ryan asked.

"Claude Ray."

Jen gasped as Zach shot toward the man. But it wasn't he who reached the latest addition to the party first. Rather it was Mariah, her skirt hiked up around her knees, who tackled the man as he tried to run the instant he realized he'd been made.

A collective gasp when up around the tent. Jennifer hid her smile against Ryan's jacket sleeve.

Mariah had the man named Claude Ray facedown on the ground and was tugging his arms behind his back. "I knew I'd catch up with you again," she said, grabbing a silk ribbon from her hair and winding it around his wrists. "And this time I'm going to make sure you stand trial if I have to guard the sheriff's office to do it."

Ryan chuckled softly, his hand lightly caressing the small of Jen's back. "You can take the girl off the ranch…" he whispered to Jen so he wouldn't break the shocked silence that had settled over the tent.

Zach stepped up to his bride and her detainee. He looked around the stunned group and swept an arm toward his wife. "Ladies and gentlemen, I'd like to present my bride, Mariah Clayborn Letterman."

Mariah looked up at him as if just realizing what she had done and where she had done it. A blush stained her pretty cheeks as she accepted her husband's outstretched hand. She slowly got to her feet to a smattering of applause that quickly escalated into a standing ovation.

Jennifer tightened her grip on Ryan's arm and sighed. "Apart from ours, of course, this is the best wedding I've been to in a long, long time."

* * * * *

HARLEQUIN®

ROMANTIC

SUSPENSE

Get your heart racing this holiday season with double the pulse-pounding action.

Christmas Confidential

Featuring

Holiday Protector by **Marilyn Pappano**

Miri Duncan doesn't care that it's almost Christmas. She's got bigger worries on her mind. But surviving the trip to Georgia from Texas is going to be her biggest challenge. Days in a car with the man who broke her heart and helped send her to prison—private investigator Dean Montgomery.

A Chance Reunion by **Linda Conrad**

When the husband Elana Novak left behind five years ago shows up in her new California home she knows danger is coming her way. To protect the man she is quickly falling for Elana must convince private investigator Gage Chance that she is a different person. But Gage isn't about to let her walk away…even with the bad guys right on their heels.

Available December 2012 wherever books are sold!

www.Harlequin.com

HRS27801

Harlequin® Desire is proud to present

ONE WINTER'S NIGHT

by New York Times *bestselling author*

Brenda Jackson

Alpha Blake tightened her coat around her. Not only would she be late for her appointment with Riley Westmoreland, but because of her flat tire they would have to change the location of the meeting and Mr. Westmoreland would be the one driving her there. This was totally embarrassing, when she had been trying to make a good impression.

She turned up the heat in her car. Even with a steady stream of hot air coming in through the car vents, she still felt cold, too cold, and wondered if she would ever get used to the Denver weather. Of course, it was too late to think about that now. It was her first winter here, and she didn't have any choice but to grin and bear it. When she'd moved, she'd felt that getting as far away from Daytona Beach as she could was essential to her peace of mind. But who in her right mind would prefer blistering-cold Denver to sunny Daytona Beach? Only a person wanting to start a new life and put a painful past behind her.

Her attention was snagged by an SUV that pulled off the road and parked in front of her. The door swung open and long denim-clad, boot-wearing legs appeared before a man stepped out of the truck. She met his gaze through the windshield and forgot to breathe. Walking toward her car was a man who was so dangerously masculine, so heart-stoppingly virile, that her brain went momentarily numb.

He was tall, and the Stetson on his head made him appear taller. But his height was secondary to the sharp

HDEXP1212

handsomeness of his features.

Her gaze slid all over him as he moved his long limbs toward her vehicle in a walk that was so agile and self-assured, she envied the confidence he exuded with every step. Her breasts suddenly peaked, and she could actually feel blood rushing through her veins.

She didn't have to guess who this man was.

He was Riley Westmoreland.

Find out if Riley and Alpha mix business with pleasure in

ONE WINTER'S NIGHT

by Brenda Jackson

Available December 2012

Only from Harlequin® Desire